Melody for L

Also published by New Guild

S.O.S. – Men Against the Sea
Elvis in Wonderland
Privy to the Mayor's Council/The Helper
(a two-story anthology)

For my parents, with love and gratitude

MELODY
FOR LIZZIE

by
Evelyn Orange

NEW
GUILD

A New Guild Book

Published by New Era Writer's Guild (UK) Ltd
5 Cogdean Walk, Corfe Mullen
Wimborne Minster, Dorset BH21 3XB

PO Box 11476
Bloubergrant 7443, South Africa
Tel: (+21) 557 6281
Fax (+21) 557 0704

PO Box 100-806
North Shore Mail Centre
Auckland 10, New Zealand
Tel/fax: (+9) 443 8069

ISBN 1 899694 05 6

This book was designed, typeset and produced by
Crispin Goodall Design Ltd
463 Ashley Road
Poole, Dorset BH14 OAX

Printed in the Republic of South Africa by
CTP Book Printers (Pty) Ltd
P.O. Box 6060, Parow East 7501

Chapter 1

"This is what I want! Oh, this is really what I want!"

Elizabeth whispered ecstatically to herself through the whirl of noise in the music hall foyer. It didn't matter that no one could hear – the words were just bursting to escape into the glittering space around her. One day, she vowed, she would be a real part of this magical world, not just ordinary Elizabeth Belmont, but a star! Her name would appear on one of the rainbow-coloured bills before which she now stood, lost in admiration.

The show had been one of the best ever. It didn't matter that she'd had to watch it from the highest viewpoint in the building, squashed on the cheapest wooden benches between the sweaty bodies of the gallery crowd. Tonight there had been the added difficulty of two bright yellow feathers on a hat in the row in front, sticking up right in her line of vision. They had bobbed up and down in time to Harry Champion's songs, risen about a foot when they all thought Cirnoc the handcuff king would be too late escaping from his latest tortuous predicament (though of course he did, in the nick of time), and swayed from side to side as the Onda Troupe of acrobats leaped and tumbled from one end of the stage to the other.

If she'd been grand enough to be watching from one of the magnificent ivory and gold boxes near the stage, she thought, she wouldn't have had such an obstruction. She had gazed down at the interval, marvelling at the elegant attire of those who occupied the red plush seats in the Grand Circle and Balcony.

Now for a few precious minutes she could mingle with the wealthier crowd in the crimson and gold foyer. No one had seen her slip in from the street, blending into the shadows with her dark skirt and jacket, scarcely noticing that her straw hat had been knocked askew in her haste to rush down the gallery stairs.

She sighed in admiration at the soft pastel gowns and warm furs of the ladies, the expensive suits worn by their moustachioed escorts, the glitter of jewels and flashes of gold at wrist, throat and fingers.

A snowy fur collar passed within inches of her as she stood in the shadows beneath the brass banister. With a start, Elizabeth saw a long pink glove float to the floor in the wake of the departing lady. Quickly she darted forward to retrieve it, then touched the soft fur collar to attract the attention of its owner.

"Your glove, Madam – you dropped it."

The lady swung round with a nod of her huge pink ostrich-feather headdress. Her bow-shaped mouth parted in a smile of amusement as she saw the eager face of the young girl at her shoulder.

"Thanks, love, don't want to lose that, do I?"

Startled by the rough local voice coming from the vision of loveliness, Elizabeth noticed that her face was powdered, her cheeks touched with rouge, and her lips definitely enhanced in their rosy prettiness. She must be one of the promenade tarts, hanging on the arm of the middle-aged gentleman who had picked her up for the evening. As she swept out of the door with her admirer, Elizabeth couldn't help but envy her finery – borrowed, no doubt, but still impressive.

"Elizabeth! What were you doing, talking to that creature? Your father would be horrified if he knew you were consorting with trollops!"

With her lips widening into a mischievous smile, Elizabeth turned to the elderly woman who had appeared at her side. "Oh, Ella, I was only giving her back her glove. You won't tell Father, will you?"

Ella took her hand and tucked it firmly around her own plump elbow. Her eyes twinkled. "No, I won't . . . and I suppose you want me to overlook the fact that you rushed off without a second glance, leaving your poor old neighbour to struggle down from the gallery on her own."

"Oh, I'm sorry, Ella. I just wanted to see all the lovely gowns. You were all right, weren't you?" The last of the patrons from the Grand Circle had now left the theatre, as they emerged in their wake into the bitter January night. The smell of soot, dust and horse dung invaded their nostrils, and the rumble of carriages and cabs, the brisk staccato rhythm of trotting horses, and in the distance the rattle of trains passing through nearby Clapham Junction station rang in their ears.

"Well, I'm still in one piece, aren't I?" Ella stated dryly. "Though in the crush I had to hit a young feller with my umbrella, as his hands were going places I didn't like. And he just gave a big, stupid grin, cheeky blighter!"

Elizabeth giggled at the scene this conjured up in her mind. "Oh, Ella, you didn't!" She swung round in a circle, arms outstretched, still bubbling with adrenaline from the show.

"Mind out!" Ella pulled Elizabeth back from the edge of the pavement with a jerk. "Watch where you're going, miss, or you'll end up under a carriage." Ella shook her head in affectionate despair. "It's time you came back down to earth now. Every time we come to the music hall, you get higher and higher."

Linked arm-in-arm with her older companion again, Elizabeth waved to two men carrying violin cases who rounded the corner from the stage door. "But, Ella, I'm fifteen now, and getting nearer the age when

I can go on the stage."

They turned up the alley to the stage door. "And what do you propose to do on the stage, love?" Ella said with the patience born of having heard the same words many times.

"Oh, maybe dance – I've been practising the steps my friend Belinda taught me. And Father says I'm playing the piccolo very well. I play his every day. He's going to buy me one of my own as soon as he can afford it."

Ella just smiled, letting her young companion rattle on enthusiastically. The cold night air stung her flushed cheeks with a welcome freshness after the stuffy interior of the music hall. She'd never seen the girl look so happy, she thought as she plodded along at her side, her stays creaking slightly at each step. Perhaps she would go on the stage some day, but Ella knew music hall life first hand, and doubted Elizabeth had the maturity to cope with the stresses yet. She herself had rehearsed many acts, playing the piano in the pit at a smaller hall nearby, and knew that life for the artistes was short on glamour, a fickle world which couldn't guarantee anyone a steady job. One minute the public loved the performers, the next they were whistled off the stage.

"Now, there's an example for you," she murmured, half to herself, as they neared the lamp lighting the stage door.

"What was that, Ella? Oh, look, it's Uncle George!"

So saying, Elizabeth rushed towards the pool of light, displaying a good twelve inches of black woollen stockings and boots beneath her flannel petticoats. "For all as if she was ten years old," Ella mused with a shake of her head.

"Uncle George!"

The taller of the two men waiting outside the stage door lifted his grey head, a grin of pleasure splitting his face as he recognised the whirlwind approaching.

"Why it's young Elizabeth – quite a young lady, too." He reached out to take her in a warm embrace.

Elizabeth responded with a hug, but gasped as her arms almost met around his frail body. His clothes hung limp as if on a hatstand, and smelt damp and musty like an old cupboard. She stood back, biting her lip, unsure what to say. He looked so battered, so unkempt.

"And what about a hug for me, pet?"

Eyes warming, Elizabeth turned to the shorter of the two men, casting off her worries as she threw herself into his arms. "Father, oh, you were wonderful. I was so proud of you. Madame Grisard's dance would have been *nothing* without your solo." She planted a kiss on his fine black moustache. It had been such a thrill to see her own father stepping up from his usual place in the orchestra, to take a special bow.

Henry Belmont laughed at this unreserved praise, but his eyes, as blue as his daughter's, kindled at her words. He held her close, touching his lips to her forehead. "Grisard is quite a good dancer, but I don't think I'll get a big review in *The Times* tomorrow," he joked. He looked up. "Enjoy the show, Ella? It was good of you to bring Lizzie."

Ella's face creased into one of her ready smiles. "Don't mention it, Henry. I enjoyed it – it was worth taking a night off."

"Is Uncle George coming back with us?" Elizabeth asked as the group set off along St John's Hill.

"Yes, yes, I am. I can't resist the allure of the wondrous Miss Belmont – so grown-up, she is now. Wearing her hair up, long gracious skirts . . ."

The girl laughed. "Well, I've been working at Miss Franklin's Ladies' Outfitter's for eighteen months. I'm learning to take measurements for gowns, now, and as I have a neat hand she lets me write out bills."

"Well, I never did. Perhaps you can measure me for a gown tonight."

Giggling, Elizabeth took George's arm. "Don't be silly, you're a gentleman. I only measure ladies."

Henry smiled as he listened to their banter. It would do his friend good, he thought, to have Elizabeth's artless company for a while. He dropped behind, taking Ella's round arm in his own.

"Where's George been, all this time?" Ella asked in a low voice.

Henry sighed. "I don't know. It's been over a year since I saw him. I don't suppose he's had one booking in all that time. I think he's living rough, in the clothes he stands up in."

Ella shook her head sadly. "Pity – he was a good comedian in his day. Still could have been, if it wasn't for the drink."

The lights of the Falcon Public House lit a swarm of activity around its doors. Laughter and loud voices joined the noise of traffic. Ella nodded across the road.

"I suppose he was in there while the show was on?"

"I expect so, though where he got the money, I don't know. He would've been better spending it on a good meal. I'll try and get him to eat something with us."

"How long will you put him up?"

"Tonight, at least. He probably won't stay any longer. But we haven't the space to have him for more than a night or two."

The two walked along in companionable silence, listening to the chatter of Elizabeth and the responses of their old friend. They passed Arding and Hobbs' impressive store to make their way up Lavender Hill, watching for an opportunity to cross the road. By the time they reached the new library building, the traffic had thinned, offering them space to scuttle to the other side ahead of two unoccupied horse cabs which were trotting briskly towards Clapham Junction.

A short walk brought them to the residential streets, where they turned off to the left. The rows of terraced houses were still in the frosty darkness, a hazy glow of gas light glimmering from a few windows. A door closed nearby, answered by a barking dog, quickly silenced. Their steps echoed back to them from the low-walled street.

As they approached the end of the road, and the house where Ella and the Belmonts roomed, George turned to Henry.

"Well, here you are. I'll be off, then."

"Now, George, you said you'd stay tonight, at least. I told you it's no trouble."

"No, I can't, really. Very kind of you, and all that, but . . ."

"Lizzie, off you go with Ella. You get ready for bed, while I persuade this old renegade to come in."

"But, Father . . ."

"No arguments, now. You've been at work today, you'll be tired. I promise you George'll be here in the morning."

Still grumbling, Elizabeth let herself be ushered through the gate and up the short pathway to the door. She turned back with a longing look, before Ella placed her arm around the girl's shoulders to guide her inside.

"Now the . . . ah . . . ladies have retired, how about a nip at the hostelry?" George offered with bland innocence as soon as they were alone.

"You old fraud!" Henry scolded with a shake of his head. "You meant this all along!"

"It's not far to that one up the road – what's it called?"

"The Crown. But I don't want to leave Lizzie . . ." Henry noticed with satisfaction the flicker of gaslight in the upstairs front room. Still in her jacket and straw hat, Elizabeth appeared at the window to draw the curtains. Henry gave her a confident wave, then motioned to her to go away from the window. He saw her shoulders heave in a reluctant sigh, but she complied with his wish.

"Oh, that young lady won't miss us for a minute or two. Come on, for old times' sake. It's not like you to be slow to agree to a drop."

The naked longing in his friend's rheumy eyes moved Henry finally. With a nod, he turned back up the road towards the Crown. As they reached the glow and noise, he touched the inner pocket of his coat briefly, remembering his piccolo tucked inside. It would be safe enough there, but he still let George go ahead to the bar, pushing his way through the crowds of working men enjoying a Saturday night drink. The air was heavy with the smell of beer, sweat and smoke.

George laid a frayed cuff on the polished bar. "Whisky, Henry?"

George ordered two whiskies, eyes swivelling to Henry when the barman named the price. With a sigh, Henry pulled his last half sovereign from his pocket, and watched with regret as it spun on the bar. One drink each, he promised silently – at the most, two. That money was all he had to feed himself and Elizabeth till he was paid again the following week.

George really was in a bad way this time, Henry thought as he noted the trembling hand that raised the glass to his lips. His face was a network of purple broken veins, his eyes so sunken beneath the bushy brows that you couldn't even tell their colour. From time to time he gave a harsh, dry cough, which hadn't been there last time he'd turned up. No one would ever offer him a booking again, despite the bravado of his claims.

His only pleasure seemed to be the drink, and reminiscing about old times. Henry kept his own dreams and plans to himself. He'd been hoping for a break soon, but he couldn't taunt the old comedian with his aspirations. He was old himself for starting afresh, over fifty now. He'd spent his music-hall life moving from pit to pit as part of the "band". Yet now a new trend could bring him out into the limelight, if he played his cards right – or rather, his tunes right. Instrumental virtuosi were popping up at all the halls, playing popular melodies, embellished and brilliant, as deft and dangerous to the ear as the acrobats were to the eye. Henry had already played special solos from the orchestra, as in the music for the French dancer Grisard, and was beginning to shed the anonymity of the pit musician. He was hoping an opportunity would come soon, but who knew if he would succeed.

Some time later – he wasn't sure how long – they emerged into the biting air of the night. Henry found himself pressing a shilling into George's hand, before they set off towards home. No sooner had they entered the quiet streets once more than the old comedian began to sing, in a loud baritone, a song which had been popular in his heyday.

"He'd fly through the air with the greatest of ease,
A daring young man on the flying trapeze,
His movements were graceful, all the girls he could please,
And my love he's stolen away . . .
Once I was happy but now I'm forlorn . . ."

Just as Henry was taking his shoulder firmly to hush him, a window was flung up nearby.

"Stop that bleedin' row, or yer'll get a bottle over yer 'ead!" With curlers wound as tight as cocoons in her hair, the woman showed an expression so fierce that Henry believed she would carry out her threat. Recognising Mrs Roland, the plasterer's wife, he ducked his head smartly, in the same motion remarking to himself that she was definitely more refined when her sleep wasn't disturbed.

"That's enough, George," he urged. He took his arm and led him across to the other side of the street, noticing that their steps wandered a little uncertainly. "We have to be quiet – some people are asleep."

George turned a bloodshot eye on him. "Are they, now? Could do with some sleep m'self." He stopped suddenly as they reached a street-lamp, regarding it solemnly for a moment, before sliding to the ground, one arm round it affectionately.

"No, George, you can't sleep here. Come on, I'll take you home." Henry leaned forward to put both hands in George's armpits, to haul him to his feet. Somehow he had to get him back to their rooms, before he passed out completely. Surprisingly, George was able to resist Henry's attempts to put him back on his legs, struggling for a few moments with startling strength. Then suddenly he flopped, becoming a dead weight. Henry stumbled forward, tripping right over his prostrate friend. He fell heavily against the lamp-post, hitting his chest and the side of his head with a resounding clang.

Winded, Henry clung to the cold metal for a few seconds until the stars cleared from his vision. Lucky I've got a thick skull, he told himself as he gingerly felt the side of his head. Then he felt his ribs.

Suddenly he was agonisingly sober, when he remembered that his piccolo had been tucked in his breast pocket. The night was instantly chill as he reached inside his coat for the precious instrument, the tool of his trade. He drew it out carefully and examined it in the pale gaslight. It couldn't be true! Three of the delicate silver keys had snapped off, and there, irreparable, was a crack just on the joint of the wood where the two parts fitted together.

Henry closed his eyes, his mouth twisted in a grimace of rage, and thumped his closed fist heavily against the lamp-post. Oblivious, George was still sitting on the ground, his lips uttering fragments of the song.

Half-demented with rage, Henry seized his companion's shoulder, and began to heave him to his feet.

"Get up, get *up*!" he muttered, struggling to turn the stupidly drunken George into an upright human being. Henry tried to block the implications of this disaster from his mind as he concentrated on getting George back to their lodging.

Thankfully George was fairly quiet for the rest of their lurching journey. Their progress was slow, but at last Henry came to his own gate. He kicked it open with one foot, and dragged George up the path before he took it into his head to wander off. It was a miracle that they managed to get up the stairs without George falling or breaking the mirror on the halfway landing. Locked together, they staggered into the main room of the Belmonts' living quarters.

Henry dropped George onto the low bed beneath the window, and swung his legs up so that he was lying full length. Immediately George was unconscious, snoring in his stupor. Henry pushed him over so that the noise decreased, then stood back with a sigh.

He lit the gas-lamp, turning down the hissing flame. The comfortable familiarity of home did little to dispel his troubles. It was an unpretentious room, furnished with three wooden chairs and a table, of which the scrubbed wooden surface was usually hidden by a fringed tablecloth. Elizabeth would have folded it into a drawer before coming to the music hall. Some washing – underwear, stockings, a shirt and a dark blue dress – hung near the small cooking range to catch some warmth from the embers of the fire in the grate. On the high fireplace, a few items of pottery were mingled with a large, ugly wooden clock and some family photographs. Several pictures cut from magazines enlivened the plain walls, the whole being reflected in a large mirror above the fireplace. A faded rug filled the floor space between the bed and the table.

He removed his overcoat, hung it on the back of the door, then slumped into a chair at the table, resting his head wearily on his hands.

How could it be! This was the end of all his dreams, for he would be certain to lose his job on Monday. He had been engaged particularly for his piccolo playing, and, although he could go back to playing the flute, he was rusty after all this time and would need weeks of practice to come up to scratch.

There was no time! Somehow he and Elizabeth had to live. There were a few possessions which could be pawned or sold, and he could borrow next week's rent from Ella, but who could tell when he would be able to pay it back? He'd never gone seriously into debt before.

He reached up to the mantelpiece to lift down a faded photograph in a gilded frame. "Oh, Jessie, my darling," he whispered to the sweet face that smiled at him. "What am I to do now?" He touched the photograph gently, as if by doing so he could bring to life the image of his dead wife.

"It looks as if your family were right about me."

"A music-hall musician!" raged the Reverend Joseph Lander, drawing his large frame up to its full height, a good five inches taller than Henry. "It's not enough that you meet my daughter clandestinely, but you now ask my permission to marry her. The answer, sir, is no, and always shall be no!"

Jessica Lander wrung her hands, and her large grey eyes gazed in anguish at Henry. He longed to caress that soft light brown hair, to comfort her in the face of her father's wrath.

The minister of the Presbyterian church had not finished. "You're not even from these parts, are you, Belmont? And hardly of a class suitable to marry one of my daughters."

"My father has an ironmonger's shop in the north-east of England, in Sunderland. I've been working in Sheffield for six months."

"And you thought you'd take my daughter back to your father's business? He's retiring and passing it on to you?"

"Well . . . no. I left home when I was sixteen. I've had no contact with him for nearly twenty years."

"So," Mr Lander continued bleakly, his face like granite, "you've had no steady job, and you expect to support a wife and family just by playing the flute? You propose to introduce my daughter to a world full of sin, and you expect me to give you my blessing?"

"But we love each other, Papa." Jessica darted forward, her dark brown dress rustling, to touch his arm. He swung round sharply, dislodging her hand so that she stumbled back a few steps. Henry's eyes blazed fury at his actions, but he said nothing for the moment. He knew he was at a disadvantage.

"I'll speak to you later, you wanton! To think that a child of mine would meet alone in public with a man her family had never even met – and not even one of her own class!"

Jessica's face set in stubborn lines. "I'm not a child, Papa. I'm twenty-five. Sophie was married at twenty-two!"

"Your sister always had more sense than you. She's married to a fine gentleman, a good church-goer. I don't expect your . . . *friend*", he spoke the word with a sneer, "has ever stepped inside the House of God."

"I've never done anything wrong, sir. I've lived an upright life – and I work hard."

Reverend Lander stepped towards the fireplace, and took hold of the bell-pull. "I have nothing more to say to you, my man. You will leave this house forthwith, and never attempt to see my daughter again."

Henry fumed silently at the attitude of the man. But he rammed his bowler hat, newly purchased for the interview, back on his head, and stalked out of the house without waiting for the servant. Poor, sweet Jessie. Her father had obviously expected her to remain his docile companion for the rest of his life. She'd told him to expect little from the interview, for even those suitors considered respectable had been given short shrift. Not that she'd given them any encouragement – the dull, pompous men like Andrew Wyatt, husband of her sister Sophie, had bored her.

Henry had never dreamed, when he met Jessica by an obscure chance, three weeks earlier, that he would have fallen so deeply in love with this gentle young woman. Reverend Lander should never have let her go alone to visit an ailing member of his congregation – but the older woman who usually accompanied her was away visiting relations. Three urchins had been baiting her mercilessly when Henry had appeared on the scene, so he'd sent them away with a shout and a cuff. At first she'd just been grateful to be rescued, but, as he accompanied her to her destination, they talked, and laughed, and a spark had ignited.

Her father would have been even more incensed if he'd learned that she'd visited the music hall with their maid Annie – and he would have had apoplexy if he'd heard her comment, eyes shining, that it had been the most exciting evening of her life! Henry grinned, his anger dissipating. There was more to Jessica than met the eye!

So her family had discovered a few days later, when meek, obedient Jessica had calmly packed a valise when her father was out, and walked from the house into the arms of her suitor. They took the next train to London, and were married as soon as they could purchase a licence in the capital.

The break with Jessica's family had been complete. Despite her distress, it made no difference to her decision. From the moment the gleaming new wedding ring was placed on her finger, her eyes never lost the brightness which the excitement of her new life brought to them. She loved attending the shows whenever she could. All through the hardships, the poor lodgings, the scraping to make ends meet, the hopes and despair of their married years, she had never regretted leaving her comfortable, but stagnant, family home.

Two years later, Elizabeth had been born. Henry then had a steady engagement with a small music hall in south London, his best position yet, and he always looked for an opening at one of the West End halls. That would have given him the boost to his wages that he needed. But the opportunity never came. Instead he moved to the newly-opened Grand Palace of Varieties in Battersea, which paid slightly better than his previous position.

Elizabeth was six years old when Jessica had given birth prematurely to a baby boy, who did not survive more than a few hours. It had been a long and difficult labour, from which she never recovered. It was a decline which lasted three years, but which left Elizabeth motherless at nine. After the funeral, Henry sat down at the very table on which he now rested his elbows, and wrote to his wife's family, informing them of her death. There was no reply. But Henry felt at least that he had done his duty and was free to grieve in peace with his daughter.

Shrugging off the ghosts of old memories, Henry now stood up, replacing the photograph on the mantelpiece. Softly he moved over to the bedroom door, opening it a crack so that the dim light fell across the sleeping girl on the bed. How peacefully she slept, unaware of the catastrophe that would have to be faced tomorrow. She looked so young – too young to be thrown on a merciless world. The pitiful amount she earned at the outfitter's could not hope to feed them both, and pay the rent.

She'd been itching to escape from that dreary shop, to the colour and lights of the halls. Henry was proud of her musical ability, and had encouraged her from an early age to play both flute and piccolo. He had hoped to buy her an instrument of her own, but now that was out of the question. She had also learned to play Ella's piano, but he couldn't see her in a job like Ella's, in the pit of a music hall. Henry had been planning for years, and, if only his own break would come, then they could make a double musical act.

She did not stir. Her lovely hair, far blonder than Jessie's had ever been, fanned out on the pillow around her head. Even in the dim gaslight, it gleamed brightly. It wouldn't do to disturb her so late. He pulled the door to noiselessly and resumed his place at the table.

Drawing the damaged piccolo from his pocket, his heart contracted in anguish again. There was no way it could be repaired. He felt again for the broken silver keys, which had slipped to one corner of the pocket, but this time felt the crackle of paper beneath his fingers. With a jolt he remembered the letter he had received early that day, which he had read incredulously and stuffed angrily into that very pocket. Then, it had seemed ridiculous, but now . . .

The letter was from his wife's elder sister, Sophie. In it she informed Henry tersely that her father had died after a long illness, and she would be in London with her husband seeing to some of the business that had been brought about by the will.

She declared the intention of calling to see them, "*for I feel duty bound to do something for my sister's child, now that my father, the main cause of the family rift, is gone. My husband's family are benefactors to a girls' boarding school nearby. If you would wish it, Elizabeth could be placed here at a reduced fee to complete her education. I know how difficult it must be for you to decide what is right for a motherless child, especially in the uncertain world of entertainment . . .* " (at this insult to his upbringing of his own daughter, Henry had nearly thrown away the letter) "*and I hope that you will consider this offer for her sake. I realise that Elizabeth may already be studying at a good school in London. In this case my offer is of no use to you, but I feel that I should like to visit my niece, and I trust that I shall see you both at two o'clock on Sunday afternoon. Unless I hear any word to the contrary, I shall wait on you at your residence.*" With the usual formal greeting, Sophie Wyatt closed her missive in her neat copperplate handwriting.

Henry rubbed his eyes wearily. The woman clearly had no idea of a musician's pay, if she thought he had enough money to pay for school fees! He'd done as he'd promised Jessica, and let Elizabeth have an extra year at school instead of leaving at the age of twelve, but she'd spent most of the time helping with the younger children. He knew that she deserved more, as she was bright, but at least she'd found a decent job where she could use her brain a little. Her wages had meant that they could eat better, have their boots soled more often, and replace some of their household effects.

Of course, he couldn't have dreamed of being parted from his darling Lizzie – especially to send her to a prim young ladies' establishment. If there had been somewhere he could have afforded in London, maybe he would have been tempted. A good education could have opened up a better future for her. Still, he thought, as he gave a huge yawn, he would have to be practical. Tomorrow they would have to decide how they were going to survive until he found a new job. They could have done without a visit from Jessica's stiff-necked sister, but it was too late to put her off now.

Feeling sick at heart, Henry divested himself of the old black suit, wondering how long it would be before he next had an opportunity to wear it. He washed out his dry mouth with a glass of water, before turning down the gas and settling himself for a few hours' sleep in his wooden armchair, with a blanket to cover him.

Chapter 2

Elizabeth pulled the laces of her corsets tighter and studied her reflection in the old fly-spotted mirror with satisfaction. In the past year her figure had undeniably grown more womanly. Her breasts were plump and firm, accentuating her narrow waist and rounding hips. Deftly she tied the ribbons on her bloomers and chemise, reflecting with a sigh that it would be a long time before she would have any money to spare for ribbons again. It had been such a treat to buy them with the few coppers she was able to keep for herself from her weekly wages.

She found a flannel petticoat and slipped into it, then reached inside the wardrobe for her skirt. Her good working dress had been washed yesterday and was not yet dry, so the old black skirt would have to do. It still showed the line where it had been let down after she left school and began to wear long skirts. Even her blouse had become faded and dull after countless launderings. As she hung the clothes on the wardrobe door, she noticed with a sinking heart that the waistband of her skirt was fraying again. It had been repaired so many times that there was hardly anything left to hold the stitches. She and her father both needed new clothes urgently – but where would the money come from now? Disheartened, she sat down on the bed. Through the closed door she could hear her father practising his flute. Tomorrow he would have to begin the long trek to look for work – and who would employ an ageing musician who had not played the flute for years?

Oh, if only she had some prospects, instead of a paltry job in an outfitter's shop. Her friend Belinda was already making her way on the music-hall stage as a singer and dancer, of the type known as "serio-comic". She had begun as a dancer, and now, at the age of nineteen, had earned enough money to break away from her down-at-heel origins. At present she was in the north of England, with a small part in a pantomime.

I could do it too! Elizabeth thought defiantly. After all, Belinda had been fifteen, too, when she started dancing on the stage, in the chorus at one of the West End halls. It would pay more money than her job in a shop, at least! Rummaging in the bottom drawer of the tallboy, Elizabeth found a battered toffee-tin which housed the old sticks of make-up that Belinda had passed on to her when the pantomime job came up.

Belinda had taught her some dancing steps, and she had learned many songs from the halls through her visits, and from Ella's song-sheets. With a few strokes, she applied the make-up to her face, finishing with an extravagant pair of bow lips. How she longed for a beautiful set of curving lips like Belinda's, instead of her straight-set mouth. Blinking at her reflection, she struck an enticing pose, one hand on her hip, the other extended gracefully.

After springing on to the bed so that she could see the effect of her appearance from head to toe, Elizabeth began to hum a song, twirling and posturing in her stockinged feet, as energetically as was possible on the sagging surface of the bed. It was much easier to dance in the main room, where she would sometimes take the mirror, if she had enough energy after a day's work and also fitting in her housework. She would perform to her own reflection as if to an audience of thousands – but only when Henry was out at work. He wasn't keen on her ideas of following Belinda.

As she came to the last line of the song, she leaned on an imaginary parasol, and bent forward to blow a kiss into the mirror.

"Lizzie! What are you up to?"

Elizabeth's head jerked round to face her father. She made an incongruous picture in her petticoats, with her long hair snaking down her back to her waist, and her lips red with carmine.

"What's that on your face? Don't you know what time it is? Your aunt's due here in ten minutes."

"But I've plenty of time – I'm nearly ready." To underline her argument, she pulled on the skirt and blouse as she spoke.

"I wouldn't count on anything – she may be early. No, leave your hair loose," he added, as she reached for the pins to put it up.

"I don't want to look like a child, Father."

"Nonsense! Your hair is lovely. You've plenty of years ahead of you when you'll have to pin it out of sight. Here, wipe off that red stuff."

With a barely audible sigh, Elizabeth accepted the outstretched handkerchief and began to rub her face, feeling like a chastised infant. Then she looked up and caught Henry's wry smile.

"I shouldn't worry about bow lips," he said in amusement. "Your mouth's much prettier the way it is . . . and it's perfect for playing the piccolo."

Her features broke into a smile, lopsided with a smudge of red at one corner of her mouth. Henry took the handkerchief and rubbed her lips with it, then pressed it back into her hand.

"Go and wash," he murmured affectionately.

Sophie Wyatt fought with her feelings as she gazed from the cab that carried her through the drizzle past the shuttered shops on Lavender Hill. She'd never forgiven Henry Belmont for luring her sister away from her home to a life of almost certain squalor, and, ultimately, to her death. Their father had been right to oppose the marriage, she thought. And Sophie was right, too, when she refused to listen to Jessica's entreaties to intercede for her.

The years since Jessica had run away had been fraught with problems for Sophie. She bowed to her father's wishes by leaving her sister's letters unanswered. But Sophie began to understand her sister better when Reverend Lander became more frail and it was necessary to bring him to live with her family. It was then that she discovered how difficult he had become to live with, so irascible and unbending. Although she would never have gone behind her father's back, having promised not to make any contact, Sophie vowed that, once he had gone, she would make her peace with Jessica.

But the chance to fulfil her vow was denied her when the news of Jessica's death reached them. Poor, darling Jessica! So, now, in an attempt to assuage her conscience, she had decided to see what she could do for her niece Elizabeth, Jessica's only daughter.

Sophie felt a surge of relief as the horse-cab drew to a halt outside a modest terraced house. When her husband, Andrew, had told her that Battersea was near the docks, she'd had grave misgivings about the sort of area her niece had been brought up in. This, though not of the quality she was used to, was a reasonable area. She accepted the cabbie's help to climb down, placing her foot gingerly on the tiny step so far from the ground, taking care to keep her black skirt away from the muddy wheel before she was on firm ground again.

The warmth of her fur stole was comforting around her shoulders in the damp chill of the afternoon. Just as she was settling it into place, she became aware of two small, pale faces gaping at her over the wall from the neighbouring garden.

"Don't stare, children. Don't you know it's rude to stare?" Sophie snapped at them as she unlatched the gate, ignoring the muffled laughter that accompanied her up the short path. Three smart raps on the knocker brought a small elderly woman to the door. This unexpected appearance took Sophie by surprise for a moment.

"Oh, er, is Mr Belmont at home?"

"I 'spect so. You visiting 'im? I'll take yer upstairs if yer like."

As Sophie entered the gloomy hallway, she realised that the house was divided into flats. Rooms! The Belmonts lived in cheap rooms! Her original misgivings returned as she followed the landlady up the narrow staircase.

Perhaps if Sophie Wyatt had smiled more often her face would have been softer and more welcoming. Neither of the Lander girls had been blessed with stunning looks, but the gentle expression that had given Jessica prettiness had never graced her elder sister's features. Sophie's mouth set into its usual firmness, a habit which had engraved small lines around her lips. A constant frown etched itself between her brows, and deepened at each step of her ascent.

"A visitor for yer, Mr Belmont."

The landlady's peremptory knock was answered immediately. "Thanks, Mrs Cooper. Won't you come in, Mrs Wyatt?"

Sophie's shrewd eyes weighed up the man who had charmed her sister enough to make her forsake home and family. Henry Belmont must be about the same age as her husband, but there was a vitality about him that Andrew had lost years ago. His hair and moustache were still black, those blue eyes vivid, and the smile still attractive. Sophie remembered how Jessica had remarked on how handsome he was, though she'd stressed that she hadn't fallen in love with his looks. Foolish child!

"Good afternoon, Mr Belmont. I trust you received my letter?" Sophie's voice was brisk and clipped, with an authority that Jessica's had never had.

"Yes, we were expecting you. May I introduce my daughter Elizabeth?"

The girl was hanging up a towel by the sink. In the same moment as Sophie took in the basic amenities of the room, she studied Jessica's child for some resemblance to her dead sister. Acute disappointment stabbed her – save for the small, slightly tilted nose, there was none at all. The blue eyes, so like Henry's, regarded her steadily for a moment. Her mouth, too, was a fuller, feminine version of her father's. The blonde hair which tumbled to her waist made her look younger than her fifteen years.

"How do you do, aunt?" Elizabeth offered her hand, which Sophie took tentatively.

Unable to speak for a moment, her hopes of finding another Jessica dashed, Sophie Wyatt gave a small smile.

"Let me take your coat," Henry offered. Murmuring thanks, she unpinned her fur collar, then removed the coat, which Henry laid on the low bed. She decided also to take off her hat, as she expected to be there for some time. They had much to discuss.

"Won't you sit down?"

Sophie's lips tightened further as she took in the three wooden upright chairs, the only seats in the room, arranged round the fireplace. An attempt at some comfort had been made by placing a faded cushion on each chair. Suppressing a sigh, she lowered herself slowly onto the largest chair, avoiding the worn wooden arms. Finger by finger she removed the black gloves, placing them on her lap along with her small reticule.

Elizabeth sat next to her, and Henry took the seat opposite. An awkward silence followed. Sophie thought that Henry Belmont seemed ill-at-ease, almost distant, as if his thoughts were elsewhere. She started as her niece jumped quickly to her feet.

"Would you like some tea, Aunt Sophie?" Elizabeth's voice was breathless, and her hands clutched the back of the chair nervously.

"That would be very pleasant, after my journey." Sophie hesitated to add that it was not even 3 o'clock yet, hardly time for afternoon tea. Her eyes followed the girl as she crossed to the tap to fill the kettle. The plain dresser from which she took the cups and saucers was badly chipped and scratched, but at least it looked clean. Judging by their shabby circumstances, she concluded that the child must do all the housework.

Henry seemed to find himself again, asking politely about Sophie's journey. She answered all his questions courteously, and explained a little about her husband's business in London.

"But should we not discuss the purpose of my visit?" Sophie said at last, while accepting the cup of tea Elizabeth handed to her.

"I'm afraid . . ." Henry hesitated, "I'm afraid it's out of the question. For various reasons."

Sophie quickly scrutinised the cup she was holding, and, finding it acceptably clean and uncracked, took a tentative sip. She had come prepared for opposition, and was able to meet it head on.

"Then Elizabeth is still continuing her education?"

"No . . ."

Elizabeth swung round quickly, holding the half-filled cup she had been pouring for her father. "What is it? Has this something to do with me?"

"Then your father has not told you?" exclaimed her aunt, astonished.

"No! He only told me that you would be coming to visit us today. Father, why didn't you say something, if it concerns me?" She slammed the cup down on the dresser, slopping some of the tea over.

"That's quite enough, Elizabeth." Henry's level tone silenced her immediately – the very fact that he had called her by her full name, and not his pet diminutive, told her that he was in earnest.

Sophie's mouth hardened into a disapproving line. "I think you at least ought to explain my proposals to the girl, Mr Belmont."

Her proprietary manner goaded Henry into retaliation. Who did this woman think she was, coming into his home and telling him what he ought to say to his own child?

"I felt that there was no need to do so, seeing as there was no possibility of accepting," he informed her stiffly.

"Why is that?" Sophie demanded sharply.

"Our . . . finances could not take it."

"Not even reduced fees?"

"Nothing. You see . . ." He paused, reluctant to admit their catastrophe.

Elizabeth, sensing his dilemma, came to stand by him loyally, her arm on his shoulder. "I don't know what this is all about . . . but what my father means is that he has lost his job. We are virtually penniless."

"I don't understand. How did you come to lose it?"

Henry sighed, put his arm around Elizabeth's waist, and drew her to him. "My instrument is broken, and I've no means of buying another. I've neither the capital, nor the guarantee of money to come. Without an instrument, I can no longer play in the band. Tomorrow I go to look for another job."

"And I've decided that I'm going to be a dancer," his daughter added quickly. "No, Father," as Henry began to protest, "I know Belinda could get me a job that would bring more money than working at the shop."

Sophie, shocked for an instant by Elizabeth's proposal, gathered herself together, and interrupted their proud wrangling. "This is where I must break in," she insisted. This could go no further. "I can be of help to my sister's child."

The Belmonts fell silent, waiting to hear what she had to say.

"This is how I see it. You are left with the problem of how to earn your daily bread, indeed, how to live. If there were only one person to support, would that not be easier?" Without waiting for the logical answer, Sophie continued. "Then what I propose is that Elizabeth comes to live with my family. We are comfortably situated, not rich, but another mouth would make little difference – and also she can finish her education at Stavington, the school I mentioned in my letter."

She laid the cup and saucer on the table firmly, waiting for their reaction. Father and daughter stared at her, both stunned.

At last Henry spoke. "I must thank you for your generous offer, Mrs Wyatt, and . . ." he hesitated, frowning, trying to sort out his conflicting emotions. It took only a moment to make his decision. "I feel that I would like to accept, for my daughter's sake. It's what her mother would have wished."

"No! No, Father, you can't send me away, please, no!" Elizabeth flung her arms round his neck, burying her face in his jacket. Her shoulders shook with noisy sobs.

"Hush, Lizzie, don't cry," he murmured, holding her in his arms, stroking her hair. "It's only for a little while, until I can get on my feet, and then we'll be together again. Just think what a wonderful opportunity this is – you'll learn to be a lady, after all. Think how pleased your mother would have been." So he ran on, comforting the girl, until the tears ceased, and she was still.

Sophie watched the scene, lips pressed together in disapproval. What a disgraceful exhibition! Truly, the girl was totally lacking in discipline – and how could Henry Belmont show such emotion in front of a virtual stranger? Her own three children would never have been allowed to behave in such a manner, even in private. Elizabeth had to be taken away from this atmosphere and cured of this unnatural dependence on her father. She could still hope that there was time to rub out the effects of her upbringing – the girl was young enough.

"There now! Go and wash your face, Lizzie," Henry said gently, kissing the top of her head.

Elizabeth obeyed meekly, her features set into lines of misery. Sophie calmly continued to drink her tea. No word was spoken while the girl bathed her face in cold water, then dried her burning cheeks.

"Perhaps you'd like to take that music down to Ella, pet, and let us talk together for a while," continued Henry. Elizabeth opened her mouth to protest, but, seeing her father's steady gaze, turned to fetch the music from the window-sill. She stood for a moment in the doorway, looking from one to the other, tears still poised to fall from her eyes. Henry could not face her accusing stare. His eyes dropped to look at his clenched knuckles until the door closed softly behind her.

In an uncomfortable atmosphere, Henry poured some more tea for his visitor and for himself, then sat down opposite Sophie. "You understand that it's very hard for Lizzie – it's six years now since her mother died, and we only have each other," he explained.

"This would be an opportunity for Elizabeth to have the benefit of feminine relations," Sophie returned, "for obviously a father cannot tell a young girl . . . all she needs to know."

"Oh, she's had female influence. Our good friend Ella Greaves has been very kind to my girl. Ella's a widow, and has no children of her own. I think she sees in Lizzie the child she always wanted. I'm very grateful to her."

"But Elizabeth has not had a proper education."

"Maybe not what you would call 'proper' – the London County Council school covered little in the way of fancy learning. But she's bright, you know. She writes accounts and bills at a ladies' outfitter's, and she plays the piccolo brilliantly. I've hardly had to give her any instruction."

Sophie Wyatt smiled wryly. "I hardly feel that playing the piccolo would be an asset for a genteel girl."

Henry's eyes narrowed. "Mrs Wyatt, we don't live the sort of lives where genteel manners are an asset. It's hard work earning a living round here, and we've done fine up till now. My daughter knows how to spin out the week's money at the market. She can cook, sew, do the laundry, clean our rooms. This education you offer her is really of no practical use to people like us. No matter how we behave, polite society looks down on us because we are connected with the world of entertainment. I'm accepting your offer – truly, a very kind offer – so that my daughter may be fed and clothed while I look for work." And it galls me to have to do so, he wanted to add.

Sophie regarded him coolly. "I'm sure Elizabeth will benefit from contact with her mother's relations. For all that my sister chose to forsake her family to marry you, I can't believe that she would have wished her child to work in a shop . . . or worse, to be a dancer on the stage."

"You and I don't understand each other, Mrs Wyatt, and I doubt if we would ever grow to like each other. Jessie was very happy in the years we had together, but of course you wouldn't believe that." He glanced at the sepia-tinted photograph on the mantelpiece. "Unfortunately, the music profession is in a poor way, and wages haven't risen in line with prices, otherwise we would have been better off. I'm not proud of the situation we find ourselves in. But I love my daughter, and, though I hate to part with her, I think she'll benefit."

An icy silence followed, in which Sophie searched for some biting reply to Henry's frankness. She suppressed a shiver. The fire was burning low, and Henry hadn't added any more coal. A glance at the scuttle revealed that there were only a few lumps at the bottom, and she guessed that they were all that was left. She decided to hasten their interview to a close. In any case, the cab driver would be returning for her shortly.

"Elizabeth will be able to stay at Stavington School until she is eighteen years of age. Do you propose to take her away as soon as you find work?"

"No . . ." Henry pondered for a few moments. "I'll be playing my old flute until I have some capital to buy a new instrument . . . but if things go well I could pay her fees myself. If we had more money, then it would be in her interest to have a better education, to be able to mix with all types of people." He stroked his moustache, imagining what it would be like to be wealthy. With a sigh, he dragged his thoughts back to reality. "I only want what's best for my girl."

Sophie nodded. "I understand. I have two daughters myself. Now, what I propose is this . . ."

Through an uneasy truce, they plotted Elizabeth's future, arranging dates and times, until agreement was reached. As Henry finally saw Sophie to the door, he had to admit to himself that life would never be the same for himself, or for Elizabeth. Whether it would truly be for the best, he could only hope – but they were committed now. Their future was in Sophie Wyatt's tight, black-gloved hands.

Chapter 3

A loud roar woke Elizabeth with a start, and she gasped in shock as her head hit a hard surface, knocking her hat from her head. A scream rose in her throat as her eyes opened to find only blackness. Then her panic subsided as the train hurtled from a tunnel into weak winter sunshine.

She bent forward to retrieve her hat from the floor, ignoring the throbbing pain in the place where her head had struck the window. She was alone in the carriage, the other two ladies having gone to the dining car for luncheon. Longing to dispel the dragging loneliness that had stalked her since leaving London, Elizabeth reached up to the leather strap and pulled the window down about a foot, letting an icy breeze flood the carriage.

The fresh air cleared the fog of sleep from her brain. The beauty of a winter landscape spread out before her eyes. It softened the pain of homesickness which had already invaded her, only a few hours after leaving Battersea. It had been a gloomy day in the capital, but here in central England clear skies had touched the landscape with frost. To a city-bred girl, the sight of pale sunlight bathing the endless stretch of fields was breathtakingly beautiful. Hoar-frosted trees stood in stark outline against the golden sky. Sluggish rivers and rushing streams flowed beneath the bridges over which the train sped, eating up the miles on its way north.

When she heard women's voices in the corridor, Elizabeth quickly pushed up the window. The two elderly ladies bustled into the compartment as she opened her copy of *Pride and Prejudice*, and innocently immersed herself in Jane Austen's prose.

"Such a delightful luncheon, wasn't it, Letitia?" cooed the smaller of the two, giving a sweet smile marred by her brown teeth. "The trout was absolutely delicious, don't you agree?"

"My dear sister is forgetting that I had the poached halibut, but, indeed, it was delicious." The taller, dark-haired lady directed a smile of shining false teeth towards Elizabeth. "Such a shame you declined to join us, my dear."

"Oh, truly, I'm not hungry. I've been fine here." Her eyes gave a surreptitious scan of the seat and floor in case any tell-tale crumbs remained from her cheese sandwich. She moved her foot so that the sole of her boot covered the few she'd noticed.

"Oh, I see you're reading one of my favourite books!" exclaimed the elder sister. "Our governess was so devoted to Jane Austen that we

25

became quite besotted with her books. *Sense and Sensibility*, *Northanger Abbey*, *Emma* . . . Have you read *Emma*, my dear? I know that was always Letitia's favourite."

Elizabeth smiled weakly, wishing she was still asleep. It was difficult to remain in her own thoughts with the two Miss Trents prattling away. Thankfully, their lively minds would not wait for an answer when they darted a question at her, and they were quite happy batting comments back and forth with each other. It was a relief to see them depart at Newark. Their places were taken by an elderly clergyman and his portly wife, and a smartly dressed man with a briefcase. For the rest of the journey there was no more conversation, only the rustling of the two men's newspapers, and the click of knitting needles.

In the end it turned out to be worse without the chatter of the two elderly women. The silence gave her a chance to brood on the home she had left behind her. . . though it had become less of a home in the past week, with the threat of her departure hanging over her, and the need to eat. Their clock had made the journey to the pawnbroker's, along with a large mirror in a rosewood frame and a Chinese walking-stick with a carved handle, which had been a present from an oriental entertainer who had befriended Henry. This money had gone to pay back Ella, and had bought their food for the week.

There was enough left over for rent for the next two weeks – but how would her father survive once she was gone? Ella would do all she could, but she wasn't well off either, and, in any case, Henry hated being in debt, and would rather strip his home around him than feel that he was living on someone else's money.

Elizabeth had suppressed the tears that were aching to be shed, knowing that it would only make it worse for both of them if she made a fuss. She had to believe that each day brought another chance of some work for her father. That morning, Henry had tucked the old flute-case under his arm as he accompanied Elizabeth to the station. At least he looked reasonably respectable, his tweed jacket having been hastily patched once more by Elizabeth in the days before her departure.

How hard she had tried to remain calm, a young lady rather than a frightened child. But as they entered the vast cavern of the station the sight of the monstrous steam engines filled her with trepidation. She'd never been on a train before in her life, and the thought of the long journey, alone, to an unknown future, struck her mute with apprehension.

Henry continued to talk and joke, to mask their unhappiness. Elizabeth's silent face, turned to him in censure, broke his flow. He sighed.

"Yes, I know. Talking doesn't make it any easier." He put his free arm around her shoulders. They walked in silence until they found a second-class carriage. The Wyatts had sent the ticket two days ago, and Elizabeth would have gladly exchanged it for a third-class place, but Henry wouldn't hear of it. The money was better spent on her journey, he insisted, and she wouldn't want to antagonise her relations from the start.

"Twenty minutes," he murmured now, glancing at the station clock. "I'll take your bag onto the train."

They sat by the window, saying little. Words seemed trivial at a moment like this. Henry cupped her hand, which was slightly roughened from housework, and consoled himself with the thought that it would soon be as soft as a lady's.

The waiting which had at first seemed interminable suddenly ended with the arrival of the two Miss Trents. Henry felt obliged to help them arrange their bags and hat-boxes, by which time the train was almost due to depart. Suddenly filled with anxiety, Elizabeth jumped to her feet to follow her father to the door.

He turned back to where she stood, her fingers gripping the sill of the open window.

"Father . . . "

The shrill whistle of the guard drowned any words she could have spoken. The train gave a lurch. Elizabeth stretched her hand out of the window to Henry, who clasped it briefly before it was carried away from him. A sob tore from her throat.

"Write often, Lizzie," Henry called.

She nodded through her tears, her throat aching with the unspoken words of love. Slowly her father's shape shrank into the distance, then disappeared from sight as the train rattled from the station. Wiping her tears on one of Henry's precious handkerchiefs, she leaned her head against the door. She stayed there until she felt composed enough to re-enter the carriage where the two ladies waited. Smiling politely at their remarks, she feigned tiredness, closing her eyes to the harsh light, until the exhaustion of parting overcame her, and she slept in earnest.

Henry scarcely noticed the horse-drawn traffic circulating on Pancras Road. His eyes still saw his daughter's face gazing through the railway carriage window. How he'd longed to open the door and snatch her into his arms again, to take her home . . . home! Suddenly he could no longer face the thought of looking for work that day.

He took an omnibus south of the river to Battersea. As he walked up the road to their lodging, children scampered around him, as it was school lunch-break. Mothers stood chatting in the doorways, scarcely glancing at Henry as he passed – he was just another man out of work, not an unusual sight here. On a street corner an organ-grinder was churning out a popular music-hall ditty, while some of the children danced and others chanted the words. How Elizabeth had loved to dance as a child, nimble and dainty, singing with her tuneful young voice. A sigh escaped from him as he unlatched the gate.

The hallway was gloomy, the flat on the landing silent and unwelcoming. For a moment he wondered why he had come home, after all. Then he remembered, with a surge of relief, that Ella would still be at home.

She didn't seem surprised to see him.

"Hello, Henry." Her voice was gentle.

"Have you . . . a pot of tea going, Ella? I can't face our place."

She took his coat, and the flute, her face soft with understanding. "Of course. Sit down."

A fire burned in the grate. Ella moved the kettle across to heat, then made herself busy gathering cups and saucers. From above the fireplace a photograph of Ella's dead husband watched the domestic scene, flanked by floral plates. Beside the armchair a stocking lay discarded on a workbox, a darning needle hastily pinned in it when Ella had answered the door.

Henry leaned back in the chair and closed his eyes, thinking to himself that there was no other face he would rather see than Ella's at that moment. He let the warmth and comfort of the little room embrace him, putting off the moment when he would have to return to the empty flat upstairs.

Elizabeth's spirits sank lower as they approached Sheffield. As daylight faded, the flames and fumes of the crowding industry flared brighter, and the roar and thump of gigantic machinery intruded into their safe little compartment. What sort of place had she come to?

After what had seemed like a journey into hell, the train finally drew into Sheffield Victoria station. With a hiss of escaping steam, the engine groaned to a halt. Scarcely any light filtered down through the glass and fretwork of the station roof as the short winter day rapidly dwindled. The narrow platforms swarmed with people. Elizabeth doubted she would ever find her relations in all the mêlée. Would all her cousins be there to meet her? The thought filled her with terror.

The other passengers quickly left the train, leaving Elizabeth fumbling anxiously with her hair, trying to push the pins into place so that her hat held firmly to her head. Hesitantly she trailed in the wake of the minister and his wife, searching anxiously for Aunt Sophie in the bustle.

For a moment Elizabeth was distracted by the bitter wind clutch-

ing at her ankles. She stumbled forward onto the platform, with her
carpet bag lurching ahead of her, and gasped as the full icy blast caught
her. She was unaware that she had been spotted, until Aunt Sophie's
brisk voice pealed in her ear.

"So there you are, Elizabeth! Dear, dear, what have you been doing?
John, give me your handkerchief."

Elizabeth's head whirled round, and she saw her aunt, a tall youth
and an older man in the clothing of a servant standing at her side.
Sophie whisked the handkerchief from the youth's hand, and began
to apply it briskly with a hard finger to her niece's face. "Tut! You
must have been leaning out of the window. Just look at those smuts."

With her composure in shreds, Elizabeth submitted meekly to the
rubbing of the handkerchief, which left her face burning and sore.
"There! That's a little better. Gregg, take Miss Belmont's bag. This is
your cousin John, my dear. He kindly offered to escort me today, as he's
home from school for a few days."

Elizabeth murmured a shy greeting to the youth, who, she guessed,
was a little older than herself. He was taller than her, and there was
the hint of a moustache beginning to appear on his upper lip. But she
was taken aback when John's eye closed in a wink, and felt her cheeks
growing even redder. How stupid she must look.

She realised as they walked out of the station that there were smuts
on her jacket, and there must be on her blouse, too. What a bedrag-
gled appearance she must present to her relations – and she'd so wanted
to make a good impression.

Some acrid fumes, borne on the wind, caught Elizabeth's throat.
"What's that awful stink?" she exclaimed, coughing.

Sophie raised one eyebrow. "That is the smell of industry, Elizabeth.
And we don't consider, er, *stink* to be a genteel way of speaking."

John grinned at his cousin's discomfort, but took the sting from
his mother's words by adding, "It's much stronger here in the centre
of the city. The prevailing wind takes it off to the east, so we don't find
it affects us, as we live west of the centre."

Gregg, the servant, hoisted her bag into the back of a trap that had
been watched over by a small boy. The boy caught the coin that John
tossed him, then scarpered off, his ragged boots flapping as he ran.

Elizabeth nursed her hurt pride all through the journey, scarcely
noticing the fine shops they passed once they had left the station envi-
rons. Her attention was caught briefly when John pointed out the new
University building. With its crenellated brick turrets, it looked more
like a castle than a place of learning to her startled eyes. Apparently
the King would be coming to the official opening in the summer. I
won't be here then, she told herself fiercely.

The horse toiled ever upwards, towards a residential area. Then, after a long run on the flat, Gregg drove the trap off the road on to a quieter avenue, up a steep hill. A sharp turn brought them into a driveway, where a grey stone house stood well back from the street, hidden from view by tall hedges.

The wide expanse of lawn in front of the house was dull from recently melted snow, but was impressive enough to show that the Wyatts were residents of some standing. The stone balustrade at the front door was smart and new, and the plants trailing round the porchway neatly pruned. The grandeur of her new home perturbed Elizabeth even more, and her legs trembled as she alighted from the trap.

Her eyes grew large in wonder at the sight which met her when the uniformed maid opened the front door. A patterned red carpet swept towards a wide staircase, and up to the landing. Two huge polished mirrors flanked the front door, reflecting the magnificent hall-stand, the tables, the many pictures . . . it was so much! Just like a window pageant in one of the expensive stores in London.

Her aunt touched her shoulder briefly.

"Elizabeth, give your coat and hat to Gertie," she instructed, while taking the pin from her own hat and laying them on the hall-stand. John helped his mother with her coat, while Elizabeth's numb fingers fumbled with her jacket buttons. At last they were free, and she struggled out of the sleeves. She raised her eyes to meet the merriest face she had ever seen.

"I'll take your coat now, miss," the maid announced in a thick Yorkshire accent. Her eyes twinkled beneath the starched linen cap which was anchored severely to her unruly brown curls. Elizabeth could only stare in amazement at this unexpected apparition in her aunt's house. Somehow she had imagined her aunt's servants would all be sombre and middle-aged – but this girl was only a few years older than herself.

"Let us withdraw," Sophie announced. "We'll take tea now, Gertie. Please inform Cook that dinner will be on time as we were not delayed."

"Yes, Madam," the maid replied, crossing her eyes behind Sophie's back. Elizabeth gave a splutter of laughter, quickly turned into a cough as her aunt looked round. All innocence, Gertie hung up the coats, then disappeared down the hallway towards the kitchen.

"This way, Elizabeth. I expect you are hungry after your long journey."

"A . . . a little, but I did have some bread and . . . oh!" Her voice trailed away in awe as they entered the drawing room. It was as big as the whole Battersea flat, with sweeping draperies at each end shutting out the winter twilight, and the lamps which had recently been lit bathing everything in a welcoming glow.

"Sit here, my dear." Sophie indicated a large upholstered chair near the fire, which blazed in a huge marble fireplace.

Elizabeth paused for a moment before lowering herself uneasily into the armchair. She was anxious that there might be more smuts on her clothes which could soil the pale upholstery, so she perched stiffly on the edge. The maid brought the tea, but, as Sophie watched her every move, she did not glance in Elizabeth's direction.

The next half hour was an ordeal for Elizabeth. She accepted the cup of tea that her aunt poured for her, but refused any cake as she was afraid of upsetting anything. The emotion of the day caught up with her, bringing with it a fog of weariness. She longed for some privacy, but she would have to wait until the maid had unpacked her paltry belongings before she could escape to the room she would be sharing with her youngest cousin, Caroline.

It was a relief when Gertie returned, to inform her mistress that Miss Elizabeth's "things" were now unpacked.

"Good. Would you like to go to your room now, Elizabeth? I will show you round the house later, but in the hours before dinner you may like to rest and bathe. Gertie will draw a bath for you, if you require. Gertie, show Miss Elizabeth to Miss Caroline's room."

Grateful to escape at last, Elizabeth followed the maid upstairs. Caroline's room was at the back of the house, down a long corridor which separated it from the other rooms. Gertie flung open a door on the way down the corridor.

"That's the bathroom, Miss. Shall I prepare a bath for you? It would certainly get rid of those smuts."

Elizabeth's hands flew to her cheeks. "Oh, are they still there? I thought my aunt had scrubbed them all off."

"Here you are – Miss Caroline's room. That's your bed there, in the corner. Your skirt's in the wardrobe, along with your two blouses, and your undergarments are in the second drawer of the tallboy. I . . . er . . . didn't know what to do with the songs, so I put them in the same drawer."

"Thank you." Elizabeth's voice was uncertain, being unused to the attentions of a servant.

Suddenly, Gertie threw off her maid's correctness, her words flooding out in enthusiasm. "Is it true, Miss, is it? That your father's on the music hall?"

Elizabeth took a step back, startled by Gertie's sudden outburst. "Well . . . yes, in a way. He's . . . he was a pit musician at the Grand Palace of Varieties in Battersea. But he's unemployed now."

Gertie clasped her hands together, eyes shining. "Oh, Miss! I can't believe I'm actually talkin' to someone who really knows about the music hall. I go every week, on my day off – just to the gallery, of course. But I've seen all the famous names who've been here – George Formby, Marie Lloyd, Albert Chevalier, lots of them. Have you met them?"

Elizabeth sat on the bed, wishing Gertie would leave her alone. She was so tired! "No . . . Father was just a pit musician. But he's played for all the best-known stars."

Gertie's eyes sparkled, and she squeezed Elizabeth's arm. "I can see we're going to get on fine. I'll just run that bath for you, then I'll have to get back to the kitchen to help Cook, otherwise she'll be complaining to Her Ladyship."

"Her Ladyship?"

Gertie giggled. "Yes, that's what I call Mrs Wyatt . . . only to myself, of course. Haven't you noticed how high and mighty she is? Oh, but of course she's your auntie, isn't she? Maybe I shouldn't say that . . ."

Elizabeth couldn't resist a smile. "You don't have to worry. I've only just met Aunt Sophie, and I've never met my cousins – except for John, today. I'm sure they look down on me."

"Well, don't let them squash you." Gertie was already halfway out of the door. "And watch out for dear little Caroline – the Brat, I call her. I've got names for them all," she chuckled, then vanished.

The room was blissfully quiet without the whirlwind presence of the maid. Elizabeth turned towards the polished mirror, so different to the fly-speckled glass she had been accustomed to all her life in London. Her pale face looked back at her, a few black smudges still apparent on her skin. It would be lovely to have a bath, but unfortunately she would have to put on one of her old blouses afterwards, as this one was too dirty.

A loud rap on the door startled her as she was opening the wardrobe. "Bath's ready, Miss!"

"Thanks, Gertie."

The bathroom was the most wonderful place Elizabeth had seen in her entire life – hot water out of taps, a flushing water closet, and a big iron bath on feet, with scented soap to wash herself. She sponged over her hair, knowing there wouldn't be time to dry it if she washed it properly, but at least it would help.

Elizabeth put on her underwear again, leaving off her stockings, then returned to the bedroom. Swinging her feet up on to the bed, she promised herself just a few moments before she would dress again. Drawing up the coverlet, she drifted off into exhausted sleep.

A hand roughly shaking her shoulder brought her back to consciousness with a start. Panic raced through her as she saw the unfamiliar surroundings, expecting to have woken in her own bed in Battersea.

Then reality flooded back when her eyes focused on a dark-haired girl wearing a starched white blouse and a navy blue skirt, one hand smothering a giggle.

"You do look funny, with your hair all tangled up!"

Elizabeth felt a burst of resentment at her rude awakening. So this was her twelve-year-old cousin, Caroline, to be her companion at that girls' boarding school. The light in her cousin's eye looked suspiciously like triumph. But Elizabeth had no wish for any confrontations so early in their relationship, so she merely brushed back her hair with one hand.

"I'm sorry, I didn't mean to fall asleep. Did your mother send for me?"

"Yes, it's almost dinner time. Mama sent me to see if you had changed yet."

"Obviously not," Elizabeth retorted as she swung her bare legs to the floor. She began pulling on her black woollen stockings.

"What are you wearing – surely not that old thing?" Caroline exclaimed as she caught sight of Elizabeth's blouse hanging on the wardrobe door.

"My best blouse needs washing. That's all I have." Elizabeth spoke firmly to squash any further comment from her cousin. She took the blouse from its hanger, put it on and buttoned it up briskly, then retrieved her skirt from the bedside chair and put that back on too. While she brushed her hair so hard that it crackled with energy she watched Caroline in the mirror. Elizabeth had been prepared to make friends with her cousins, but this girl had immediately placed a barrier between them. So Gertie called her the Brat? Well, Elizabeth would be able to answer Caroline in kind – a childhood playing on the streets of Battersea had made her amply able to defend herself from sharp retorts.

Maybe she would fare better with her elder cousin, Violet, who was after all eighteen, and would be less eager to score over her.

"Is Violet here yet?"

"No, Violet is spending the weekend with the Cunninghams. She's supposed to be staying with Adela, but it's really to be with her precious Harold." Caroline scowled ferociously at the mention of this last name. Elizabeth gathered that he was not a favourite of Caroline's.

"Who's Harold?"

"Don't you know anything?" snapped Caroline. "Violet and Harold are getting married in August. He's the son of someone Papa knows through business. Still, when she goes I'll be able to have her room, and won't be stuck here at the back of the house." *With you*, Elizabeth was certain she wanted to add.

Well, I'll be just as glad to be on my own, she thought. Then added, but I won't be here in August.

To Elizabeth's surprise, Caroline brought a blouse and skirt from the wardrobe. "I shall be glad to get out of these clothes. I always feel so dusty after travelling."

Elizabeth felt that her eyes were being opened to a whole new existence. To change clothes for a whim, and not because they needed washing! And not to have to worry if they would be dry in time to wear again.

Caroline's eyes followed her as she put the last pins in her hair. The downward curve of her mouth spoke plainer than words that her cousin found her clothes distasteful. Elizabeth could stand it no longer.

"I'm going downstairs now."

One day, Miss Caroline Wyatt, she thought as she left the bedroom, one day I'll have the money to wear the very finest gowns – and I'll earn it myself!

Dinner was as much of a nightmare as the rest of the day had been, made worse by the fact that Elizabeth felt herself to be under the scrutiny of the whole Wyatt household. As a result, her appetite deserted her. It was such a trial always to have to watch everyone else's movements so that she could copy them absolutely. How dreadful it would be if she made some horrendous mistake, showing herself up for the poor relation she was.

One consolation was that Caroline was so taken with showing off to her parents that she hardly noticed what her cousin was doing. She told long elaborate stories about her friends at school, and how the mistresses had praised her, until her father broke his silence.

"Caroline. Eat your dinner – otherwise you will be sent to finish it in the kitchen."

It was obviously a very real threat, for the girl frowned mutinously, but turned her attention to her plate immediately. Elizabeth, at her side, could see John hiding a grin. The rest of the meal was spent virtually in silence, which gave Elizabeth a chance to study her new family.

Sophie's husband, whom she had been told to call "Uncle Andrew", looked much older than his wife, as he was white-haired, and had a constant frown between his brows. Elizabeth wondered what sort of relationship he had with his children. Somehow she couldn't imagine them laughing with him the way she did with her own father. Quickly she suppressed this thought, as it brought tears of homesickness to her eyes. Still, she expected that banking was a very serious job, so it would need a very serious person to become involved in it.

Sophie was very pleasant, smiling frequently at Elizabeth as if trying to make her feel welcome. But the amiability felt false, somehow. She remembered how solemn Sophie had been the day she had come to Battersea. Maybe that was because her father had just died, but she hadn't seemed to be grieving, just disapproving.

John was a quiet young man, but he, out of all of her new family, seemed the least critical, and treated her like a normal person. But she was afraid to let herself like him. After all, he too came from this privileged background, and probably only saw her as a curiosity. He would probably disown her in front of his schoolfriends.

As for Caroline, well, Elizabeth would have to learn to get along with her. On Sunday they would be going to Stavington School together, and somehow Elizabeth thought that this would be even more difficult with Caroline beside her. Over the weekend she would have to try to befriend her. Being a few years older, it would be her place to make the effort, as her father had always encouraged her. But something told her that Caroline would be a difficult task.

Later, as she lay in bed, listening to Caroline breathing deeply in sleep on the other side of the room, Elizabeth was tempted to give way to the waves of loneliness which overwhelmed her. The bed she lay on was softer than any she had ever slept in, but she longed for the familiar creaking bedstead at Battersea. The lights were still on downstairs. What were they saying about her? Then she turned over, angry at herself for letting it worry her. What did it matter? Shuddering, she hugged her arms to her chest, bringing the folds of her old nightgown up to her face, still with the smell of the soap she always used to launder the clothes. She wouldn't cry!

At last the heaviness of her limbs overwhelmed her, as her thoughts dissolved into disjointed images, and brought the relief of sleep.

In the end she saw little of Caroline over the weekend, as her cousin complained of a stomach-ache on Saturday, and stayed in bed most of the time. Elizabeth suspected that the illness was imaginary, so that Caroline could avoid having to entertain her strange cousin. But, to her great surprise, Elizabeth discovered that Uncle Andrew was giving up his Saturday afternoon to drive her round the city. John elected to join them, which was a relief. The thought of several hours in the company of dull Mr Wyatt was more than she could bear.

It was a relief to be out of the house, to sit back without thinking and watch the new impressive buildings passing. Sheffield certainly seemed a more interesting place than she had first thought. John added a few of his own remarks on the drive. When they turned into Pinstone Street, he turned to her with an impish grin, pointing out the Empire Music Hall in nearby Charles Street.

"Vesta Tilley is top of the bill this week. I suppose you've heard of her?"

"Heard of her? Why, she's wonderful. She can impersonate all sorts of men, though she's best as a young johnny-about-town. I saw her perform at the Grand Palace of Varieties in Battersea. I even saw her backstage, when I went to meet my father after the band-call."

"Band-call?" John was mystified.

"Oh, that's what we call the first rehearsal that the acts have with the band. They try out their songs to get the timing right, that sort of thing. It's very important to the performer, otherwise the act might fall flat." Her eyes wistfully followed the façade of the theatre as it receded from the moving trap. "I don't suppose you've been there? Even to the pantomime?"

Andrew Wyatt gave an exclamation of displeasure. "We would never step inside such a place. We do not consider it a fit source of entertainment for our children. And I won't ask, young sir, how you knew what act is top of the bill." He turned censorious eyes on his son, his thin mouth drawn down. John turned his head away, though his eye caught Elizabeth's, and closed in a wink. But it was little consolation to her. That would be the last time she would mention the music hall in her uncle's hearing. She swung round in her seat, eyes gazing unseeing at the passing buildings.

So this is how it would be! Her background was despised in this middle-class world. No one would understand her love of the theatre, or share it with her. In that moment she understood how alone she was, but the knowledge generated a small kernel of strength which was the beginning of a new independence. She would learn to fit in for now, and save her dreams for the future.

Sunday found Caroline still uncommunicative, demanding her mother's attention as she sat looking miserable in the drawing room for most of the day, clutching the supposed stomach-ache. Elizabeth was despatched upstairs to arrange her belongings in a black box, with brass handles, which Gertie had brought in for her. The box had been Caroline's until her elder sister had left school last summer, and had passed on a cedarwood trunk to her.

The brass-handled box had been inadequate for Caroline's clothes and possessions, but looked cavernous when Elizabeth had laid all her clothing in it. Violet had given her two of her older blouses to tide her over until she was measured for a proper school uniform. Beneath these went her few sheets of music, given to her by Ella – some waltzes, a polka, and two songs currently in vogue through the popularity of Marie Lloyd.

Suddenly tempted, she took the sheets of music from the box, and hurried downstairs to the parlour where the upright piano stood. Surely, if she played softly, no one would mind. Uncle Andrew had gone down to the church, as he was officiating at the morning service. At least she had been spared that, in order to pack. Her aunt was in the kitchen discussing household business with the cook, and surely would be out of earshot.

A few hesitant chords told her that this was a good piano, much better than Ella's old instrument with the tinny sound. The waltz was one of her favourites, and it drove back the loneliness of the past few days. The music was so familiar that her mind could stray back to Battersea while the notes poured out of her.

Elizabeth remembered the first time she had been allowed to put her chubby, six-year-old's fingers on the keys of Ella's piano, her high-pitched laugh mingling with Ella's chuckles as she fumbled to imitate the sounds of the few notes she had been taught. Her parents had stood in the shadows, watching with amusement and pride at her responsiveness. Later memories also surfaced – of the time after her mother's death when she spent so many hours with Ella learning the notes properly; and, more recently, of Ella playing popular tunes from the music hall, with Elizabeth singing the words or dancing with her skirts raised above her knees.

People might have thought it was quite enough for performers to work the halls all week, without making music in their spare time – but music was everything to Ella and Henry, and Henry's dream of a solo spot had never waned. On Sunday afternoons he would bring his piccolo showpieces – polkas and variations – to Ella's rooms so that he could try them out with accompaniment. More often, recently, he had handed over the piccolo to Elizabeth, for her to play while he listened and criticised. Afterwards, the three of them would go to buy some saveloys and pease pudding for their supper, which on a fine summer evening they would eat on Clapham Common, or in Battersea Park.

Elizabeth's fingers faltered at the memories. She became aware how cold the room was, as the fire had not been lit. Blowing on her fingers, she was weary of playing now that the memories had become painful. Instead, she reached for the music sitting on the piano lid, curious to see what the Wyatts judged to be "proper" music. There were some songs by Schubert, Arne, and Henry Bishop – some of the serious artistes had been known to sing these on the halls, so they were quite familiar to her. There was also a book of hymns, and some piano music. *Chopin – Nocturnes* it said on the cover. A beautiful leather-bound copy with gold lettering, it was hardly used. As she opened the cover, an inscription leaped out at her: "*To Jessica with fondest love – Sophie*", and, underneath, "*Christmas 1885*".

This had been her mother's! With a sudden shock, she realised that she had stepped into her mother's world, her only world until she had run away with Henry Belmont. How hard it must have been to leave these comforts, and to break with her family so completely. Had she found it as difficult to adapt to a new society as Elizabeth was finding it now?

The book slipped from her fingers as the door opened behind her.

"Ah, Elizabeth. I thought it must be you, when I heard the music." Her aunt stood in the doorway, one hand resting on the brass doorknob.

"I'm sorry, I didn't mean . . ."

"Don't worry. I'm glad that you want to play the pianoforte. It is sadly neglected, for none of my family has shown any particular aptitude for the instrument." She bent to pick up the book Elizabeth had dropped. "What is this? Ah, Jessica's book." A tender smile graced her features, taking years off her appearance. "Would you like to have this music, as a keepsake in memory of your mother? Perhaps you could learn to play some of the music."

"Oh, that would be lovely," Elizabeth exclaimed, warming to this unexpected gesture. It moved her enough to add, "But I can hardly remember my mother."

"Of course. Poor child." Sophie reached out to touch her niece on the shoulder. "I hope that you will come to me, in place of your mother, should you need any advice or help."

Elizabeth's face softened to a smile. Though she could scarcely imagine taking any problems to her aunt, she welcomed this overture of friendship.

"And you must feel free to play the pianoforte whenever you wish . . . though," Sophie added almost apologetically, "not on a Sunday. This is the day we observe for Church and rest."

Clutching the Chopin album to her breast, Elizabeth watched her aunt's graceful departure in silence. For a few moments she had felt that she had done something that merited approval – then suddenly this last comment! How hard it was going to be to learn their ways and manners. But the music in her hands gave her some comfort. She liked to think that her mother, too, had been a misfit here, and had gone away with Henry Belmont to find true fulfilment. It was with this small hope that Elizabeth ran back upstairs to her room, and laid the book reverently at the bottom of her box.

Chapter 4

It was a clear, crisp winter day when Belinda Grey stepped off the tram on Lavender Hill. A young labourer, leaning against the wall, stopped smoking his pipe long enough to emit a whistle of admiration at the slim ankle that was revealed for an instant beneath the long skirt. The answering twinkle in Belinda's eye caught him momentarily off guard. The smart brown outfit, piped with orange, and the large hat surmounted by two matching plumes indicated a young lady of means – but no well-brought-up miss would have taken his appreciation in such a way. He stared after her, scratching his head with the stem of his pipe.

Belinda was quite unperturbed. She felt pleased with herself today. She had arrived back from her engagement in the north just two days earlier, with some extra money in her pocket, and already two jobs booked and the promise of another. The outfit was new, bought the previous day from a shop right up in town. It made her feel that she had arrived at last – she was able to buy good clothes, and the future seemed bright. She and her friend Patty had even had a few days' holiday at the seaside for the first time ever!

Now she couldn't wait to share her good fortune with young Elizabeth Belmont. How the girl would adore to hear the news of Belinda's time in the pantomime. It was Saturday afternoon, and her friend would have finished work for the week.

People stared at the young woman as she walked down the side streets. For Belinda, born in a slum, had emerged into womanhood with style. At nineteen, she was tall and graceful as a result of her dancing career. Large brown eyes and a wide, full-lipped mouth gave her a striking appearance, crowned by thick chestnut hair that glowed with red glints in the sunlight. She knew her talent was not great, but she had a winning personality, was ready and eager to laugh, and possessed an attractive voice. Coupled with her looks and dancing ability, these attributes made her a good "act". Audiences liked her. Perhaps, with a truly great song, she could even make it to the top of the bill.

But Belinda didn't care about fame. She loved to play to the audiences, to sense their admiration – or envy – and she revelled in the feel of her own independence. She had dragged herself from poverty to sufficiency through sheer hard work, and it was a wonderful sensation.

Belinda could not deny that she felt very pleased with life as she knocked at the door of her friend's lodgings. Within a few moments, the leathery face of the landlady appeared in the doorway.

"Oh, it's you. Come to see the Belmonts?"

"Yes, can I come in?"

"Well, I suppose you'd better." Mrs Cooper drew in her lips with what looked suspiciously like disapproval as she took in the fine new clothes and smart hat. "But your friend isn't here."

Momentarily nonplussed, Belinda halted in mid-step. "What do you mean? Lizbeth's out?"

"Gone away to relatives . . . but he's still here. Been a few changes."

Glancing back at the spectral Mrs Cooper, Belinda advanced up the stairs. Well! She had not expected this at all.

A brisk knock on the door soon summoned Henry. It was unusual to see him so untidy – hair standing up in peaks, shirt only half-fastened, braces loosened.

"Belinda! Why, what are you doing here? Come in."

Hastily he swept some clothes from the chair, while running one hand over his head to try to neaten his appearance. He reached for his tweed jacket to cover his undress.

"I hear Lizbeth's gone – and you don't look as if you'll be here much longer." She nodded to the two crates by the window, packed with kitchen goods wrapped in newspaper.

"No, I'm moving tomorrow. This place is too big just for me, and, anyway, I haven't the money for it. We've had a bit of trouble, Lizzie and me. Lost my job last week . . . broke my piccolo. There's no money for another, until I get a job playing the old flute. I'm going to a room in Balham. I've enough money for two weeks' rent. Maybe something will have turned up by then."

"And what about Lizbeth? The old bag downstairs said she'd gone to relatives. I didn't think you had any."

Henry pulled up the other chair, and sat down wearily. "Not mine – they're her mother's family. Jessie's sister, Sophie, is married to a wealthy cove in Sheffield, and they're sending my Lizzie to school with their daughter. It seemed the only thing to do – she'll be looked after, and get a good education on top of it."

Belinda stood up, her face troubled. "But she's so far away! She'll miss all this like hell – and she'll miss you."

"D'you think I don't know that?" retorted Henry defensively. "But don't you understand? I've no money, and no prospect of any wages. I'm too old to change my job, be a labourer or something – anyway there's nothing at the docks now. Half of them are laid off at the moment, till something turns up." He muttered the last into his clenched hands, on which he rested his chin dolefully.

Belinda laid a hand on his shoulder. "Oh, listen to me! I'm sorry, Mr Belmont. It's really knocked the feet from under me, and I'm taking it out on you when you must be down in the dumps." She moved over to the window and gazed down into the back yard. "If only I could help in some way. I'm doing all right now."

Henry's face lightened in amusement. "Yes, I can see you're making a bob or two. But I can't take any money from my daughter's friend. Yet who would have believed that skinny little Belinda should grow up into a young woman with her own means?"

A warm smile enlivened Belinda's face. "It still seems like a miracle to me – but I feel I owe it to you."

"To me? You've done it all for yourself!"

"No, I couldn't have done it without you and Mrs Belmont. She made me believe I was a real person, not just a piece of rubbish in the gutter, and you showed me how to change my life by going on the halls."

"Jessie . . . yes . . ." The thought of his wife reminded Henry of his lack of hospitality. "I'm sorry I haven't anything to offer you. If you'd come yesterday there would've been tea and biscuits, but I've packed the last food, and I'm eating with Ella till I leave tomorrow."

Belinda turned back to Henry with a smile. "Oh, don't mind me. I just came to see Lizbeth, and now she's not here. Maybe, if I had the address of the school, I could write her a letter . . . though I ain't much good at that sort of thing."

Henry scribbled the address on the back of an old envelope, and Belinda slipped it into a pocket in her skirt.

As Henry saw her to the door, she turned back to him briefly. "I hope you get a job soon . . . but I'm sure you will. You're a good musician, Mr Belmont."

Henry smiled a sad acknowledgement of her compliment. "It's a matter of finding an opening – if there are no jobs, how can I find one?"

Belinda nodded in agreement, pressing his hand. "I'll keep my fingers crossed," she said, before slipping out into the winter sunshine, blinking at the brightness.

As she turned to look for the last time at the familiar lodgings, Belinda recalled her first meeting with the Belmonts. Six-year-old Elizabeth had fallen on the way home from school while playing a rough-and-tumble game with other children. Belinda, at ten already growing like a weed, had picked her up, mopped her bloodied knees, and marched her home. It was not that Elizabeth demanded the attention – rather, it was Belinda who had wanted to be needed, to be a protector instead of a victim. As the youngest in her family, she'd always been either bullied or ignored.

Jessica Belmont, advanced in her second pregnancy, had taken pity on this child, with her elbows protruding from her dress, and her toes pinched in fourth-hand boots that were far too small. Belinda sensed that she was not resented there, and took it upon herself to

41

escort "Lizbeth" home from school each day.

Gradually she began to make herself useful, helping Jessica as her movements became more awkward and difficult. Belinda was a strong, bright girl, whose appearance began to take on a new neatness. The Belmonts had little enough money to spare, but there was no cost in combing hair, washing some clothes, and passing on an old pair of Jessica's boots to this child, who was only too happy to feel wanted. Her own family cared little enough for her whereabouts.

It was one of the biggest disappointments of Belinda's life when Jessica's baby died. She had so looked forward to helping to look after him, but instead the tiny scrap of humanity had hardly greeted the world before he left it. But Jessie Belmont had grown to depend upon the strong, willing girl, and in the difficult months following the birth Belinda found she was needed more than ever. She learned to cook and clean, ran errands with Elizabeth, and even on occasion took messages or food to Henry at his work in the music hall on St John's Hill.

It was here that Belinda's eyes were really opened. In the plush, dim interior, ordinary people became gods – they shone in the limelight. There she met Maggie Holland, who lived in the next street to her own family, and who danced for a living in the chorus. At the age of twelve, Belinda finally persuaded Maggie to show her the dancing steps properly. And it was then she discovered her goal in life – she wanted to be up there in the limelight. Once or twice she persuaded her elder brother, Joe, to take her to the gallery, where she sat amongst the sweaty bodies and shouted and clapped along with them. Oh, to be down there on the stage, lapping up the applause with the other dancing girls. The men loved their bare legs, a sight never seen decently outside the theatre.

When Belinda was fourteen, Jessica Belmont died. Belinda shared the grief of the family, and gave to them most of her spare time from her factory job. But Jessica had taught her neatness and self-respect, which gave her the courage, a year later, to audition at the Grand Theatre, where she took up a proud place in the line of dancing girls.

Belinda's ambition had not stopped there. The Belmonts saw less and less of her as she worked at her own solo act. By the time she was eighteen, she had broken away from the chorus, and was getting small engagements as a solo artiste. This year was the second in which she had been engaged for pantomime. So Elizabeth had grown up in the wake of her friend's success. The girls became closer as they grew older, despite the fact that Belinda moved away from Battersea to share a small apartment with her friends Patty and Dora.

Belinda's own home held few happy memories, so it was a wrench to know now that she would never return to the Belmonts' rooms. Sighing, she made her way to the tram stop to wait for the next transport back over the river.

Elizabeth's spirits were bleak as she gazed out across the barren winter landscape, searching her mind for something positive to write to her father. There was no comfort for her in the rugged beauty of the Derbyshire peaks.

After a fortnight there she still felt an outsider – there was so much that she didn't know, had never learned. A council school in London did not educate young ladies. She was trying to apply herself, but her lack of knowledge had left her far behind the other girls. Nobody had actually laughed at her ignorance, but there had been a few whispers. Her pride smarted, for she knew she wasn't stupid. Yet, in other ways, they seemed to regard her with awe, being a girl who had earned her living in London, and with such an unorthodox background! She had lived a life they would never know.

Her cousin Caroline had been unable to keep to herself the exciting news about Elizabeth's origins, which now every girl in the school seemed to know. Caroline found herself to be rather a celebrity, having introduced her unconventional cousin, who proved to be quite a novelty. At first Elizabeth had talked a little to her about her life in London, but, once she found that each bit of information was immediately relayed to every other pupil at the school, she stopped. There was no one here who could understand her love for her father and her ambitions for the future.

The dormitory door slammed. Caroline's face intruded into her thoughts.

"So here you are! We've been singing hymns with Miss Bailey in the music room. Why didn't you come?"

Elizabeth moved back from the window and sat on her bed. "I didn't feel like singing hymns, and I didn't have to." She folded the letter she had started and slipped it into the front of her blouse. She had once caught Caroline trying to read one of her letters, and wouldn't put it past her to try again. She was such a nosy child!

Four more girls burst into the dormitory.

"Penelope, you're lucky that Miss Mead didn't see you running up the stairs!" exclaimed one.

The girl at the front of the group laughed defiantly. "I've had enough of hymns for one day! I wish my brother would send me some music-hall songs. Then we could have a lark! He went with a friend to the Empire Music Hall in London and saw Marie Lloyd. They said that her songs were ever so naughty. How she gets away with it, I can't tell."

"You mean . . . she uses . . . rude words?" asked the girl who had reprimanded her.

Elizabeth knew that Penelope had started the conversation to bait her, but could not stop herself from interposing. "Of course not!" she exclaimed. "She uses her actions to suggest it."

"What do you mean . . . how do you know?" Penelope demanded.

"I've seen her! My father played for her last year."

"What was she like? Show us!"

Elizabeth pushed them aside, and clambered up onto the long table which they used sometimes as a work-table in the evenings. She hitched up her skirt to her knees, and began to sing:

> "*When you're giving folks advice,*
> *Or you're telling stories nice,*
> *I shouldn't tell the end if I were you,*
> *For to cut it short is best,*
> *You can let them guess the rest,*
> *Twiggy voo, my boys, Twiggy voo?*"

All the little innuendos were there – the hand on waist, the sway of the hips, the big wink. Delighted, the other girls laughed and clapped at each nuance.

"What's going on here?"

Guiltily, the girls swung round to face the door. There stood a tall girl, her dark hair pinned up stylishly round a hair frame.

Abashed, Elizabeth climbed down from the table.

The other girl scrutinised her. "Why, I don't know you – you must be new."

Blushing with embarrassment, Elizabeth stammered, "I'm Elizabeth Belmont."

Caroline darted forward. "It's my cousin from London. She started here a fortnight ago."

The senior girl nodded briefly at this interruption, then turned back to Elizabeth with a friendly smile. It quite transformed the serious features, lighting up her grey eyes. "My name is Frances Whittingham. I hope you'll be happy here. But I must warn you that I noticed that Miss Underwood is looking in on each dormitory. I heard the noise from here as I was passing. She doesn't take kindly to dancing on the tables." Her eyes twinkled mischievously.

With startled cries, the girls rushed to their own beds, leaving Elizabeth with Frances. "Thank you. It was kind of you to let us know."

"I can't wait now – but sometime you must explain to me what you were doing. Goodbye."

Caroline sidled up to Elizabeth once Frances had gone. "That was a long conversation for Frances Whittingham. She's such an odd girl, spends all her time buried in Latin and Greek books. She even wants to go to university. Imagine! It's no life for a young lady, my Mama says."

Elizabeth considered this new acquaintance with interest. Another young woman with ideas other than marriage! Perhaps she wasn't unique in this school after all.

Frances Whittingham was the third child of the director of a Sheffield steel company. Her two elder brothers, Alfred and Gerald, were at Cambridge University, and had encouraged their bright sister in her unladylike ambitions. Her father had learned to be proud that his daughter should show such intelligence, and had promised that she would have the proper coaching required once she reached the age of seventeen, but he had also been adamant that she should complete a suitable education for a young lady, at Stavington School.

Though it was a more enlightened school than many at the time, Frances still feared that she was academically far behind her brothers. Weekends were spent poring over Virgil and Ovid, and studying any other books she thought might advance her academic career.

A week after the scene in the dormitory, she tried to concentrate on John Milton's *Areopagitica*, while flurries of rain blew against the windows. She had been working for two solid hours, and daylight had sunk into twilight early for the time of year. Frances sighed and stretched her arms. Perhaps if she went to the kitchens, she could persuade one of the staff to give her a cup of tea.

Pinning up a stray strand of hair, she left her study bedroom that she shared with another girl. She still gloried in the whispering sound of her long skirt and underskirts as she walked along the landing – it was a welcome privilege to be a senior girl, and to dress as an adult, though her sixteenth birthday was still a few weeks away.

Rounding the corner, she gave a cry of surprise as she almost bumped into Elizabeth Belmont. "Elizabeth! What are you doing here?" Then she frowned. In the dim light of the corridor, it seemed as if she could see tears on the girl's cheeks. "What's wrong?"

Elizabeth wiped a hand across each cheek. "I didn't want anyone to see me. It's foolish, really, but I've had a letter from my father. The show he was playing for has folded, and it means I can't go home for Easter now. I'll have to stay with Aunt Sophie and Uncle Andrew." She straightened her shoulders. "Well, there's no point being miserable about it – it won't change matters." She would have walked away, but Frances caught her arm.

"Don't go. Come to my room to have a cup of tea. The girl I share with has gone away this weekend, and I was just going to ask for a drink in the kitchen. Do come."

"I'd like that. Thank you."

Clutching their cups, the girls sat side by side on the window-seat, Frances' books pushed to one side.

"So you don't like it here . . . still?"

Elizabeth shook her head. "I never wanted to come, and my father didn't want to send me, either. If he hadn't lost his job, I would still be working in the shop at Battersea, instead of being stared at and laughed at by these girls . . . oh, I'm sorry, I didn't mean . . ."

"No, don't apologise. Most of them are too narrow-minded to be polite to someone who's different. And you have so many differences – especially your accent. Where does it come from? I've never heard anyone speak like you."

Elizabeth smiled. "It's my own – from the Battersea of my home, with some of my father's north-eastern accent. I believe I spoke more like you when my mother was alive. I think it's coming back."

"Yes, it's not quite so strange as it was."

With a sigh, Elizabeth put down her cup and saucer. "I'll never catch up with them in lessons, though. I was always good at our lessons in Battersea, but I just haven't done the same things in school. I can add up a bill, and measure a lady for a dress, or shop for food in the market and cook it – but it's not what a 'lady' does. And I can play the piccolo and the piano."

Frances looked at her quickly, interested. "The piano? Are you having lessons here?"

"No. I didn't know that I could."

"Well, you must ask your aunt and uncle immediately if you can have lessons. That at least will be something that you can do as well as the other girls."

"Maybe you're right. But why should you be so interested in me?"

Frances stood up and walked restlessly to the centre of the room. "Don't you understand? It's because I'm different, too. They think I'm a freak, with my head always buried in a book. People have warned my mother many times that I will end up an old maid because no man will want to marry a woman who can talk to him as an intellectual equal. But my mother says she would have acted the same as I have, had she been given the chance. And there are so many more things that women can do now – they are becoming doctors and lawyers, not just ornaments or baby-producing machines."

Stunned by this openness, Elizabeth sat up. It seemed to put her own feelings into words. "I want a career, too . . . but it's not quite like your idea. I want to go on the stage."

"As an actress?"

"No . . . promise me you won't tell anyone this? I want to be a dancer, or a musician. My father says I have talent, that I can play the flute and piccolo almost as well as he does. I haven't told anyone here . . . nor the Wyatts. Everyone seems to disapprove of my life in London. I suppose you do, too."

Frances considered for a moment. "To be honest, I don't know enough about it. I've only seen it from the outside. We used to go to the pantomime at the Theatre Royal when I was younger. Earlier this month we saw Henry Irving as Shylock in *The Merchant of Venice*. My family don't disapprove of the theatre, unlike the strict Presbyterians like your aunt's family." She sat down beside Elizabeth and grasped her arm in an unusually impulsive gesture. "I'm so glad you have ambitions, too. You're the first girl I've ever known here who hasn't wanted just to be married as soon as she possibly can. I do hope we'll be friends."

They smiled warmly at each other in the glowing firelight.

It was a consolation to Elizabeth to have found a friend in the alien world of Stavington. The days weren't so long when there was someone to confide in, and this helped her over the times when she missed London so badly. Before she knew it, they were into the summer months, the time she had promised herself she would be going home. There had been more work coming Henry's way, but there was still no end in sight for her ordeal.

Often she daydreamed that Henry might turn up unannounced at the school, wearing fine clothes, or driving a motor car, and that she would walk out with him, full of pride, with the admiring eyes of the other girls following her. Occasionally, parents would take their daughters out at the weekends, but never Henry.

But what did arrive unexpectedly one June Saturday was a small package for Elizabeth, wrapped in thick brown paper, sealed with string and sealing wax. Through the paper she could feel a wooden box, and it was quite heavy.

Frances was with her when she received it. "What could it be? It's the wrong shape for a cake."

"Too narrow," Elizabeth agreed, snipping the string with Frances' nail scissors. She tore off the paper, and found two envelopes inside, one large and one small, as well as a black wooden box.

The small envelope contained a letter, in a hasty scrawl, as much as she ever received from Henry. "It's from my father," she stated, and began to read.

"*Dear Lizzie,*

Much as I would love to see your face when you open my little gift, the reason I have been able to afford it is because I have saved so hard over the past few months. I have one just like it for myself, so we have a pair. Use it well, my

pet, and we'll be able to use them together when you join me again.
    Your ever loving
    Father"

As excitement welled within her, Elizabeth began to realise what the present must be. She opened the little black box to reveal two small black tubes, one decorated with a row of silver discs. "Oh, wonderful!" Her eyes shone.

Frances was mystified. "What on earth is it?"

"It's a piccolo! Father bought it for me – my very own instrument!" Eagerly she took the two pieces from the velvet-lined box, and fitted them together. Tentatively, she blew a note. A high-pitched squeak came from the opposite end.

Frances' hands flew to her ears. "Oh, that's shrill!"

Elizabeth laughed and tried again. She played a few notes, and made a sweeter sound. "I'm so out of practice! But I won't be, soon. I'll practise hard for Father. Oh, isn't it wonderful, Frances?"

Frances lifted up the other envelope. "You haven't opened this, yet."

Reluctant to lay down her piccolo, Elizabeth reached for the second envelope slowly. Tearing it open, she said, "It's a piece of music – oh, look, it's called 'Melody for Lizzie' – and here's another note. '*This is your very own waltz, Lizzie. It was written by the son of someone Ella knows, who wants to write for the music hall. I bought it for you.*'"

"Oh, Frances." Elizabeth's voice was choked with happiness.

"Go on, play it for me!"

Elizabeth smiled. "Oh, no, not until I can play it really well. Then I'll show you what a pretty instrument the piccolo is." So saying, she clutched her two gifts to her, smiling in anticipation. At last she could start to prepare for her future . . . surely this was the beginning of all her dreams.

Chapter 5

"Spare a copper, miss!" Two barefoot boys stretched out thin grimy arms to the tall young "lady" who strode purposefully down the street. Above their heads, seagulls from the nearby docks screeched over a scrap that the two urchins could well have done with.

"Get along with yer! I ain't got anything for the likes o' you!" Belinda retorted over her shoulder. Startled at her vivid London accent, they stopped, open-mouthed, and let her carry on down the street. Two women standing gossiping against a wall followed her with their eyes. Belinda ignored them, clutching the brown-paper parcel more tightly in her arms.

At the end of the street, she marched up to the last ramshackle cottage and thumped her fist on the door. Eventually it was answered by a tall woman in a faded dress. Her once lovely chestnut hair was streaked with grey around her forehead and temples, her face set into a dull resignation.

"Oh! It's you. You'd better come in, then."

Belinda sighed. Some welcome. "Janey!" she exclaimed, noticing a tell-tale thickening of her elder sister's waist. "You're not expecting again?"

"I don't have much choice – not when Bob comes in drunk on a Friday night. It's easier to let 'im have 'is way. You know 'e ain't a bad man – 'e don't knock me around, like Pa used to hit Ma." She returned to the potatoes she had been peeling.

"Where is Pa, anyway?"

"In the back." Janey indicated the back room with a jerk of her head. "Hasn't got up yet, lazy sod. How 'e held 'is job as long as 'e did, I'll never know. At least Frank's more reliable." Frank was the eldest brother, who had taken over their father's job when he became too often the worse for drink. Frank and his wife Annie lived in the next street. Joe, a year younger, had run off to be a soldier as soon as he was old enough, glad to be away from the crowded household.

Belinda went to pick up Janey's youngest child, a one-year-old boy who was whingeing at the side door. She rocked him back and forth until his eyelids drooped and he slept, oblivious to the talk of the two women.

"How's Tom's leg?" Their other brother, now twenty-three, had suffered an accident as a boy, laming him for life.

"Oh, 'e manages. It was pretty bad last month in the wet weather, but when work came up again at the docks 'e was all right to be taken

49

on."

"And you? You all right?"

Janey's smile was grim. "I 'ave ter be all right. No one else ter look after them all, is there? Not now you're off in the fancy West End."

Belinda knew she should not be angry, but it always upset her when Janey made such remarks. A little guilt, maybe, because she had escaped? "You know I can earn more money there than anywhere else. If I'd stayed 'ere an' married an' 'ad as many kids as you, there wouldn't 'ave been any more money."

This new baby would be Janey's sixth, though one had died soon after birth. She knew the carping was partly despair on Janey's part, and some jealousy. It was no joy to be stuck with four kids at twenty-five, and another on the way, not to mention a drunken sot of a father and a crippled brother. At least Belinda had been given a chance.

With a sigh, she laid the sleeping child in the cot by the fire, and reached into the bodice of her dress for the packet of money she brought them each month. "There's an extra two quid this time. It'll help you buy something for the new one. And there are some clothes you can cut down for the girls."

There was no point staying longer. Janey would always scorn her offer to help with the chores, and she didn't want to meet her father when he finally got up, crotchety and bleary from the previous night's drinking. Janey had given up trying to stop him by keeping him short of money, for he only filched it from any of his family's pockets, or borrowed it from his cronies until one of them came round, demanding to have the loan returned from another of the Grey family.

She took a different route back to the tram stop to avoid the two boys who had accosted her on the way there. If she was tempted to give them a copper, they would only pester her each time she came back.

The visit home always left a cloud of gloom hanging over her. It wasn't that she was ashamed of her background – all her friends had come from similar origins. It was just that her family never made her welcome, and now she was beginning to make some money they made her feel as if she had earned it at their expense. Sometimes she wondered if they would prefer it if she disappeared completely.

To dispel the gloom, Belinda wondered whether she should take a tram straight to the theatre – or maybe she would go to Francis and Day's to look at songs. What she needed was a really snappy number, and maybe they could put her in touch with a songwriter with some good new material.

It was a relief to join the bustle of the London traffic, to see people who seemed to have a purpose in life. Even the journey to Charing Cross Road raised Belinda's spirits. She found two interesting songs by new writers who might possibly be willing to produce something for her in the future – it was worth the money to try them out. Leaving the door, she paused for a moment, blinking in the sunlight after the dim shop interior.

"Ouch!" She gave a yelp of pain as the person standing nearest to her stepped back on to her toe.

"Oh, I do beg your pardon, Madam," he exclaimed earnestly, raising his straw boater. Belinda saw a tall, fair young man with the healthy golden skin of the young leisured rich used to long hours spent boating or playing outdoor sports. "I do hope I haven't caused you too much discomfort – so bad-mannered of me!"

His consternation was so sincere that Belinda couldn't repress an amused smile. "I think I can still walk – the damage ain't beyond repair."

"You've dropped your purchases." He bent hurriedly to retrieve them, and placed them in her hands. "Why . . . excuse me, but don't I know you?"

"Know me?" Belinda raised an eyebrow. Was he trying his luck with a pretty girl?

"Of course, you're . . . you're Miss Belinda Grey. I saw you at the Tivoli last week. May I say . . . you're even more charming in person."

She chuckled. "Thank you, Mr . . . ?"

"Bertram Chard, Miss Grey. Could I make so bold as . . . to invite you to take tea with me, as an apology for my clumsiness?"

"Sorry, but I'm off to the theatre now. Some other time, maybe. It's been a pleasure, Mr Chard." Smiling, she tucked the songs under her arm and walked off into the crowd, leaving Bertram Chard still clutching his boater to his chest.

Several young men had recognised her on the street before. "Miss Belinda Grey, serio-comic" had scarcely risen higher than the foot of the bill, so it was quite a thrill to her. Belinda thought little more of her most recent encounter until the following week, when she was playing at the Bedford, in Camden Town. As she entered the stage door for the first evening performance, the stage doorkeeper handed her a bunch of violets.

"A young gent left these, Miss Grey, and there's a note with them."

"Thanks, Sam," Belinda replied, and hurried along to her dressing room. She had opened the card, and was reading it in surprise, when one of the other artistes who shared the room burst through the door.

"Flowers on a Wednesday? Lucky you. Who are they from?"

"A young man I bumped into last week – Bertram Chard. Have you heard of him? He sounded like a toff."

"Chard? The only Chard I know of is Richard, who was a right rip until his father died and he became the Earl. If your Bertram is his young brother, it means he's the Honourable Bertram Chard."

"Well, I'll find out soon enough – he's invited me to dinner after the last performance."

Envy sparked in the other woman's eyes. "Make the most of him, dearie – it's not every day the aristocracy open their coffers for the likes of us."

But Bertie Chard did not look like an aristocrat as he stood turning his silk top hat nervously in his hands in the lamplight outside the stage door. Belinda felt ridiculously old as she met his flushed countenance with a welcoming smile. He took her arm gently and manoeuvred her with surprising ease to an awaiting cab.

"I'm so glad you like the flowers," he offered, seeing them pinned to the front of her coat.

"They're beautiful." She had changed into an evening dress which experience had taught her to keep in her dressing room for such occasions. There had only been a few invitations before now, but somehow she felt much more at ease with this eager young man than with the older, more practised "stage door johnnies".

They had a quiet table beneath a large plant which kept them hidden from most of the other diners at the Carlton. It was obvious that her escort was known by the waiters.

"A little bird told me that you're not plain 'Mr Chard'. Is that true?"

With a grimace of mock distaste, he said, "Found out . . . I was hoping to remain anonymous, so to speak."

"After bringing me here? It wasn't the best way to hide your roots!" Her eyes danced. Then she added, soberly, "I never expected to actually dine here. I come from the real dregs of Battersea – if you saw my family, you'd never want to be with me again."

His hand caught hers quickly. "No! Don't say that – you're the loveliest young lady I've ever had the good fortune to meet. Don't you realise how charming and alive you are? Please, you must call me Bertie – all my friends do – and may I call you Belinda?"

"Oh, Mr Chard – Bertie – of course, don't be daft! But you're surely too young to have met many young ladies."

He threw back his head and laughed. "I'm not so young. I graduated from Oxford two years ago. So I must be a few years older than you."

"Yes," she replied, with a giggle. Fancy thinking he was just a boy! An intense pleasure washed over her. She realised that she was going to enjoy herself this evening.

Later, he helped her into a cab, and sat silently and decorously beside her until they reached her lodgings. When they arrived, he leaned out of the window.

"Wait here, cabbie, until I see the young lady to her door."

A smile tugged at the corner of Belinda's mouth on hearing herself called a young lady. How Patty would have laughed if she had heard him.

In the shelter of the alleyway he took her hand into the warmth of his own. His face was ghostly in the reflection of the street-lamp.

"Dear Belinda, I hope this will be the first of many evenings we'll spend in each other's company. I hope you've enjoyed yourself."

"It's been . . . really lovely. Thanks awfully . . ."

He stopped her declarations with a wave of his hand. "I've had all the reward I need, just being with you. I'll be back in London next week. Can we dine again?"

"Of course . . ."

"Then I'll meet you next Wednesday, after the last house? Wonderful!" He exclaimed, seeing her excited nod. "Goodnight, lovely Belinda," and with a wave of his hat he returned to the cab.

Still clutching the violets against her breast, Belinda watched his departure as if through a golden haze. It wasn't the champagne, though that had been heavenly. No – it was being treated so genteelly, like a real lady, and he meant it, too. He wasn't teasing her, or leading her on.

"I can't believe this is really happening to me," she whispered to herself as she mounted the stairs to the rooms she shared with her friends.

As Bertie had hoped, they began to meet regularly. He spent much of his time in Hampshire at the family home, where his widowed mother lived, but still managed to see Belinda whenever he was in London.

"Thank goodness the old way, where the second son was expected to make a career in the army, doesn't still prevail. I've no taste for soldiering." Instead, he had a mind to put his money into business. "A friend of mine from Oxford is going to manufacture motor cars. He needs a partner, and I'd like to have a good solid interest in something. Anyway, I like the idea of building for the future – I'd like to go in for something completely up-to-date."

Belinda understood that his family concerns were close to his heart and never questioned the time between his visits. It was lovely to be able to write to Elizabeth and describe him to her – much better than talking to Dora or Patty, the girls who shared rooms with her. Dora was engaged to be married and only interested in her own affairs, and Patty was always with some man or another, having "a good time", as she would always say. She would spend a couple of days weeping over the latest departed swain, then would find another one – or two – to replace them quickly enough. But this was the first time Belinda had had a regular "beau". Although Elizabeth was so much younger, Belinda knew that she would understand.

For the first time ever, Belinda kept up a regular correspondence with her friend. She loved telling her about Bertie, about how he always treated her like a lady instead of a common little tart. Many other men had tried to make her give in to their advances, but Bertie never had. Belinda knew that she was rapidly falling in love with him.

Elizabeth mostly poured out her own longings to be back in London, though there was the excitement of her cousin Violet's wedding in August to relay. She confessed that she'd been a model of gentility in her new chiffon gown of pale yellow, a gift from her aunt. Belinda began to realise that, despite her constant longing for London, Elizabeth was beginning to show a self-sufficiency she'd never had before. Perhaps it was doing her good after all to be separated from her father.

In the autumn, Belinda wrote with a piece of exciting news. She had been engaged for a small part in pantomime at Nottingham. There was no chance that she could visit the school – rehearsals were intensive at the beginning of her stay, then the performance would fill most of the time. In any case, she didn't expect that the headmistress of Stavington would accept a visit from a pantomime artiste! Maybe Elizabeth could come to Nottingham?

Elizabeth folded up this letter with a pang of envy, and tucked it into her top drawer until she had decided what course of action to take. She was now sharing a room with Frances, and had the right, as a senior pupil, to put up her hair and wear long skirts at school. The girls could now spend the evenings talking to each other of their hopes and passions.

But it seemed that Frances, too, had had an interesting letter. Elizabeth was beginning to see a new side of Frances. Usually so calm and serious over her books, occasionally her fervour for her beliefs erupted. She now burst into the room, aglow with excitement.

"Listen, listen to this, Elizabeth! It's from my Aunt Victoria in Manchester!"

Her companion, busy hanging her school skirt in the wardrobe, stood in her white cotton chemise and drawers, amazed at the light that beamed from Frances' eyes.

"Oh, don't bother about undressing now! Put on a robe while I tell you about what Aunt Victoria says – it's so exciting."

Elizabeth wondered, while struggling into the robe flung to her by Frances, what could be so exciting about Manchester, but it was apparently not so much the city as one of its female inhabitants. A Mrs Pankhurst and her daughters had set women's hearts aflame, and their aim was to win the vote!

"The vote?" Elizabeth murmured. "But why should we vote?"

"Oh!" exclaimed her friend, fists clenched, "You shouldn't say that, Elizabeth! Think of all the intelligent, responsible women in the world who are denied a part in the decisions of their country because of their sex."

"I hadn't thought of it that way," she admitted. "Do you want the vote, then?"

"Of course! Just as soon as I am able, I shall join the fight. Great things are planned. Already they have shown that they mean business. Aunt Victoria told me that there has been a society formed in London – the Women's Social and Political Union. We will get degrees from universities, and we will vote, too. We must show men that we're as good as they are!"

Elizabeth sat on the bed, never having seen Frances so enthusiastic about anything before. "What does your family think of all this?"

Frances dropped her dramatic pose, and came to sit by her friend on the bed. "Oh, I'm not fighting them. The boys are sometimes a bit insufferable, but Papa believes in women's abilities." She smiled mischievously. "My mother had to be strong-willed to put up with him all this time – and, for all his strictness, she has drilled him well!"

They laughed, and made their preparations for bed. But, as Elizabeth lay beneath her coverlet in the darkness, she wondered whether Frances would approve of a jaunt out of school to Nottingham. It seemed so frivolous in comparison to the other girl's vision of great things.

"Henry! Henry Belmont!"

Henry looked up, roused from his reverie, and was confronted by a multitude of colours in the mirrors of the music-hall bar. He swung round quickly, searching the milling crowd. A small, athletic man, dressed in a threadbare jacket, materialised from the mass of noise. His mobile brown face was creased into a vivid smile.

"Henry, my old pal. What are you doing here?"

"Stan Fisher! It's good to see you! And how are you these days?"

Stan grabbed a stool and dragged it to the bar, where he climbed on to it nimbly. "Me? Oh, not so bad. But you . . . you ain't answered my question."

"I'm standing in for Bill Smith – he's away in Bournemouth for a week."

"Bournemouth!" Stan's grin widened. "In weather like this, he can't have gone with his missus!"

Henry chuckled as he called the barman over to order Stan a drink.

"No steady job, then, Henry?"

Henry sighed. "No. I'm between jobs just now. Finished a show last week."

"Nothing lined up then?"

Henry shook his head. Stan took a mouthful of whisky, and swilled it around his mouth before swallowing it. "I really thought you would hit the big time, Henry, the way things were going. You should at least be playing for a big hall, somewhere like the Alhambra, or the Coliseum."

Henry shrugged. "It just didn't work out like that. I had a bit of bad luck at the wrong time – broke my instrument. Still, enough of me. What are you doing now?"

"Oh, I been out of touch a while. This laid me up." He tapped his knee. "Looking around for a new opening now, much like you."

Henry nodded.

"But how's that sweet little daughter of yours?" Stan asked, leaning forward eagerly.

"Lizzie? She's not so little now. Nearly sixteen years old, and quite a young lady."

"Didn't she want to play the halls?"

"Oh yes, stage-struck for sure. But she's up in Derbyshire, at school. She's staying with her aunt."

"Didn't know you had a sister, Henry."

"Not my sister – my wife's. Starchy family, but I shouldn't complain. They've been good to my girl when I was in a bad spot."

"Wouldn't she rather be in London?" Stan asked. "You know, a little looker like her wouldn't half grace someone's act. They'd fall over themselves to hire her."

Henry was more guarded. "My Lizzie's gracing no one's act – she's going to be an act. And if she comes in with anyone, it'll be me."

Stan drained his glass. "Good little musician, eh?"

Henry smiled slowly. "Beautiful."

"Say, look, Henry, I've been thinking. There's a 'try-out' next week that I'm going to. Got to make a start again. There's an agent I know who's interested in my act. He might take a liking to your sort of turn."

"What, piccolo acrobatics?"

"Why not? You got anything you can use?"

Henry was thoughtful. "Yes, but they'd eat me alive at a try-out. My type of turn isn't for the Friday-nighters. If I got the 'bird' it wouldn't impress an agent."

"No, no. This is a great opportunity – none of your tough audiences. This is on a Tuesday night – a one-off run for better turns, wanting a new opportunity. The chap running it knows me from before. He tipped me off a fortnight ago. He'll let you in on it too, if he knows you're an experienced performer."

Henry shook his head. "But I'm not an experienced soloist. I'm usually down there in the pit, not up in the limelight."

Stan pushed his stool back in exasperation. "Well, if you ain't willing to take a risk, you'll never get anywhere."

"No. Tell me more." Realisation was beginning to dawn on Henry – here was a new chance for the old dream. They put their heads together, oblivious to the noise around them, as they discussed plans and possibilities.

Chapter 6

Ella turned from her seat at the piano.

"I have to go to the Hall now, Henry. No time left for rehearsal."

Henry wiped his mouth. "Yes, fine, Ella. Off you go."

She shifted her ample bulk from the stool, and squeezed his arm gently. "Now, don't you worry, Henry. You're a fine piccolo player."

"Oh, yes, yes," muttered Henry. "I know I can play it . . . it's just remembering it all . . . and at my age . . ."

"Oh, don't think of it! Just play, give it all you've got! Then you'll come out on top."

Henry smiled at her gently, while she gathered her odds and ends of music for the hall. Ella had been a great help to him in the past week, rehearsing at all hours of the day. He had worked up three numbers, the crowning item being 'Melody for Lizzie'. He had a new arrangement of the piece – the original had just been a melody, hauntingly beautiful.

He had never met the composer, James Adamson, for he lived somewhere out in Kent. Ella had in fact introduced his music to Henry. Her sister had sent a song, written by Adamson, who was the son of an acquaintance of hers. Knowing that Ella was involved with the music halls, her sister had hoped that it might provide an opening for Adamson. Impressed, Henry had written back, suggesting that the young man might write a piccolo solo for him, dedicated to his daughter. Within a week, 'Melody for Lizzie' had arrived, and from that moment it had been Henry's favourite piece. Adamson's music had so far not found much wider favour with other artistes, but Henry knew that 'Melody' was good.

As Henry travelled to the theatre by tram, his best jacket carefully folded on one arm, he nervously touched his music, going over the notes in his head. There was that difficult part near the end – how could he possibly remember all the notes? The tunes ran around in his brain, all jumbled together. He shied away as a man stumbled on the footplate of the tram, knocking his arm. The man shot a curious look at Henry, but he was oblivious, caring only for the safety of the small black instrument tucked into his jacket pocket.

There were six of them in the same dressing room at the theatre. It was a small building, but that was just as well, for such a bill as this could not hope to fill a large auditorium. The other artistes were subdued in mood – two "patter" comics smoking pipes in the corner, and a trick cyclist "warming up" with knee-bends by the cupboard. Yet another comic was talking in an undertone to Stan, who was wiping the strings of his violin, which he incorporated into his own comedy act. Henry nodded to them as he entered, then started to prepare himself for the performance. He was too early, he knew – but rather that than be in a panic at the last moment.

One by one the others left the dressing room, to do their "spot". Henry was straightening his bow tie when a hand touched his shoulder. It was one of the "patter" comedians, offering him a hip-flask. When Henry shook his head, the man shrugged, took a quick swig himself, and stuffed the flask into his inner pocket before swaggering off after his partner.

All too soon it was Henry's turn. He stood in the wings, gazing out into the auditorium. A mass of undefinable faces surrounded the stage. The stage blazed in the light, where the two comedians prattled to each other. Intermittent bursts of laughter came from the audience – they were doing all right. Then the band struck up, heralding the end of the act. A swift-moving, bantering song brought the two men back into the heavy darkness of the wings. The one with the hip-flask noticed Henry, and whispered "Best of luck, mate," before he disappeared down the steps to the dressing room.

There was a chairman to introduce the acts – rather out-of-date these days, but he skilfully stilled the applause that had accompanied the two comics off the stage.

This was it! Henry was hardly aware of the announcement bellowing forth to the waiting audience, who shifted warily in their seats as they wondered what entertainment the next act would bring them. He wiped each hand in turn down his trouser legs, and licked his dry lips.

Then suddenly there he was on the stage, in a sea of brightness, below him the conductor waving his stick to the introduction of his first number. He knew the man from an earlier engagement, and all at once he felt at ease, almost as if he were sitting in his normal place in the pit. Placing the piccolo to his mouth, he felt the satisfaction of producing the sweet sounds he had always loved. The notes trilled out, and soared over that dim mass of faces.

There! The first piece over so soon! He smiled at them all, and leaned forward as the ripples of applause faded. "This next number," he confided, "was written for a slim lady dressed in black, who likes silver jewellery." He nodded at them, and tapped the piccolo. A sprinkling of laughter followed, as his meaning became clear. Launching into a bright polka, he saw that they were enjoying it – the rhythms in this happy music were appealing. Again there was light applause at the end.

Once more he addressed them. "My final number is for a beautiful young lady – dedicated to her, and played for her. It is called 'Melody for Lizzie'.'' He signalled to the conductor, who directed the opening bars, and Henry joined in. The music began softly, as a haunting melody that mounted to a climax, portraying in its varied tones a sweet young girl. It then progressed into a variation, quick and happy, through which Henry saw Elizabeth playing as a child on the streets of Battersea. There followed a slow passage in a minor mode, through which he portrayed all the pain and sorrow of their separation. Then it was back again to happiness, this time triumphant, with flourishes, surely symbolising Elizabeth reunited with himself, glowing with success. Up and up, faster and faster towards the final climax, his fingers flew over the silver keys.

It was over. The applause rang out. Henry, exhausted and relieved, bent into a deep bow. Below him, the conductor smiled. Henry acknowledged the orchestra, then with a final bow left the stage. He was sweating profusely under the black tail-coat. He knew he had played well. The audience seemed to like the act, and it looked as if he had chosen the right music. But he was a seasoned performer, and he knew that there was a measure of politeness in the applause. Well, at least he had survived. There were acts tonight which had done very well – he couldn't claim to have equalled them. Stan had been one of the most successful, which was good.

He cleared up his belongings in the dressing room. In the distance could be heard the shrill voice of a serio-comic, an aspiring Vesta Victoria maybe, with her sweet innocence. Henry took little notice, mulling over his few slips, wondering what he would tell Elizabeth. She had known nothing of his adventure. He somehow could not bear to tell her of failure, after his precarious life of the past year. Again he thought back to that fateful night last February.

George – what had happened to him? And where was he now? Henry wondered sadly if he was still managing to exist. He pushed open the dressing-room door and stepped into the corridor, still lost in thought.

Two men were waiting outside.

"Good evening," said one, a tall, heavily built man. He held out a business card, which Henry took dazedly.

"Carter Willson," he read. "Artistes' Agent. Piccadilly, London."

"I liked your act," Willson stated briefly. "I could offer you some work – not much to begin with, but it could lead to more. Are you interested in being signed on my books?"

Startled, Henry stared at the man, wondering incongruously how long it would be before the buttons straining on the front of the agent's bulging coat burst open from sheer force. "Well . . . yes, of course," he managed to answer.

"Right. I'll expect you at my office tomorrow morning, 10 o'clock sharp. Bring your instrument – and your band parts. There may be something going."

With a stiff nod, the man left Henry standing, half disbelieving, by the dressing room door. Carter Willson – not the biggest London agent, by a long shot. But it was work. Work that he badly needed. Immediately his mind leaped forward, thinking of his daughter. Too much to expect big money, but at least there could be an opening for Elizabeth, when she finished at school. Silently he thanked Stan for giving him this opportunity, and the good luck which had brought them together that night. Whistling, he sauntered out of the stage door, Willson's business card tucked in his pocket alongside his piccolo.

Elizabeth was involved in plans of her own. Frances had been enthusiastic when she heard of Belinda's invitation to Nottingham.

"But of course we must go!"

"Then you'd like to come?"

"Of course – you don't think I'd miss a chance to go backstage in a theatre, or to meet your friend Belinda? A real theatrical player!"

Elizabeth sighed. "It's all very well, but how are we going to get there?" There was a brief silence.

"Listen, I've thought of a plan," Frances announced. "We'll have to go by train, and say that we're off to Sheffield for the day. We can tell them that my father will be meeting us in Derby, as he has business there . . . or some similar excuse."

"That would be marvellous . . . if only they would believe us!"

"Oh, they will – I'm a good liar." They laughed conspiratorially.

After supper they spread out a railway timetable on Frances' bed. The two pored over the hours and destinations, working out their journey in minute detail. They were so engrossed that they were unaware of the door opening softly, until a shrill voice interrupted their discussion.

"Oh, where are you going?"

Guiltily, the two girls looked up.

"Caroline! What do you mean by coming in here without knocking?" Elizabeth demanded in irritation.

"I heard you!" the young girl exclaimed, ignoring the question. "You're going somewhere, aren't you?"

"That's none of your business," Frances stared coolly at the intruder. "Just go off to bed, like a good little girl."

Caroline stamped her foot. "I'm not a little girl, I'm thirteen! You're mean to say so . . . and you're mean if you don't take me with you."

"Oh, you wouldn't be interested," Elizabeth said, trying another tactic.

"Oh, no? Well, I heard you talking about a theatre . . . and I want to go too!"

The two conspirators looked at each other in despair. "No, you can't come," Frances stated flatly.

"Oh, yes I can – if you don't take me with you, I'll tell Miss Mead."

Elizabeth walked over the window and clutched the ledge tightly. "She would, you know," she told Frances quietly.

"Little sneak," Frances hissed venomously, closing the timetable with a slap. She turned to Elizabeth. "Well, I suppose it's all off."

Elizabeth swung round again. "No – I want to go. We'll just have to take her with us." As Frances sighed, she added quickly, "But she'll have to pay for herself."

"And you'll jolly well do as you're told!" Frances insisted, frowning at the interloper. "We'll make all the plans, as we know more about it."

Caroline nodded, excitement welling up inside her. She was happy to do as she was told, now that she had won her victory and was going to take part in a wonderful adventure. Though it strained her curiosity to its limit, she agreed to leave them alone. Hugging the secret to herself, she rushed off to her dormitory.

Left alone, the two older girls groaned. Elizabeth despaired of her cousin. She seemed to be growing into a little spy. Caroline seemed to wish to live her life through everyone else – she was never content with her own company or friends of her own age, but must always be prying into other people's secrets. In this way she had haunted her older sister Violet until her marriage, and now she had turned in the same way to Elizabeth.

They managed to plan most of the jaunt without further interruption from Caroline. They had it all arranged exactly. Leaving early in the morning, they hoped to be in Nottingham for noon, to spend most of the day with Belinda. If they left by 7 o'clock in the evening, they would be back in time for supper. Frances had spun a tale about meeting her father in Derby, and this had been accepted by the mistress on duty.

They reached Nottingham without mishap, tumbling eagerly out onto the platform amidst the clouds of steam escaping from the engine. Elizabeth and Frances led the way, Caroline trotting in their wake, mouth agape. It was the first time she had been away from home without the company of an adult. The station looked far more awe-inspiring without an older person for protection.

Elizabeth found the right tram without any trouble, with the experience born of living in a capital city. The Saturday streets were thronged with people, carriages and the occasional motor car weaving around the tram as it rattled through the city centre.

Belinda was waiting for them at the stage door, wearing a smart green costume which offset the red glints in her hair. Elizabeth had never seen her look so pretty or so happy. She positively bubbled with well-being, impulsively embracing Elizabeth.

"Lizbeth – you look so grown-up."

"You look wonderful. How exciting, to have such a good part. You're a real success."

Introductions were made. Belinda scrutinised Frances. Perhaps this was not a girl she would have chosen to have as her own friend, but she looked strong-minded and no doubt loyal, which was what Elizabeth needed just now. The younger Caroline Belinda appraised briefly, having been warned in advance that anything spoken in her presence would be bound to find its way back to the Wyatt household. Nevertheless, Belinda greeted them both warmly.

They ate some lunch at a small tea-shop where they could sit and talk in comfort, then Belinda took them back to the theatre. With a laugh and a wink, she dismissed the stage doorkeeper's objections and slipped them into the theatre for the duration of the rehearsal.

The activity backstage left Frances and Caroline breathless with wonder. Elizabeth held Caroline's arm firmly for fear she would get in the way of the scene-shifters and lighting-operators going about their work. Opening was only a week away now, and there was no time to be wasted. The familiar smell of the theatre assailed Elizabeth's nostrils like a whiff of home, and her eyes stung momentarily with tears. Then she dragged Caroline through the door to the auditorium, Frances following close on their heels.

In the dimness amidst the plush seats and the glow of the lights, Elizabeth almost expected to see her father down there in the pit in front of the stage, playing in the orchestra. She had seen the top stars of the pantomime before, in London. It was a thrill to watch them again now, the comedian cracking impromptu jokes which made the chorus girls dissolve into fits of giggles. A pang of envy shot through her when she saw Belinda on the stage.

"It's wonderful, Elizabeth," Frances whispered to her as the rehearsal drew to a close. "I can see now why you find it so exciting."

Elizabeth nodded, saying nothing in case Caroline, on her other side, should hear.

When it was finally over, they returned backstage to meet Belinda in her dressing room. She laughed and chattered while changing out of her rehearsal clothes, glad to exchange news with Elizabeth. Caroline fiddled with the sticks of make-up, asking questions about how it was used.

Their conversation halted abruptly at the sound of a knock on the door.

"Who could that be?" Belinda said, a frown creasing her forehead. "I'm not expecting anyone. Answer it, would you please, Lizbeth?"

Obligingly, Elizabeth pulled open the door to find a tall young man, dressed impeccably, his hair tumbled appealingly over one eye.

"Oh . . . I beg your pardon. I thought this was Miss Grey's dressing room."

"Bertie!" With a flurry of skirts, Belinda ran to him. "What are you doing here?" Elizabeth was touched by the joy that lit his face.

"I persuaded my partner that we might want to open our motor-car factory near here," he replied, "so I came to spy out the land, so to speak. And it just so happens that my favourite young lady is also in the region . . ."

Belinda's laugh was almost ecstatic. "But let me introduce you to my friend Lizbeth . . . and her cousin Caroline, and her friend Frances."

Bertie greeted them all politely, but only had eyes for Belinda. Elizabeth was amazed at this unexpected bonus – so this was the Honorable Bertram Chard, Belinda's young gentleman. Eventually, he tore his gaze from Belinda, and turned to smile at the other three.

"Well, where am I taking all you lovely young ladies?"

"Oh . . . I'm afraid we can't," Frances said firmly.

"What? Surely you must eat?"

"No, really," Elizabeth added. "We must catch the train at 7 o'clock."

"But you said that the train at 8 would be the latest we could catch," Caroline argued.

"Yes, the latest – but that would be cutting it very fine for catching our connection." Frances insisted. "We want to be safe."

Caroline scowled into the mirror.

Bertie's mouth twisted in amusement. "Now girls, don't let's quarrel. Are you coming or not?"

"Oh, why must you both be so mean?" Caroline jumped to her feet, glaring at Elizabeth. "It would be such fun. And I'm so hungry!"

It was true of all of them. There would be nothing except dry biscuits to eat on the train. Elizabeth and Frances exchanged glances. Then Frances sighed. "Very well. But we must make our way to the station in plenty of time."

Caroline laughed excitedly, her mood amiable once more. The five trooped from the theatre, and took a tram to the restaurant which Belinda had chosen.

There was much laughter with the meal, but Elizabeth could not enjoy it for chafing to be away. They left while Bertie was smoking an after-dinner cigar, his fingers playing nonchalantly with Belinda's. The three schoolgirls departed quickly, feeling better for having eaten, and hurried down to the station.

They were in plenty of time for the 8 o'clock train, and Elizabeth breathed more easily. She sat quietly throughout the journey, gazing unseeing out into the darkness, thinking how lucky Belinda was to have such a wonderful part, not to mention a handsome admirer. She woke from her thoughts as the train ground into Matlock. The girls jumped out on to the platform, huddling together in the chill November night. Frances stopped the nearest guard.

"Excuse me, can you tell me where we catch the train for Bakewell?"

"Bakewell? Sorry, Miss, the train's been cancelled. Engine trouble."

They froze in horror. "Cancelled! Oh, what are we going to do?"

Chapter 7

The guard took a book from his pocket. "See, don't worry – there's still a train to Rowsley. That's due in half an hour."

"But that's five miles from Bakewell!" Elizabeth exclaimed.

Frances frowned. "It's only three miles to school if we cut across country. We'll just have to take it, for we haven't anywhere to stay."

Their spirits subdued, the trio sat huddled in the waiting room over a meagre fire which the guard had kindly left burning for them. The train, when it came, was virtually empty, and all the heat had long been lost. They sat in silence for most of the journey, in miserable anticipation of the last leg still to come.

Only two other people got off at Rowsley and they were too preoccupied with themselves to worry about three schoolgirls, unusual though it was to see young girls out alone, especially so late. The girls stared down the main street in trepidation. Beyond stretched the utter blackness of the open moors. Two old gas street-lamps cast a mellow light on the main street, and the occasional light glowed behind an upstairs curtain. They set off immediately, the sound of their boots echoing in the deserted street.

Soon they were on the open road. With relief they noticed that there was a moon, though it dipped in and out behind the rushing clouds. The wind stung their cheeks, and chilled them through their thick garments.

When they had been walking for nearly two miles, they branched off on a footpath, flanked on either side by tall bushes. It was darker this way, and they clung on to each other's coats for fear of losing contact. More sheltered from the wind, they were aware of each other's steady breathing as they hurried on towards the school.

Suddenly Caroline gave a cry and fell forward, pushing Frances to the ground.

"Oh, oh, my ankle – I've hurt it," Caroline wailed.

The two older girls sighed in desperation – for this to happen now!

"Can you walk on it?" Elizabeth asked. Caroline's only answer was to sob more loudly.

"Oh, pull yourself together!" Frances said, gripping the girl's shoulders. "If it wasn't for you, insisting on going for that meal, we wouldn't be here!"

"I . . . want to go . . . home!" Caroline sobbed.

Elizabeth's mouth set. "We're going to have to carry her," she told her friend.

"What?"

"We can't leave her here . . . and it must be so late. What time do you think it is now?"

Frances considered for a moment. "It must be past 11 o'clock." She shivered. "I wonder what they've been doing about us?"

Elizabeth shook her head. "Don't let's think about it yet. We'd better just get back."

She persuaded Caroline to climb onto her back, with an extra push up from Frances, and they set off again, more slowly now. Caroline was heavy-boned, and not much smaller than her cousin, who staggered valiantly under her burden. They changed over at intervals, Frances taking turns to carry the injured girl.

At last the silhouette of Stavington came into view. With renewed vigour, the two girls struck out again for the safety of its walls. They followed the curve of the garden wall until they came to the old door to the vegetable garden. It was never padlocked, but had an inner latch. Elizabeth could just get her hand through a rotten plank of wood, though it scraped her fingers in the effort. But at last the catch yielded, and they carried Caroline into the vegetable garden.

The kitchen door was locked fast, and there was no sign of light from any of the windows.

"I expect someone must be waiting up for us," Elizabeth said dismally.

"Let's try and sneak in without being seen. Then we can pretend we've been in for hours. We'll just be reprimanded for not reporting at the right time."

Frances led the way to the front door. Peeping into the hallway, she found there was an oil-lamp casting a dull glow. No one was in sight, so she beckoned to the other two. Elizabeth held Caroline's hand as she limped across to the stairs.

They had reached the first landing, when, suddenly, "Girls! Where have you been?" The icy voice rang out in the hallway. Frances dropped the bag in shock, while Caroline sat down abruptly on the stairs and burst into tears. A look of dismay passed between Frances and Elizabeth over her head.

The next morning at 9 o'clock, Elizabeth sat outside Miss Mead's office, gazing pensively at her hands clasped in her lap. She turned as she heard the door open. Frances emerged, her face grim, and could do no more than squeeze her friend's shoulder before Miss Mead appeared in the doorway behind her.

"Elizabeth, will you come in now?"

The girl followed her into the office.

"Sit down, please." The headmistress walked over to the window, and stood looking out for a minute. Elizabeth sighed silently, wishing that she would finish the ordeal swiftly. Miss Mead turned quickly, and sighed.

"I'm very disappointed in you, Elizabeth. I had thought that you were settling in quite well here, but it seems I was mistaken. I am shocked that you should have induced these two other girls to accompany you on such a . . . disgraceful jaunt. That you should have influenced Frances Whittingham is bad enough – but your cousin Caroline, a child of thirteen, and the daughter of your benefactors . . . how ungrateful you have been!"

Elizabeth bit back the angry reply that rose to her lips. If it hadn't been for Caroline . . . and it must have been she who told all to Miss Mead, not Frances.

"We have overlooked much in taking you as a pupil here. One of your background could not be expected to fit in well in such an establishment. Your previous schooling has been barely adequate, as you have found. It was only in deference to your uncle that we chose to disregard these great disadvantages.

"In view of the circumstances, I feel that I would be perfectly justified in asking him to remove you from the school."

Elizabeth's head jerked up. Leave? But she could not! Her father was still struggling, and it could ruin his chances if she had to go back now. Miss Mead went on.

"But I decided to speak to your uncle first. I told him that I would be willing to give you a second chance, but of course I would understand if he wished to remove his support. He also decided to give you a chance to redeem yourself. So you understand that you will have to conform to the ideas of this school while you are a pupil here, and remember that you are especially indebted to those who have given you a place here, amongst the daughters of respectable people."

"Yes, Miss Mead. Thank you."

"You may go now."

Thankfully, Elizabeth escaped into the hallway. She would not have to leave, then. Much as she wished to go home, her practical nature knew that this was not the time.

But what had Miss Mead said? "Respectable people." So . . . Elizabeth was not respectable, because her father was in the halls! She had suspected that they disapproved of her, but it had never been said in so many words. Well! She would suffer their attitude, and show them how respectable she could be.

Elizabeth stopped on the landing and gazed out at the crags. There lay the south – and her father. Only three more weeks, and maybe she would be free of this discipline. Before then she would be sixteen. She was growing up quickly, and already had the body of a woman, which reminded her that in time she would be far from here, and ready to go on the stage.

"Penny for your thoughts, Bel?"

Belinda turned to Bertie with a smile, then picked up the hem of her skirt to avoid a puddle. How fresh the park looked after its sprinkling of rain. The sun sparkled on the pond, where a few children fed the greedy ducks.

"Oh, nothing in particular, dear. Just admiring the day. It's quite warm for March." She couldn't tell him that she'd been wondering how long they would go on like this. He'd been more than gentlemanly with her for so long, and she was beginning to wonder if there was something strange about him. Maybe he didn't care for women in that way? She didn't dare ask.

"You look so lovely, Bel. I've never seen you so assured."

She shook her head. "I can't believe how well things are going. I've been offered a tour for the summer, in the south, and the audiences seem to become more enthusiastic every week."

He grabbed her waist, swinging her round. "That's because you're in love – it's radiating from every part of you."

Belinda laughed. "Stop it, Bertie!" she scolded, disengaging herself. "You're shocking everyone."

"But it's true, isn't it?" He tucked her hand under his arm, and turned on to a quieter path. His face became more serious. "Bel, there's something very important I must discuss with you."

"What is it, Bertie?" Her heart sickeningly skipped a beat – he looked so serious. Was this the end of their friendship?

"I . . . I feel it's unfair to . . . what I mean is . . . my family . . . oh, Bel."

She felt the strength drain from her. So this was the finish of their love.

Then Bertie cleared his throat and took her other hand so that they stood facing each other. "I'm making this even more difficult, I can see from your face. Don't think I want to end things, dear. I love you very much, Bel. But what I have to say is, we can never marry. There won't be another girl like you for me; but I have to do my duty by the family. It's up to me to produce an heir. My brother Richard has been married for six years and there has been no sign of a child. So it means that one day I shall have to find a suitable young lady to be my wife."

"Oh, Bertie," her voice caught on something between a sob and a laugh, "As if I would have expected you to marry me – me, a real guttersnipe. You goose, it means so much to me just to be with you." Heedless of any passers-by, she leaned forward and kissed his cheek.

Arm in arm, they continued their stroll.

"But I hope you won't be offended at what I'm going to ask you now. I'm buying a flat in town, as I need to stay here more often for business. It's too much trouble to open up the family town house out of season, just for me. So, when I'm settled in my flat, would you . . . consider occasionally staying with me?"

"Yes, Bertie." Her reply was immediate, laced with a feeling of relief. "You've waited a long time to ask me – not like others, who seem to have expected it. But, for you, I will – and I mean it."

And she had meant it, then. Just a few weeks later she was in his apartment, eating a meal provided by his manservant, who had then retired discreetly to leave them alone.

Belinda savoured the last spoonful of her crème brûlée and reached for her glass of dessert wine. Immediately, Bertie lifted the half-full bottle and motioned as if to refill her glass. Swiftly she covered the rim.

"No, no more. I'm not used to so much wine."

"Want to keep a clear head, eh?" he responded teasingly.

Belinda's cheeks coloured, and she quickly added, "Do you want to smoke?"

"No, not this evening." His eyes were bright in the electric light. Belinda thought how unnatural it looked, despite its novelty and convenience. Then she shivered.

"Please excuse me for a moment." She pushed back her chair, and swept aside her cream silk evening dress, carefully chosen for the occasion. In the bathroom, she regarded her reflection with distaste, strongly shadowed by the light, and felt a stab of doubt. Why had she agreed to come to the flat? At the time, it had seemed so right, and exciting, but, now the reality was upon her, her courage was failing.

It was silly to feel this way – after all, lots of other music hall artistes had lovers – and she did love Bertie. If he hadn't asked me, I would have been disappointed, she argued. I hope I can please him. I've never done this before. I hope it won't hurt.

There really was no need to be afraid, she told herself – it was her own dear Bertie out there. But this was a liberty that she had allowed no other man. Sighing, she splashed her face with cold water and dried it on one of the soft towels by the basin.

When she returned to the drawing room, Bertie had banked up the fire with more coal. She could not meet his eyes.

"Bel . . . come here, darling."

She let herself be drawn into his embrace. He kissed her forehead. "You're nervous, naturally. I won't rush you into anything – if you don't want to go on, then we needn't."

"Oh, Bertie . . . I really don't know what I want to do." Her voice trembled.

He touched her cheek, then pulled her gently towards him, moulding her body against his as their lips met. Belinda's resistance began to melt as she responded to his touch. They sank to the settee, bodies straining against each other. Belinda felt his hand slide between her petticoats to find the soft skin above her stockings, and the last of her hesitancy vanished. Tomorrow, and the real world, could wait.

Henry was soon playing two halls a night. As he was not a big name, he had to earn as much as he could in as little time as possible. It was also Willson's way of getting him known. Henry's name would be before audiences at the Hackney Empire and several miles away at the Shepherd's Bush Empire, all in the same time-span. His jaunty melodies, easy personality and sparkling playing found reasonable favour with the audiences.

It was hard work, polishing up new pieces for his repertoire during the day, speeding across London by night in a hired cab. But the money was so much better than a pit musician's wage, and he was in the limelight at last.

Somehow the audiences did not look the same from up there on the stage. The staring mass of sweaty bodies behaved differently to each artiste. To the stars, they were a catalyst, a sounding-board for the act; to the poor acts, a ruthless judge. Henry was somewhere in the middle – he knew he was not a star. He was a "filler", but they liked him, and he loved being there. The excitement, the challenge of thrilling them with his music, and the heady satisfaction of playing well – it was all like a drug to him.

Elizabeth came home to a different world at Easter. There were new "digs" at last – two bigger rooms to live in. It was back in Battersea, near their old rooms, where Ella still lived. In the bedroom was a huge dressing table with a large mirror quite as polished as any in the Wyatt house. She only stayed for a week, because of Henry's long hours, and money was still not abundant. But in that time she managed to slip into the music hall, where she watched her father from one of the boxes, with Ella by her side.

Ella, too, was thrilled at Henry's new success. Elizabeth was sure that their friend's face glowed with as much pride as her own did, as he played. Then, at Henry's final item, he announced that it was written for his lovely daughter, who was in the audience tonight, and the spotlight swung round to capture her in a pool of brilliance. Blushing, she waved at the audience, who murmured and clapped heartily, then waved to Henry who gave her one of his special smiles. The spotlight swung back to the stage, to illuminate him as he played their special melody.

The show moved on. It was Henry's second "spot" of the day, so he was finished at last. Smiling to himself, he left the stage moments before a roar of applause greeted the top-of-the-bill artiste – Albert Chevalier. As the strains of one of Chevalier's newer numbers wafted into Henry's ears, he mused that it would not be long before the audience would call for the coster-singer's famous number, 'My Old Dutch'. With his expressive, simple delivery, he knew how to wring a tear out of people from all levels of society, not just the working-class music hall audience.

But Henry was in no mood for Chevalier's ballads tonight. He felt that he had played especially well, knowing that Elizabeth was out there listening to him. He had arranged with the "spot" operator to turn the light on her, to give her a thrill.

"Ow! mind where you're going!"

His attention was brought back to the present with a jolt as he collided with another artiste ascending the stairs.

"I do beg your pardon, miss!" he exclaimed, catching the woman's arm to steady her. A pert face looked up into his – it had pointed features, screwed up in indignation, topped by an unruly mop of unnaturally red hair. Probably pure mouse, he noted mentally. But she had arresting greenish eyes, which crinkled at the corners now as her pique vanished into a smile.

"Daydreaming, I see!" she scolded. "You're the piccolo player, ain't you – Henry Belmont?"

"Yes, that's right. But I'm afraid I don't know you. What do you do?" He looked at her keenly, trying to place her. She was dressed in a gaudy outfit, with an abundance of frills on the knee-length skirt. Lovely legs – not a peep of light between them – and dainty feet too.

She giggled. "It's quite obvious, don't you think? I'm a dancer . . . but not just any dancer," she added quickly. "I'm a principal dancing girl. Some day I'm going to be a star!"

Henry laughed, delighted at her determination. She was certainly no child, probably around thirty, but would look twenty on the stage. "Well, Miss . . . ?"

"Florence Royle."

" . . . Miss Florence Royle, I wish you every success. And I'll try not to dim your prospects by knocking you downstairs in future." So saying, he gave her a mock chivalrous bow, and she skipped up the rest of the stairs, waving her foot at him when she reached the top. Chuckling, he went to his dressing room.

Chapter 8

"Mrs Wyatt sent me to help you pack, Miss."

Elizabeth swung round in irritation from the music she had been studying. "There's really no need, Gertie. I thought this was your afternoon off, anyway."

Gertie's wiry hair looked as subdued as her expression. "Her Ladyship wants me here for the dinner party this evening, so she said I'd have to put it off till tomorrow. I don't know what my Archie's going to say about this. We were going to the early house at the Empire Palace."

Elizabeth frowned. "Archie? I thought your young man was called Charlie."

Gertie shrugged, pulling the door closed behind her. "Oh, him. He were carrying on wi' Mary Little, the maid at number twenty-three, and never let on. Archie's much nicer, he were the butcher's lad, and he's just got put up to a proper apprenticeship."

Gertie had obviously decided to stay and chat, so Elizabeth put the music to one side. Experience had taught her that once Gertie made up her mind to stay there was no dissuading her. Although she could be a bit of a nuisance at times, she wasn't an unpleasant girl, and Elizabeth felt sorry for her. She was obviously completely out of place in service. Her trips to the music hall had convinced her that it was the most glamorous place in the world, and every little titbit about the halls was precious.

"It'll be so dull here without you, Miss." Gertie moaned as she hauled the black box from beside the wardrobe to a more accessible place. "I missed you when you were in London for those three weeks, but I didn't expect you to be going off again so soon."

Elizabeth took a dress from the wardrobe, handing it to the maid. "You can't really mean that, Gertie. I hardly ever see you."

Gertie folded the dress carefully. "Oh, this is pretty. But it's true, I miss your stories. You haven't told me anything about your time in London."

Elizabeth suppressed a sigh. Sometimes she wished Gertie didn't idolise her quite so much. Some things were private, to be shared only with Frances, not relayed in detail to just anyone. "We didn't do an awful lot. We spent most of the time rehearsing duets, when Father wasn't at the theatre."

Gertie's eyes were luminous. "Did you go to see him again, Miss? Who was on the bill?"

"I went once to each hall – just the two. Kate Carney was top of the bill at one, and Little Tich at the other."

"Ooh, I'd love to see them. Tell me about it, please, Miss. Is the little feller as marvellous as they say?" The thrill in Gertie's face made Elizabeth feel guilty about being so grudging.

She smiled. "Well, this time he was dressed as a Spanish dancer. He dances so neatly, just like a young woman . . ."

Packing was forgotten as Gertie's attention was riveted.

Elizabeth longed to open a window to let the August air into her aunt's front parlour. If only Frances would arrive before she melted, she thought as she fanned herself with her gloves. It had been quite a rush in the end to finish packing, as Gertie had wanted to know about every act she had seen on the stage in London. The maid was now setting up the table for the evening's dinner party. Elizabeth wondered how Archie would take his love's absence that evening. Well, Gertie never seemed to be without an admirer for long, though it wasn't surprising, as she was exceptionally pretty.

A strange rumble disturbed her thoughts, escalating to a roar. Elizabeth rose to her feet in amazement at the sight of a motor car approaching the Wyatts' house. A figure swathed in veils waved to her from the front seat as the vehicle drew to a halt.

"Frances!" Elizabeth cried, half in disbelief, hurrying to open the front door. She almost tripped over her skirt in her haste to run down the steps.

Frances raised the veil. "Elizabeth! What do you think about my father's latest acquisition? Magnificent, isn't it?"

"Yes, but noisy!" came the wry reply. "Are we really going to travel all the way to Totley in this?"

"Of course. My excellent chauffeur is entirely trustworthy. This is Alfred, my eldest brother."

The young man removed his goggles and cap, smiled briefly at Elizabeth as he took her hand, then jumped out to check the car.

The Wyatts' manservant, Gregg, loaded Elizabeth's trunk quickly. All that was left was for Elizabeth to give her aunt a quick kiss on the cheek, before she joined Frances on the leather seat.

"Here's a veil to protect you from the dust. Wrap it right round your hat and tuck it in well. I've also brought my mother's motoring coat. You don't want to spoil your costume."

Elizabeth laughed with the novelty of it all as she tucked the veil under her chin. "I must look like a bundle of washing!" she exclaimed.

"Oh, much prettier," Frances returned. "Let's be on our way, Alfred."

"Ready? Here we go." Alfred released the brake and the engine escalated to a roar. Frances and Elizabeth gave up any hope of holding a conversation over the noise.

On this hot, August day, the air was heavy with the smell of industry. As they travelled out of the city, Elizabeth was conscious more than ever of the difference to her home in London. The air seemed completely still in this huge basin of the Pennines, and through the haze she watched the people at their daily business.

When they finally reached the Whittinghams' home, Arthur stopped the engine, leaving a breathless silence. As Elizabeth stepped from the vehicle, she unwound the heavy veil that Frances had lent her and inhaled the fresh scent of her surroundings.

The sky was becoming overcast, especially in the direction of the north-east, where Sheffield's industry disgorged its waste into the clouds. Here in Totley, however, the open spaces, fresh with the promise of rain, could have been fifty miles away from the stinking city, rather than only five. The very colour of the foliage was deeper, as if newly painted on a canvas.

The house itself was mid-Victorian, with two acres of grounds. The view of the village was sheltered by trees, and formed a small hidden park at the end of the grounds. There was a stone path leading down to the brook.

A fair-haired young man bounded across the gravel to meet them.

"Miss Belmont! May I take your luggage?" His genial face immediately made her feel welcome. She gave up trying to brush the dust from her hat, and turned to him with an answering smile.

Frances stepped forward quickly. "Elizabeth, may I introduce my brother Gerald?"

"How do you do," Elizabeth murmured. "You must call me Elizabeth, please."

Gerald took her hand in greeting, then reached over for her bag. Frances linked arms with Elizabeth as they strolled into the front hall, while her brother vaulted up the stairs with great strides.

"That's Gerald for you! Always bouncing with energy. You would think that he would lose most of it in term time with all his rugby and cricket, but he still has plenty left over for the holiday."

"He's at Cambridge, isn't he?" Elizabeth asked.

Frances nodded. "He's going back for his second year soon. And," she added, her eyes burning with passion, "next year I shall be accompanying him."

Elizabeth smiled at Frances and squeezed her arm in encouragement as they went to greet her mother. Elizabeth had met Mrs Whittingham briefly at the school speech day last summer, and had taken to her immediately. Now Mrs Whittingham impulsively embraced and kissed Elizabeth without the slightest hesitation.

That one generous gesture seemed to Elizabeth to set the atmosphere of the whole visit. She and Frances spent much time with the two elder brothers, Alfred and Gerald. Young Edward was only thirteen, and more interested in fishing with the other boys from the village. Cissie, Frances' eleven-year-old sister, was surprisingly shy for a member of such a large family, but was affectionately babied by everyone, especially the two young men. She was currently enjoying a craze for scraps and pressed flowers, and would spend hours happily on her own, cutting and pasting in her large scrapbook.

Mr Whittingham spent his days at the offices of the steelworks in Sheffield. A serious, intense man, he was graciously welcoming to his daughter's guest. Generally quiet, he would appear to be uninterested in the family's conversations most of the time, but, from the carefully worded comments he occasionally interposed, it was clear that he was aware of every word. Elizabeth noticed that the family became immediately correct and precise in their behaviour as soon as he appeared – obviously Mr Whittingham held the last word in his household.

Elizabeth felt more a part of this family than she did of the strict and repressed household of the Wyatts, with Caroline following her every move, and her aunt's frowning judgement at each step. The Whittingham home seemed untrammelled in comparison. Maybe it was because there were more children. Mrs Whittingham nevertheless encouraged all their interests.

The time was filled with walks, games of tennis, and musical evenings when they sang from songsheets of famous songs and ballads. Elizabeth was even persuaded to entertain them with her piccolo, to enthusiastic applause. The Whittinghams did not frown on her association with the halls, though of course they only visited them for the pantomime, a family entertainment. Each night Elizabeth went to bed brimming with happiness. She and Frances would lie talking in their adjacent beds until their voices were drowned in yawns.

One of the high spots of the visit was a play they performed. As Mrs Whittingham loved the stage, she took part along with all the young people, seeming more like a sister to them than a mother. Apparently these amateur theatricals took place three or four times a year. Mr Whittingham was a patient audience. To Elizabeth it was a breath of home.

Frances, in fun, had cast Gerald as the hero and Elizabeth as the heroine of the piece, declaring that they could not have brother and sister playing the parts. It was a great lark, they all agreed. Gerald threw all his energy into the part, even attempting with gusto the trite love duet at the end, at which they all bent double with helpless laughter.

The visit romped towards its end all too soon. There was now only one day left in the company of the Whittinghams, and the following day Elizabeth would return to Sheffield. After the great excitement of the play-acting, Alfred suggested a more peaceful pastime for their last day, so they decided to walk down their quiet stretch of the brook. It was pleasantly warm weather, and the two girls sat chatting happily beneath the shade of the trees and their sunshades, while Alfred and Gerald tossed stones into the brook. They ate a picnic on the riverbank, then played a modified game of cricket in the warmth of the afternoon. A comfortable stroll brought them home in time for afternoon tea.

When they turned to take the path up to the house, Elizabeth felt a grip of restraint on her arm.

"You two go on ahead," Gerald told Frances and Alfred. "Elizabeth and I will put the cricket equipment away."

"Very well, then, but don't be too long, for Mother will be waiting for us."

Elizabeth folded her parasol and helped Gerald stow the bats and stumps in the shed. He turned the key deftly, then turned to his companion.

"Elizabeth . . ." He spoke her name slowly, and she felt startled at the intensity of his gaze. A slow blush crept up her cheeks. He leaped in an instant to her side, taking her hands impulsively.

"How lovely you are!" He spoke quickly. "Dear Elizabeth . . . I hope you won't be offended by my declaring my feelings for you?"

"Oh . . . no, Gerald, no." But she had an insane desire to laugh at his earnestness. Then, in an instant, it was forgotten.

"Then . . . may I . . .?" He bent lower, and very gently kissed her. The soft touch of his lips was delightful, a hesitant tasting of unknown fruits. Their lips moved softly together, as if murmuring silent endearments. Through half-closed eyes the girl marvelled at the closeness of his young face – how soft it was, not like the rough feel of her father's cheek. They drew apart. A smile slowly touched Elizabeth's lips as she gazed at him.

A sudden call through the trees broke the spell. "Hey there! Gerald! Come on, tea's ready."

"Yes, right away, Alfred!" he shouted back, taking her hand to hurry back to the house.

"You will let me write to you, Elizabeth?"

The girl shook her head wistfully. "It's no use, Gerald. All of our letters are strictly scrutinised at school. They would never allow it."

"But there must be a way. We can't part like this." He squeezed her fingers anxiously. There was no further opportunity for conversation. They dropped hands as the house came into view.

The next morning, as Gerald helped her into the motor car, he whispered, "I shall find a way . . . I shall."

She smiled at him, and fixed the veil in place, still remembering with excitement the feel of his lips on hers. As long as she could see the family grouped on the lawn, she waved to their diminishing figures, and especially to one. When they were gone, she faced the road ahead, hugging to herself this new experience.

Chapter 9

The summer had now fled, and autumn was rapidly dwindling into winter. Back at school, Elizabeth faced the discipline sullenly. How could she waste her time here, while her father was making his name in the halls? She longed to be forging her own career.

Then she would think of Gerald – and his memory always brought an excited flutter within her. From time to time, she would pause in what she was doing, and her eyes would lose sight of their immediate surroundings, seeing only that summer day by the brook. It was wonderful that a young man should wish to kiss her as Gerald had done.

Sometimes, when she was alone for the night in her room, she would loosen the heavy cotton nightdress and let it slip to the floor, studying her reflection in the mirror. She had seen such firm, plump breasts, tiny waist and round, moulded hips in the pictures of models and dancers which were sold as postcards in the back streets. It was the kind of body that men desired, and the fashions of the day were made for her figure. Yet her young body lay hidden under starchy outmoded skirts and blouses, and Elizabeth could only gaze in envy at the postcards sent to her by her father, showing the music-hall artistes in all their finery.

Elizabeth chose to stay at school during the half-term break. She was growing increasingly tired of Caroline's constant attention, especially as Winifred, the girl who had taken Frances' place in the shared room, was away so often. The excuse she gave for staying at Stavington was that she wished to do some extra work. School studies had become no easier, and still required a lot of attention. But, in fact, she spent most of the time playing her piccolo away from the hearing of the other girls, and also lost herself in examining fashion plates that Belinda had sent from London.

She thrust one guiltily under her pillow at the sound of a knock on her door. One of the younger girls stood in the doorway.

"Miss Mead sent me to tell you that you have two visitors in the vestibule."

"Thank you, Maude," she replied, surprised at this unexpected turn, and hurried to the hallway.

"Frances!" she exclaimed, upon recognising them, ". . . and Mrs Whittingham."

Both looked supremely elegant. Frances wore a smart navy-blue tailored skirt, "Gibson Girl" style high-necked blouse and tight-fitting hip-length jacket. She sported a rather masculine style of homburg hat. Draped over one arm was a heavy motoring coat. Mrs Whittingham smiled. "We were on our way to Bakewell to visit some friends of mine, and when Frances mentioned that you were staying at school we thought you might like to see some familiar faces."

"How kind of you! What a lovely surprise."

"We're in our motor car," explained Frances. "You'd better wrap up well, and bring a veil."

As Elizabeth rejoined them in the hallway, coated and tying a veil over her hat, she asked, "Did you motor all this way by yourselves? I didn't know that either of you knew how to drive the motor car."

Frances laughed. "Yes, I've driven it around Totley, but we have a willing chauffeur today." She spoke these words as they emerged from the doorway, and Elizabeth, recognising the young man standing beside the vehicle, stopped abruptly.

"Gerald?" she asked, turning to Frances.

"Yes," her friend replied, squeezing her arm. "It was my mother's idea. She was tired of hearing his woes of how he would never see you again, so she decided on this little ploy to get you together."

Astonished, Elizabeth shook her head. "But I don't understand . . . your mother doesn't mind?"

Frances regarded her quizzically. "Why should she? You're my friend, aren't you? Anyway, she dotes on Gerald. Come on – let's not waste any time."

Gerald caught Elizabeth's gloved hands impulsively as they met, his eyes crinkling with his smile.

"Gerald . . . how nice to see you," she said, meaning every word. Her breath was quick with excitement as he helped her into the motor car after his mother and sister. Then he replaced his goggles and cap, and put on a huge motoring coat over his Norfolk jacket and trousers.

They entered the village in a cloud of dust and with a roar of the engine. Startled onlookers scurried out of the way, needing no encouragement from Gerald's touch on the hooter.

"Well, I think we have woken up the whole countryside," announced Mrs Whittingham dryly as she descended to firm ground once more. "As it's not too cold, why don't you young people walk around the village, while I am chatting to Matilda. Then you could come in later for tea."

"Oh, Mama, I think I shall join you. I would like a rest after all that jolting and noise. Gerald can show Elizabeth the village."

With a barely concealed smile at this uncharacteristic speech from her brisk daughter, Mrs Whittingham conceded. "Very well. But don't stay out so long that you become chilled."

As the door closed behind them, Gerald took her arm gently. "At last! I thought we'd never be alone. Have you missed me, dear Elizabeth?"

As always, the girl felt quite bowled over by Gerald's exuberance. "Well . . . we hardly know each other."

He smiled. "That's just what I wish to alter. Tell me what you have been doing since I last saw you."

They strolled along the street, avoiding the group of children playing "diabolo" with rods and strings on one corner. Elizabeth steered the conversation away from Stavington, towards her hopes for the future.

"When you are a famous star, I shall send endless bouquets to your dressing room!"

"Oh, Gerald!" she laughed. "That won't be for years, if ever. I'm not even sure what I shall do on the stage. My father thinks I should perform on the piccolo with him, but it's such a specialised type of act that I don't know if it will ever be popular enough to make me a star."

At that he stopped and took her hands. "You would be popular at anything – people would pay just to look at you!"

The heat rose in her cheeks. "Don't say that, Gerald. I'm not as attractive as many other girls."

"What nonsense! Any man would be willing to lay his heart at your feet."

Startled at such effusive words, Elizabeth could only shake her head. Gerald's vigorous declarations left her a little frightened. "I think we'd better return to the others now," she advised. "Gerald . . ."

"Yes?"

"Nothing . . . only . . . remember that I want to go on the stage. I'm not ready for anything . . . serious."

His face relaxed into a charming smile. "I know," he reassured her. "You mustn't mind me – I'm known for my enthusiasm even for my flirtations."

Laughing with relief, Elizabeth could not help exclaiming, "How many flirtations have you had at the age of nineteen?"

"I reached my twentieth birthday last month. But to answer your question – enough, enough. But none so sweet as this."

Sharing their mirth, they entered the gate of the house and went to raise the doorknocker. What fun she would have in writing of this to Belinda, and to her dear friend Ella, back in London, thought Elizabeth mischievously.

Ella lifted the kettle from the range and poured the water into the brown teapot.

"I've had another letter from Elizabeth," she informed Henry through the steam.

Henry stretched out his legs to the fire, glad of the warmth in

Ella's little parlour. The winter had closed in on London, bringing the thick November fogs and icy winds. He still came to visit Ella on some Sundays, harking back to the days before Elizabeth had gone north. Even then, the occasions were becoming less numerous – maybe once a month, or even six weeks, and that only while he was in London. Ella, never very expansive, accepted these appearances for the company they brought, and never asked him why he didn't come more often. She loved Elizabeth as if she were her own daughter, and knew that she had been more of a mother to the girl in recent years than any other woman. More than that, the letters held confidences made as if to a trusted friend. Ella valued this, and knew that Henry would always be eager to hear any news of his daughter that she might not have included in a letter to him. Her pride would not let him see how precious his company was to her.

"What does she say?" he asked Ella now.

"Oh, much the same – that she is longing for Christmas, so that she can be back in London. Belinda has been offered a job as principal boy in a pantomime in a north London hall. She sounded envious."

Henry chuckled, and took the cup of tea she had poured for him. "Trust Lizzie! She would be."

"Any more news of that young man?"

"No – nothing since the meeting in October."

"Do you think she cares for him?"

Ella shook her head. "No, she's just flattered. What girl wouldn't be? But I doubt if it'll last. She has her eyes too firmly fixed on the stage."

"Good," Henry smiled. "I'm glad you think that. She's too young to be thinking of love."

Ella sat down in the chair opposite him. "Henry, she's nearly seventeen. Don't forget that she's growing up. Haven't you noticed the change in her since she left?"

He sighed, thinking the question superfluous. "Yes, of course. She wears her hair up, and skirts down to the ground."

"No, not just her appearance – her letters, her attitude to life. She's had a lot to overcome, and all on her own."

"But I don't regret her going, Ella, even though I miss her. It's done her good to live without me."

Ella was quiet for a moment. "Yes, I know, Henry," she spoke softly. "I miss her, too. But she's been away eighteen months now."

"I'll pay for her schooling as long as she needs it – I don't want my daughter to feel out of place in any society."

Ella said no more, even though she disagreed. She was beginning to think that it was time Elizabeth was back in London for the good of all of them. Her real home was here.

After a pause, Henry said, "I don't suppose you've heard of a dancer called Florence Royle?"

"Florence Royle? Where did you come across her?"

"Oh, at the Hoxton Empire. She wants to be a star."

Ella snorted. "Doesn't everyone! But what makes little Florrie Higgins think she'll make it above all the others? It's a far cry from the docklands. Do you think she'll get to the top?"

"Oh, I'm no judge of dancers." He drank his tea, Ella's reaction making him unwilling to discuss the subject further.

Ella watched him closely, feeling suddenly less buoyant. Yes, she thought sadly, I can guess what you are a judge of. She recalled Florence from eighteen years ago, pretty and curvaceous at the age of fifteen, with her gap-toothed grasping mother pushing her on the halls. Ella had played for her audition, while the assembled men had drooled over her shapely legs and plump pointed breasts pushed up high behind her bodice. That young woman had learned to survive from necessity, and was not afraid of wielding her power over men to her own ends. It seemed that she had added another to her list of followers. Ella drank her tea silently.

Only one week of term remained. Elizabeth, newly seventeen, spent the weekend in Sheffield, packing most of her clothes ready to be sent to London for Christmas. Henry had bought her a new trunk in London that summer, so that she wouldn't feel like a poor relation any more, using her cousins' cast-offs.

Elizabeth was alone in the house with her aunt and uncle that weekend, as Caroline had a cold and had decided to stay at school rather than face the enervating journey to Sheffield.

On Sunday evening they had had a small soirée, when Elizabeth had played some Mendelssohn on the parlour piano. The atmosphere of the evening had been restrained and correct, her aunt's friends in their expensive pastel evening gowns and modest jewels praising her accomplishment. Elizabeth had spent most of Sunday packing, and finishing off some schoolwork for the end of term. It had been agreed that she would stay in Sheffield until Monday afternoon so that she could see her trunk onto the train, to be sent ahead to London. Those last four days of school would seem so long, knowing that on Saturday she would be back with her father.

Only one more night in Sheffield, Elizabeth thought as she brushed her hair before the mirror in Caroline's old room. Then school for a few days, and home. I'll play my piano pieces for Ella – she'll see a big improvement.

With a start, Elizabeth realised that her Mendelssohn book was still on top of the parlour piano. Slipping out into the corridor, she made her way back down the stairs, her thin shoes making no noise against the thick stair-carpet.

The lamplight from the drawing room spilled out into the hallway from the half-open doorway. Her aunt and uncle were talking about the friends they had entertained the day before.

Elizabeth groped her way into the parlour, and found the music by the dim light from the hallway. She came out and closed the door softly. At that instant she heard her name mentioned by her aunt, and froze. It was wrong to eavesdrop, she knew, but she could not help but hear.

"It is wonderful how Elizabeth has improved in the time she has been with us," her aunt's voice floated out into the hall.

"Yes, I agree. Her manner is much better. One would hardly guess her origins," came the deeper-toned reply of Andrew Wyatt. "It's just as well she doesn't speak of her father in company these days. It would do my business connections no good if it were known that your niece's father is a music-hall musician."

Sophie sighed. "How I wish we had thought to bring her here sooner after Jessica died. Indeed, I regret that dear Jessica ever made that disastrous marriage. Henry Belmont was – is – a wastrel. He has no idea of how to bring up a child, no reliability. If they had never married, my sister might still be alive today."

Elizabeth stood in the cold hallway, burning with fury. Her fists clenched with rage, she burst into the warm glow of the drawing room.

"How dare you! How dare you say my father is a wastrel! He's a good, kind man, and my mother loved him."

Andrew rose from his comfortable armchair, holding a smoking cigar between his fingers. "Elizabeth! It is shameful to listen at doors," he intoned ominously.

"Listen? I couldn't help but hear as I passed. I came to collect my music."

"My dear child . . ." began Sophie.

"No!" the girl almost shrieked. Tears threatened to overcome her, and suddenly she drew herself back, trembling with the effort of keeping calm. "I shall return to London tomorrow with my trunk. I can no longer stay in a house where my father – the man my mother loved – is held in contempt." With dignity she surveyed the two before her. "I thank you for your generosity in our time of need. But you may rest assured that every penny will be paid back to you. Good night, Aunt Sophie, Uncle Andrew." So saying, she turned smartly and left the room before they could utter a word.

Sophie raised one hand to her lace collar. "Well!" she breathed.

"Well!" Shocked, she sat down, while her husband took a long inhalation from his cigar. The air seemed still to ring with the wild words of their niece, preventing any further speech.

Upstairs in her bedroom, Elizabeth gave way to the rage and humiliation that had threatened to engulf her in the drawing room. Sobbing, she tore the pins from her hair and wrenched the dress from her back. In her chemise and petticoats, she threw herself onto the bed, and buried her face in the pillow.

Later, when she was calmer, she took off the rest of her clothes and put on her flannel nightdress. Even then she could not still the trembling of her limbs. It was a restless night, a fitful sleep broken with recollections of her rage.

A milky winter sun crept through the windows the next morning as Elizabeth cleared the last of her belongings from the dressing table. A subdued knock broke the silence.

"Come in."

A wan-faced Gertie sidled in. "Mrs Wyatt sent me to see if you were ready. Oh, Miss, is it true? That you're going home to London and never coming back?"

"Yes, Gertie, it's true." Elizabeth's voice was level, cool.

"I'll miss you ever so. Your stories have made this place bearable. Miss . . . I were wondering . . ."

Elizabeth placed her mother's hairbrushes and mirror in the old carpet bag she had brought with her nearly two years ago. She looked up at the maid's hesitancy. "Yes?"

"I . . . I were wondering if you would mind . . . well, if you might give me your address in London . . . so I could write sometimes, or you could send me some news about how you're faring. Miss, I just know you're going to be famous, and it'd be so nice to hear about it . . . please?"

Elizabeth thought for a moment. Gertie couldn't be said to be a friend. But it was a small thing to do to help her. "Very well. Here's a piece of paper." She scribbled the address of Henry's current lodgings on a scrap, thrusting it into the maid's chapped hands. Her solemn face broke into a glorious smile.

"Oh, thanks, Miss. I won't be a nuisance. Just once in a while, a little note. I'll tell Mrs Wyatt you're ready."

Pale but calm, Elizabeth descended the stairs to travel with her trunk to the station. Limply she accepted Andrew's hand, and turned an impassive face to her aunt to kiss, though she felt no affection for either of them. It was as well to uphold dignity in front of the servants.

Then, as she was about to step into the carriage, she turned to Sophie. The anger left Elizabeth's eyes, and in its place was an immense sadness. Gently she extended her hand.

"Goodbye, Aunt Sophie. I'm sorry it had to come to this."

Then the carriage moved off down the drive and she was gone. Sophie stared after it, unseeing. Those words – they were not the words of a child. Her voice was so like Jessica's. Why had she never noticed before? Sophie had longed to find something of her sister in her niece, and it was only now that she could see the great resemblance, in her every action. Why did she feel such an overwhelming sense of failure? Shivering, she turned away from the sight of the retreating carriage.

Chapter 10

The train arrived at St Pancras station in London at 3.30 in the afternoon. Elizabeth had had five hours to mull over the events of the previous evening. How would her father take this unexpected arrival? She was nearly a week early, and, though she thrilled with the daring of having changed her own future, a small nagging doubt kept worming its way into her thoughts. What if she had upset all her father's plans?

She decided to take the tram to Belinda's lodgings first to ask her advice. Resolutely, she set out across the road to walk to the tram stop. All around her was the bustle of pre-Christmas London. Street-vendors cried out, advertising their wares, a newspaper boy shouted the latest headline, and the glow of a chestnut stall warmed the murky December afternoon.

A young stall-holder called to her as she passed. Her quick response was to avert her face – she was not interested in buying anything, especially as she had so little money with her.

"Lizbeth Belmont!"

She turned suddenly, wondering who had called her.

"It *is* you!" came the exclamation.

"Johnny Riley! What are you doing so far from Battersea?" Her face lit up with pleasure. Before her stood a wiry young man, muffled up against the cold, with his cap pulled halfway over his eyes.

"Got meself a stall – my old man's mate needed 'elp, so I stepped in. Been doin' it a year, now." His mouth stretched into a grin. "I see you ain't done so badly either. Saw your old man's name up outside the Shepherd's Bush Empire last month."

Elizabeth smiled. "Yes, 'e's 'ad a good break." She automatically slipped back into the odd accent that had so upset her mother's relatives. "I've been away – but I'm back now, for good. I've missed the old Smoke." She looked up to the sky, heavy with grimy winter clouds.

Johnny studied the line of her neck in appreciation. "Hey, Lizbeth," he said softly, "you've turned into a real smasher. Come out with me tonight?"

Cocky as ever, the girl thought, and laughed. "Sorry, I can't – I've only just got back, and I've got to find my father. Anyway, I'm set to go on the halls – really, not just a bit 'ere an' there. So I'll be working when you're free."

The young man shoved his hands into his pockets, and smiled, undaunted. "I bet you will, too. I'll come an' clap for you when you're on at the Hippodrome."

"An' I'll blow you a kiss – like this," she demonstrated, moving off down the street. "Got to go now, Johnny."

He waved after her. "I'll be watching for your name in lights," he called. His gaze followed her, taking in the neat ankles peeping out from beneath her skirts as she hurried round the corner.

It was completely dark when Elizabeth knocked at the door of the lodgings where Belinda lived with her two dancer friends. Her stomach was grinding with hunger now, for she'd had no food on the train. With relief she noticed that there was a light on in the room upstairs. The idea of being alone on the streets in the dark was far from appealing.

Her knock was answered by the landlady, who recognised her with a grim nod. Elizabeth was allowed to climb to the first floor on her own, and she rapped quickly on the door to the girls' rooms.

"Lizbeth! What are you doing here?"

Belinda's appearance was startling, quite unlike her normal self. Her skirt and blouse were crumpled. Half her hair had tumbled down and had been left unattended – and had she been crying?

"Come in, quickly." Belinda's melodious voice was unusually subdued, almost a whisper.

Following her anxiously into the dimly lit room, Elizabeth began, "Belinda, what's wrong . . . why . . . ?"

"Shhh!" was the swift reply. "Come over here," Belinda hissed. "Let me take your things."

Elizabeth removed the pins from her hat and took it off. Then she unbuttoned her coat and laid it over a wooden chair.

"So you've run away from school?"

"No, not exactly. My aunt knew I was leaving. They won't want me back. But time enough for my story. Belinda, what has happened? Why the hush?"

She sat down on the settle at Belinda's gesture. "It's Patty. She's very ill, but sleeping at last. I thought you might be the nurse we've hired. Of course, she wasn't due for another hour, but I have to work, and can't leave her alone like this."

Shocked, Elizabeth asked, "Is it . . . very serious?"

"Serious enough – some young 'masher' got her in trouble and wouldn't take the blame. But he was quick enough to give her the money to be ripped apart so no one need know," she added bitterly. Jumping to her feet, she paced the room, twisting her hands in anguish. "He needn't have got her pregnant – there are ways. Why? Why did she ever let him do it?"

Elizabeth was faced with a side of Belinda she had never seen before

– where had such acrimony come from? On impulse she ran to her friend's side. "Don't cry, Belinda. Will she be all right?"

Belinda wiped her eyes with one hand. "She was bleeding when she came home on Saturday. I was alone – Dora's in Southampton for the season. I got the doctor straight away, and he at least managed to stop the blood. But she's weak and feverish. We have a nurse at night to look after her, and the doctor told me she should be better in a week or so." Then she started up vehemently again. "God, these butchers! She'll never be the same again. Give me that handkerchief, will you, Lizbeth?" So saying, she blew her nose, wiped her cheeks. "Well, moping won't help. Do you want something to eat? I must have something before I go out. You can tell me your tale while I prepare it."

Belinda calmed once she was busy with her hands. Elizabeth realised with a shock that her friend's bitterness could be a sign of fear that some day she might find herself in the same plight as Patty. After all, she assumed that Belinda was Bertie Chard's mistress, for she had mentioned several times that she had stayed at his London flat. The least she could do now was to try to take Belinda's mind off this near-tragedy, so she launched into a detailed account of the past two days. As her tale unfolded, she realised the enormity of what she had done.

"I've really made a mess of it, haven't I?" She bit her lip. "Father wasn't planning on having me home for good just yet. Do you think he'll be angry?"

"He'll be glad to see you – he misses you more than he admits."

"Does he?" Elizabeth's eyes shone. "Do you think he'll let me go on the stage now?"

"I'm sure he will. Go to him tomorrow."

Elizabeth left Belinda's rooms just after noon the following day, reassured that her father would not be dismayed at her appearance. In the light of a new day her apprehension appeared absurd, and as the tram rattled nearer Battersea she felt a thrill of happiness now that she was about to see him once more.

Resolutely she knocked at the door of the lodgings, and waited impatiently for the bolts to be scraped back. The landlady eyed her resentfully.

"Yes? Who d'ye want?"

"Oh, please . . . is Mr Belmont at home? I'm his daughter. Do you remember me?"

The woman peered out into the bright daylight and nodded, accepting her identity. "He wasn't expecting you, was he, love?"

Disappointment descended on Elizabeth. "Then he's not in?"

"No, love. He's rehearsin', up at the Palace. Left word he wouldn't be back till after the show." She took pity on the girl. "Want to come to my room for a cuppa?"

Elizabeth considered the offer for a moment – it was tempting. "No, thanks, I really must find him."

She took her leave and hurried back up the street, skirting a ragged group of children noisily playing hopscotch. A tinny tune floated by from an organ-grinder in the next street. As she walked, she counted the coins left in her purse – just enough to get her back to the West End.

At last she found the theatre, and slipped round the side to look for the stage door. The street was deserted, and there was an unlit gaslight above the artistes' entrance. Without hesitation Elizabeth opened the heavy door and stepped inside to the welcome warmth. The stage door-keeper, who had been relaxing with a newspaper, jumped to his feet and quickly resumed his role as guardian, blustering at her.

"Now, now, young lady, you can't come in 'ere – artistes only, you know."

"Excuse me," she replied. "But could you possibly tell me which dressing room my father has? I really must see him."

The doorkeeper snorted into his moustache. "An' who's yer father, then? Charles Coborn? An' I expect your mother's Marie Lloyd!"

Exasperated, Elizabeth exclaimed, "No! Of course not. He's Henry Belmont, the piccolo player. Please will you let me go to him?"

He regarded her quizzically. "How am I to know that you're tellin' the truth? We get enough stage-struck young misses hopin' to get a sight of a star."

The girl thought for a moment, then delved into her carpet bag. With a flourish she brought out the piccolo, and unwrapped it. "There! Will that convince you? Or should I play it?"

Amazed, the doorkeeper stared at her. Then his mouth widened in amusement. "No, no, I believe you. It's not every young gel who keeps one o' them in her bag! Up the stairs, third door on the right – that's where yer Pa lives. Go an' play it to him."

Smiling her thanks, Elizabeth deftly wrapped up the piccolo again and slipped it into the bag, then grasped her skirt to ascend the old stone staircase. Already she could smell the familiar dusty theatre smell which she so loved; it brought a pang of longing to her. Further up, she came into a corridor, brightly lit, where the sound of voices told her that some of the rooms were already occupied by the artistes preparing for the first house. Two dancing girls, no older than Elizabeth, hurried down the corridor towards her, giving the stranger only a flickering glance, and disappeared through one of the doors.

The third door was near the end of the corridor. On the outside were the names of the occupants: "Briggs and Morter", "Max Merrin",

"Henry Belmont". There were voices within – how many, she could not judge through the thickness of the wood. She hesitated for a moment, then knocked rapidly on the door. The voices stopped abruptly. Then came a murmur, and seconds later the door was flung wide by a red-haired woman in a black gauze dressing-gown that reached her knees. Beneath this were a pair of shapely calves encased in spangled tights, and white satin dancing shoes on her feet. Her eyes were smudged with the remains of old make-up as if she had removed it hurriedly after a show. Her face registered blank surprise as she took in the appearance of the visitor.

Henry's voice came from within the dressing room. "Who is it, Florence?"

The dancer stepped back so that Henry could see the doorway from his chair by the mirror. Slowly he stood up, eyes fixed on the figure standing there.

In a small voice, Elizabeth answered his question. "It's me, Father."

"Lizzie," he whispered, then, louder, "Lizzie, is it really you?" as he covered the distance between them in large strides. Then, laughing delightedly, he took her in his arms. Her response was swift, and they clung to each other tightly. Then Henry held her back at arm's length. "My little lass – I hardly recognised you at first. How grown-up you look."

"I'm seventeen now, Father."

"And quite a young lady." Then he frowned. "But what are you doing here so soon?"

Her face froze, and she looked away. "Please . . . I . . . I'd rather not talk about it. I . . . disagreed with my aunt and uncle."

Florence Royle set her mouth grimly. "I think I'd better leave you, Henry," she interposed, piqued at being ignored during the reunion. Henry looked up, suddenly realising that there was another person present.

"Oh, yes of course. Forgive me, Florence. Elizabeth, may I introduce you to Miss Florence Royle. She's a dancer here. Florence, my daughter, Elizabeth."

The dancer smiled coolly, and murmured, "Delighted, I'm sure," in a tone which caused Elizabeth's hackles to rise.

"How do you do," she said stiffly.

Florence nodded to them both, then left the room, closing the door firmly behind her. Henry seemed unaware of the antagonism passing between Florence and his daughter. He put his arm round Elizabeth's shoulders and guided her to a seat.

"Now, Lizzie, you can't just arrive and tell me that you've had a quarrel and expect me to accept it with no further explanation. What about school? Do they know that you're here?"

"I'm not going back there, Father!" the girl blurted out. "I've never fitted in properly – and what good can it do me now? I want to earn my living. I'm old enough, now. I'm seventeen."

Henry looked at her, absorbing the full picture of the young woman before him, brimming over with life. "And you are, too, by God!" As his mind leaped onwards, he forgot about explanations. "Have you brought your piccolo with you?"

"Of course!"

"And have you been practising those duets I sent you?"

She nodded.

"Good! Lizzie, before the month's out, I'm going to have you on the stage with me."

"Oh, Father – so soon?" Her eyes blazed with excitement.

"And why not? Haven't I been preparing you for this all these years? We'll show them – 'The Belmonts: piccolos superb'!"

Elizabeth's delighted laugh rang round the dressing room.

Belinda arrived early at Bertie's flat on the following Sunday afternoon. It was to be their last meeting before Christmas, and Belinda had thought long and agonisingly about whether she should continue to see him after the festive season was over. She felt overwhelmed with a constant dread of being "caught", like Patty. How could she ever abort Bertie's child? That morning she had visited Battersea with presents of warm clothes for all the family – that way her father wouldn't have money to spend on drink. Next week a large hamper would arrive to tide them over the darkest time of the year; thus she felt her obligations were fulfilled. But after the week of caring for Patty, and the anguished hours of trying to reach a decision over Bertie, the sight of her sister trying to cope with five children and a recalcitrant father had only served to depress her further.

"It's the same old trap," she had told herself. "Have I fought to escape that only to fall into it because I've been swept off my feet? A child is the last thing I want now."

Standing in the bay window of the flat, she watched the twilight slowly engulf the street. A nursemaid hurried past from the park, wheeling a perambulator, with a little boy in a bundle of warm clothes clutching the side and trotting to keep up. Belinda stared from behind the lace curtains until the figures turned the corner. Her mind was made up. It had to end now.

The flat was glowing with warmth by the time Bertie's cab drew up. He bounded up the stairs to the front door before the cabbie even had time to whip up his horse, and the clop-clop of hooves receded into the distance while Bertie opened the door to the flat.

"Bel!" His face was glowing with cold. "Have you just arrived? You're still wearing your hat and coat. Still, that won't stop me." So saying, he put his hands on her shoulders and kissed her hungrily on the lips.

Belinda closed her eyes, feeling his love wash over her. Without waiting for her greeting, he grabbed her still-gloved hand and pulled her over to the fire.

"Now, I can't wait to see if you like your Christmas present. It took me weeks to decide – so you have to open it now." He delved into his coat pocket and withdrew a small jeweller's case, which he held out to her. Belinda paused, unable to take it. "Go on . . . for my sake . . . open it now!"

She removed her hat and gloves, then accepted the case from him. Opening it, she saw the most exquisite star-shaped brooch, set with diamonds.

"For my own star. Look at the back," urged Bertie.

Belinda turned it over, and a delicate engraving of two letter Bs entwined together caught the light. Belinda's face crumpled, sudden tears overflowing onto her cheeks.

"Bel! Belinda, my darling! What's wrong?" In consternation, Bertie flung his hat onto an armchair, and folded her in his arms. Then, in gasping sobs, she poured out the tale of Patty's trouble, of her own dreadful week of worried nursing. She withheld the deep doubts that had assailed her, and her resolution, but Bertie sensed the fears she felt for herself. Stroking her hair, her face, he pulled her down to sit by him on the settee.

"Never fear that I would deny a child, my love. If it happened to us – God forbid – I would see that you had everything you needed to look after the child. Or to have it adopted and schooled well. I would care for you."

As she listened to his gentle voice, and felt the caress of his hands, Belinda's tears dried.

God forgive me – I love him so much. I can't give him up now. As long as he wants me . . . So thinking, she rested her head on his shoulder.

The pantomime season was now upon the music halls. Stars who spent the rest of the year entertaining the working class and men of the higher classes who had a taste for "winking the other eye" humour, now stepped into a family entertainment. It was a time for exchanging roles – the firm-limbed serio-comic would don breeches as the principal boy, and the red-nosed comedian would emerge in petticoats as the pantomime dame. Middle-class families could now see in the flesh the artistes whom they could only know about through hearsay during the rest of the year.

Henry finished his "two halls nightly" engagements the weekend before Christmas, and stepped into his seasonal job. Frederick Radley, manager of a small east London hall, had hired Henry for a small guest spot as the Pied Piper in his more conventional pantomime of 'Mother Goose'. Henry was delighted – no racing across London by carriage from hall to hall. Just one hall, and a reasonable wage to boot. And, best of all, it left him more time for Elizabeth, even more important now that she was to be prepared for the stage.

As soon as Christmas was over, they sorted through their repertoire, setting aside the duller numbers. It would be wise to use material already familiar to the audience from Henry's act, refurbished as duets – and, of course, 'Melody for Lizzie'. Henry planned her début for February, after the pantomime was finished, and a new season of variety would be starting.

When the pantomime engagement was drawing to a close, Henry announced that they must make an excursion to buy a suitable stage dress for Elizabeth.

"But where shall we go, Father?"

"Why, to the best! Maison Lucile, why not?"

"But surely that'll be too expensive?"

He waved her protestations aside. "You must have the best, Lizzie. An evening gown of the finest cut will stun them – and that's what we want! They're going to take notice of you straight away."

Nothing could match the excitement of entering the establishment of an exclusive couturier who had designed costumes for such famous shows as 'The Merry Widow', when the hard times were still fresh in Elizabeth's memory. They both knew it was a gamble. Henry was comfortable now, with engagements assured until May, and more possibilities in the offing. But he was not "top-of-the-bill" material, and he was unlikely to be offered work at one of the top West End halls. If the dual act was a flop, they would again be penniless.

She clutched the dress-box tightly as they travelled home in the hired cab which Henry had thought would add class to their arrival and departure. The final fitting had proved Henry right – it was a dress fit for a star. Not the creamy pastels and lace of high fashion, which her father had brushed aside, but a deep rose pink, the dress cut low across the shoulders and fringed in a sweep from shoulder to floor. Elizabeth had not realised before how good Henry's eye was for a dress. She could not lace her corsets tightly, for she had to be able to breathe deeply to play the piccolo, so instead he had insisted that attention be drawn to the milky white skin of her shoulders.

In the quietness of her Battersea rented room, she slipped on the magnificent creation. Standing in the light of the hissing gaslamp on a grey winter's afternoon, Elizabeth felt like a flower on a midden. It seemed to be Henry's reaction, too, when he first saw her.

"By God, they're going to love you!"

Elizabeth laughed, and stepped forward to hug him. "They're supposed to love my playing, not my looks!"

"Ah, but I haven't sat in the orchestra pit for all these years without using my eyes, pet. Or this." He tapped his head. "I can't wait to see the reaction."

Elizabeth gave a shiver of anticipation. The day was drawing near.

But it was not so near as they had hoped.

Henry had two six-week contracts after Christmas, one south of the river, the other in a hall nearly in the West End. During the morning and early afternoon they would practise, first separately, then together. Twice a week they would go round to Ella's rooms, and she would play the orchestral accompaniments on the piano.

But Elizabeth noticed that Henry seemed more and more preoccupied when he came in at night, after downing a "jar" with his colleagues in the bar, or a public house. Finally, a fortnight before Elizabeth was due to make her debut, he came in looking graver than usual.

"Father, what is it?" she asked anxiously as she took his hat.

Touching her arm, he guided her into their sitting room and drew up a seat to the fire before he spoke. "Lizzie, my love – things are not all well with the music halls. We're coming out on strike."

She gasped. "But who? And why?"

"All the artistes in the Variety unions, and the musicians, and the stage-hands."

"But why now, Father, when you're doing so well?"

He gave a quick bark of laughter. "Maybe for a few weeks, but for how long? No, pet, I'm doing better than before, but only top-of-the-bill artistes are doing really well. And too many people are in the situation I was in not so long ago – really on the breadline. We have to make the contracts fair – we've a genuine quarrel with the managers. Some won't protect employees against injury, conditions in dressing rooms are often poor, and most of us suffer from the barring clause."

"What's the barring clause?"

"It means that . . . just say I had a contract to appear in a West End hall in six months' time, but I was offered the chance of a job in another hall in the next street this year. The manager of the hall which had booked me for six months ahead could forbid me to appear at the rival hall."

"But that's monstrous!" exclaimed the girl. "I didn't know that could happen."

"It can and does – and that's what we aim to stop. From tomorrow night, we're on strike."

Elizabeth knelt on the floor beside her father, her eyes troubled. "But how will we live?"

He stroked her hair affectionately. "No worries this time. The federation will pay us something for as long as it takes us."

"And how long will that be?"

"Who knows – but I can't see your début going ahead as planned. I'm sorry, Lizzie."

Henry went out later than usual the following night. It was his intention to join the pickets at one of the halls where he normally performed, he told Elizabeth. He arrived back after 11 o'clock. His face was ruddy with cold, and his hat and the shoulders of his coat damp from the snow that had melted into them.

"You're wet, Father," she exclaimed with concern. "Let me take your coat."

Once he was seated by the fire, with a mug of steaming cocoa in his hands, he told her of the evening's work. He handed her a few soggy handbills, which they had been handing out to passers-by. "The following stars will not be appearing at this hall until further notice," declared in bold red lettering, and then proceeded to list several prominent performers, followed by the main grievances of the artistes.

"Are many of the stars in sympathy with you?" Elizabeth asked. "Surely it can't mean so much to them."

"Oh, yes, they support us. Marie Kendall, Arthur Roberts, Gus Elen, to name but a few. They know that everyone can't be at the top, and most of them had humble beginnings."

"And what of the public?"

He considered for a moment. "I think they're more curious than anything else at present. Of course, not all artistes are in a union, so some of the halls can still put on a show."

"Father, can't I help in some way?"

He frowned. "You, Lizzie? But it's not exciting work. It's cold and means a lot of standing around."

"Yes, but don't you understand? I do so want to go on the stage, and all this means waiting, and waiting. At least if I can help you with this I feel that I'm benefiting my future career."

He paused, gazing into her face, vivacious with enthusiasm. "All right, my Lizzie, you can come with me on Saturday. But you must promise to wrap up warmly."

She jumped up and hugged him boisterously.

However, she was not so exuberant on the night of her first venture into the real world of music hall. What a way to start my career! she thought as they stood in the gaslight outside the hall, thrusting leaflets upon any passer-by who would take them. Henry had introduced her to the other pickets, who stared curiously when they arrived. There were five members of the orchestra, three members of a juggling act, a singer of humorous baritone songs, two comics and two female acrobats. They conversed happily with Elizabeth, in good spirits despite the fact that they had earned considerably less money than usual that week. One of the violinists shared some roast chestnuts with the Belmonts, while chatting to Henry about musical topics. The two acrobats offered Elizabeth their commiseration on missing her début, and offered her a few tips on how to win over an audience.

The highlight of the evening came with the arrival of Marie Kendall, the serio-comic, with her husband Steve McCarthy. They had come to cheer on the pickets before going on to the Oxford Music Hall to join the propaganda distributors.

"You keep it up! We're all behind you," she had exclaimed to them, to hearty cheers from the little band.

"Now there's a fine woman," Henry stated as the artiste left them. "With people like that with us, we must win. The audiences might not miss us, but they can't do without their stars."

The strike stretched on for nearly three weeks. Elizabeth read in the newspaper with concern that Marie Kendall and her husband had been arrested for obstruction outside the Oxford Music Hall. They weren't the only people to be arrested during the course of the strike. Then the Alliance of the Artistes' unions hired the Scala Theatre with the intention of raising money for the cause through a gala performance. At last, talks began between the managers and the "employees" – but more than two weeks had passed since the start of the strike before the pickets were withdrawn from the "barred" halls.

The 4th of February, the date chosen for Elizabeth's first appearance in her father's act, had come and gone. But ten days later, with the promise of a new settlement for the strikers, Henry was buoyant, and planned that she should step into the limelight the following Monday.

They rehearsed with Ella on the Sunday, before the run-through with the orchestra on the following day. Elizabeth could already feel the fluttering of excitement in her stomach. When they had finished practising, she packed up her music carefully.

"Oh, Ella, do you think they'll like me?"

The older woman put an arm round her shoulders. "Of course they will! You play beautifully, and they always love a pretty girl. Just go along with your father. He'll help you through the first performance, and after that you'll wonder why you were so worried."

Elizabeth laughed nervously. "I don't want to let Father down."

"Nonsense!" Then Ella regarded her seriously. "Are you sure it's what you want?"

"A life in the halls? But you know I've always wanted it, Ella."

She shook her head. "My dear, I know. But it's a life which will cut you off from many people – the hard work, the late hours, the stigma of belonging to the stage."

Elizabeth hugged her impulsively. "Dear Ella, you mustn't worry about me. I've lived in the atmosphere of the halls all my life – I know what it's like, and I'm sure it's the only life for me."

With a gentle smile, Ella said, "Well, I hope that you find success, and happiness." Later, when they were saying their farewells, she took Elizabeth's arm. "Remember, love, whatever happens, I'll always be there. Don't forget that."

And as they set off to walk home in the dusk Elizabeth waved back to Ella with a feeling of warmth and security.

Tomorrow – it was almost upon her at last!

Chapter 11

Elizabeth stood in the wings, her face a dim oval in the darkness. On stage, her father played a vivacious polka, his fingers nimbly working up and down on the silver keys of the piccolo. He walked back and forth as he played, putting on comic faces, stretching his eyes, frowning, raising his eyebrows, winking – it was amazing what he could do while his lips were occupied.

In the last moments of her anonymity, she took several deep breaths to relieve the tightness in her chest. She was thankful that they were not directly after the top-of-the-bill act, George Robey, the famed "Prime Minister of Mirth". It would have been too much for a début, to play to an audience strung to such tautness.

Despite her nerves, she hadn't been able to help laughing while watching Robey from the wings, in his absurd mock-clerical costume with the mobile accentuated eyebrows beneath the bowler hat. His cane twirling, he would deliver the most spicy jokes as if totally unaware of the innuendos, then with feigned anger he would turn on his audience, who were helpless with mirth, and say, "Desist! Temper your hilarity with a modicum of reserve. I beg you . . ."

It was an ingenious method of raising even more laughs, to feign outrage at his audience's reaction. Few of them could have understood the ridiculously long words which he scattered amongst his soliloquies, but they only served to make his act funnier. He had the air of a gentleman comedian, but somehow was close to his audience, yelling the occasional "Shurrup!". Elizabeth had laughed tonight along with the crowd until her sides ached.

But now the audience sat more quietly, their mirth spent and calmed by an acrobatic trio and a blackface singer. Now they were watching a stocky figure in an evening suit performing in the pool of light.

Henry played the final note with a flourish and bowed low to the applause which followed. In the darkness, his daughter blotted her damp fingers nervously on her evening dress, and stepped as near to the stage as she could without being seen. This was her moment.

Henry signalled to the bandmaster to strike up the next piece of music. The orchestra vamped quietly, while Henry played a simple melody all through. When he came to repeat it, he played the first line, then stopped in mock horror as it came back to him from off-stage, vividly elaborated. Pretending indignation, he played the next part with many flourishes – only to have them played back even more brilliantly. He stopped and thought, while the orchestra kept up its "um-tee-tum" background. Then he tried again – and the same happened. Finally, he threw up his hands. If that was the way it was going to be . . . The two piccolos joined together in a duet – imitating, complementing, harmonising - and finished with a surge of musical acrobatics. The audience clapped appreciatively.

Then Henry put his finger to his lips and tiptoed over to the curtain. Forming his mouth into a round "O", he extended his hand and brought forth Elizabeth, charming in her rose gown. A murmur rippled round the theatre and another round of applause broke out. She curtseyed deeply, thrilled at the ovation, but careful not to trip and spoil the effect.

When the noise died down, Henry again nodded to the conductor and they began to play 'Melody for Lizzie', which Elizabeth joined after the first time through. In her pauses she smiled happily, relaxed at last on the stage where she knew she belonged. As they took their final bow, Henry squeezed her hand, beaming with pride at his daughter.

As they hustled their way through the wings, she whispered, "They liked me, Father, they liked me!"

"Of course they did, my pet! And you played like an angel."

She laughed. "Angels play harps, not piccolos!"

Gently he pinched her cheek. "This angel plays a piccolo – and I think this calls for a celebration."

He left her to change while he cleared up his belongings, and they met at the stage door. As a treat, they hired a cab to take them home. While they were being jogged along, Henry produced his surprise.

"Champagne!" Elizabeth exclaimed. "I've never had it before. Will I like it, Father?"

He chuckled. "I hope you will! I don't want to drink it all myself."

They hurried up to their little flat. While Elizabeth lit the gaslights and stoked up the fire, Henry searched for two glasses. They laughed as they drank to their future in the halls, and planned more for their act.

"We won't always have old glasses!" Henry exclaimed. "Soon, I hope we'll have real champagne crystal." He held his glass high. "To you, Lizzie."

Her blue eyes sparkled over the rim of the glass.

With the start of her stage career, Elizabeth was flung into a new routine that altered her whole way of life. Rehearsals and performances – at least two a night – left her feeling drained by the end of the week, and on Sundays she had to do the washing, which previously she had managed to do on weekdays. There were always plenty of Henry's shirts to be washed and wrung out through the heavy mangle, and shirt collars to be scrubbed clean, before she started on her own garments. Then they all had to be ironed and folded away.

At least they had enough money now to buy clothes, instead of mending and making do with old garments. Another engagement came their way within two weeks of Elizabeth joining Henry's act, and "The Belmonts" started to climb the bill.

People began to notice the piccolo players. Henry was right that the audience liked a pretty girl, especially one as engaging as his daughter.

It was late March when Frederick Radley, owner of the Diamond Music Hall in south London, returned from a trip to France. Radley was a man determined to make his mark. He had inherited the Diamond from his father five years earlier. Now, at thirty-eight years of age, he had amassed enough money to take over another music hall, nearer the West End, and he was fitting it out completely. Consequently he was looking for the most promising acts to grace the stage of "Radley's Palace". He had booked two already on the Continent – an acrobat, and a magician who had held the Parisian audiences spellbound.

He didn't expect to find anything suitable at the Diamond, which he had left ticking over in the hands of his deputy manager. Still, he had to look in at the theatre to make sure that everything was in order.

The dancer Florence Royle had trapped him immediately he stepped into the auditorium at the interval of the first house. He wondered if she might after all be a possible future act for his new hall. He had noticed before that the dancer had ambitions to climb up the bill. Stroking his moustache, he listened while she talked gaily of what had happened in his absence. Her hand rested gently on his arm, and he was aware that she was trying to start some kind of flirtation.

He reached into the breast pocket of his suit for a cigar and struck a match to light it. As he looked up, he stopped suddenly, arrested by the sight of a young woman pausing in the doorway.

"That girl," he exclaimed, heedlessly breaking in on Florence's words. "Who is she?"

Annoyed, the dancer snapped her head around. She took in the poised stance of the young woman in her rose evening gown, her hair glinting in the soft gaslight.

"Oh, that's Elizabeth Belmont, Henry Belmont's daughter. She plays in his act now."

"Does she, by Jove!" he muttered as he placed the cigar between his lips and drew on it. He watched as the girl located her father amongst the men talking by the bar, and walked over to say something to him. She only stayed for a few moments, as all eyes were on her, amazed at the sight of a respectable young woman in the male preserve of the bar.

Florence pressed her lips tightly together. That girl spoiled every-thing! Just when it looked as if Radley was considering her act for his new hall, the Belmont chit took his attention completely.

His gaze followed Elizabeth out of the door, drinking in every curve of her body. He muttered a few words in reply to Florence's attempt at conversation, then excused himself and went to the front of the house. Finding the deputy manager, he questioned him mercilessly about the Belmonts. Then he slipped in at the back of the main box and watched the piccolo duo avidly from behind the draping cur-tains. What creamy shoulders! What a delightful bosom! She was so lovely it made his groin ache just to look at her.

Her image haunted him throughout the cab journey home. As he strode into the house, his mind still imagining her stripped of her rose evening dress, a female voice called out to him from the drawing room.

"Frederick? Is that you?"

His heart sank, his fired body growing cold and heavy. "Constance? Are you still up?"

A sallow, dark-haired woman appeared in the doorway. He realised that she had changed into a revealing evening gown. Her sagging body only served to make the contrast with the luscious Belmont girl even stronger. Radley's wife gave him a loving smile. "Come in here, Fred-erick. I've poured you a brandy. I thought you would like one before bed."

His heart sank. Why, oh why had he hinted that he might visit her tonight? God knew, it was years since he'd felt any desire for her. In the past there had been a couple of mistresses who had satisfied his needs, and made his marriage tolerable. Trouble was – the woman was lone-ly. Their eleven-year-old son, Malcolm, was away at school, and she had nothing to occupy her. Maybe if there had been a daughter to stay at home with her . . .

The thought only brought to mind another man's daughter. I never knew she existed, he thought.

"Not tonight, Constance. I've got work to do before I turn in." He spoke curtly as he moved towards his study.

Constance Radley bravely tightened her trembling lip, turning away from her husband's coldness.

Early the next morning he left the house and went to the nearest florist, where he ordered two dozen red roses and sent them to Eliza-beth Belmont's address, with the request that she and her father call on him that afternoon at the theatre.

Elizabeth stared at the card, dumbfounded. "What can it mean, Father?"

Henry took the card from her, read it quickly, and shrugged. "Who knows? But he's the owner, and it must be something important. At least it can't be anything bad, not if he sends you roses."

Still dazed, she said, "But I can't understand it. Why should the owner send these? Surely a note to us both would have been enough?"

"I don't know, love. But look, put the flowers in water. You don't want them to droop."

But, as he watched her arranging the roses, humming delightedly to herself, Henry felt an undefined pang of foreboding. What could it mean, indeed?

The meeting itself had a strange atmosphere. Radley ushered them into his office, holding a chair for Elizabeth, offering Henry a fine cigar. Henry sniffed it, found it to be as good as was to be expected from the manager's box, and accepted the proffered light willingly. Once seated, Radley launched into an explanation.

"You must be wondering what this interview is about," he said, leaning back and placing the tips of his fingers together carefully. "You may have heard that I've taken over another music hall, to open shortly under the name of Radley's Palace."

The Belmonts watched him, waiting for more as he tipped his seat forward and leaned towards them.

"I've been looking for acts to book for my opening season, and have decided to offer you both a six-week contract."

Henry opened his mouth to say something, but Radley went on quickly, ". . . renewable of course after the initial period is up. So . . . may I send details of the contract to your agent?" His eyes came to rest on Elizabeth.

"Of course . . . we would be delighted," Henry answered. "But when would it start?"

"My new hall is to open at the beginning of May. I know, of course, that your contract at the Diamond runs two weeks into May but I suggest that we transfer those two weeks to a contract for Radley's Palace."

Henry nodded. "What about the salary?"

"I had thought . . . forty pounds a week."

Elizabeth gasped. It was more than twice what they were earning at present.

"Mr Radley . . ." Henry stuttered, and stopped.

Radley tore his gaze from the girl, and turned to her father. "You agree?"

"Of . . . of course. We have no other comparable offers."

"Good. Then I'll send the details to your agent tomorrow. We will determine your position on the bill nearer the date, but you can rest assured that it will be considerably higher than at present."

The interview was at a close. Radley saw them to the door. Elizabeth turned to him on the point of leaving.

"Thank you, Mr Radley. And may I also thank you for your flowers."

"My pleasure, Miss Belmont."

He closed the door after them, his pulse racing. She even had a lovely speaking voice! Her presence had almost been too intoxicating. But at least he had secured her for his new music hall, at a price he doubted many would offer to a little-known duo at this stage of their career. He moved to the window, and waited until he saw them emerge onto the pavement, talking intimately, her hat bobbing up and down with the movement of her head. He watched as Henry helped her up into the waiting cab. The cabbie whipped up his horse and they trotted off round the corner.

With a sigh, Radley dragged himself away from the window and sat at his desk staring blankly at the pile of papers in front of him.

Radley did not later regret engaging the Belmonts at the higher fee, as his impetuosity had brought him a sound business investment. Audiences took to the new act, welcoming them with enthusiasm, laughing at Henry's quips, and applauding appreciatively at the end. Elizabeth received three bouquets in their first week, plus a single rose accompanied by a card signed "*Johnny*", with "*Blow me a kiss now*" scribbled underneath. She had laughed, remembering the young coster and their meeting on her first night back in London, fresh from the Sheffield train.

Ella found a clipping about them in a newspaper and brought it round triumphantly on the Sunday. Delighted, the Belmonts had bent over it, Henry reading it out loud: "*. . . a brilliant new act. Not only is Miss Elizabeth Belmont a joy to hear, but she is also lovely to behold. Grace of movement and the thrill of virtuosic playing point to a successful career for this new duo.*" Then he laughed. "*An act to which you could take your daughter.*"

Elizabeth's eyes shone with happiness and she hugged Ella for bringing the clipping. "May we keep it?" she begged.

"Of course," murmured Ella, delighted at the girl's excitement.

Elizabeth pasted it into a large book, along with their first handbills. As the months went by, more and more souvenirs were pasted alongside these, including their first poses captured by camera on postcards. These, more than anything else, gave Elizabeth a thrill, as she looked at her own face smiling back at her from the card. On an impulse, she sent one off to Frances. At least she should not be shocked.

The lodgings at Battersea could contain them no longer. In late July they moved to a smart house overlooking Battersea Park. They could even afford the paid help they required to run such an establishment – a cook and a maid. No more scrubbing and working at the mangle for Miss Belmont! Now that they were more settled in their act, it meant that Elizabeth had more free time to herself.

It was at this time that Belinda would occasionally ask her to accompany herself and Bertie when he had a friend in town. During that summer they shared many boat trips and picnics. Occasionally, Elizabeth thought of Gerald Whittingham with a stab of guilt – she had never even told him her London address. Still, Frances would have passed it on to him had he asked, so she didn't feel that she had treated him too badly, and what fun they were having. Life was aglow, and, looking at Belinda's happy, contented face, at Bertie's side, she could almost believe that life would be one eternal summer.

Radley was aware of a change in Elizabeth. There was more confidence in her manner, as she became used to the caprices of the audiences from night to night. A bad audience would wash over her, and a good night would leave her contented and calm, rather than excited as she had been at the beginning. It only made him want her all the more. He had never felt like this about any other woman; the others had been casual affairs, women who had gratified his pleasure for a short time, but his interest in them had soon waned. That he should be so fired by this child in a woman's body!

He had sensed that he would have to tread warily this time. However, as August moved in, he decided that he could wait no longer. He determined to act when he met her coming from the stage door of Radley's Palace after she and her father had been rehearsing a new number with the orchestra.

Elizabeth would have merely nodded at him coolly, but he stepped into her path, whipping off his hat.

"Excuse me, Miss Belmont, I wonder if I might ask you something?"

Startled at this opening, she looked at him with wide eyes from beneath the brim of her lemon gauze hat. His tanned face was strikingly handsome with its strongly defined bones offset by a glossy brown moustache. But she didn't like to see it so close to her own, almost touching her hat as he bent down. She leaned back a little.

"Oh, of course, Mr Radley," she finally replied.

He cleared his throat, then launched forth. "Would you do me the honour of dining with me this evening, after the show? There is something I wish to discuss with you."

"I'm afraid we cannot. My father is travelling to Southampton to meet a French instrument-maker. Perhaps tomorrow night would be suitable, for he should be back by early afternoon."

"No, no, there is no need for that." It was better, he thought, if she believed that he had wished to see them both. He could introduce the matter more delicately. "It will suffice to have your company alone. I take it your father will have no objections?"

She creased her brow a little. "No, I suppose not. Where do you wish to meet me?"

"Come to my office when you are ready, and I'll arrange for my carriage to meet us at the main door. The crowds should have dispersed by then."

With little further conversation, they parted. On entering the darkness of the theatre, Radley found that his heart was pounding. Cursing himself for a fool, he ran up the stairs to the door into the auditorium, ignoring all those who called "Good day" to him, his mind mulling over his possible approach for that evening.

The gaslight shimmered over her hair, gilding the odd wisps which had escaped the pins and curled over her forehead and at the base of her neck. Radley congratulated himself for having the idea of hiring a room to themselves, which meant that no one else could enjoy the sight of the young woman before him. Her evening gown was of the palest blue, laced tighter than those she wore on stage, to show off her slender waist.

Every movement of her smooth, rounded arms, as she lifted fork to mouth or raised her wine glass, had been watched avidly by the manager. He now drank his port, while she toyed with the remains of a cream meringue on her plate.

"Mr Radley, I think the time has come for you to explain what you want of us."

Carefully he laid down his glass, and looked straight into her eyes. This was no time for prevaricating. "Not your father, my dear. This evening's business is with you."

"With me? Why, I . . ." her voice tailed off.

"You may not be aware of the admiration I hold for you," he continued. "When I engaged you for the Palace I wasn't fully aware of your potential as an artiste. But I was aware of you . . . as a woman." He paused, and, when she made no reply, he went on. "As it turned out, you and your father have become very successful. But it wasn't monetary gain which prompted my action. I wanted you near me. And I want to make you . . . nearer. Do you understand what I am proposing?"

She had been gazing as if mesmerised into her empty plate. Slowly she lifted her head until her eyes met his. "You are a married man, Mr Radley," she said in a quiet, level voice.

"Yes," he acknowledged. "It isn't marriage I'm proposing, as you know. It would be an arrangement which would be . . . not without advantages for you. I would look after you. I'm a wealthy man."

A flush crept up her face and spread down across her neck and shoulders. She gripped the edge of the table, and when she spoke her voice was tight.

"How dare you, Mr Radley. I may be an artiste, but I do have my morals. I wouldn't accept a penny from you, save what I earn honestly. I would rather die than do what you ask of me." With shaking hands she reached for her gloves. "Please ring for my wrap. I wish to go home now."

Breathing slowly, Radley watched her with a frown between his brows. "Very well," he conceded, "if that's what you wish."

He rang for the waiter, and when he appeared curtly demanded the bill, and "Madam's wrap". The waiter returned almost immediately with Elizabeth's fur draped over one arm. While Radley dealt with the bill, she took the fur and quickly wrapped it round her chilled shoulders.

As they left the restaurant, she held back. "Please call me a cab."

"Now don't be unreasonable. My carriage is here."

"I have enough money to get me home." Spotting a free cab, she raised her arm quickly and caught the cabbie's eye. This accomplished, she turned to Radley. "If you wish to terminate our engagement at the Palace, it will be perfectly acceptable to me," she announced coldly.

With an exclamation of annoyance, he took her arm. "Elizabeth! Please be reasonable."

Furious, she shook herself free. "Miss Belmont, if you please!" she hissed, and called out her destination to the cabbie. She wrenched open the door, but was not quick enough to evade Radley's last remark.

"Your engagement stands," he said. "And so does my offer."

Speechless with rage, she knocked on the ceiling of the cab, at which the driver clicked up his horse to a trot.

Radley remained motionless, glowering beneath a street-lamp. His offer had been rejected outright. However, he wasn't a man to admit defeat. He would work out a way to make her yield, somehow. He leaped into his own carriage and barked to the driver to return home.

Henry had bought two new piccolos from the French instrument-maker, and was delighted both at their craftsmanship and at the sound they made. Filled with enthusiasm, he hardly spared a moment to listen to his daughter's explanation of the previous night.

I can't tell him what the manager asked, she thought desperately. What if he thought I'd encouraged him? I know now I shouldn't have gone alone with him, after all he's a married man, and why else should a man take a woman alone to dinner? It's not something my aunt would have approved of. Elizabeth found it was a help to remember that, when trying to do the right thing.

Finally Elizabeth told Henry that Radley had only wished to reward them for a job well done, and to ask how long they would be willing to continue at Radley's Palace. He had in fact asked her this quite early on in the evening, so it was no fabrication.

"Well, it seems funny to pay for an expensive meal just for that. Nice place?"

"Yes," she stated, hoping he wouldn't ask for a description. It would be better not to reveal that they had been alone in a private room.

"Look, see how beautifully the key work is made. And look at the head joint – it's lined with silver. Go on, try it. What a sweet sound. I couldn't believe it when he told me how reasonable it was."

Obediently, Elizabeth played a few notes on the piccolo, relieved that Henry's attention was so taken with the new instruments. All she had to hope was that Radley didn't suddenly terminate their contract. He wouldn't, would he?

To her relief, the situation didn't change. As the weeks passed, she made sure she avoided the manager as much as possible. It was a relief when their contract finished at the end of August. Henry accepted a new contract to run from mid-October to the beginning of the pantomime season in December. There would also be more work for them in the spring at Radley's Palace. It was good, steady work, so Elizabeth could hardly complain.

They had a successful run at the Bedford Music Hall in Camden Town, coupled with appearances at the New Battersea Empire where Ella worked, the first time they had ever all played together professionally. The Battersea theatre was the second spot, which meant that after the last house they only had a short journey home.

Elizabeth yawned cavernously. "Another Saturday night over. What time is it, Father?"

Henry switched off the light above the dressing-room mirror, and slipped his watch out of his pocket. "Quarter past 11. Not bad. We should be home by half past. Ready, pet?"

Her eyes were smarting a little from the cold cream she had used to remove her make-up. She dabbed them with a handkerchief. "Yes, let's go. I'm looking forward to a rest tomorrow."

Gathering their stage clothes and instruments, they headed for the stage door.

"'Night, Bill," Henry called to the doorkeeper.

"Wait, Mr Belmont. There's a woman here says she knows you." He waved his pipe towards a seat in the corner, where a small female figure sat hunched over a threadbare holdall.

Henry frowned. He felt no recognition at all for this stranger, who lifted her head eagerly at the sound of the voices.

Elizabeth, following her father, gasped. "Gertie! What are you doing here?"

Henry turned to his daughter. "You know her?"

"She's Aunt Sophie's maid, from Sheffield."

"No more, I'm not. I've left service. I got here on the train at tea-time."

"But . . . why?"

Gertie stood up, the limp rag doll of a few moments earlier now charged with energy. "I couldn't stand it any more. I've come to make my fortune – I'm going on the halls."

Elizabeth and Henry were saved any reply as the stage door burst open, and two performers rushed through with only minutes to spare before their act was due on stage. "Stupid place to stand!" one snarled as he nearly careered headlong into the three standing just inside the door. Henry grabbed Elizabeth's arm, sweeping her to one side.

"It's time we were gone," he said once the running footsteps had disappeared towards the dressing rooms. "Where are you staying, Gertie?"

"Well . . ." she looked sheepish. "I haven't decided . . . I mean, I don't know . . . you see, I've only got two shillings left, after the train fare."

Elizabeth looked at Henry. A small expression of agreement passed between them. "Well, you can come home with us tonight. Tomorrow we'll decide what's the best thing to do."

Gertie's face was radiant. "Oh, thanks, Miss. I don't know what I would have done."

"Mind," Elizabeth said as they made their way down the steps, "we don't have a spare bed. It'll have to be cushions."

"I don't mind. You're really kind." Gertie chattered happily through-out the whole journey, thoroughly excited by the trip in the hansom cab, though it was very cramped with the three of them, plus costumes.

Their cook had left a cold meal for them, and Gertie shared this gratefully, as she had eaten nothing since leaving Sheffield.

"I told Mrs Wyatt I'd got another job, and she didn't ask where. Maybe she thought it were in service, but I'm not doing that again, if I can help it. But I'll do anything for you, Miss, just till I get on the stage."

"What did your family say about all this?" Henry asked.

"Well, it doesn't affect them, you know. I've got four brothers and three sisters, all older than me. There's only our Effie who's younger, and she's in service too. And when Frank said he wasn't ready to get married, well, I knew I'd had enough."

"Frank? What happened to Archie?"

"Oh, that were ages ago. Frank and I'd been walking out for near on four months, and I thought he'd get me out of service. Well, that's all water under the bridge now. I'm here in London to make my fortune."

Elizabeth looked at her father in despair. How she wished she'd never written to Gertie. She'd only sent a couple of notes, and a handbill which she thought would thrill her. Now Gertie seemed to think that it was easy to make a name on the halls.

Seeing Elizabeth's expression, Henry quickly said, "Well, we'll talk about that tomorrow. It's time we turned in."

Henry thought about Gertie overnight, and decided that the best idea would be to take her to Belinda, for she had an inventive mind and might come up with a solution.

Luckily, Belinda was at home that weekend, as Bertie was attending a house-party in Gloucestershire. She was glad to see Elizabeth and her unexpected visitor, as Dora and Patty were both out.

Belinda looked Gertie up and down, seeing a small, neat figure, a pretty smile, dimpled cheeks, and luxuriant, wavy brown hair. "Well, you're presentable enough – what can you do?"

Gertie wriggled uncomfortably. "I don't know. I thought you might be able to tell me."

Belinda laughed. "It ain't for me to tell you. Surely you have some ideas. Can you dance? Sing? Do acrobatics?"

"I . . . I don't know. I could try . . ."

"Do you know 'The Boy I Love is Up in The Gallery'?" It was a popular music-hall song.

"I . . . think so." Gertie took a deep breath, and began to sing in a wavering voice.

Elizabeth's face took on a pained expression. "That's no good. Let's forget about singing. What about dancing?"

"Try these steps with me." Belinda hummed a tune, executing a simple sequence. Gertie stumbled along valiantly after her, but it was clear that her talent did not lie in that direction either.

Elizabeth sat down with a sigh. "Well, Gertie, you'll need to find someone who'll take you into their act just to look pretty."

"Maybe I could learn to dance if I tried really hard, did some every day."

Belinda patted her arm. "Maybe. But in the meantime, you might think of becoming a dresser. Some of the quick-change acts need someone to help them dress in the wings. I'll keep my eyes open, and Lizbeth will too."

Gertie nodded, a little subdued.

There was no other solution than to take Gertie back home again. Tilly, their maid, was quite huffy whenever she did anything in the house, but Gertie seemed not to notice, happily lending a hand whenever she thought it necessary.

By the end of the week, Belinda had heard of a quick-change artiste who needed another dresser. Gertie was despatched to see her, and declared suitable. The artiste was off to Bristol at the weekend to start a tour, so the little Yorkshire woman was bundled off with her belongings, and disappeared out of Elizabeth's life once more.

Chapter 12

"A letter for you, Lizzie. Sheffield postmark."

Elizabeth, who was busy unhooking her boots, straightened up quickly, the button-hook poised in mid-air. "Oh, no, surely not something about Gertie." It was only a few days since her departure, and the house was blessedly quiet again. Tilly was even thawing a little, her fifteen-year-old pride mollified by the Belmonts' insistence that they couldn't have a better maid than herself.

Quickly, Elizabeth tore open the envelope. Then her frown disappeared, sheer pleasure replacing it. "I ought to have recognised the writing. It's from Frances. She's coming to London next week with her brother, Gerald, to see one of his friends. They want to come to one of our performances."

"We'll be back at Radley's Palace for our last spot, and there are some good acts on – Kate Carney and George Formby, for a start."

"And the Belmonts!" she added.

He hugged her, laughing. "Yes, the Belmonts, too. It'll be a good bill."

Elizabeth sent her reply the next day, but, once it had gone, she couldn't help wondering how she should behave towards Gerald. Would he expect to continue their flirtation after all this time? Surely not – they hadn't been in contact since she left school. Frances had kept up a correspondence, full of news about her success in entering Cambridge University. The life sounded very intense, with the serious lectures and strict chaperonage. Frances was thriving on it, but to Elizabeth there was no comparison with the bright lights of the music hall.

When the evening finally arrived, her stomach fluttered with an apprehension she had not felt since that first week of her performing career. She still felt the excitement of playing in public, knowing that a second's lapse in concentration could break the flow of memory, or cause a wrong note to intrude. But real nerves had never troubled her since then.

As they ran through the stage doorway, the Palace doorkeeper called out, "Flowers for Miss Belmont!"

Henry grasped them and passed them to Elizabeth, who was already unbuttoning her coat as she hurried along in front of him. Deftly she flicked over the card, smiling excitedly.

"Is it from your guests?" her father asked, pushing open the dressing-room door.

"Yes. Frances writes *Best of luck from all of us. We look forward to meet-*

ing you after the show." Elizabeth placed the posy in a jar by the window, and poured a little water from the jug set out for their use. She flopped into a chair, opened her make-up box and dusted some powder across her bosom. On studying her reflection carefully, she decided that her eye make-up needed no touching up, so she replaced the powder puff and snapped the box shut.

Henry was twisting the ends of his moustache while checking in the mirror that there were no specks of fluff on his black tail-coat. A deep sigh from Elizabeth made him turn round.

"Tired, my pet?"

She stretched her arms up to the ceiling. "What a long day this has seemed! How will I stay awake to entertain them? They'll think me so dull!"

Henry's eyes twinkled. "Not at all, you wait and see. Once you're on stage you'll wake up. You know what it's like – the applause always runs through your body like fresh blood in your veins."

It was true. As they faced the audience, ready to begin the act, Elizabeth's energy levels leaped up, and she felt the familiar excitement. Gone were the nerves and the anxiety that she needed to play especially well for her friends. She was the music, part of a duet of sound played through the intricate pipe held in her hands.

The last notes of 'Melody for Lizzie' burst from their piccolos in a wild flourish, and were met with the crash of applause. The limelight illuminated their smiling faces while they bowed to acknowledge the appreciation of the crowd.

Henry's arm rested lightly on her shoulders as they left the stage, then climbed to their dressing room. Behind them blared the tinny music for a number by the dancing girls.

"Well, they will have enjoyed that, Lizzie."

"Do you think so? I felt it went well, didn't you?"

He nodded. "Enough time now to change before they arrive. Where will you go?"

"Oh, I believe Gerald has a place he frequents when in Town. I shall wear my ivory satin, and send the red dress home."

She began to remove her make-up, wiping every trace from her face. Only women of dubious morals would be seen wearing cosmetics outside the theatre. Then she noticed that Henry wasn't removing his tail-coat, as he usually did after the last show.

"But what about you, Father? Aren't you going home?"

"No, not yet. Seeing as my daughter is going to be out enjoying herself, I've arranged a little company."

He began to unhook her dress while he spoke.

"Company? What do you mean?"

"Well, only one person." He released the dress so that she could step out of it. She lifted down a hanger from the wall and arranged the dress carefully over it.

"It's Florrie."

"Florrie?" She turned to him, not recognising the name.

"Oh, you've met her once or twice. Florence Royle, a dancer in fact, a soloist."

The girl's eyes narrowed. Of course, she remembered her now – the dancer in the spangled tights who had been in her father's dressing room last year when Elizabeth had arrived from Sheffield.

"I didn't think that she was friendly with you now." Elizabeth reached for the ivory dress and stepped into it.

"Oh, it's for old times' sake. She's taking up a year's contract in America, beginning in February. She sails next Friday. I thought it would be nice to say goodbye."

Elizabeth felt suddenly flat. She couldn't say why the thought of Florence with her father should fill her with such distaste, except that she had never liked Florence. It was difficult trying to think of a suitable comment to make now. Fortunately, she had no need to supply any reply. A flurry of knocking on the door jerked her back to the immediate present.

"Oh, quick, help me with my dress!" she exclaimed, reaching for her necklace which she clipped on while Henry fastened the last of the tiny hooks. Smoothing the material over her hips, she looked to him for confirmation of her presentability, which he gave with a nod of his head and an appreciative smile.

If it hadn't been for Henry's revelation, her evening would have been one of unclouded enjoyment. Frances was as full of enthusiasm as ever, though dressed quite severely in brown. It was part of her new self, she explained, for she was taking life seriously now, and all her fellow undergraduates were constantly trying to display an air of non-frivolity.

Gerald shook hands with Henry, and in turn introduced his own friend, William Hareton, who was in his final year at Cambridge and due to enter his father's law firm when he graduated. In every way, Gerald seemed to overshadow him. William was shorter by two or three inches, and his hair and fine moustache were of a nondescript light brown. He slipped unobtrusively into the background once the introductions had been made.

"We did enjoy the show!" exclaimed Frances. "What a magnificent woman Kate Carney is. She knows just how to put across a song. And what a superb hat she was wearing!"

Elizabeth laughed. "Yes, she's the original 'coster' girl, with her pearly outfits and hats. I wondered whether I should try that sort of dress, all pearl buttons."

"Oh, no, it wouldn't be in keeping with your music." The soft voice of William Hareton came from behind her, insistently. "It's too refined for a cockney outfit."

Amused to hear their act so described, Elizabeth turned to him with a smile on her lips. The look of intensity in his eyes gave her an unexpected frisson of pleasure.

Then Gerald interrupted. "I personally thought you were the most attractive act on the stage!"

"Well, that makes me very happy," she exclaimed, turning to kiss Henry goodbye as he left. The rest of them followed almost immediately.

Frances talked enthusiastically about her new way of life. She had come specially to see her aunt's new home in Belgravia, to which she had moved from Manchester. Apparently the two women had spent the day locked in delighted discussion of the latest developments in the fight for women's suffrage.

"It's so wonderful," Frances enthused over the rumbling of their taxi cab, "to see it all first-hand."

"To see London?" Elizabeth asked.

"No, no, don't you realise? The WSPU!"

"What on earth is that?"

"Oh, Elizabeth. Surely you remember? The Women's Social and Political Union – more commonly known now as the Suffragettes!"

Elizabeth recalled the vigorous correspondence between Frances and her politically minded aunt in Manchester. She had thought that, now Frances was at university, she would not have time to take part in political activities.

At this moment, Gerald butted in. "Here we are, thank goodness. Once Frances climbs onto her box, she won't come down for hours. Let's go in while we have the chance!"

He spoke playfully, but Elizabeth noticed the flash of annoyance in Frances' eyes.

"Well, at least it's for the good of the country, not mere frivolity like horse-racing. You and William talked about nothing else all the way to the theatre!" she retorted.

Gerald merely grinned, while his friend looked vaguely uncomfortable. William opened the cab door and jumped out, holding it steady for them to pass through. Elizabeth gave him a warm smile of thanks, and was amused to see a hint of pink appear in his cheeks.

The restaurant Gerald had chosen was richly decorated in red plush, with heavy velvet curtains tied back with gold tassels. The food was deli-

115

cious, but Elizabeth's appetite was meagre after hearing her father's plans for the evening. She kept thinking of him with Florence Royle, wondering what they were doing, and each time the question formed in her mind she felt a twist inside her.

Frances and Gerald dominated the conversation, while Elizabeth made what seemed to be the right responses. Time after time she found her mind wandering, only to become aware of William Hareton's earnest face turned in her direction. Eventually, she found her own cheeks growing warm, as yet again their eyes met. Suddenly she wanted to know more about him.

It was growing late, however. Their meal was over, and Elizabeth was desperately tired. Time and time again she tried to think of something with which to open a conversation with William Hareton, but only found herself making dull replies to Frances' questions. All too soon they were in a cab, trundling along through darkened streets to her home, before the others went on to where they were staying.

Her thanks were sincere. It had been a lovely evening despite her weariness and absent-mindedness.

"I'll send you details of some meetings," Frances said as she kissed Elizabeth's cheek.

"Meetings?" she returned, mystified.

"Of the WSPU. You agreed you would go."

"Did I?" She couldn't remember having said anything, and was cross with herself for not having paid closer attention to the conversation.

"Yes. You must see for yourself what it's really like. I shall be in London from time to time to attend various meetings and rallies. We can go together sometimes. We'll show Mr Campbell-Bannerman what women are really made of!" The fire of the militant suffragette blazed from her eyes.

Over her shoulder, Gerald caught Elizabeth's eye and winked. Stifling a giggle, she replied, "Oh, of course, do send me the literature, Frances. I'll certainly read it."

Then, serious once more, she gave her hand to the quiet young gentleman. "Goodbye, Mr Hareton. It's been a pleasure meeting you."

He almost stood up in the carriage, but was hampered by the low ceiling. "No, no, the pleasure is mine, Miss Belmont. I hope we shall meet again."

"Perhaps." She smiled sweetly at him, then turned to bid Gerald goodbye. Still she could feel William's eyes upon her, but she avoided his glance, much as she ached to look up again. Who knew if their paths would ever cross again?

His features were imprinted on her mind's eye as she entered the house. But as soon as she saw the darkened parlour her heart sank in the knowledge that her father wasn't home yet. He would have waited for her, wouldn't have gone to bed without saying goodnight. The warmth of her own evening fled for good, and unease settled on her like a dark cloak.

She couldn't sleep until she heard the furtive rattle of the front door, signalling Henry's arrival some two hours later. Even then she lay awake, listening, longing to ask him about his evening but fearing an answer she didn't want to hear. The rumble of early morning traffic had already started when she finally drifted from consciousness into welcome sleep.

Well, at least Florence was out of reach now, an ocean separating them. Henry had said little to Elizabeth about their night out together, and she could only hope that her father would forget the dancer now. No doubt Florence would find plenty of amusement in the vaudeville halls of the United States. With any luck she would find a permanent attachment, and would settle there.

The anniversary of the début of "The Belmonts" passed in February. It was difficult for Elizabeth to comprehend that she had been an artiste for only a year. Their rise to fame had been remarkably swift, mainly due to Henry's original reputation as a soloist, but undeniably helped by the influence of Frederick Radley. They were finally free of their contract with him. In the new year they finished their engagements at Radley's Palace, appearing instead in Leicester Square, in the very heart of the West End.

It was a thrill to be on the same bill as some of the really big names. Eugene Stratton, the blackface singer and dancer, Vesta Victoria, and Little Tich all graced the same stage as the Belmonts. Elizabeth would always make a point of standing in the wings to watch Little Tich. The performances of this tiny man never failed to thrill her. His ingenious dance routines in character costumes were amazing, and he even imitated female dancers to perfection. Always, there would be his "big boot" dance, the favourite of his audiences, which they wouldn't let him leave out of his act. The boots were three feet long, and on these he would balance and dance with incredible skill. Yet Elizabeth in the wings would see the fatigue and strain on the diminutive features after the curtain had hidden him from the audiences. What the artiste would do to please his public! Even the top artistes didn't have an easy time of it.

With no worries now on account of Florence and Henry, Elizabeth was able to immerse herself in her work and social life. New pieces needed rehearsing, and new arrangements of old material. From time to time there would be a new item from James Adamson, the composer of 'Melody for Lizzie', and these they usually bought. Elizabeth had

little time to read the pamphlets that Frances sent her, along with letters urging her to join the fight for the vote. As Elizabeth pointed out,
most of the meetings took place while she was at work. It was taxing
enough to be a performer, without becoming involved in strenuous
political struggles.

A new revolution in fashion styles that year discarded the old tightly
laced corset, to Elizabeth's relief. She and Belinda rushed out to
order some new gowns immediately, and, when they were delivered,
tried them on in Elizabeth's spacious bedroom at the Battersea house.

"What a difference!" Elizabeth exclaimed as she scrutinized the new
long straight corset that reached nearly to her knees. "How free my
waist feels – and you know that I never laced tightly for the stage because
of needing to breathe freely."

"It's strange to be without all those petticoats. There aren't even any
frills or lace on this dress. Help me hook up the back, Lizbeth."

"How elegant," they breathed, examining their reflections in the
large glass. Belinda looked so tall in her narrow dress with its swirl of
fabric at the hem. Elizabeth's was intricately tasselled and embroidered
on the high bodice, which reached to just below her bust. Finally, they
added the widest hats they had ever owned, festooned with ostrich feathers.

"I'll have to find a new song for this outfit!" exclaimed Belinda. "I
can't keep singing the same old numbers when I'm dressed in a wild
new fashion. Do you think your composer could write me one?"

Elizabeth laughed while pinning her hat to her hair. "James Adamson isn't our composer. Our agent has his address. I'm sure he'll be
glad of your custom. Look, do you think I should pad out my hair? My
hat keeps slipping to one side or the other."

As Belinda adjusted her friend's hat, a thought crossed her mind.
"Why, look at the pair of us – not what your friend Frances would be
doing. We're like a pair of fashion plates. Do you think Frances talks
of anything except intellectual matters?"

"We're working women – it's part of our jobs to appear in the height
of fashion. Forget Frances and her suffragettes. Isn't this exciting?
Just wait until Bertie sees you in your new gown."

The very mention of his name was like a taste of honey to Belinda.
She twirled so that she could study her back view in the mirror.

"You'll turn a few heads, too. What about Felix Hampton, Bertie's
old school chum?"

"I say, old gel!" mimicked Elizabeth, rounding her thumb and
forefinger into a monocle shape, which she placed over her right eye,
"You look absolutely topping, what?"

They shrieked with laughter at her impersonation of the young gentleman who fancied himself as a 'masher'. Downstairs in the parlour, Henry heard their hilarity and smiled to himself.

There was no doubt that the battle for women's suffrage was becoming more energetic. In February, Mrs Pankhurst, leader and idol of the aspiring women, was sent to prison for six weeks. She emerged full of indignation at the treatment of women inmates, and ready to begin a crusade for better conditions. Frances wrote to Elizabeth that she, too, would risk imprisonment for the sake of the cause.

In early June the non-militant suffrage society, the Suffragists, staged a spectacular march from the Embankment to the Albert Hall, displaying an impressive array of women workers. Writers, artists, factory workers and typists all congregated beneath embroidered banners denoting their trades, and walked eagerly to listen to several speakers at the Albert Hall. Mrs Pankhurst walked with them, but Frances merely watched from the side, for the main WSPU wasn't taking part.

The next day Frances took a tram to Battersea, her thoughts teeming with plans and ideas. It was her aim to enlist Elizabeth's support for her own society. She hoped that her friend would take little persuasion, having already shown that she believed in some of the ideas of the WSPU. It was Frances' duty to convert Elizabeth fully to their side.

When Frances arrived at the Belmonts' house, she paused for a moment to appraise its exterior. She had never seen the theatrical "rooms" in which her friend had spent her childhood, but she had passed through many districts of huddled streets of a similar appearance. This house must have been a considerable contrast, she mused. There was a faint twist of envy within her as she surveyed their home, built in warm red brick and surrounded by trees and well-kept lawn.

Frances' parents' house was far bigger, located in a beautiful setting, and nothing could equal its village peacefulness. But Elizabeth had earned a share in this house through her own work, and wasn't dependent on any male member of the population to keep her. Frances couldn't help but be aware that she was only at Cambridge due to her father's money. Once she had completed her three years there, she was determined to be independent.

Resolutely she strode up the path and knocked on the door. It was answered by a small, pale girl in black who looked no older than twelve, but was more likely to be aged fourteen or fifteen, seeing as she was in service. She certainly seemed quite confident, and told Frances that she would inform Miss Belmont of her presence. In a moment, Elizabeth appeared in the hallway, and ran to embrace Frances. She was invited in to take tea with them, and Tilly took her hat and coat.

119

Elizabeth's father was in the back parlour, and with him an elderly woman whom Frances had never seen before. She was neatly dressed, but her clothes were wearing thin at the sleeves and hem. She stood up at the same time as Henry, and warmly pressed Frances' hand when Elizabeth introduced them. "Frances, this is our dear friend, Ella."

"I may call you Frances, my dear?" Receiving a nod, Ella continued, "It's lovely to meet you after all this time. I've heard so much about you."

Frances smiled, immediately liking this gentle woman with her soft voice inclined to slip into a Kentish accent. "And I've been looking forward to meeting you, also. Elizabeth loved the letters you wrote to her at school."

Elizabeth handed a cup of tea to her friend, and talk dwelt on light matters for a while. Ella left after half an hour, for she wanted to go back home to feed her cat. "He's getting too old to hunt, and misses his food if I don't put it out for him," she explained, and kissed Elizabeth affectionately. Ella waved away Henry's offer to find a cab for her, insisting that the tram was quite good enough. It would only be a few stops.

After her departure, Henry excused himself with the remark that he was sure the girls wanted to talk alone.

"He's probably gone for a smoke in the garden," Elizabeth said. "He feels that it isn't right to light his pipe in front of us." She walked over to the bureau and brought out an envelope. "Look at these, Frances." She took from the envelope a collection of four postcards, and showed them to her friend. Two were portraits of Henry with Elizabeth, in one holding their piccolos, and in the other playing them. The other two were views of Elizabeth alone, highlighting her new fashions. In the first she carried her piccolo, and in the second was in the typical pose of an artiste – wearing a gorgeous hat that weighed down her head with flowers, and in her new embroidered dress, smiling beguilingly at the camera.

Frances frowned. "That's quite nice, Elizabeth, but don't you feel that you are cheapening yourself just a little, to play to men's desires? After all, they won't be purchasing these cards of you on your own because of your skill at playing. They'll pin them up in their offices out of sight of their wives and sweethearts, where they can dream illicit thoughts of you."

The other blushed. "It's all part of the music hall – you know that, Frances. They'll see the cards and will want to come to the halls to see the act."

"Yes, but don't you see? You could do so much more for women if you kept above these things. You're what you call an 'artiste' – people will pay money to hear you play. If only you would support women's suffrage, it would prove a point for our cause. You are equal to men on the stage – a partner with your father. Join with me and support our campaign for 'Votes for Women'!"

Elizabeth sat down, sighing. "It's all very well to say that, Frances, but you know that the very nature of my work means that I'm busy when your meetings are on. Sunday is my only free day, for we're always rehearsing. We even practised a new number this afternoon, with Ella."

Frances was undaunted. She explained that there was to be a huge rally at Hyde Park on Sunday the 21st of June, with plenty of speakers. "If only you could hear them talk, it would inspire you – I'm just one voice, and I can't speak like they do. You have never been to a meeting. Come to this, promise me! It's going to be a wonderful day."

Elizabeth paused for a moment. Then she looked up. "Very well, I'll come. But I won't promise to become a supporter of your cause. The choice will be mine alone."

Frances nodded, her face bright with satisfaction. The first step was taken – she would convince her that there could be no peace for any woman until they had won the vote.

The Sunday of the rally was one of the best of the summer. Frances' white dress blazed in the brightness, a stark contrast to Elizabeth's dark blue. The two young women set off from Battersea together, their destination Trafalgar Square, one of seven rally points where women had arranged to meet at around noon.

Elizabeth gasped at the sight of so many women together, stretching in a procession that reached round three sides of the square.

"Look, that's Mrs Bernard Shaw – and over there, Mrs Grant Allen. What a privilege to be taking part with them!" Frances enthused.

Elizabeth gazed in wonder at a large banner which declared '*La Solidarité des Femmes*'. Seeing the direction of her eyes, Frances added, "The French 'Feministes'. Wonderful, isn't it?"

Despite the girls' early arrival, some of the other participants were late, so the start of the march was delayed. It was almost 1.45 when they left, and all were relieved to be on the move at last. Eventually, they streamed through the Grosvenor Gate to join the massive crowds already assembled in Hyde Park. Small islands in the throng were created by about twenty platforms, mostly carts or wagons.

"What's that furniture van doing in the centre?" Elizabeth murmured as their group headed for one of the platforms.

At that moment, a woman's voice began to shout instructions through a megaphone, from the direction of the van. "It must be the control centre," Frances replied, without faltering in her step. Her face was glowing with exercise and excitement.

Two of Frances' friends joined them while they waited for the proceedings to start. Leaving them to their animated discussion, Elizabeth watched the crowds in fascination. Although women were in the majority, there were some men, there either to support female relatives or just out of curiosity.

A trumpet fanfare rang out across the park. At the signal, a young woman dressed in white climbed onto the cart beside them.

"Women of Britain! We call upon you all today to bear witness to our struggle. For centuries the women of this country have been oppressed, bowing to the wishes of their men. And now the time has come to change this!"

Elizabeth, sandwiched between Frances and one of her university friends, found herself caught up in the fervour of the speaker. She listened entranced as the young woman denounced the new Prime Minister, Mr Asquith, and the Government.

"If the law-makers of this country are all men, how can women hope to better their lot? Who are men to say that we have inferior minds? Given the chance of a proper education, women can reach unchartered heights. It is only men's fear which is keeping us back. If we had the vote, we could change all this. The vote is just the beginning. Through this we will better the lot of our children, our old people, the sick, the unemployed."

Yes, that's true, Elizabeth thought, along with many others in the audience. Another fanfare blared out.

"This meeting calls upon the Government to give the vote to women without delay."

Elizabeth found herself raising a cheer, along with the other women. Beside her, Frances waved and cheered excitedly, turning to her friend with a smile of triumph as she saw the effect that the speech had had on her.

"Votes for Women!" they chorused, and then repeated the impassioned slogan.

With echoes of chanting and cheering still ringing in the air, the meeting broke up. Crowds began to head for the park gates.

"Oh . . . is that the end?" Elizabeth asked. It was just past 5 o'clock.

"For most people, yes – but not for us. Alexandra has offered to take us to meet Mrs Pethick Lawrence, one of the leaders of our cause."

Elizabeth clutched at her hat as she was jostled from behind by the departing crowds. She moved closer to the wagon for shelter. To her surprise, she noticed a young man pushing against the tide of people, coming towards them. With a jolt, she recognised him as Gerald's friend.

"Why, it's Mr Hareton!" she exclaimed.

Frances swung round sharply, scrutinising the newcomer through narrowed eyes.

"Miss Belmont! Miss Whittingham! I've been trying to attract your attention . . . but the crowds!"

"An interesting afternoon, don't you agree?" Elizabeth declared.

He smiled, hardly aware of Frances, despite his greeting to her. "Oh, undoubtedly. I wondered if you would care to discuss it over a cup of tea with me . . . er, both of you, of course."

Frances' mouth twisted. "I regret that I am engaged now, with Miss Gordon and Miss Smithers. Elizabeth, of course, may do as she wishes."

Elizabeth glanced from one to the other, wondering what she should do. Suddenly, the thought of being displayed as a "celebrity" to other women was extremely unattractive.

"I do believe I would like a cup of tea," she announced brightly. "Thank you so much for your invitation, Frances, but I'm quite parched after an afternoon in the sun."

She took her leave politely, promising to keep in touch with Frances, who looked at her dismally, saying little. Elizabeth was quite aware of her disapproval, but unrepentant.

As they wove their way through the crowds, William's hand at her elbow, she turned to him with a mischievous smile. "I fear I've offended Frances. She wants me to become an active member of the cause."

He took her to a wooden bench, and spread his handkerchief for her to sit upon. "How do you feel about that?"

She shook her head. "I'm not sure. This afternoon it all seemed much clearer . . . and seeing so many women all together, all believing the same . . . I was quite ready to throw in my lot with them."

"And what do you think now?"

She considered for a moment. "No, I don't think I shall, after all. Oh, I'm not against it, don't think that. I believe that there's a lot of good in the movement. No, it's more a selfish reason. Frances is a student, and has time to think about these things. I'm in quite a different situation. I perform every night of the week except Sunday, and I have to practise and rehearse every day. Life has been much easier since our success, as we now have other people to cook our meals and clean our house. But it's tiring work. Often we don't get to bed before 2 o'clock in the morning. It's not an easy life, not as glamorous as many people think."

"Yet still you continue – why?"

She laughed. "Why? because we love it. I was born to it. I have some wonderful friends." She thought of Belinda and Ella. Then she continued, more softly. "The thrill . . . of success." She looked up into his face. "Can you understand that?"

"Yes, I believe I can." Then, as if embarrassed by the intimacy of the conversation, he looked round quickly. "The crowds are thinning. Shall we go in search of our tea now?"

Elizabeth nodded, and they set off in the wake of the dispersing crowds. It was about an hour before they found a tea-shop with two free seats, but they were happy to walk together, talking as they had been unable to do at their first meeting.

"It was such an amazing coincidence, to meet you there in the park," she exclaimed after they had placed their order with the waitress.

"Ah, no, not such a coincidence. I knew you would be with the procession leaving Trafalgar Square – Gerald told me," he explained. "I searched for you all the time the women were congregating, expecting every minute that the procession would leave before I could find you. Thank goodness for the delay! I finally discovered you, and followed you to Hyde Park." He paused, then, seeing her look of bewildered surprise, continued, "I just had to see you again, Miss Belmont. It seemed the only way to meet you."

"But you could have called at our house."

He shook his head. "No, I would have had to ask Gerald for your address, and I didn't want him to know. It was only in passing that he mentioned about today, so I knew that this would be the best way."

The young woman's cheeks flamed, and she hastily averted her eyes to look from the tea-shop window instead of at her companion's face. Her heart was fluttering faster than it had ever done before a performance.

William leaned forward. "May I see you again? It must seem very rude of me to ask after such a short acquaintance, but I really would like to meet soon."

She turned back to him, a smile beginning to light her face. "Yes . . . I believe I would like to see you again, too, Mr Hareton."

"Oh, please, call me William. And may I call you Elizabeth?"

She nodded her assent, at which he tentatively closed his hand over hers, as it rested on the spotless white tablecloth.

Chapter 13

When Henry looked back in later years, he would think to himself that he had never seen his daughter so innocently beautiful as in those summer months when her love for William Hareton was first growing. Happiness shone from her face, even in repose, when a secret smile would rest on her features.

Henry was happy to let them meet every Sunday afternoon. Throughout July and August they would stroll happily through the parks, and when it was wet they would seek shelter, scarcely heeding the bad weather in the joy of being together. William was a charming companion. He would often bring her a nosegay, bought for a few farthings from a flower-seller, to pin to her dress. Though it was his genuine, serious manner which had first attracted her, Elizabeth discovered that William had a ready wit, bringing a delighted laugh to her voice with his quips.

William would talk with pride and affection about his family. He was the elder of two boys. His brother, Edwin, was in his last year at Winchester College, and was a bright boy with designs on a career in the City. His uncle was already eminent in that field. But William himself had accepted without challenge that his destined career was the law. It was the "Family Profession". He always spoke these two words as if they began with capital letters. The Haretons had been in the legal profession for four generations, and he wasn't going to break the tradition. He had always known it would be his destiny, and had been brought up to prepare himself for it with pride.

He kept his work very much to himself. To divulge any information about his clients, even to Elizabeth who had no idea who any of the people were, would have been unforgivable. His profession was sacred. "It is not for ladies to be involved," he explained.

His companion gave a wry laugh. "I shouldn't let my friend Frances hear you saying that. The suffragettes believe women can enter all professions."

William shook his head in disbelief. "It's a vain hope. They will never win women the vote if they continue to be so outrageous. It makes people think that they are unworthy."

There was no way to change his mind. Elizabeth smiled and shook her head fondly.

The Belmonts were still playing the London halls, though there was the hint of a tour in January. Elizabeth was relieved it was so far off, for she was eager to have William's company each weekend, and sometimes between shows if there was enough time between two "houses".

Henry accepted another ten-week contract at Radley's Palace, starting in September. The terms were good, but he noticed immediately that his daughter's face clouded at the news.

"What's wrong, Lizzie? It's a good contract."

"I know, Father . . . but somehow I . . . I can't like Mr Radley."

"Why not? He's not such a bad fellow. Maybe a bit pompous, but he's always been good to us. And you made your début at one of his halls."

She shook her head, unwilling to explain. It was good money, too good to lose if Henry was angered by what Radley had offered her. He would be, too. Elizabeth knew how much Henry valued her – his talented, virtuous daughter.

They took a band-call on the Monday morning at Radley's Palace. The rehearsal went smoothly, for most of the musicians were familiar with the main numbers. They were the last act to rehearse that morning, so the theatre was almost empty. Henry was happy to be able to chat with Mr Gemmling, the musical director, now bent with age. Henry had played under him for many years at the start of his career as a pit musician, and was eager to hear news of other musicians they had both known.

With her instrument already cleaned out and packed away, Elizabeth strolled down into the stalls to wait for her father. After only a few minutes she became aware of a movement at her side.

"Miss Belmont . . ."

She started in surprise at finding Frederick Radley at her elbow. In the dim light of the auditorium she had not seen him approaching.

"May I say . . . how enchanting you look. You haven't changed – at least, any change has been for the better. And your act – more polished, superb."

Turning her head away from him to look towards her father, she replied coldly, "Thank you, Mr Radley. My increased experience has no doubt helped the act. It's now over eighteen months since I began my career."

There was silence for a few moments. A vague murmur of voices rose from the pit where Henry and the musical director were conversing. Then Radley continued in a low voice, loud enough only for his companion to hear.

"I . . . trust that you remember the . . . circumstances of our last meeting?"

"I haven't forgotten, Mr Radley." Her voice too was quiet, level, not betraying the anger which began to spark within her.

"Seeing you today . . . I know that I feel the same for you. Won't you reconsider – have dinner with me tonight?"

She stood up quickly, trembling. "Mr Radley, I find your offer insulting to my character. My answer remains the same. Please don't ask me again." It was all she could do to keep her voice low, in her indignation. Knowing William, to consider such a man as Radley was impossible, unthinkable.

The manager also rose to his feet, holding his black silk hat to his chest. "I shall not ask you again, as you wish. But, should you ever change your mind, the offer will always stand."

Her eyes blazed. "I won't change my mind. Please excuse me. I believe my father is waiting for me."

Elizabeth managed to avoid most contact with Radley during their engagement at his music hall. It was the one sour taste amongst the flavours of that time of happiness. While she was with William it was a joy to forget everything but their contentment with each other. Henry was concerned that they seemed to be alone together so much, a situation which lacked propriety considering that they were young and so obviously attracted to each other. All he could do was insist that they meet at the Belmonts' home more often.

Henry was prepared to like William, but couldn't help wondering how Elizabeth's young man would react to him at their first meeting. Henry hadn't been born to the same privileges as the Haretons; his father had owned a shop, was a tradesman, and spoke with the local accent of the north-east. Henry, too, had never lost this vernacular, though he had modified it since he had been in London, so he could be understood. Like Elizabeth, he had the ability to imitate the speech of the upper middle class, but he only did it in moments of extreme need. He felt as if he were acting a part at such times, so he seldom used it.

Elizabeth never worried about her father's way of speaking. It was a part of his character. So he decided to act as himself for the benefit of her young admirer.

On the afternoon of their first meeting, Elizabeth wandered aimlessly around the parlour, fingering the fringed shawl draped over the piano, touching the flowers in the tall vase on the table, and brushing the curtains aside to glance into the garden.

"Is it 3 o'clock yet?"

Henry folded his newspaper and regarded her in amusement. "The clock still says we have five minutes. Sit down, pet. He won't forget."

She threw herself into the nearest armchair with a flounce which hearkened back to the Elizabeth of the pinafores and black stockings. "Oh, I know. But I do wish he would hurry."

As if in response to this wish, the knocker resounded through the hallway. Elizabeth started to her feet. "He's here!" Without waiting for their maid to answer the door, she ran through to get there first. Henry, suddenly less sure of himself, cleared his throat and laid the newspaper on the table, listening to his daughter's excited half-whisper and the deeper voice that answered her.

At his first sight of William, Henry was impressed by the young man's quiet self-assurance. He had a pleasant smile and an easy manner. Henry was gratified to see the admiration in William's eyes whenever they followed Elizabeth's movements. But beneath his pleasure there was a hint of an emotion he was unwilling to name. He pushed it to the back of his mind, and the afternoon passed pleasantly enough.

He tried to put his feelings into words the following Sunday when he was at Ella's, drinking tea in the pattern of their old neighbourly friendship. They talked often and long about Elizabeth, the focus of both their lives. Henry knew that Ella missed her more than she admitted, so he made a point of talking about his daughter with their friend.

"You may be losing her quicker than you think, Henry."

He contradicted Ella's statement brusquely. "Oh, I don't believe that, Ella. She's still little more than a child."

She shook her head. "I don't see a child there now – she's a beautiful woman, nearly nineteen, ready for the sort of love a young man can give her. You'll have to let her go some day."

"Some day, yes. But I don't feel that William Hareton is right for her."

"Is it really William Hareton, or is it just that you want her to stay your little Lizzie? If she wants to go, what could you do to make her change her mind?"

"She's under age, Ella."

"She's also your beloved daughter, Henry – and what have you ever been able to refuse her?"

He was silent for a moment, then he spoke again. "I know I won't be able to oppose her if it's what she really wants – but could you see Lizzie for ever in the world of middle-class respectability? The wife of a solicitor? With a father in the halls?"

Ella smiled. "It does seem a little far-fetched. But if young Hareton is big enough, he'll be able to accept her for herself."

"Yes . . . I do feel he cares for her. What his family feels about the attachment, I've no idea. Lizzie has never met them. I'm not really sure if they know she exists."

"Well, we must let things run their course. You can't stop her falling in love with a good-looking, charming young man."

The objects of this discussion were themselves involved in a review of the previous Sunday. Elizabeth had been eager to find out William's opinion of her father. Half-apprehensive, she had hedged around the subject, then had been unable to contain her curiosity.

"Well, William, what did you think of my father?"

He laughed at her unveiled eagerness, then his face relaxed into a more serious mould as he searched for the right words. "Well . . . he's very much like he is on stage."

"What do you mean by that?"

"He . . . likes to make an impression on people. To make them laugh, and to make them admire you."

She frowned. "You really think that? I didn't realise that's how he appeared."

"Oh yes, he thinks as much of you as you do of him." Seeing that she did not fully understand his meaning, he added, exasperated, "You think the world of each other. Do you think I measure up to your father?"

"But what are you talking of? You're completely different, and you don't have to measure up to him. He's my father . . . and you . . ."

Tempted to believe her, his arm slid around her waist and drew her near enough for him to kiss her lips. "What am I, then?"

"You're my own William." Her eyes beamed love. Their discussion forgotten, they entwined hands and walked in companionable silence. But William had not quite spoken all of his thoughts. Later, as they were saying goodbye, he added, "There's just one thing that puzzles me, Elizabeth. Why do you speak differently when you're with your father?"

"Do I?"

"Yes. I hadn't heard you talking that way before."

She laughed. "But it's the way we've always spoken. My father comes from the north-east of England. I was brought up in south London. It's natural that I should speak like the people who taught me."

"But you don't talk in that accent to me."

She shook her head. "But you talk in a different way to my father. I learned to speak like this when I was at school. It feels natural to me now to speak with people in their own manner."

Mystified by her ability, William could only wonder what other differences he had yet to discover about her. Charmed though he was by this lovely young woman, he was becoming more aware of her strange background, which was difficult to reconcile with his own world.

Elizabeth had some idea of the direction that his thoughts were taking. It was a relief to her that she had never been tempted by Radley's offer. Henry and his daughter could give the appearance of respectability now that they had enough money. The morality of artistes was frequently being called into question. But that was a stigma which had always gone with the theatre. There were many who lived moral lives –

look at Vesta Tilley. She was married to a theatrical manager and lived a life free of scandal. She, too, had been protected by her father almost up to the moment of her marriage. Elizabeth admired this petite, dark-haired impersonator with fervour. She was so elegant, too. The young woman was careful to mention her more than any other artiste who might be of doubtful character to a middle-class Edwardian.

What Elizabeth had not sensed was the thrill of excitement it gave William to be involved with a music-hall star. He had known young men who were able to "keep" dancing girls and actresses who did not care – or hope – for marriage. Not that he considered such a path. His own morals had to be impeccable. He could see that this young woman was not like the "fancy pieces" of his acquaintances. But the nearness of her white shoulders and the curving breasts beneath her demure dresses were enough to send a man wild. Without realising it, Elizabeth had absorbed the sensuality of the music-hall stars, women who used their sexuality to stir up their audiences.

As October drew in, the weather changed, and frequently they were unable to spend Sunday outside. They rode trams, and also went more often to Elizabeth's home. Still William didn't speak of taking her to visit his family. He told her that they would have to be prepared carefully for the fact that she appeared regularly on the stage. He had mentioned that he had met a young lady and was hoping that they could all have tea one Sunday, but that was all. Frequently he told them that his Sunday outings were with Gerald Whittingham.

"But what about your other friends, William? Couldn't I meet them? That at least would be a step."

"I don't have many friends in London. They mostly live in the country." He paused, thoughtful. "Yes, you're right. We must arrange something." The idea seemed to take root with a vengeance. Suddenly he was enthusiastic. "Yes, you'll see – I'll sort something out."

She was smiling with him, happy that their future was making progress.

He was quick to make arrangements. The next Sunday, he met her in Hyde Park with the news that they were going to visit one of his friends.

"He has a place near here, where he often spends Sundays."

"Oh, I wish I'd known sooner, William. I'm totally unprepared for meeting anyone."

"But you're prepared for meeting me, my dearest. You would charm anyone. Especially in that delightful gown – is it new?"

Her cheeks flushed slightly. He had noticed – she had worn it especially for him. It always charmed her how William appreciated her clothes. He did indeed have an eye for detail, like a good lawyer!

It was only a short walk to the flat. William rang the bell quickly, and stood rubbing his hands together with unaccustomed nervousness as they waited for an answer. Elizabeth examined the surroundings. They were faceless, red-brick flats, somehow masculine in outward appearance. The road was quiet, with windows, discreetly blank, staring on to the iron railings that bordered the pavement.

"He doesn't seem to be here yet."

"Perhaps we should walk round the block for a few minutes until he arrives," Elizabeth suggested.

"No, there's no need for that. Look – he gave me a spare key in case this should happen. He said he might be delayed, and that we could go in and make ourselves at home." He pulled a key from his pocket, and, while fumbling to insert it in the lock, dropped it. The key tumbled down to Elizabeth's feet. On picking it up, she realised that she had never seen William so nervous. His cheeks coloured as she handed it back to him.

They entered a dark corridor, and climbed to the first storey. William produced a second key which let them into the flat itself. Elizabeth wandered into the large sitting room, which looked out on to the main road. It was decorated in sombre hues, except for an Indian carpet which relieved the severity. To one side was a small kitchen, and next to it a closed door. Looking the other way, she saw another door opening into a bedroom. All that was visible was a large wardrobe, and, reflected in its mirror, a bed with a white counterpane. Everything was very neat, almost untouched. She shivered.

Immediately, William was solicitous. "Are you cold? I'll light the fire." The coals were already laid in the grate, and it didn't take long to coax a blaze. Eventually Elizabeth felt warm enough to take off her coat. Removing her hat, she tucked the pin into the brim, and placed it on the coatstand by the door. She sat gently on the edge of the settee, looking at her hands.

"Do you think your friend will be long?"

"Oh, I don't know." William seemed strangely elated. "In the mean time, I'll make some tea to warm you up, shall I?"

Her lips curved in amusement at this new idea of William acting in a domestic fashion, and she nodded. While he clattered about clumsily in the kitchen, Elizabeth took in her surroundings. Her own reflection gazed back from the big mirror above the fireplace. The furniture was solidly Victorian, but the plain walls deferred to the latest fashions. Finding little to interest her in the main body of the room, she fell to examining the rich colours of the carpet until William brought her tea.

He kept up a steady stream of conversation, while she answered little. Her confusion increased. William finally came to sit next to her and slid his arm around her waist. She rested her head on his shoulder, but couldn't bring herself to relax. Her suspicions were growing. Finally, she sat up straight, and held William away firmly.

"William . . . your friend . . . he's not coming, is he?"

"It's only been half an hour. He could still come."

"No, please. I mean that he never was going to come."

The young man was silent for a few moments. When he spoke, the false brightness had gone from his voice. "No, you're right. I asked him if I could come here because I wanted to be alone with you."

She absorbed his words, trying to understand their full meaning. His hand stroked her shoulder. Her eyes strayed to the open door, with the wardrobe mirror reflecting the neatly made bed. "Alone with me – for that?" She turned back sharply to meet his gaze. His eyes could not hold hers, flickering uneasily away. But his hand did not cease its stroking movement.

Then he was closer, both arms around her rigid body. His lips were in her hair, on her neck, his voice pleading, "Oh, please, my dearest . . . will you? Will you do this for me?" She felt his lips on her cheek, then closing over her mouth, and she was dissolving inside. Almost unwillingly, her arms stole round him. It was different, so breathlessly far from those kisses in the park, or stolen in the parlour when they had been alone. The firmness of his hands on her body quickened her senses, until their hot breath mingled.

Without giving her time for further protests, he clasped her firmly in his arms and took her through with him to the bedroom. Surprised by his action, Elizabeth felt her protests swept aside.

But as he laid her on the white counterpane and reached for the hooks of her dress, she cried out, "Oh, no, William."

Stunned, he stopped. "But don't you want me, Elizabeth? Please, my love, won't you be mine completely? Mine always?" His voice was thick with desire.

"Yours always . . . do you really mean that?"

He nodded steadily.

"Oh, William . . ."

Sensing her softening, he renewed his advances, releasing at last the hooks and pulling her dress away. Her own fingers helped him to free her breasts of the restricting corsets, and she shuddered at the touch of his cool hands on her warm bare flesh. As they cupped the roundness of her breasts, she felt a responding fullness and tingling in her thighs and between her legs. She had never known such sensation could be possible, and her longing for fulfilment increased at his every touch. Swiftly she helped him remove the rest of her garments, while he discarded his own clothes with a breathless urgency.

The instant of contact came with a pain which cut across all sensation. Suddenly she was aware of the man-smell on top of her, and had a moment of lucidity. "What am I doing?" Then as the exciting new sensations spread through her body, she was lost again, only aware of the heaving, thrusting weight on top of her.

William drew to a shuddering halt, panting. He pulled away from her, satisfied, and laid his head across her breasts. Elizabeth's arms lay at her sides, trembling. Slowly she put one hand to his hair, and traced the curve of his head. His arms still grasped her shoulders.

It was dark when they dressed. Elizabeth was silent, accepting his caresses mutely. What he had said, about being together always – what had he really meant?

"Why so quiet, my darling?" he probed, stroking her cheek.

Her dark eyes gazed back at him, resentful of his need to ask. But why hedge? "I could have a child."

"Is that what worries you? But my dearest, don't be afraid. What does that matter when we are to be married anyway?"

The darkness lifted from her. "You mean it? You really mean to marry me, William?" She clutched his arm ecstatically.

"Of course I do. Next Sunday you'll meet my family, I promise. I'll make the arrangements this week, and we'll meet on Saturday, between your shows, to confirm the time."

"The time?" Realisation dawned. "Oh, Lord, I must go home. It's so late. Father will be worried."

They took a taxi back to Battersea, their hands entwined with a new intimacy. Elizabeth now chatted happily, alive with plans for the future. To be William's wife! She leaned contentedly against the warmth of his body.

They kissed goodbye in the darkness of the cab before they reached the Belmonts' home. William didn't come into the house, but directed the cabbie to take him back to Richmond. Elizabeth watched the retreating vehicle for a few moments before she hurried inside to break the wonderful news, that she was to be married, to her father.

Elizabeth could tell Henry little of their plans. There had been so little time to discuss anything about the future. One thing she did know was that William expected her to give up performing – it was out of the question that a man in his profession should have a connection with the music hall. He, and his wife, had to be above reproach.

Henry brooded over the news, though he didn't let Elizabeth see it. Much as he loved to see his daughter so happy, he knew that this was the moment he had been dreading – losing Elizabeth for ever. He was wary of something in William Hareton – all this talk of respectability. . . Elizabeth was young enough, and infatuated enough, to be influenced by her husband. Perhaps he would begin to turn Elizabeth away from her father, and he would lose her, lose what grandchildren they might give him.

Whenever he saw her shining face, dreaming with unspoken longings and hopes, he was angry with himself for being a suspicious, selfish man. He longed to talk to Ella, to unburden himself of this intolerable worry, to hear her reassurance.

Elizabeth performed that week as if inspired. She would tell no one of her forthcoming marriage, not until she was wearing her fiancé's ring and had met his family. On the Saturday afternoon she left for the theatre in high hopes. They had only one hall to play in this week, which meant there was no travelling across London. A new contract began for them the next Monday.

Henry could tell that Elizabeth's mind was not on the music. She played technically well, with no slips, but it was almost mechanical. Her deepest emotions were with William, not with the music.

As they left the stage, Henry slapped her playfully. "Go on! Off you go to that young man of yours!"

Laughing, she hugged him and ran ahead to the dressing room. Within minutes she had removed her stage make-up and changed into her outdoor clothes. Her hand was on the doorknob when she paused to turn back to Henry.

"Oh Father, I'm so happy." She stepped forward and clasped him briefly in her arms, before darting out of the door with a final smile for him. Henry's eyes lingered on the closed door, picturing her hurrying to meet William. How young she had looked, standing there by the door. He hoped that William would care for her dearly. He sighed and finished his own ablutions. The evening suit went on a hanger with his starched shirt, to be replaced by his older jacket and trousers so that he could go out for a walk to pass the time between the "houses".

He changed again in plenty of time, finding it strange without Elizabeth to chatter to him. He glanced at the silver watch and chain he now sported. She should have been here by now. The programme had already begun. A small worm of doubt writhed inside him. All kinds of visions of possible harm lurked beneath his consciousness. Almost without realising it he began to pace the floor . . . back and forth. Again he whipped out the watch. Only two minutes had passed. He flung open the door, and his restless eyes raked the corridor. Only a few dancing girls chatted at the far end, oblivious of a father's anxiety.

He closed the door again, and sat down in the old wooden chair in front of the mirror. The damp coldness of perspiration began beneath his clean shirt. His hands were slippery as he reached for his piccolo and worked his fingers up and down on the keys.

At that moment he heard a faint sound outside the door – the soft brush of heavy material, the scrabble of buttons against wood, then a muffled noise like a voice choking. He had already risen to his feet when the door opened.

His daughter stood in the doorway, huddled, all the spark extinguished.

"Lizzie, my darling, what is it?" For one awful moment he thought she had been injured. Then, as she hurled herself into his arms, sobbing, he realised that she had come to no physical harm. With one free hand, he pushed the door to, then held her tightly in his arms. He had never known her to cry like this. The sobs tore loudly at her throat in an uncontrollable anguish. He let her weep until the main storm had passed, then lifted her chin.

"What has happened, my pet?"

The tears still ran unchecked from her eyes as she choked out the words, "It's . . . all over . . . he won't . . . marry me."

Henry's arms stole round her again. "Oh, my little love, my dearest child." He rocked her back and forth, as if it could somehow lessen the hurt. Sharp anger towards William Hareton thrust up inside him. How could William do this to his lovely Lizzie?

The knock of the call-boy startled them both.

"Five minutes, please!"

Elizabeth looked at her father, her breath still heaving.

"You must get dressed, Lizzie! Quickly!"

"Oh, no, Father, I can't go on now. Please don't make me!"

He could see that she was on the verge of breakdown again. Blind anger towards Hareton's callousness surged up in him again, and he grabbed her shoulders.

"Listen to me, Lizzie! All those people out there have come to listen to us. Us, not me! Are you going to let them down?" He made his features look at her accusingly. "Are you going to let me down?" he added softly.

She pulled away from him swiftly, feeling rejected, anger strengthening her.

"All right," she muttered. "I'll go on."

There was no time to change her dress now. All that could be done was to repair her swollen face with make-up. Henry didn't speak to her again before the act, afraid lest any words of sympathy might break down the façade of defiance he had roused.

Her performance was strong, strident, lacking any feeling – only anger and defiance came across, for she knew she could sustain nothing else. They took their bows to a moderately enthusiastic audience. Henry sighed with relief as they left the stage and four acrobats rushed past to tumble over the boards into the limelight. He put his arm around

Elizabeth's shoulders in the backstage gloom, guiding her stumbling feet.

"My brave girl," he whispered tenderly.

In the privacy of their dressing room, Elizabeth sought the protection of his arms again, giving way once more to tears of rejection.

As Henry comforted her, he realised with a guilty stab that beneath his resentment towards William Hareton was a flood of relief. Elizabeth was not to be taken from him! He laid his cheek on her hair.

Chapter 14

Ella sighed as she looked at Elizabeth's downcast face. It was now two weeks since the break with William, and still Elizabeth wouldn't speak about him. It was heartbreaking to see her joy snuffed out. Even her voice sounded dull.

The two women were alone in Ella's rooms, the only sounds being the crackle of coal burning in the hearth and the click of Ella's knitting needles. Charlie, Ella's ageing tabby cat, was sleeping contentedly on Elizabeth's lap.

"Lizzie, love, wouldn't it help to tell me about it? You've been bottling it up for too long." There was no need to explain further what she meant.

"I can't stop thinking about it – I wish I could. If I talk I'm afraid it'll make it more vivid." Elizabeth's eyes glinted with unshed tears.

"It doesn't work that way – it's more like giving away your pain when you talk to someone. I won't tell anyone, if you don't want me to. I only want to help."

"Dear Ella, you're so good to me." There was a silence, in which Ella took up her knitting again, thinking her words had done no good.

Then Elizabeth's voice began softly. "It was a sunny day, so we decided to walk in the park. But I could tell as soon as we met that something was troubling William. He didn't talk much until we reached the lake . . ."

William had fingered his hat uneasily while he spoke. "Elizabeth, I . . . I'm sorry, but you won't be able to meet my family tomorrow."

With a sick feeling in her stomach, she looked at him despairingly. "But why not? What has happened?"

He turned his head away and gazed towards the half-naked trees, shedding dry leaves onto the grass with every gust of wind. "I told them . . . about us. About you, your father, your time at school and . . . and the music hall."

Her hands clenched in anguish. It wasn't difficult to guess what his next words would be. "They said they wouldn't meet me," she whispered.

His eyes turned back to her, bright and sad. "I'm so sorry, my love."

"But . . . but surely that can't matter! We still have each other . . . our love!"

"Elizabeth," he insisted softly, "I can't break with them. We can't live on love alone. We have to eat, to have a home."

"But I earn money – I have enough for both of us. My father and I are making more and more as the weeks go by."

His face went stiff. "I couldn't live on my wife's earnings!"

"You need not, William!" she pleaded. "I could give you the money to set up on your own."

"Elizabeth, I don't have the experience for such a venture. Anyway . . . I have my pride."

Suddenly she was angry. "Your pride! And does your pride mean to separate us?"

He replied very quietly. "I'm sorry, it must be. There's no point in continuing our relationship now."

There was a prolonged silence while the finality of his words sank in. At last she spoke. "Goodbye, William," she said to his shamed back. He swung round to see her fleeing across the grass back to the pathway, surprisingly fleet despite her narrow skirts.

"Elizabeth! Elizabeth!" he called, contrite. He had meant to see her back to the theatre safely, instead of which she had left him wildly and without his being able to calm her. He began to run after her, but she darted out of the gate and was lost from view amongst the pedestrians. By the time he reached the entrance to the park, she had found a taxi cab and was already speeding away from him.

Elizabeth had directed the taxi to the West End, but had paid off the cabbie before they reached the theatre. In a haze of anguish, she had wandered through the streets, past the theatres, scarcely aware of her surroundings. Unable to understand how he could hurt her like this, she went over every meeting, wondering if there was anything she had said or done to turn him from her.

Her thoughts turned to that last Sunday, though she never told Ella of their intimacy. She relived his tenderness and apparent sincerity when he had declared that they would marry. It was hardest to accept that William thought more of his pride and family traditions than he did of her honour. The surrender of her body had been reluctant, and had only been done because she believed his declaration of love and intentions to marry her. The most wounding suspicion was that he had never in fact intended to carry out his promise, but had only spoken it in the heat of passion.

It was comforting to unburden herself to Ella because she never criticised. She just accepted, offered consolation, and occasionally a word of advice for the future. Ella, more than anyone, didn't believe in looking back on sorrows. She had known hurt, too, as a young woman. Then she had married good, dependable Sam Greaves, who had been comfortable if not exciting, and Ella had grown to love him dearly. There had only once been the hope of a child, but, heartbreakingly, she had miscarried, and there had never been any more. So it had been a great comfort to her to become a kind of mother to Elizabeth as she grew up.

After pouring out her misery, Elizabeth laid her hand on Ella's, adding softly, "Do you know what is so wonderful about you, Ella? You're always there when I need you. You'll always listen."

Ella smiled, with a hint of sadness which went unnoticed by her companion. "Yes, love, I'm always here. When you, or your father, need a friend, I'm here."

Elizabeth prayed silently through the week that followed that she would have no greater need of Ella's help. That stolen afternoon in October could have started a baby, which she would have welcomed had she been married, but could now only be a source of unhappiness.

Henry, too, worried about this. He never mentioned it to his daughter, but broached the subject instead to the one person who might have had her confidence.

"Ella, did Lizzie ever speak to you about . . . what they did, on those Sunday afternoons?"

"Why, she told me about the walks in the parks, what he said to her, that sort of thing."

"No, I mean, how . . . far . . . it went with them." He sighed. "I haven't the courage to ask my own daughter about her . . . virtue."

Ella sat down opposite Henry, her features serious. "You don't need the courage, Henry. If she's in trouble, she'll tell us. Myself, I don't believe it went further than a few kisses or cuddles. They were only engaged less than a week – I can't see Elizabeth giving in lightly."

Henry was relieved. "You've taken a great burden from me, Ella. I was afraid that he might have just offered to marry her because there was a baby on the way. You know, I sometimes wonder if you know more about my daughter than I do."

She shook her head. "No, that's something I can't believe. Sometimes it's just easier to talk to someone who isn't so close. And some things are easier to say to another woman."

In the end, Elizabeth had no need to divulge her secret. By the beginning of November, she knew that there would be no child. In an effort to fill the emptiness of her life, she threw herself wholeheartedly into her work. The smiles came seldom to her face, and, even when she did laugh, almost immediately the dark memory of her betrayal flooded back.

Gradually the life of the stage absorbed her again. They were engaged as special guest artistes for a pantomime in Southampton. Lizzie was to be Tom, the Piper's son, with Henry as the Piper. It was the first time she had appeared in a breeches role, and was self-conscious at first, showing so much leg in public. But the cut of the costume showed her figure to advantage, and she made a charming "boy". There was no doubt that the male members of the audience found plenty of reason to return to see the pantomime over and over again. The steady stream of nosegays and bouquets sent to her dressing room testified to that. Yet Elizabeth never answered them. For weeks she would scan them with her heart beating unreasonably wildly, but when the hoped-for name did not appear she tossed them aside in disappointment.

Henry did his best to cheer her up, and cracked endless jokes to see her sadness lift for a moment. But he knew that some sort of flame had ceased to spark within her, and would often hold her close in a wordless expression of his affection. Elizabeth was grateful for his presence, and talked endlessly about their work – anything rather than the subject of William.

The crowning moment of their career came later that year. Their agent contacted Henry to inform him that they had the offer of an engagement at the Coliseum, Oswald Stoll's magnificent four-year-old theatre in St Martin's Lane. It had gained a reputation for "respectable" entertainment. Only the best had a chance of appearing there, and only if they could not offend anyone's delicate feelings. The Belmonts were offered a ten-week season beginning at the end of February.

Henry was thrilled. They must have fresh material, new music. He wrote at once to James Adamson in Kent, the composer of 'Melody for Lizzie', asking for a new number. Henry himself spent many hours rearranging old material, and working on a new selection from one of the popular shows now running at one of the London theatres. They practised the new music endlessly, with Ella's help.

It was a relief when the pantomime season ended. They had a week's break before beginning at the Coliseum. Henry had to re-engage their "taxi" service – a driver with his horse and cab – to take them regularly from theatre to theatre, because they had another engagement running concurrently with the Coliseum job. Henry worried frequently whether they would have their timing right, as they needed enough time to warm up before going on stage. A small delay could ruin their schedule.

In many ways the pantomime was an easier engagement – only one theatre each night. The rehearsals for the new job had been hard, especially as they had been unable to try the new numbers in a smaller hall.

Concerned thoughts about the new engagement ran through Henry's mind as he wiped off the last of his make-up on the final night of their pantomime. He was relieved to hear Elizabeth humming snatches of one of the new numbers while she dressed behind the screen. It was the first time he had heard her singing since the previous October.

That niggling pain was there in his chest again. He massaged it gently, frowning. It would be necessary to be more careful about his food, eat more slowly. It was hard to accept that his digestion was not as good as it used to be.

"I think we've been quite a success, don't you?" Lizzie said as she emerged from behind the screen, fixing a brooch at her throat. Then she stopped. "Father, what is it?"

He smiled sheepishly. "Oh, a touch of indigestion, pet. I don't suppose you could get me a glass of water?"

"Yes, yes of course." She paused in the doorway for an instant, regarding her father with a hint of a crease on her brow. Then she hurried away to carry out his request.

The pain was passing. Henry caught sight of his face in the mirror and froze, shocked. His skin looked grey – not that of a young man any more. He looked old.

All the practice and planning were paying off. There were good reviews for their new numbers, and the passage between the theatres was smooth and efficient. Their driver also took them home after the second engagement, which was a relief for their weary bodies.

The money was good. "But we earn every penny of it!" Henry declared. They had never worked harder. Still, he was happy to see that Elizabeth was living for her work. It was a beginning, he told himself. Sooner or later there would be someone else to heal the wound. In the mean time, let her make the most of the heady applause, the adulation. There were no stars in her eyes, as there had been two years before, but he could see that she responded to the ovations. "That girl is a born artiste," he mused. The old wild enthusiasm and the charming openness had darkened to a calm assurance, almost cold, but somehow admirable.

"Well, do you like playing the Coliseum?" he asked her one day at the end of their third week, as they rushed out of the stage door and leaped into the waiting cab.

"It's a beautiful theatre," Elizabeth replied, "very grand, and it makes me feel grand to be performing there. Oh, Father, we've really made it now, haven't we? We're truly a success."

He kissed the top of her head as the vehicle moved off. "Of course we are, pet. But I never doubted we would be. I even heard a street organ playing 'Melody for Lizzie' last week."

She leant her head on his shoulder, at which he laid his arm across her shoulders while she watched the passing buildings. Suddenly she felt his hand tighten on her upper arm, and turned to see his face contorted in pain in the light of the passing gas-lamps. His free hand was pressed to his chest.

"Father! Father, what's wrong?"

He could not speak, could only gaze at her out of anguished eyes as he slid into the corner of the seat. Terror gripped her. "Father!" she shrieked. Then she jumped unsteadily to her feet in the moving cab, and rapped hysterically on the partition separating them from the driver. "Stop! Oh, stop, stop!"

They cancelled all engagements. The theatres bustled on in their brightness and hubbub, while Elizabeth sat at home staring at her father's ashen face, night after night. It had been quite a serious heart attack, the doctor told her, but there was no reason why he should not make a full recovery, with careful nursing. In response, Elizabeth moved her bed into her father's dressing room, to be on hand should he need her at all.

It was when she was clearing the small cupboard in the dressing room that she found the bottle of hair dye. It was half-empty. How long he had been using it, she had no idea. Henry had always had dark hair, still had, she had thought; it was a shock to realise that he needed to enhance it. Oh yes, there was no place for an old artiste on the halls. Immediately she remembered George Medway, the old comedian who had dropped down and down, and out of their lives completely since that fateful night when Henry broke his piccolo. But Uncle George had been old – not like her father.

With a hollow heart she replaced the bottle in the cupboard and walked softly into Henry's bedroom. He was sleeping, as he did most of the time now, but the dim gas-light beside the bed could not soften the ravaged features. Lying there, ill and helpless, it was a sharp shock to Elizabeth to see how old Henry looked. He was . . . she calculated . . . fifty-six – fifty-six! Many men didn't live to be that age.

Her position beside the bed, gazing at the sick man in consternation, was undisturbed when she heard the door open behind her. Expecting to see their maid, she turned her head slowly. Then she gave a soft cry, and flew into Ella's waiting arms.

"Don't worry, my lamb, I'm here to help you."

Elizabeth looked down. Ella was carrying a checked bag stuffed to bulging.

"Yes," the older woman added gently. "I'm going to stay just as long as you – both of you – need me."

With Ella's presence, the house changed. Everything seemed brighter, brisker. Even Henry seemed to rally, but Elizabeth could not tell whether it was natural improvement or due to Ella's nursing. He still looked frail. The flesh hung in folds around his neck, and even his dressing-gown sagged on his shoulders. His hair had now reverted to its natural grey, changing his appearance dramatically.

At the beginning of April the Court announcements heralded the forthcoming marriage of Miss Mary Argyll Stewart to the Honourable Bertram Albert Edward Chard. The names leaped into Elizabeth's line of vision when she was reading the newspaper to Henry one day, causing her hands to shake so much that it caught Henry's attention.

"What's the matter?"

"Oh, nothing, Father. I'm just trying to make the newspaper lie flat – there's an article on the Stage Society that I thought might interest you." Henry had never been told about Belinda's long-standing affair with Bertie – their jaunts last year had been with unnamed young men. Now Elizabeth's immediate reaction was to rush to her friend – surely now she needed a confidante, and she couldn't talk to her family.

She found Belinda at home the following noon, looking especially smart in a new hobble skirt. She smiled a welcome.

"Lizbeth! Come in. Tell me how your father is. He must be getting on well for you to be here."

Elizabeth removed her hat and gloves, astounded that Belinda appeared so fresh and happy – could it be that she was unaware of the announcement?

"He's improving. Ella's looking after him, so I don't feel the need to be with him all the time. She's been trying to make me go out, but I haven't really felt very sociable. I don't have much to talk about, now."

"Ah, but if you went out more it would give you more to talk about."

"I really came to see how you are, Belinda."

The bright façade slipped from her friend's face, her smile dropping to heaviness. "Oh . . . so you saw *The Times*."

"You look . . . surprisingly well. How long have you known?"

Belinda sat down by the window, the daylight now highlighting the pallor of her face. Elizabeth could see that her cheeks had been touched with rouge.

"I've always known, right from the start, that one day this would happen. I didn't know when it would be – nor did Bertie. But . . . knowing didn't make it hurt any less." Her voice cracked on the last sentence. For a moment she sought to control her shaking lips, then added, "Every time we met, I expected him to say, 'It's all over, I've found the girl I will marry, and we must part.' So every time he didn't say it was a blessed gift. But then, the time did come." With a sob, she brought out a lace-edged handkerchief and buried her face in it.

Elizabeth rushed to her side. "I'm sorry, Belinda, I didn't mean to upset you by making you talk about it."

Wiping away the tears, Belinda shook her head quickly. "The pain will deaden. I suppose I'll even learn not to love him, and not to burn with jealousy at the thought of them together. I'm becoming a very good actress – I even managed not to cry when he told me."

Elizabeth squeezed her shoulders sympathetically. "You had more strength than I did."

With a sigh, Belinda dropped her hands to her lap. "No, maybe it was a little easier for me because I was prepared, or maybe I was just numb with shock at hearing the words. I suppose I hoped that we would go on for years as we were." She looked up at Elizabeth. "I never asked you much about William – does it still hurt?"

Elizabeth turned and walked away with a swift movement.

"Not the same way as at first. I . . . grew to hate him, you know. He wasn't prepared to save our love. I would have waited, for years if necessary. But now – it's just a blankness. I feel nothing for him. But I hope I won't meet him again."

"I don't hate Bertie – he never lied to me. I always knew it would only be for a while." There was a radiance in her eyes, still bright with tears. "I don't regret it. He did love me. Look, he sent those flowers."

With a gasp, Elizabeth noticed the enormous basket of spring flowers in the corner, festooned with lace and ribbons.

"But you'll never see him again?" she asked.

"No. That was our agreement. What shall I do with myself, now?"

"Work, work, work," Elizabeth stated firmly, almost harshly. "It's the only way." She walked over to the flowers and touched them with her fingertips.

Poor Lizzie, Belinda thought through her own sorrow. She's never recovered from William. There's a hardness I never thought to see in her. She needs to get back to the stage, or find a new interest, and escape from the worry of her father.

Dr Richardson made his usual visit one Monday morning, while Elizabeth waited downstairs. Ella was at her rooms for the day, as she was to return there permanently at the end of the week. The young woman thought how much she would miss her, as she sat in the parlour trying to read a book. The lavender perfume of Ella's clothes lingered in this room, over the scent of the spring flowers in the vase in the window, comforting in its presence.

The sound of footsteps on the landing roused her. As soon as Dr Richardson's eyes met her own, Elizabeth sensed that today was different. He did not smile so readily – there was a gravity in his face beneath the veneer of pleasantness.

"Miss Belmont," he said solemnly, "may we talk for a moment?"

Her mouth went dry. "Will you come into the parlour?" He followed her, declining a seat, and standing by the window instead. Elizabeth's hand clutched the mantelpiece as if to gain courage.

"I have examined your father today, and can say that he is making a good recovery."

Her grip relaxed on the wood.

". . . but there is one matter which I must make clear. This has been a serious attack. To avoid the possibility of another, I regret that your father must never play the piccolo again. The strain . . . on his heart."

For a moment Elizabeth could not breathe. Then her voice returned. "Have you told him this?"

"Yes, I have. I think it would be best if you go to him now. As you can imagine, it has been . . . quite a blow to him."

"Yes, of course, doctor."

As soon as he had left, Elizabeth hurried upstairs, her anxious footsteps thudding on the stair-carpet. She paused for a moment outside Henry's bedroom, then knocked gently. There was no reply. Pushing open the door, she took a few steps into the room.

He was sitting in the big oak chair from the parlour that had been brought upstairs and placed by the window. He looked shrunken in his nightgown, the thick wool dressing-gown bundled on top, emphasising his thin wrists as they lay on the wooden arms of the chair. His gaze was directed out of the window, but took in nothing. Tears started into her eyes.

"Father . . ." she murmured.

He turned his head at the sound of her voice. "He told you, then?"

She nodded, unable to speak for the pain at seeing him thus.

His head dropped down. "I'm finished, Lizzie." There was a strange croak in his voice that she had never heard before.

"No, no, don't say that!" She was on her knees, arms around him, holding him. "We'll find a way, Father. We will!" She laid her head on his lap, as she used to as a child.

His hand came down to stroke her hair.

The motor cab rumbled steadily along in the wake of an electric tram, the driver whistling some unrecognisable melody to himself over the din of the engine. From the dim recesses of the interior, Elizabeth stared out at the Strand. Horses and motor traffic mingled on the busy thoroughfare. The animals were fewer in number now than they had been the first time she had come this way by taxi, only a few years ago. Then it had been a horse cab. This was the first time she had taken a motor cab, and it certainly wasn't unusual to do so now. It didn't attract any attention from the numerous pedestrians out enjoying the April sunshine.

But there was little joy in Elizabeth's heart as she clutched her parasol and gloves. Her outfit was a picture of charm. It was one of her stage dresses, and as such was cut a little lower than was customary for a day dress, but neither was it obviously an evening gown. A smart jacket buttoning up to the neck hid her décolletage for the moment, but she would know later whether there was any need to show it.

Her heart began to pound once they reached the West End. It was two months since she had been in this area, and even longer since she had been to this particular theatre.

With a shaking hand, she paid the cabbie and told him to keep the change. Her resolve very nearly failed her as she stood alone on the pavement, facing the stage door. Then the image of her father passed across her vision – the lost, aimless man of the past months, the ghost of the man he had been. She took a deep breath and plunged forward. She could no longer bear to see her father destroyed.

It was a week now since she had recalled the words he had once said to her, years ago, "Lizzie, when I'm too old to play the piccolo, I want to carry on in the pit – with a baton. I'd love to conduct the band, be with the 'boys' forever. They're a great bunch, the musicians."

These words had come back to her when Ella mentioned that she had heard that Gemmling, Radley's band director, was giving up. He was a frail old man now, at least twenty years older than her father. The plan had been forming in her mind since then. Much as she disliked Radley, and hated the thought of begging a favour from him, she knew that she had to do this for Henry.

The stage doorkeeper jumped to his feet in surprise when she entered. "Why, Miss Belmont! It's a long time since you've been here. And how is your father?"

"Recovering slowly, Jack. Missing all of this, of course." She had told no one of his inability to play. "Is Mr Radley here? I have an appointment for 11 o'clock."

"Of course, Miss. Go right up. And I'm glad to hear Mr Belmont's better. Please give him my regards."

"I will do, thank you." Slipping through into the darkened auditorium, she walked up the aisle. The heavy door moved smoothly at her touch.

Radley's office was situated behind the dress circle. He only used it during the day, so its door was unmarked. If he wanted to be in the theatre during the evening, he would use one of the boxes. Elizabeth had been in it only once before, when they had had their last engagement here at Radley's Palace. It was much finer than the old office where he had first offered them a contract to play at the new hall. She knocked on the door, and, at the muffled reply, stepped inside.

Radley sprang to his feet the moment she entered. He had only just lit a cigar, but immediately crushed it out in the ashtray.

"My dear Miss Belmont!" he exclaimed, approaching her with a show of his strong white teeth in a smile. "Do sit down. May I take your coat?"

"Not just now, thank you," the young woman demurred. She sat on one of the leather chairs, propping up her parasol on the arm. Looking now at this man, she could see how women found him attractive. He hadn't let his body run to fat – it was lean and muscular beneath the impeccable suit. The slicked hair was only showing a few grey hairs at the temples. He exuded an air of success.

"Now, what can I do for you? You said it was urgent. Do you want a solo spot?"

"No, no, it's not for myself that I am here." She moved closer to the desk. "I hear that Gemmling is to retire next month."

"Yes, that's true."

"Do you have a replacement yet?"

Radley put his fingertips together and pursed his lips. "No, a few possibilities, but . . ."

"Then I have a favour to ask of you, Mr Radley. Would you offer the job to my father?"

He sat up in surprise. "To your father?" His quick mind grasped the situation immediately. Henry Belmont was an excellent musician. He could probably do the job as well as anyone – and he had pit experience. But this obviously meant a lot to his daughter. She had always worshipped the man, he knew. The manager began to see a way to get what he had always wanted.

"But Miss Belmont, why should I offer the job to him?" His voice was cool. "I've had some very experienced directors expressing interest in it. True, your father has been a good musician with a long career in the halls. But what advantage would there be for me in offering the position to him?"

Elizabeth was in no situation to search for his motives, or to be too proud to beg. "Oh, please, Mr Radley. You've no idea how much this could mean to him. Now he's unable to play, it could mend him again. Please do this. I'd do anything. . ." She stopped.

"Anything?" the manager asked quietly.

Elizabeth's thoughts raced as she realised the implication of his words. She rose to her feet and walked to the window, her hands rubbing together reflectively.

Can I do it? she wondered. She knew that she would be sullied for ever in the eyes of the world. For the first time in months she allowed herself to remember that intimate afternoon with William, but the pain of his rejection still mingled with the memory of that tenderness. Then she recalled the empty months stretching since, the hours of watching over her sick father, during which she had learned to hate the young man for his cold silence, and then her hate had turned to blank indifference.

I don't care about my body any more, she thought. Her only cares were for her father, and she truly would do anything to see his self-esteem restored. Slowly her fingers moved down her coat, unfastening the buttons. Then she turned with great dignity, her face impassive.

"Yes, Mr Radley. I'll do anything you wish, if you'll make my father conductor of your band."

Radley could scarcely believe his luck. He approached her swiftly. "Elizabeth . . ." he uttered, his voice choked with desire.

"But there is one condition," she added in a hard tone, totally indifferent to his hand stroking her neck. "He must never know that I have had anything to do with it. And you must do everything in your power to make sure that he never knows . . . about this." Her voice dropped to a whisper for the last two words.

Radley's hands were on her shoulders, in her hair, caressing her. "I promise," he said softly, as he drew her towards him.

Chapter 15

The letter arrived before the end of the week. There had been little post except bills since Henry's illness, so the formally addressed envelope with the seal of Radley's Palace on the back stood out amongst the rest of the letters. Henry eyed it curiously, and, putting the others aside, tore open this envelope first. Elizabeth stood by his chair, having just handed the day's post to him. Her fingers trembled slightly as they rested on the upholstery.

Disbelief and wonder began to show on Henry's ravaged features. "Lizzie! Lizzie, listen to this!" His voice was strong and vibrant, as she remembered it from before his illness.

"Frederick Radley wants a conductor, and he has written to me, offering me the position. He's heard of my illness, and wondered if I would like this opportunity to get back to the halls." His eyes were shining when he swung round to face her.

Tears pricked Elizabeth's own eyes as she bent forward to kiss him, her arms firm about his neck.

"Oh, Father, I'm so happy for you. What a wonderful thing to happen."

"I wonder why he chose me? It's some time since we played for him."

She moved away from the chair guiltily, and walked to the window. "Well, he must have always admired your ability, Father. That's all I can think. But," desperately changing the subject, "why worry about reasons? The job is offered, and you must write at once and accept it."

Henry paused thoughtfully in the action of dipping his pen into the inkwell that she brought him.

"A month – do you think I'll be fit enough?"

"Of course you will! Look how well you have been recently. You'll be good as new!" She laughed, but stopped as it caught in her throat.

The letter was soon penned and signed. "I'll insist that you play on my first night! No . . ." as the protests rose to her lips, "I'll do all I can for my daughter's career."

"But I'm so out of practice – and I'm nothing without you, Father."

"Rubbish, Lizzie! You'll be brilliant as a soloist. With your ability, and your looks!" He took both her hands. "But, seriously, pet, you must do this. Please . . . do this for me."

"Very well, then." She bent forward to kiss his forehead lightly. "I'll go and post this straight away."

Her step to the door was light, but all was heaviness within her at the thought of what she was already doing for Henry. Still, a solo career could easily take her away from Radley, and would mean that she need not always be at his beck and call. Perhaps it wouldn't be such a bad idea after all.

There was a touch of warmth in the spring air as she left the house to walk to the post box. Her feet blindly followed the pavement, her eyes turned inwards, reliving the past few days. It seemed unbelievable that no one had noticed that she was different. It was as if she didn't belong to herself, for she had given her body over to a man as a chattel, to be used for his pleasure.

Only a few days after their "agreement" had been struck, a note had arrived for her, secreted in a small nosegay of flowers. With it had been a key, and the address of a flat in Chelsea. The only other words on the note had been "*Tomorrow, 1pm*". Slowly, Elizabeth had crushed the card to a ball, and dropped it into the fire. So . . . he hadn't wasted any time.

The following afternoon, dressed in a dark, narrow-skirted costume with a matching veiled hat, Elizabeth had walked along the road named in Radley's note. The key dug into the palm of her hand, safe inside her glove. As she looked for the number of the building, she was struck by the irony that this street was so like the one where William had brought her that rainy October afternoon. It had a discreet frontage, which a young lady could approach with no hint of suspicion.

The shiny new key slid into the lock with no resistance. Its rasp of metal against metal made her jump and glance round furtively, as if it declared her business to all the inhabitants of the neighbourhood. Quickly she buried herself in the concealing obscurity of the hallway.

Her heart pounding, she stripped the kid gloves from her hands, damp with perspiration. Again she was conscious of the similarity to the day with William, for once more she had been directed to a first-floor apartment. The stairs creaked with bold announcement of her ascent. There was only one door on the first floor landing, so she applied her knuckles gently.

A crack of light appeared in the doorway, forming an incongruous halo around Radley's head as he held the door open for her to enter. "May I take your coat?" he offered, shutting out the darkness of the corridor.

They were silent as he lifted her coat from her shoulders and she unpinned the hat and voluminous veil, laying them on a cabinet by the lace-curtained windows. Immediately Elizabeth was aware of the luxury of this apartment. Her feet sank into the deep carpet at each step. The air was filled with the warmth of a crackling fire. A silken shawl draped the couch, and a bowl of fresh spring flowers held their heads up towards the sunlight that streamed in through the windows.

"Would you like something to drink, to warm you?"

"No, thank you," she murmured. Her hands gripped the back of a chair. "Mr Radley, I have come here for a purpose. Please let us . . . fulfil this . . . purpose immediately." She couldn't hide the tremor in her voice.

Radley was swift in coming to her side.

"Elizabeth . . . why, you're trembling." He raised one hand to her cheek, at which she flinched away, her breath catching on a sob of fear. Carefully he disengaged her hands from their grip on the chair-back, and led her towards a chair in front of the fire. This was a Radley she had never seen before. His voice low, he talked to her gently as if she were a young child, until she was leaning against him, her hair loose on her shoulders, silken beneath his stroking hands. She felt drained, all strength ebbing from her.

Then with a start she pushed him away from her, and stood up. "Which door is the bedroom?" she uttered through stiff lips.

"This one." He pointed to the nearest door.

"Give me a few minutes," she said brusquely, and hurried through the doorway. Even the bedroom was warm. Very carefully she unbuttoned her blouse and unhooked her skirt. Opening the wardrobe, she found some clothes hangers and dutifully hung up each article of clothing as she removed it. Loosening her corset, she stepped from it, then folded it on a velvet-covered chair by the window. Dressed only in her chemise and bloomers, she pulled the door open slightly.

"I'm ready."

The stiffness of fear crept into her limbs at his approach. His jacket and waistcoat discarded, the muscles of his chest swelled under the crisp lawn of his shirt. He was far taller and broader than William had been. Panic fought in her to escape as his arms came round her – strong, compelling arms, searching for those sensitive parts of her through the folds of her chemise.

Then he was murmuring to her again – soft words, mellowing endearments – and those experienced hands began awakening her body against her will. This was so different to that first time in the cold room with William, warmed only by their passion and love.

Afterwards, she rose from the bed, leaving him smoking a cigar amongst the tumbled sheets. One by one she put on each of her garments, under Radley's scrutinising eye.

"So . . . it wasn't the first time for you."

"No," Elizabeth replied coldly, speaking to his reflection in the mirror, "it wasn't my first time. I'm sorry if it disappointed you, Mr Radley, if you had hoped for a virgin. I trust the agreement will still hold, despite this drawback."

"God Almighty, you're touchy!" he cried out, stung by her barb, grinding out his cigar in the ashtray on the bedside table. "Can't you see that I just want you? To feel you, touch you, have you soft against me?"

"You have paid for the privilege, sir."

"Paid! You make it sound as if you're a whore!"

Tears sprang into her eyes. "I'm no better than they are."

Incensed, he sprang from the bed. Immediately she averted her eyes so that she wouldn't see his nakedness. The sight of his maleness made him even more menacing.

"Elizabeth." He now spoke gently, pleading. "Can't you see how much I care for you? If only you could grow to . . . like me a little. How happy I could make you, if only there could be more between us than . . . business."

With a look sharp as broken glass, she raised her eyes to his. "Never ask that of me, Mr Radley. You have my agreement – but not that."

She had slunk home in the afternoon sunshine, avoiding the eyes of people she passed. With relief she managed to enter the house without meeting her father, and ran a hot bath in which she soaked until her skin glowed red as a burn, wishing she could wash away the shame of the afternoon. And, as if her skin showed the manager's handprints like soot on her white flesh, she took to wearing high-necked, long-sleeved gowns and blouses.

There had only been the one rendezvous before Henry started work, as Elizabeth knew that she couldn't disguise her absences when her father was around the house all day. In any case, he wanted to hear her practising, and to discuss future programmes.

However, as soon as Henry began to take regular band-calls, and then took over the evening performances, Elizabeth was free to do as Radley wished. It was then that she was glad of her father's insistence that she resume her career. The manager was piqued by this development, but knew that he could hardly deny Henry's wish to give his daughter a "spot" on the grounds that he wished to enjoy the delights of her body while her father was otherwise engaged.

Almost immediately the audiences took Elizabeth to their hearts. They found her charming and fresh, with an innocent air overlaying the ripeness of her body. Gradually, as she overcame her shyness at performing alone, and her fingers threw off the rustiness of those months of inactivity, her playing grew bolder and sparkled with a brilliance that thrilled her public. Her agent was soon providing her with bookings more numerous than ever before. Henry was delighted, especially as she always included 'Melody for Lizzie' as her encore piece when she played at Radley's Palace. And for Elizabeth herself there was the reward of seeing Henry regaining some of his old vigour.

Several young men paused on their way to their business in the City as they set eyes on two charming young women amongst the mid-morning travellers at Waterloo Station. Behind them, a porter wheeled a gigantic trunk, big enough to hold both the young beauties, hats and all.

While the porter saw to the stowing-away of his burden, the chestnut-haired member of the pair mounted carefully into one of the carriages of the Southampton train. The other gazed sadly at her from the platform.

"I'm going to miss you terribly, Belinda."

Her friend laughed. "What – with all of these young beaux? The Honourable Monty couldn't wait to get me out of the way, so that he could make an approach to you. And what about Rutherford? He's heir to thousands, and he couldn't take his eyes off you when we were at Claridge's last week."

Since resuming her career, Elizabeth had joined Belinda occasionally for a social jaunt after performances. It gave her an alibi when she needed to meet Radley.

She now smiled in half-pain. "It wouldn't matter so much if you weren't going to the other side of the world. Do remember to write often!"

Belinda stretched one hand out of the carriage window to touch her shoulder. "Of course I will. I'll tell you about all those handsome Australians. Maybe I'll tempt you to come too!"

Elizabeth stepped back. "Oh, no, not me."

"But why, love? There's no great hold for you here. There's a whole world out there waiting to be discovered."

"Maybe I'm not as brave as you."

Belinda's face lost its bantering glow. "No, I don't believe that. You've probably more courage than me. Why, look at me, running away, half across the world!"

Sympathy welled in the younger woman. "You haven't forgotten Bertie at all, then."

Belinda cocked her head on one side. "No, it's just that it will be easier to start again in a country where I know he won't be. There'll never be anyone quite like him, for me, and it's harder to forget him when every other young man I meet knows him, and talks about him and his new wife."

"So they're married now."

"Yes, last week." She straightened up. "Enough of nostalgia! But, listen, before I leave you . . ." Belinda leaned closer out of the carriage window. "There have been whispers about you, Lizbeth. I don't know if they're true, and I won't ask, but . . . don't do anything silly. You may think that sounds odd, coming from me . . . but love has to be in the right place. Don't waste it on just anyone – remember Patty. Promise me you'll think carefully?"

Elizabeth nodded, at once frightened that her liaison was rumoured, and at the same time touched at Belinda's concern.

"Listen to Auntie Bel!" the traveller mocked herself. At that instant came the shrill whistle announcing the departure of the train. Quickly they hugged, and Elizabeth stepped back to wave. At once, both of them were weeping.

"I'll be back once the pantomime's over at Christmas!" Belinda called through her tears, alternately wiping her eyes with her lace-edged handkerchief and waving it through the open window.

Henry was looking and feeling better than he had done in years. The job at Radley's Palace suited him. He was an old hand, and knew how to get the best out of his band. It was a good little collection of instrumentalists. Many of them he knew from earlier days, and loved to chat with his old pals over a pint of beer after the band-calls. The "lads" in return respected Henry's judgement, knowing that he had once been one of them, and acknowledging his ability in making it to a respectable place on the bill as an artiste in his own right.

As his strength returned with renewed vigour to his leaner figure, Henry found his thoughts straying to matters other than his work. Now that it was August, Florence Royle, the dancer, must be back in England.

He hadn't loved any woman since Jessica, Elizabeth's mother, had died. There had always been Ella to give him a cup of tea in winter, and a nip of whisky when he was cold at heart. She had been good to Elizabeth too, his precious girl. But she'd never been more than just a good friend.

It wasn't until Elizabeth went away to school that he had realised how lonely he was. The years of hard work seemed to have dried up his need for a woman. Then he got the chance to make his name – and, suddenly, the cups of tea with Ella were not enough. He recalled his first meeting with Florence, when she had bumped into him – probably on purpose, he acknowledged now. But he was ready to be led on. What a figure she had! He could feel those long-forgotten stirrings, just thinking of her.

But she always skipped too far ahead of him. She had come to visit him before the shows when he was crawling up the bill, and would lean a plump white bosom over him, always tantalising. He was certain that they would have gone much further, if Florence hadn't taken a dislike to Elizabeth.

To Henry it was inconceivable that anyone could dislike his daughter. Florence changed whenever Elizabeth was near, becoming cold and hard. Henry realised that Elizabeth was now an attractive woman, but Florence had good looks, and a knowledge of the world to beat anything his daughter possessed. Not that Henry wished his girl any different – he wanted to protect her for better things. Florence, now, was made for a man's bed. You could see it in her eyes, he reflected. But he knew that she wanted to get places, too. The years were overtaking her, and she was aiming for the top of the bill. She hoped for Radley's influence in that sphere, and Henry hadn't been blind to her pursuit of him. But no doubt Radley was wise to her wiles and wouldn't let himself be used, for he was always cool and businesslike with her.

Henry admitted to himself that he sometimes felt a physical ache for Florence. She had been in America now for a year, dancing in vaudeville. He knew that he would have to see her somehow when she came back, and then . . .

But he couldn't let Elizabeth know what he envisaged. He had to protect her – other people could behave how they liked, but not her old Dad . . .

The dancer was standing in the foyer of Radley's Palace, dressed elegantly in a lilac hobble skirt, a veiled hat of an exactly matched shade perched on her carefully hennaed hair. Her bright newness was a contrast to the foyer of the theatre, already dingy after only two years. Henry at once turned to look at her, and recognised Florence's curvaceous figure. She hurried over with a rustling of skirts to clasp his hands.

"Henry Belmont! How are you? I heard you'd been ill and I was so worried." There was a new pronounced transatlantic drawl to her words. "Yet how well you look. How do you think I look?" She twirled round gracefully, at which Henry smiled.

"Really lovely, Florence. I heard you were a great success over in America."

Tossing her head up, she said, "I was, too. I was quite someone over there." She smiled coquettishly. "I nearly didn't come back."

"We would have missed you."

"We?" Her eyes challenged him through lowered lashes.

"*I* would – you know that, Florrie."

Her response was bright with laughter. "Well, I hope that the halls feel the need for me now. My agent is just now arranging terms with Mr Radley. I'll really show him what I'm worth!" At these last words, her eyes narrowed as if already counting the box-office receipts.

"Come for dinner with me, Florrie. I want to hear about your tour in America."

A smile rested lightly on her lips. She reached out and patted his hand. "We'll see, Henry dear. Once my act is fixed up, I'll contact you. Until then . . ." She waved a lavender-gloved hand as she vanished out of the theatre doors.

For a moment, Henry gazed after her, nonplussed. He was unsure whether or not he had been rebuffed. Then, with a shrug, he entered the auditorium to join the band, who were assembling noisily in the pit. He would just need to wait and see if she made a move.

Florence began to dance a solo spot as from the following week. Her placing on the bill was not much higher than when Radley had last engaged her. Henry suspected that this had rankled with the dancer, flushed from her success in the United States. He had seen her exchanging heated words with the act that preceded her, a comedian who had taken an extra bow and in doing so had held up her entrance.

It also became noticeable that she had taken to frequenting the bar when she knew that Radley was in the theatre. Once or twice Henry saw her approaching the manager, or engaged in vivacious conversation with him. But what became even more apparent was that Radley was not interested in her advances, which pleased Henry. He could not compete with this man, either in influence or money. Radley's years, too, were on his side. Yet Henry, sizing himself up in the glass behind the bar, saw a man of good appearance. He had let his hair grow grey, and it lent distinction to his features, he thought. His shoulders were still broad, but the flesh now sat more firmly on his frame. More to the point, he was unmarried, unattached, and interested.

It seemed at last as if the realisation of this had dawned on Florence. Henry picked his moment. The next evening he knew the manager would be in the music hall, he wandered down to the bar during the second interval. Sure enough, Florence was there, dressed in a daringly low-cut dress of a deep gold colour. She had already made her usual approach to Radley. But tonight he was in no mood to sport with her. Henry, from the other end of the bar where he sipped his whisky, furtively looked along to Radley, and saw the brief flash of irritation that crossed his features. A few more moments, and Radley had vanished into the crowd.

One of the regular "girls" of the promenade was touching Henry's shoulder, willing to offer an evening's company, but he smiled and shook his head, transporting his whisky along the bar.

"Florrie," he said gently, while signalling to the barman with his hand. He pushed a brandy towards the dancer.

Slowly the frown cleared from her brow. "Thanks, Henry," she murmured after she had taken a wild gulp. "I needed that." She draped her leg over one of the bar stools, clearly revealing the shape of her thigh.

She doesn't need to do that, thought Henry with irony. He could feel the heat pulsing through him just through being near her. He made a comment about her performance, asking her about the timing of the music – but all the while he was aware of the delicious warm flesh near him, and hardly heeded her answers.

Florence was silent for a few moments as she turned over the last of the brandy in her mouth, her red lips pursed pensively. Then she swallowed, and leaned towards her companion. "Henry, would you do me a favour?"

"Anything, Florrie."

"I want to try a new dance – but I need to rehearse with the band. Would you get the boys to come in tomorrow afternoon?"

Henry smiled roguishly. "Yes – if you promise to come to dinner with me tomorrow after the last show."

Her lips curved up, eyes crinkling in amusement. "Very well, Henry." Then she threw back her head and laughed. Heads turned in curiosity, but Henry revelled in their attention. He leaned forward and took her arm purposefully, so that all could see that he was with this engaging woman, and led her the length of the promenade.

Chapter 16

The waitress paused until the two young ladies had removed their coats and settled themselves at the window table before she took out her notebook and hurried to stand beside them. The dark one, thought the waitress as she eyed her black skirt and austere blouse, was definitely one of the "New Women". But the fair one – surely she had seen her somewhere before? Her complexion was a little dull, though, as if she hardly ever saw the air.

"We'll have tea, please, and some fresh scones with jam," Frances announced, once they had studied the menu. Folding her gloves neatly by the plate, she looked out of the window, along the Strand. "Look how many horseless carriages there are now – even motor buses. London has really changed over the past few years."

"Does your father still have a motor car?" Elizabeth asked.

"Oh, yes, but he's just bought a new one – much faster, and more reliable. He let me drive it twice this summer. It was great fun! But, surely, your father must own a motor car now?"

Elizabeth shook her head. "We rely on taxis and carriages. Our expenses wouldn't run to a chauffeur, and I wouldn't want Father to attempt to drive, after his illness. His health appears to be good, but I'm always a little apprehensive."

Frances nodded sympathetically. "That's understandable."

Their conversation paused for a moment as the waitress carefully unloaded her tray. Frances immediately took possession of the teapot and began to fill the cups. Elizabeth enquired after the other members of the Whittingham family. The eldest, Alfred, was now working in Manchester. Gerald had recently graduated from Cambridge, and was going to spend a year abroad in Germany before returning to their father's firm. But what was unbelievable was that young Edward was now sixteen and aiming to follow the three older Whittinghams to Cambridge, and little Cissie was fifteen.

"And is Cissie going to be academic, too?"

Frances pulled a face. "Not she! Cissie has all the airs and graces of a young lady, and intends to live like one! She's still at Stavington, but can't wait to be old enough to be married. She hopes that Papa will introduce her to the sons of his colleagues."

Elizabeth smiled. "Obviously she intends to become another Violet Wyatt – sorry, I should say Cunningham."

"Have you heard anything from your Wyatt relations?"

"No, nothing at all. I suppose I ought to write, but they never replied to my father's letter, which he sent just after I left, to thank them for their financial assistance. We paid back the money, too."

"It's an awkward situation. I did hear that Violet has produced two healthy children already."

"The Cunninghams must be pleased with their bargain." The girls laughed. Then Elizabeth added, "What about you, Frances? How are your political activities?"

Immediately the other young woman's eyes took on an excited glow. "That's why I'm here in London. We have a wonderful new project planned – a petition to the Prime Minister. Every day supporters are waiting outside the House of Commons to attempt to hand it to him, and we need as many women as possible to take a turn. I shall be there all of next week, before I return to university. You must join us, Elizabeth."

Elizabeth gently set down the delicate china teacup. "I'm sorry, Frances. It's really very difficult – rehearsal schedules. I'm due to play at a new venue that week, and I have some new material to rehearse with the orchestra."

"But surely you could organise your dates so that you have some time to join us?"

"No, truly – it's an important engagement, and I don't want to get a reputation for being difficult."

Frances subsided in her chair. "All right, I see how it is. I thought that now your friend Belinda was abroad you might have time for some more serious activity. But I see I was wrong."

Elizabeth swallowed an angry retort. Frances had always seemed to like Belinda – she had never suspected this resentment. One look at her friend's closed face told her that she was hurt by Elizabeth's refusal. But what more could she say? Her personal life was causing her enough problems without becoming actively involved in a political movement. If only she could confide in Frances – or anyone, for that matter. But no one would understand. They would all condemn her.

What was more damning was that, during the very week in which Frances had wanted her to join with the suffragettes, Elizabeth already had another engagement. One of Radley's business associates was staging a special night's performance in aid of charity, and the manager had persuaded her to accompany him. He had managed to convince her that it would not be compromising to be seen in his company just once – in fact, it would be beneficial to her career to be seen patronising a worthy cause. Too often the profession had the reputation for squandering money on their own shallow pleasures. He had it on good authority, that Vesta Tilley and her husband, Walter de Frece, would be there as well as the actor Beerbohm Tree. In fact, Elizabeth did not mind too much attending such a function in Radley's company. What did worry her was that, now he had persuaded her to take this step, he might prevail upon her to accompany him at other times.

Despite these misgivings, she agreed to go. Henry, to her surprise, was delighted. He saw it as a wonderful opportunity to be seen in the "right" company, especially if the press were reporting the function and mentioned her name.

"But . . . I'll be late back, Father. You won't mind?" She knew very well why Radley had told her to warn Henry of this. She couldn't meet his eyes.

"No, there's no need to worry about that. Anyway, I'll be out myself that evening, after the last house."

Surprised, Elizabeth glanced at him sharply. "Oh? Where are you going?"

"For dinner with Florence Royle."

"Again, Father? But you saw her only two days ago."

A prick of annoyance touched him. "Lizzie, I don't question your choice of friends. So I would thank you to leave me to make my own."

Hot tears stung her eyes at this reprimand. "Sorry," she muttered, turning away.

"Lizzie," he added more gently. "Don't let us quarrel. You enjoy your companions, I'll enjoy mine."

"Yes, of course," she said quickly, edging from the room before he could see how upset she was. Enjoy her companions! Who was there? Belinda was thousands of miles away, and she hardly ever saw Frances, who was either studying or bound up in her militant politics. There was only Radley . . .

When the evening of the charity benefit came, Elizabeth was surprised at how exciting it was. She had nearly always been on the other side of the footlights, or crushed into one of the cheapest seats before her career began. Here, instead, she was treated almost like royalty, in the company of so many wealthy people. There had even been a few moments of precious conversation with Vesta Tilley, whom she admired so much. In her white silk evening dress, her dark hair dressed fashionably, the gentle impersonator couldn't have looked less like the smart young "johnnies" of her act.

"I haven't had the chance to tell you this before, but I must say how beautifully you play. It's such a pleasure to see one with talent doing well."

Elizabeth flushed with pleasure, stammering her thanks.

"I'm also pleased to hear that your father is so much better. His leadership is excellent – I have never known finer. I hope to perform with him soon at Radley's Palace."

How thrilled her father would be to hear such praise! She stored up all these comments with her impressions of the evening, to be relayed to Henry afterwards. At the reception that followed the performance, she was never allowed to be bored for an instant, with people constantly clamouring for her attention. With a thrill, she realised that she was glamorous to many of those present. There were a few envious glances from the rich young women who were aware that she was seldom without a young man at her side throughout the evening.

Noticing a break in the throng, Radley edged up to her, to place a glass of champagne in her hand. "I've never seen you looking lovelier," he murmured while toasting her with his own glass.

Her eyes sparkled as brilliantly as the wine. "Oh, thank you. It's been such an exciting evening. I have spoken to so many people. Do you know, young Lord Sawley has been to see me play six times!" She laughed delightedly, the unaccustomed champagne having already gone to her head.

Radley leaned closer. "But of course, Elizabeth. You're worth beholding many times." He decided to risk stretching further, " . . . and even more worth having."

Her contented smile continued as if she hadn't heard the last part of his sentence. But she had registered every iota of its meaning, and for once it did not seem such a dreadful idea. In fact, the nearness of his broad shoulders and the expanse of his muscled chest beneath the silk evening shirt and tightly fitting black tail-coat was having a distinctly indecorous effect on her.

She turned her blue eyes languorously upon him. "How much longer do we have to stay, Frederick?"

Radley nearly dropped his champagne glass at the tone of her words. Could it really be that she was willing, for the first time ever? Almost suffocating with his eagerness, he replied in a hoarse voice, "We can leave whenever you wish." He laid down his glass before he could do anything so shameful as break it. "Now?"

"Yes," she whispered.

They took a formal leave of their host and hostess. Elizabeth then wandered out into the night air with her fur wrap draped over one arm, while Radley collected his cloak, cane and top hat. The sounds of music and conversation drifted out on the pavement with a blaze of light from all of the windows. The beams even reached so far as to light a group of people passing on the other side of the road.

"Elizabeth, my dear, you'll catch cold." Radley was at her side, taking charge of her wrap, pulling it solicitously over her shoulders. He couldn't resist a sweeping caress over her arms and shoulders, as she was so desirable in her new compliant mood. "I'll get the chauffeur. Wait here on the steps."

Pulling the fur tighter round her body, Elizabeth watched his elegant figure disappearing into the shades of night. Almost immediately, a hiss at her back caused her to swing round, startled.

"So, Elizabeth Belmont! This is why you would not join us! You had better company!"

"Frances . . . what are you doing here?"

Half-shadowed by the darkness, Frances' black coat was torn, and her hair fell down from beneath the brim of her hat onto her dirt-streaked face.

"Why . . . whatever has happened?" Elizabeth asked.

Frances smiled grimly. "Only a little skirmish with the police – quite normal, I assure you. But I don't suppose you want your fine friends to see you associating with such a scarecrow."

"It's not like that at all – it's a function in aid of charity."

"Charity!" The suffragette laughed bitterly. "I saw the way that man handled you – and you were enjoying it."

"But you don't understand . . ."

"I've seen enough to understand now. You're a disgrace to womankind. Well, Miss Belmont, the suffragettes can do without women like you, who debase themselves. And so can I!"

Elizabeth's dismay turned to sharp anger. "You've no right to accuse me – I can lead my life without your judgement!"

"Don't worry! You won't ever hear from me again!"

So saying, Frances swept round and hurried after her friends, who waited just out of earshot, a black group huddled beneath the street-lamp at the corner. A motor car passed them and approached the pool of light. Radley jumped out.

"There, my dear! We're all set. Jump in!" He made to take her elbow, at which she recoiled furiously.

"Don't touch me!" she uttered through clenched teeth. Dumbfounded by her transformation, Radley stepped back. "What's wrong? What can I have done to make you so angry?"

"Lost me my close friend, that's what!" she cried, the last word catching on a sob of sheer rage. Pushing him aside, she stepped into the car, leaving him to follow her at his will. He joined her immediately, directing the chauffeur to drive to Chelsea. Well, no matter! Maybe she would soften, despite the fact that she kept her head rigidly turned away from him so that he could not see her face. Once or twice on the journey she lifted a handkerchief to wipe her cheeks. Tears . . . he sighed. Well, it would be no different from many other times. How sweet it would have been to take her willing body, just once.

Henry flagged down a motor cab at Trafalgar Square to take Florence back to her lodgings. He gasped at the nearness of her naked shoulders as she stepped into the cab.

"Here, you'll be cold," he said to hide his embarrassment, handing in her fur stole, and followed her into the cab.

She sat close to him in the taxi, completing his sensations of well-being after a good meal and some excellent wine and port. He'd taken quite a liking to port since his fortunes had changed. It had always seemed a gentleman's drink to him. He had been struggling for long enough, so why not enjoy a little luxury now?

"Henry, come up with me. Time for a nightcap?" Florence's voice was soft and low in the darkness of the taxi.

He pinched her cheek gently. "Why not? I've always time for a pretty woman." He helped her out and paused for a moment to pay the driver. One aspect of his prosperity that he particularly enjoyed was the fact that his pockets were always full of money – enough to hire a cab whenever he took the notion, and he never had to worry about finding the extra to tip the cabbie.

It wasn't the first time he had been in Florence's apartment, but he had never been there at such a late hour. Her landlady had laid a fire in the grate, and Florence now lit it. Within moments the orange glow was spreading round the room, and with it came the beginnings of a welcome warmth.

"Let me take your coat, Henry." She slid it from his shoulders, her hands brushing his arms almost imperceptibly. It was enough to kindle a response from him. Had she meant it, or was it in fact unintentional?

"Help yourself to a drink. I'll be back in a moment." She disappeared from the room with his coat over one arm, leaving Henry alone in the glimmering half-light from the dim gas-lamp that Florence had lit on their arrival.

After pouring himself another port, Henry sat in the large chair next to the fire, stretching his feet out towards the coals. He felt younger tonight than he had done for years – being with Florence always rejuvenated him. Perhaps he was more attractive to a young woman now, he hardly dared to hope as he took a generous mouthful of the drink.

The carriage clock on the mantelpiece showed him that she had been gone ten minutes already. Where could she be? Laying his glass on a polished table, he stood up and walked to the window. He drew back the curtain a little way and gazed down into the street. It was completely deserted. For a brief moment he wondered how his daughter was faring at her charity engagement.

"Henry."

Immediately he swung round to find Florence advancing towards him. He was speechless at the sight of her in a soft silk wrap, with froths of ivory lace at the cuffs. A roguish smile played around her lips as she studied his reaction. Then her arms were around him, and he found himself kissing her, longing for her as he had done for no other woman since Jessica, his wife. But Jessica was forgotten in the soft presence of here and now, and he was engulfed.

The house was silent as Elizabeth let herself into the polished hallway. She paused for an instant, listening for any signs of Henry's presence. After all, it was past 2 o'clock, and she had been expected around midnight. Softly she made her way up the stairs, which mercifully did not creak beneath the carpet.

She made to tiptoe past Henry's room, when she noticed that the door was wide open. The bed was empty. So he wasn't home! Sighing with relief, she walked quickly past to her own room, where she undressed quickly.

But her relief was short-lived. There was only one place Henry could be now, if not at home – and that was at Florence Royle's. The knowledge settled on her like an icy cloak. She lay in bed in the darkness, thinking bitterly of the happenings of the evening. Still angry at Frances for her unjust accusations, she blamed herself in the next instant. It was true, she was immoral, but she had only done it for Henry. The final twist was that he would never know, could never know. Yet there he was with that awful scheming woman, Florence Royle, who hated her, yet who might still become her stepmother. If Henry married her, then Elizabeth knew she would cease to be Radley's mistress, for Florence would be bound to ferret out the truth. But, though she longed for an end to her current position, she couldn't hope for such a marriage for her father.

Sleep would not come. The slightest noise stirred her, with the thought that it was her father home at last. When she finally did hear him ascending the stairs, the first glow of dawn was creeping into the sky. But it brought no lightening of her burden.

Elizabeth's pale complexion and heavy eyes drew a comment from Henry when he joined her at luncheon that day. Feeling dull and numbed of feeling, she explained it away by saying that she had met Frances and had quarrelled.

"But what did you quarrel about?" asked Henry, incredulous. "I thought you were such good friends."

"Oh, it was to do with her views on . . . on the suffragettes, a woman's place."

"But what a time to bring it up."

"Please, Father. I don't want to talk about it." Her voice cracked in fear that he would ask too many questions.

"I understand, pet. Perhaps she'll come round later."

"Maybe," she replied, adding "never" to herself. And Henry didn't, couldn't, understand.

They fell into a routine existence. Elizabeth practised, rehearsed, performed, and met Radley once a week. Henry was in constant demand for rehearsals or shows. When he was free, his daughter hardly saw him, for inevitably he was to be found in the company of Florence Royle. He had learned not to speak of her in Elizabeth's presence, for she would answer coldly. Her disapproval was never spoken outright, but Henry hated to see the barrier grow between them. So instead they talked of the shows, the other acts. It hurt him that he couldn't talk to the person closest to him of his new-found happiness, but then he told himself that after all, Elizabeth was only nineteen, and was probably embarrassed that he should be having an affair with a woman who wasn't her mother.

Belinda found the hugeness of Australia thrilling after the crowded English cities she had played before. She was glad that she had bought two new songs from James Adamson before leaving her home country, for the rough-and-ready Australians loved them and her. Here, nobody cared about her origins. "London" was all one place to them, home of the King and Queen, a distant palace of a city.

The vast distances caught her breath, as did the amazing heat. The months she spent in vaudeville, before the pantomime season began, taught her what to expect from her audiences. She accepted a few invitations to supper after the shows, and found that, despite their difference of origin by thousands of miles, she was in fact nearer to these Australian men in character than she had been to Bertie Chard. She even dined with some of them more than once.

The pantomime was 'Jack and the Beanstalk', with Belinda as a charming Jack – the first time she had ever been the principal boy. Never before had she performed panto in summer weather, she mused as she stepped into a cool day gown with relief after a rehearsal. It was still only October, and really only spring, but already she found the heat considerable.

Her eyes strayed to the posy of violets on her dressing table. It was a long time since she had been able to look at violets without a stab of sorrow. But this time, instead of bringing Bertie's face to mind, they conjured up a tall, straw-haired Australian businessman, his face deeply tanned and lined from the sun.

Reg Keene arrived promptly, beaming a good-natured smile. He was nearly thirty, broad shoulders straining beneath the cloth of his suit, as if he ought to be working out in the bush rather than behind a desk.

"I see you got the violets," he said.

Belinda picked up the nosegay and pinned it to the festoons of chiffon on her hat. "They're lovely, Reg. How did it look, from the front?"

"Fine, great. You were the best, quite the most beautiful Jack – but I like you better like this."

She laughed.

"Do you ride, Miss Grey?" he asked.

"Reg, I thought we were on first name terms," she scolded. "No, I don't – but I'm willing to learn. Why?"

"Well . . . Belinda . . . I thought you might like to come out to our sheep station on Sunday. It'd make a change from the city."

She paused for a few moments, noting the faint boyish dusting of freckles over his golden skin. He wasn't handsome, like other men she had known, but somehow it seemed to make him more attractive. Her mouth curved into a smile. "I'd love to come, Reg." It would be best to make the most of this exciting country while she had the chance to explore it, she told herself.

In London, November drew in, and with it came the first of the winter's suffocating yellow smogs. Elizabeth was determined to make the journey to Ella's home that Sunday, and would not let the weather put her off. There was little time for her to see Ella, now that they lived further away. Sometimes they met for afternoon tea, but the occasions became less frequent. It had been a month since their last meeting, and she knew that Radley wouldn't expect her while the traffic had to grope almost blindly through the damp, heavy atmosphere.

The only way to get there was by walking. It was like returning to her old home in a dream. The eerie shapes of the houses loomed on either side of her, the occasional incandescence of a street-lamp sending its brightness through the cold, clinging air. Despite this, the smog was less dense than it had been during the past few days.

Holding her coat tightly round her to ward off the dampness, Elizabeth finally reached the familiar green gate, dewed with moisture, and hurried up the path. To her surprise, her knock was answered by Mrs Lane, who with her husband now occupied the first-floor flat where Elizabeth had grown up.

"Where's Ella?"

"She's in bed. It's 'er chest. It's this 'ere weather. Come in out of the cold, love."

Flushed with anxiety, Elizabeth gently opened the door to Ella's lodging. Immediately the heat of the coal fire met her, a welcome contrast to the damp that still clung to her clothes.

"Oh, Ella, if only I'd known you were ill, I would have come sooner," she cried, hurrying over to where the invalid lay, propped up by cushions in her bed. Ella's face creased into a smile of welcome.

"It's all right, dear, and anyway the weather was too bad to send you a message," she wheezed.

"Oh, but it isn't all right. When did this start?"

"With the smog. I've had a bad chest before, but never been laid up for so long."

"Have you seen a doctor?"

"Oh yes, some young bloke who insisted that I should stay in bed."

"And that's just what you'll do. I'll stay with you, and look after you until you're better."

"No, listen, Eliz . . ." She broke off as a fit of coughing shook her, while Elizabeth held her up to try to ease her breathing. It left Ella weak and gasping. When she was able to speak again, she continued. "Mrs Lane is looking after me. You have your job to go back to, and your father needs you."

Elizabeth looked away. "I hardly see him now."

Ignoring this remark, Ella went on, "There isn't enough room for you, dear. I appreciate your offer. But it would give me more comfort to know that you were safely home before dark today."

"But that means I can only stay one hour!"

Ella silenced her protests, and, with a promise that she would return later in the week, Elizabeth left, her spirits considerably lower than when she had arrived.

Henry was also shocked to hear of their friend's illness. Elizabeth suggested that he should come with her the next Sunday to visit Ella, but he demurred.

"I can't, pet, I've arranged to rehearse."

"Can't you change it?"

"No, I can't. It was arranged two weeks ago, and I've engaged some of the band to come along."

"Oh, it's for her, is it? Very well, I'll go alone."

"Lizzie . . ." he began as she swept from the room. Then he sat down with a sigh. If he called it off, Florence would be livid, because she wanted to perform the routine in the Christmas pantomime at Radley's Palace, and Henry had persuaded the manager to watch her the week after. But he couldn't forget Ella, alone and ill. Maybe he could slip round during the week.

But somehow the hours were filled, and Ella slipped from his mind. So his daughter made the trip alone. This time she took a taxi, as the smog had cleared, leaving the weather wet and windy. She had sent round extra warm blankets and some food delicacies during the week when she was unable to leave work.

Ella was much improved, but still confined to her bed. It shocked her young friend to see her looking so pale despite the heat of the fire.

"I'm not so young as I was," Ella said in response to Elizabeth's concern.

"Oh, Ella, you must come to stay with us until you are well. We can get a nurse for you."

"No, my love, I wouldn't want that. I'm happy in my little home – little enough time that I shall have here now."

"What do you mean?" Elizabeth cried sharply.

Ella smiled. "Not as bad as you think, love." She settled back on her pillows. "No, it's just that I shall have to leave here. The doctor has advised me to leave London as soon as possible. He says that another winter here could be too much for me."

"But . . . where will you go?"

"I've had a lot of time to sit and think, these past two weeks. I've decided to go and stay with my sister, Vera, in Kent. She's a widow, too, and it'll be company for both of us. I've written to suggest that I'll move after Christmas, if she'll agree."

Suddenly, Elizabeth found her eyes full of tears, spilling over onto her cheeks. "Ella, what are we going to do without you, Father and I?"

"Come here," she said softly, folding Elizabeth's head on to her shoulder to still her sobs. "I really don't think your father needs me now, Elizabeth. When you were a little girl I was glad that I was there to help you when you needed a mother's guidance. But you're a woman now, and a successful artiste."

"But, if Father had married you, then you would have been my mother – and we wouldn't be losing you now."

"Is that what you would have wished?" Ella said softly, her own eyes blurring a little.

"Oh, Ella, I would have loved to have you as my mother – instead it looks like it will be that dreadful, scheming dancer. She's wormed her way into Father's heart, using her body to hide that she has no real feelings."

"Hush, you mustn't say such things."

"But it's true . . . he's with her today."

A little tremor of pain crossed Ella's face. Elizabeth saw it, and realised then how much Ella loved her father. In silence, she put her arms round her friend and the two women held each other close, comforted in their trouble.

Chapter 17

There were plenty of Christmas cards for Elizabeth from admirers and well-wishers that year. Many came via Elizabeth's agent, along with requests of money from charities and individuals. There were also the inevitable offerings from aspiring composers of popular tunes, begging her to try their music out in her act.

The act became more important to her than she could have believed. It seemed strange that, in her wilderness of emotions, with all those close to her now having deserted her, she could put so much into her performances. But the music brought her the happiness she lacked elsewhere in her life. "It's better to put my trust in music," she reasoned. "It'll never let me down."

Truly her career was blossoming. There had been offers of tours, but only one had appealed to her – a tour involving the north-eastern circuit, the land of her father's roots. She had always wanted to visit the area, and particularly Sunderland, the town of Henry's birth, where his father had owned an ironmonger's shop all those years ago. There was no close family there now, no one who would remember the young Henry Belmont who had run away from home at the age of sixteen to become a pit musician, and who had later starred in the music halls. But now his daughter was to have a star spot at the fine new music hall, the Sunderland Empire, recently opened by the famous Vesta Tilley.

It had been worth all Radley's protests to see Henry's face when she told him. He had hugged her hard with pride to hear that she had decided to accept the tour.

"Good billing throughout, Father – six weeks in February and March, after the pantomime season."

"Oh, Lizzie, you'll love the north-east. And at Sunderland you can go down to the beach and see the tall cliffs, and the North Sea racing up the sands. It's fine and wild, and so beautiful! Maybe I can even get in touch with some old friends . . . but no, they won't remember me now." He sighed. "It's almost as good as going back myself."

She laughed in delight. "I'll save my bills for you. Can you see it – 'Miss Elizabeth Belmont, Charming Music and Novelty Performer, at the Sunderland Empire'?"

Henry set to work immediately planning new music for the tour, and making new arrangements of her most popular material. For a while they regained some of the old closeness and rapport that they had known in her childhood. Then, as Florence's pantomime season was due to open, the dancer insisted that Henry should give her extra rehearsals with the band. She was the fairy godmother in Cinderella, complete with accompanying "corps de ballet" at Radley's Palace. It was her biggest part yet, though she could have hoped for more. Still, she was determined to be the star attraction, creating storms whenever Henry's preoccupation with Elizabeth's coming tour threatened to take his attention away from her. Gradually the planning sessions became fewer, and Elizabeth was forced to use old arrangements after all. On her own she would play through the tunes sent through the post, but they were, in the main, useless.

Then in the Christmas mail came a letter which was passed on to her by her agent. It read:

"*Dear Miss Belmont,*

I have had the privilege of hearing you play on several occasions, and it delights me that you still use 'Melody for Lizzie' which your father bought from me several years ago. I am proud to be a small part in your success. I have composed another piece which you may find useful, and I should be honoured if you would include it in your act. It has come to my notice that it is the occasion of your birthday, so I hope that if you do like the music you will accept it as a gift.

Yours sincerely,

James Adamson"

Inside the envelope was a carefully folded music manuscript, beautifully copied in a neat hand. Entitled 'Skylark Waltz', it was arranged for piccolo with piano accompaniment. Immediately hope sparked in Elizabeth that this could be music worth playing. 'Melody for Lizzie' had always been popular with the audiences. A new piece by the same composer was just what she was looking for, and it would be simple for Henry to write out a few band-parts in an arrangement of the accompaniment.

They were to have a small celebration in honour of her birthday, and Elizabeth had insisted that it should include just herself, Henry and Ella. It would provide an opportune occasion to try the new music. "My birthday piece", she called it – and it proved to be charming and immediately attractive.

After Ella and Elizabeth had finished playing 'Skylark Waltz', Henry gestured with his pipe. "That fellow's definitely got talent. That's a real gem of a number. We must ask him for more."

Elizabeth folded the music between the pages of her other current numbers. Somehow it seemed to bring hope of better things to come. A new piece, promising to be popular, and Henry's interest aroused. But, more than that, there was the gesture which had prompted James Adamson to send her his creation as a birthday present. He was a vir-

170

tually unknown composer, and had sent his hard work to her for no other reward than that she should enjoy playing it. For this reason, it meant far more to her than the two-row pearl choker which Radley had presented to her the day before. It seemed ridiculous to feel this way when she had never even met James Adamson. Yet he played a significant part in her life, for it was with his music that Henry had launched his career, and subsequently his daughter's.

This year Elizabeth was not involved in the flurry of the Christmas season. There were a few private engagements at soirées of seasonal entertainments of the nobility, which proved useful for trying out 'Skylark Waltz' and one or two other pieces before the tour. She spent most of her days practising in the silence of the house. Henry was heavily involved in the pantomime at Radley's Palace, and was frequently in Florence's company when he was not working.

Just after Christmas, Henry handed her a letter on his way out to a Monday morning band-call at the theatre.

"Letter for you, pet, from Australia."

She reached out swiftly to grasp the envelope. "At last! It's been months since I last had a letter from Belinda."

"Well, enjoy the news. I'll be back late after lunch, because Radley wants us to do an extra rehearsal with the French acrobats he's engaged for after the pantomime."

Elizabeth felt the hot blood rising in her cheeks at the mention of her lover. Radley had arranged the rehearsal so that she could be back home before Henry after an assignation with him. It sickened her to think how she was deceiving her father, yet she had no more power than a caged canary to resist Radley's advances.

Elizabeth sat motionless for a moment after Henry had left her. Then her thoughts returned to the missive in her hand, and she fell eagerly to freeing the letter from its envelope. It was filled with news of the pantomime, the other artistes, and descriptions of the country – all that Elizabeth had imagined would be included, with Belinda's lively narrative bringing it all to life.

"*But, darling Elizabeth,*" she wrote in her usual effusive manner, "*I am saving my most exciting piece of news until last. You probably wondered why your naughty friend has said nothing of the fine young Australian beaux. Well, the truth is, they didn't excite me very much – or so I thought. The country itself did, and I took every chance to see as much of it as possible. Then I realised that it was mostly due to the attention of one young man. You remember that I said there would only ever be Bertie for me? Well, I still mean that – he was my great love, and I shall never forget him. But I have now had an offer of marriage, and have decided to accept, because I like it so much here. So as from January 16th I shall be Mrs Reginald Keene, wife of a young businessman in*

New South Wales.

He's tall and fair, but apart from that, nothing like Bertie. His father was a farmer back in England, and now they own a very successful sheep farm – acres and acres of it. I know that I can be the right sort of wife for Reg, and I'm sure I shall never meet anyone better for me. He knows all about my life in London, and doesn't mind – maybe because it's so far away. I believe that I can make him a good wife, and be happy.

Needless to say, I won't be returning to England after Christmas, as I originally planned. Who would have thought that this would happen? Even now I have to look at my lovely diamond ring to convince myself that this isn't all a dream.

Oh, how I wish you could be here with me for my wedding! Still, once we are settled, you must come and stay. Australia will love you – and you will adore Reggie."

With protestations of affection, Belinda had then signed off the letter. Elizabeth sank back in the chair, clutching the papers to her throat. Belinda – married! Her immediate thought was that she had been deserted by her last friend. Belinda's return had been a milestone to look forward to, and now she was gone for ever. Neither her father nor Radley would ever let her go to Australia, especially when they heard of Belinda's decision. They would fear that she too would never come back.

Blinking back tears of disappointment, Elizabeth carefully folded the letter and placed it in the bureau to await her reply. She would never tell her friend of her selfish thoughts. All she could do was to rejoice that Belinda had found happiness. She turned the tiny key on the desk front, then went to prepare herself again as a sacrifice to Radley.

Later, after their rendezvous at Radley's town apartment, which he kept only for their meetings, the manager urged her to join him at one of his social engagements. "I want to see those pearls in their proper setting", he cajoled, "on that lovely neck."

At his words, Elizabeth's fingers skimmed lightly over the skin of her throat, as if imagining the hard shape of the pearls touching her.

"No. You know I can never be seen with you in public. Already our meetings are becoming too frequent."

"But, Lizzie, you know . . ."

"Don't call me that!" she rounded on him furiously.

Now Radley was also angry. "Very well," he said in measured tones, "I'll stick to 'Elizabeth' – but you have made your bargain with me. You'll meet me when I want to, or your father may find himself dismissed without an explanation."

She grasped her hairbrush hard with trembling hands, aware that Radley was playing on her fear of Henry losing his job. She suspected that he was more than satisfied with her father's work, and was aware how well the band played under a director they liked and respected. But she didn't have the courage to call his bluff – he might just turn away a good employee to spite her, and to prove his power over her.

"And what's more," he added, striding over to grasp her shoulder, "you might show a bit more pleasure. The bargain's worth nothing to me if I have to make love to a corpse!"

Shaking herself free, she picked up the last of her belongings. "I've always kept my part of the arrangement. If you recall, your side was that we wouldn't be seen in public together! So I'll meet you when you want, and I'll give myself up to your desires, but that's as far as it goes. Now, I must leave, because my father finishes rehearsing at 2 o'clock, and will expect to find me at home when he returns." So saying, she gathered her coat and umbrella, and, with no further glances behind her, left the apartment. With unsteady hands she fixed her hat and coat in the hallway, then paused for a moment before stepping outside.

How much longer can I suffer this? she agonised, pressing one hand to her burning eyelids. One day I'll be free of you, Frederick Radley, just you see! I'll find a way.

One benefit from the reduced number of her performances during that pantomime season was that Elizabeth was free to help Ella with the arrangements for her move. She was due to leave at the end of January, just one week before Elizabeth went on tour. There were only a few small items left to pack, with just two more days left of Ella's sojourn in London.

"It will seem strange, knowing that you aren't here any more. In many ways, I still think of this house as my home."

Ella smiled. "But I hope you'll visit me often in my new home."

"Oh, I will, Ella . . . but . . . you know, sometimes it's difficult to get away." She twisted her hands together.

Gently, Ella stretched out to touch her. "Lizzie . . . what is it? There's something troubling you. Why don't you tell me?"

Fear and anxiety crossed the young woman's face in the same instant, and were just as quickly banished. "Why, there's nothing. I'm just tired."

Ella was not convinced. "You should rest more, tour or no tour. Look at you – how thin you are! No flesh on your arms."

Elizabeth looked in the mirror, and touched her gaunt cheeks. She laughed weakly. "Well, it's the price of fame and fortune. You ought to know that, Ella."

"I'm not happy about you, love. You don't look after yourself, but that's not all. You know I can help you, if only you would tell me what's wrong."

For a moment Elizabeth was sorely tempted to unburden herself of the troubles of the past year. She opened her mouth . . . then stopped. Her eyes filled with tears, and she shook her head. "I can't tell you now, Ella."

Ella's heart was wrenched as her fears were confirmed. "Well, you know where I'll be. If ever you need me . . ."

Elizabeth was rehearsing on the day of Ella's departure, so she could not wave her off from the station. Ella was glad, for it left her free to make one final visit without her young friend's knowledge before leaving London.

Leaving her last pieces of luggage piled just inside the front door, she walked out into the frosty air to find a tram to take her across the river. She had prepared her appearance carefully, her one piece of fur clipped over her winter coat. Her boots tapped hurriedly over the frosty pavements.

It was some time since she had been to Radley's Palace. The bright paint work had been recently re-touched, and the posters proudly displayed forthcoming attractions. She had little trouble gaining admission via the stage door. Wilf, the doorman, was an old friend from the Diamond music hall, and greeted her with warmth. The rehearsal, he confirmed, was due to finish at any moment. Satisfied, Ella passed into the auditorium.

All was dim save for the lights in the pit, and one blinding spot illuminating a comedian scurrying through a patter-song. He broke off to call down to Henry that he wanted the cymbal clash to come sooner, and that the orchestra must speed up more towards the end of the song. With a nod, Henry directed the players to go from the top again, and the number was repeated. After the final chords, the artiste declared himself satisfied, and the rehearsal drew to a close.

"Henry."

He turned round quickly at hearing his name. "Ella . . . of course, you're leaving today. How nice to see you."

For an instant, Ella felt gratified that he was genuinely pleased to see her. Then she pushed personal considerations aside. "I haven't just come to say goodbye – there's something I must say to you. Is there anywhere we can talk?"

"Of course. Come to my room."

He led her through the pit and the band-room where the members of the orchestra were putting away their instruments, then into his own small room. His pressed evening suit hung in one corner. The rest of the room was bare, save for a closed cupboard, and two chairs before the table and mirror. He seated Ella in one chair, and moved the other so that he could face her.

"Well, what did you want to tell me?"

"It's Lizzie, Henry. I'm worried about her. She's looking so thin and tired, lost all her bloom. There's something troubling her badly. Haven't you noticed?" she added, as Henry sat back in obvious consternation.

"No . . . well . . . no . . . you see, I don't see much of her these days. Our working hours . . ."

"When did you last have a good talk with her? You used to be so close in those days in the old lodgings. I thought you would both pine away when she went off to school. But look at you now."

"She's a grown woman now, Ella, with her own career."

"But she's still only young, Henry, and without a mother to confide in. If you don't do something soon, she's going to be ill. I'm not trying to interfere – it's not my business. But you know how much I love that girl."

Henry nodded. "Yes, I know, Ella. I'll certainly make the effort, but she's off on tour next week, and we start a new season here, so there won't be much opportunity."

Ella's heart was heavy as she left the theatre, but whether it was because of Elizabeth or because of parting from Henry she couldn't say. But her time was up, and Henry had to take over the responsibility of his daughter.

Somehow they slipped into the old routine, and Henry couldn't bring himself to stir up problems. He admitted to himself that Ella's observations were true – Elizabeth did look thin and pale. The light had gone out of her. Still, he could only bring himself to acknowledge that she was overworked and tired. He couldn't really think of any reason why she should have any worries. After all, she was successful, with a secure home, and, since the trouble over William Hareton, there had been no young man who particularly interested her. She came and went to her performances and practices, and rarely went out alone, as far as he knew. Now Belinda was married in Australia, she never made up a "foursome" with anyone else.

Before he could deliberate on the problem further, the morning of Elizabeth's departure was upon him, and she was walking down the stairs towards him, ready to depart, one small bag in her kid-gloved hand. How elegant she was! Who could believe this was a girl brought up in two rooms in Battersea. Her fine blonde hair was rolled up neatly, balancing a large feathered hat that matched exactly the spice-brown of her costume. A fox fur completed her outfit.

But the rich hues of her outfit only served to emphasise the shadows of her eyes. As Henry gazed into them, he felt as if he were gazing into deep hollow caverns. Momentary fear made him reach out to her as she stepped off the last tread of the stairs, and he folded her in his arms.

"Lizzie, pet, I wish I could come with you," he said, suddenly protective.

"Maybe you could get off for a few days, when I'm in Sunderland," she replied softly.

He regarded her steadily. "I don't mean a visit – you need someone to look after you. You've been working too hard."

She gave a rueful laugh. "That's just what Ella said."

"Well, she was right. As soon as you come back from the tour, you're going to have a proper rest. How about a stay with Ella in Kent?"

Elizabeth's eyes glistened as she took all this in. "That would be lovely. Can you arrange it for me with my agent?"

He held her close. "Yes, of course, my pet. Now hadn't we better go for that train?"

Henry walked with his daughter along the platform of King's Cross station, his arm linked with hers. As she climbed into the carriage of the train, he handed her the small bag. Her trunk had been sent on ahead to Hartlepool. He smiled ruefully.

"It seems that we spend our lives saying farewell on stations."

"Don't remind me of that other time," she said, closing her eyes with a shiver.

"No . . . well, this is different, eh? We're both doing well now. I know the north-east will love you. You belong."

Elizabeth hesitated, then began tentatively, "Father . . ."

"What, pet?"

The guard's whistle tore shrilly through the air.

"Nothing . . . just look after yourself while I'm away, won't you?"

For an instant she clung to him desperately before breaking away to take her seat in the carriage. As Henry waved to the receding train, his heart felt unaccountably heavy. He hadn't said all he had meant to. But it would be different when she returned – he would make it so.

The tour warmed up gradually. The northern audiences were curious at first, for hers was a novelty act, but soon they decided that they liked her music and her pretty face. Men and girls alike would crowd at the stage door for a glimpse of her, delighted when she spoke a few words to any of them.

"Bonny, isn't she!" they would murmur on seeing her face to face. Elizabeth would smile and ask if they had enjoyed the show, and which tune they liked best from her act. It pleased her to have the admiration of the ordinary folk, far more than that of the stage-door johnnies of the London theatres. The further north they went, the nearer to Henry's accent their speech became, despite the fact that many of the edges had been smoothed from his during the long years in the south. But it was true – as her father had said, she did feel that she belonged.

The constant touring was fatiguing, but it was thrilling to see all the new places, and to feel the mood of each new audience, then work to swing them in her favour. Generally she found them easy to please. But she had been placed well in the programmes, just after a local comic, who left them feeling buoyant and receptive. She could almost have enjoyed unreservedly the experience of the tour, except that she found that the constant stodge cooked for her by the theatrical landladies disagreed with her and gave her attacks of nausea.

But nothing could take away from the pleasure it gave her to stand at last and gaze in admiration at the fine exterior of the Sunderland Empire Theatre. It was truly a prince among music halls, not yet three years old, a domed palace of splendours, with Terpsichore the goddess surmounting the whole magnificent edifice.

But the Empire had, strangely enough, brought a figure from Elizabeth's past back into her life. While waiting for her rehearsal with the band that morning, she'd been watching the previous act with interest.

"Who's the magician? We didn't have one before on the tour," she asked the stage manager.

He scratched his bald head with the stem of his pipe. "The contortionists are out – one of them got into a brawl on Saturday night, and they're both cooling their heels in jail for a few days. So the management axed them. This is the Turkish Magician – of course, he's as Turkish as my Auntie Annie, but the audience won't care." He turned away quickly, barking to a stage hand, "Trapdoor – ready – now!" There was a puff of smoke, and the girl in her leotard disappeared from sight.

Elizabeth watched, fascinated as always, by the sleight of hand which gave the illusion of magic. The magician swaggered and strutted as if receiving rapturous applause, then directed his assistant, a rather spotty young man, to wheel forward an elaborate box, as tall as he was. The magician tapped it melodramatically on all sides, then opened the door to reveal the girl.

As she stepped forward, hands high, posturing and curtseying, Elizabeth drew a sharp breath of recognition. "Gertie!" So her aunt's former maid had achieved her ambition – to appear in the spotlight.

Gertie was waiting for her after her own band-call, changed now into a faded dress. Her looks still had their ripe prettiness, but there was a shabbiness about her that had never been there before. "Fancy us appearing on the same bill!" she twittered.

"How long have you been a magician's assistant?" Elizabeth asked curiously.

"Nearly a year now. Percy got me into it, when the other girl fell pregnant."

"Who's Percy?" As if I didn't know, thought Elizabeth.

Gertie simpered. "He's the magician's assistant. We've got a sort of understanding, you know. Oh . . . is this your dressing room?" as Elizabeth stopped outside a door. "It's lovely. But of course, you're nearly at the top of the bill. I'm in with the dancers. We usually get a dressing room just for us, but, seeing as we've just stepped in, they had to squeeze us in somewhere."

"I must go, Gertie. I have to clean out my instrument."

Gertie's face fell. Elizabeth relented. "Maybe we'll have tea one day this week, if we can fit it in."

"Oh, that would be lovely, but I spend most of the time with Percy. I'll see what he says."

Percy was obviously a big influence in Gertie's life, Elizabeth reflected as she finished packing up. Perhaps she'd found her niche at last . . .

She rested during the afternoon to prepare herself for her opening performance. Her landlady was large and friendly, and had been happy to talk about the town, delighted to find that Elizabeth's father had been a boy there.

"I know that part of town well," Mrs Thorn announced when the young woman explained that her grandfather had had an ironmonger's shop. "I don't think there's an ironmonger's at that number now – it must have been changed when your grandfather died. But I can tell you which tram to catch, if you want to go and have a look."

"Yes, I'd like that," Elizabeth told her. "Perhaps on Tuesday, before the shows."

The first house on Monday was packed, to the delight of the artistes.

"I've often played here before," confided the little comic who preceded her. "They're a choosy audience, but, if they like you, you'll be the darling of their hearts."

Thus, as Elizabeth played her opening number, a well-used skittering polka which her fingers tripped out almost without prompting, she gazed into the auditorium and tried to absorb the mood of the faces she could barely see beyond the blinding glare of the spotlight. It was with relief that she heard the ripple of applause which greeted the final chord of her first number. She followed it up quickly with 'Melody for Lizzie' and 'Skylark Waltz', and was pleased to feel them warming to her music. Then she played her trump card – as Henry had prompted her.

"Ladies and gentlemen . . ." (how thin and reedy her voice sounded on that vast expanse of stage, shouting out to the hordes of people in the auditorium) "I should like to thank you for your warm welcome. Sunderland is particularly special to me, as my father grew up here. So you see, I'm really one of you." A small murmur of appreciation greeted this announcement. "And now, in honour of my return 'home', I'm going to play some music which I'm sure you will recognise."

With a signal to the conductor, she launched into the local air 'The Keel Row', a new arrangement which Henry had made for her, combined with snatches of 'Bobby Shaftoe' and 'Ma Bonny Lad'. As she finished with a rapid flourish, the audience erupted. Cheers and shouts mingled with the rapturous applause.

Her glowing reception carried her smiling into the wings, where a plump, rosy-faced young woman was waiting to follow her on to the stage.

"Eee, pet, I never knew yer Da came from round 'ere. Yer did the right thing there – they love yer for it, an' all!" she announced with a wide grin.

"Aren't they wonderful?" was all Elizabeth could say. If only Henry could have heard them.

The comedienne laughed. "How do I follow that? I'm just like a comfortable old shoe to them now."

The applause was subsiding, and the band launched into a jaunty tune. "Wish me luck, pet. I'm on!"

Her smile was infectious, and Elizabeth couldn't help but respond to this vivacious local artiste. "You're just what they want – don't worry!" she said as the comedienne tripped onto the stage.

"Who's that?" she whispered to one of the stage-hands who was standing close by.

"That's Nora Davies – she's a real canny lass!" he announced with a wide grin. Elizabeth nodded, understanding from knowledge of her father's expressions that this meant that the man thought Nora Davies was a very nice girl. Elizabeth watched some of the act. Nora was a competent performer, completely at home in this north-eastern idiom, but it was strictly local humour. She was a useful artiste, if not a great one.

By Wednesday, Elizabeth found herself falling frequently into the company of the comedienne.

"I've played many times in Sunderland before this," Nora confided, "but this is only me second week at the Empire."

"What are the other halls like, then?"

"Oh, nothing like this – this is a real palace. It's the best theatre I ever played in, and I've played a few. Still, I bet it's nothin' on those

London theatres."

Elizabeth considered for a moment. "I wouldn't say that – all theatres are different. This is the newest music hall I've played in, but it's really the audiences that make the atmosphere. This is my first tour, and I've noticed how the audiences differ so much from town to town. Are you from Sunderland?"

Nora smiled. "Nearly. I was born in South Shields, just a stone's throw up the coast. I moved to Hartlepool when I married, because my Jim worked there. But now I live in Newcastle, because it's a good place to be near work."

"Did your husband get another job in Newcastle?"

"What, Jim? Naah, we was split up long before that. He couldn't take the stage – didn't like the other lads looking at his wife. So we split. Better for both of us. You take my word, pet, marriage and the halls just don't go together."

Elizabeth replied softly, "I think I've learned that already."

Nora was about to question her further, when she noticed how closed and downcast Elizabeth's expression was. She could learn somehow, she was sure . . . she would bide her time.

Elizabeth had found her way to Hendon, the district where Henry had once lived, and had found a baker's shop occupying the premises where her grandfather had had his ironmonger's, and where her father had started his working life. She guessed that the living quarters above the shop had changed little since the days when the Belmonts had lived there. It felt strange to be standing in the street where her father must have played as a boy. It was a busy area, between the town centre and the river. The houses looked neat, despite the dingy colours of the curtains in the windows.

She had bought a bread "bap" in the baker's as she had felt too queasy to eat breakfast when she got up. The smell of hot bread had been too much for her to resist, and she nibbled the bap now as she walked back to the tram. A few passers-by stared at the unusual spectacle of a well-dressed young lady eating as she strolled along the street.

The tang of salt was strong in the air, bringing Elizabeth to the decision that she could wait no longer to see "the North Sea rushing up the beach", as her father had described it. A young woman was pushing a battered perambulator towards her, accompanied by a small child. Elizabeth approached her and asked where she could catch a tram to the seaside. She was directed to walk back to the town centre, and there to take a tram destined for Roker.

Soon she was standing on the high promenade, gazing at the mighty breakers as they vented their fury on the base of the great limestone cliffs, and cascaded over the curved arm of the pier and over the new lighthouse that guarded the entrance to the River Wear. The strong wind which spurred the waves played round her, making her grip her large picture hat firmly, while she shivered from the wind's icy bite.

It made her giddy to watch the fury of the wind and waves, and for an instant she wished she could mingle with them in mindless anger. If only she didn't have to go back to London. To forget it all, to stay here, far from Radley. But no, she had to return to her father. Firmly she pushed such thoughts from her mind. She only had to think of now, and to live for the performances ahead of her.

All too soon Saturday was upon her, the last night of the tour. She'd had the promised tea with Gertie on Thursday, but hadn't met the amazing Percy Parker, though Gertie had given her every scrap of information about him, right down to the size of his shoes. "Percy has such narrow feet." At least she seemed reasonably content with her life.

That was more than could be said for Elizabeth. The idea of resuming her life in London made her stomach turn each time she thought of it. No matter how many times Elizabeth told herself she was being foolish, she couldn't dispel the dread on that final day of the tour.

Just think of the music, think of the music, she repeated to herself like a litany. Even her dress felt tight and uncomfortable, restricting her breathing. Somehow she got through the act without betraying her tension. Successful artistes learned to cope with the endless performances, playing even when they felt unwell, so that the audience would never suspect that they weren't enjoying every moment.

But, as Elizabeth stumbled into the darkness of the wings, out of the glare, she had to grip the curtains tightly to stop the lurching of her surroundings. The heavy drapery hid her from the view of the stagehands, and kept her out of the bustle of the changeover to the next act. As the music burst forth behind her, mingling with murmurs of laughter from the audience, Elizabeth fought the terrible waves of nausea that threatened to overcome her.

She was still standing there, temporarily paralysed, when Nora nearly bumped into her as she jumped off the stage.

"Why, Liz!" she exclaimed, "what's up?"

"I can't move . . . I feel so bad," came the anguished whisper.

Nora was quick to take charge. "Now, you lean on me. Don't worry, I'll get you back to the dressin' room, and you can lie down."

"But all the people . . ."

"Rubbish! They're all too busy to notice. Come on, here we go!" With a gentleness contrasting with her hearty cajoling, Nora took Elizabeth's arm, and supported her up the stairs to her dressing room. She left her sitting in a chair, her head laid on her arms on the table, while she hurried for a glass of water. When she returned, she said, "Here, let me loosen your dress." With a deft movement she unhooked the gown, then loosened the corset beneath. Supporting Elizabeth's head, Nora held the glass to her mouth while she drank.

"Better?" she asked, seeing that a little colour had returned to Elizabeth's lips. The rest of her face was hidden by make-up, but she could not colour her lips with carmine while playing her instrument.

Elizabeth nodded. "Sorry for being such a nuisance. I haven't been feeling my best this week."

"No . . ." Nora said slowly, studying the other carefully. "How long have you been feelin' bad?"

"Well . . . since I came away on tour. It must be the food . . ."

"Food, my eye! Listen, Liz, how many of your monthly courses have you missed?"

"What? . . .well . . . two. But I don't see . . ."

"Don't you?" Nora added vehemently. "Surely you don't expect me to believe you're that innocent?"

Elizabeth was silent, her face closed and defiant. Then her hands went up to her cheeks. "You're right, Nora. I just didn't want to think about it. But I suppose I've just got to accept the fact that it's real, and won't go away." She gazed at the other woman in misery. "What am I going to do?"

"Listen, pet, I can't help you. What do I know about you? Can't you marry the father?"

"No!" Lizzie spat out. "Anyway . . . he's married."

"Oh, God, how did you get involved with a married man? It never pays."

"I didn't do it for myself!" Elizabeth replied defensively. "He had a hold on me."

"What?"

Elizabeth found that she could tell Nora. After all, she would have no connection with any of them in the future. "My father's job."

Nora sighed. "Your father's job? Was it really worth it?"

She thought for a moment, then shook her head. "But what am I going to do now, Nora?"

Nora faced her, hands on hips. "Only you can decide that, Liz. Go back to London tomorrow, and make up your mind. You can't run away from it."

The bridge over the River Wear was quiet in the early Sunday morning. A fine sea mist hung over the ships, ghostly hulks and half-built skeletons. It glistened on the huge curve of the bridge, and on the clothes of the young woman who leaned on the wall, looking down into the grey water. She only carried the small bag which she had brought with her for her personal effects. Her theatrical trunk was already sent on ahead, along with her clothes.

Sleep hadn't come easily last night, despite her fatigue. The last show had gone well, without any recurrence of her nausea. But the vague dread was a reality. How could she return to her father, knowing that she carried Radley's child within her? It shouldn't have happened, for he had been careful – but somehow it had, and she was to bear the responsibility, the stigma. It was bad enough to be in this condition, unmarried, but to be pregnant with the child of a man she hated! She shuddered.

How far down it looked to the shifting water beneath the bridge. The parapet wasn't high. It wouldn't be difficult to climb up, and to throw herself down into oblivion.

But no, she couldn't do it to this town, with its welcoming audiences. She had felt truly at home here.

Suddenly, hope flashed within her. If only she could persuade Henry to come back here! She could play the local halls, like Nora, and never have to see Radley again. Henry need never know that his job had ever been bought by her body.

The child. There was still this growing embryo. Abortion? How could she do that and conceal it from Henry? The vision of Belinda, weeping over her friend Patty after that botched operation, rose in all its hideous reality to confront her. No, it was impossible. Anyway, this child would be part of her. Elizabeth's hands touched her waist. Three months, at the most – it wasn't noticeable yet. There would be time to think of a solution.

She picked up her bag, and walked slowly towards the railway station.

Chapter 18

Henry was at King's Cross station to meet Elizabeth. He was burning with excitement now that he was to see her again after so long. It had been impossible to get away during her tour, with the new season beginning here after the end of the pantomime. At last she was due home, and he had so much to tell her!

It seemed an eternity until the train finally approached the platform, and groaned to a halt with a massive hissing of steam. A flood of travellers poured from all the doors, hats of all shapes and sizes merging into an indistinguishable sea before Henry's eyes.

Then at last from the crowd appeared Elizabeth's small form, and his heart leaped. He waved to gain her attention. The smile with which she responded was strained, he noticed, as he pressed forward to hug her, with no heed for the other passengers.

"Lizzie, my lovely girl, you're here at last."

"Yes, Father," she said softly into his coat front.

"You look tired. Let me take your bag."

Wearily she pushed a strand of hair back into place under her hat. "Yes, it's a long journey. I'm longing to get home now."

Taking her arm, he propelled her through the crowds, and managed to find a cab with little trouble. As they jogged through the traffic, he questioned her about the tour, about the towns she had played, and especially about Sunderland.

"I liked it there, Father. And the people were so friendly, and not just the audiences. But they liked the act, too. I'd like to go back." She could see that her words pleased Henry. But that wasn't the only reason she had spoken them – she really had felt at home there, and maybe it was a way of overcoming her predicament. At least she could sow the seeds gradually in Henry's mind . . .

It would have been so comforting to have her father fussing over her, sitting her in the chair beside the fire with a hot cup of tea pressed into her hands, if only it had not compounded her guilt. She didn't know how, or when, she would confess to Henry. Of course, there was one way he need never know. She could say she was going to stay with Ella, then discreetly procure an address . . . and, by the time she arrived at Ella's, the problem would have gone.

But somehow she couldn't bring herself to make the decision. Leave it a few days . . .

"Lizzie, are you listening to me?"

Quickly she snapped back to the warm parlour. "Sorry, Father, my mind was wandering."

"Well, listen to this. James Adamson, the composer of your best melodies, is going to be in Town on Tuesday, and he wrote to me to ask if he could meet us." His daughter smiled, to show some response. "He'll be busy during the day, but I've asked him to meet us for dinner after the second show. He's written to confirm that it will suit him. So you'll have to come to the second show."

"But what about my visit to Ella?"

Henry leant forward to take her hand in both of his. "That's all arranged, pet. You're to go down on Friday. I thought you would want a few days to sort yourself out. Then you'll be free until the second week in April to stay in Kent or come back here, as you please."

Elizabeth closed her other hand over Henry's. "That's lovely, Father. Thank you so much. And, yes, of course I'll be glad to come to the second house on Tuesday. I'll be interested to meet Mr Adamson."

The first house hadn't been spectacular that Tuesday evening. The audience seemed dispirited and ill-inclined to laugh, even at the top stars. Despite this, Henry felt buoyant as he fixed his cufflinks for the second performance. He had a special surprise for Elizabeth that night, and was certain that it would please her. After buttoning his white waistcoat over the spotless shirt, he patted it over his flatter stomach and felt pleased that he had managed to stay so much fitter.

A knock sounded at the door.

"Who is it?"

"Florence," came the muffled reply.

"Florrie, where have you been?" he exclaimed while ushering her into the dressing room.

"Oh . . . busy," was the coquettish answer.

"Busy! I can imagine who with, as well! That young Wright has been sniffing round you more than is good for him."

"That 'young Wright' happens to be a very promising assistant manager. You know it'll be good for my career, Henry."

"Yes, but how much will he expect in return?"

"Are you jealous?" she teased, leaning across to tap him on the nose.

"Have you given me any reason to be?" Henry asked.

Suddenly Florence whirled round angrily. "Listen, Henry Belmont, you've got no hold over me. I do what I like!"

"Florrie! Doesn't any of it . . . of what we have been to each other . . . mean anything to you?"

But Florence wasn't in a mood to be cajoled. "What do you want of me? I'm not going to be any goody-goody little woman at your beck and call. If I can have fun elsewhere, I will. If 'young Wright' can get me to the top of the bill, I'll do anything he wants!" Then she smiled to herself and murmured, "He happens to be rather good, too."

"Why, you . . . you slut! Selling your body to get on!"

Stung, Florence retaliated. "Yes! What do you think I slept with you for? And, before you call me a slut, why don't you look to your own daughter? Do you think you both got where you are today through playing those stupid little tin whistles?"

Speechless with rage, Henry raised his arm to strike her, but, seeing her cringe before his action, he turned away swiftly. "Get out! Just get out! I never want to see you again!" he spat.

He heard the door close sharply behind him, and found that he was shaking. His heart pounded ferociously. All he could do was sink into a chair, and seethe with fury. Then he stretched towards his outdoor coat and fumbled for the hip-flask he kept in the top pocket. With unsteady hands he poured a measure into the cup and swallowed it in one. The fiery liquid burning his throat brought him back to his senses. No, of course it wasn't true about Elizabeth. Florence was only jealous – always had been, for that matter, ever since Elizabeth had been a schoolgirl. There was no need to listen to the green-tinged ravings of a jealous harpy like that. So Wright was better than Henry Belmont? Well, he could do without little trollops like her.

"Ten minutes, Mr Belmont!" came the penetrating tones of the call-boy's voice through the door. Taking another mouthful of whisky, Henry replaced the cap and tucked the silver flask into his pocket. Then he took his tail-coat down from the hanger, and put it on. He took one last look at his reflection in the mirror. Well . . . he would show Florence Royle! Of course he had made his position on his own merit! But what had she meant, anyway? Shaking his head, he pushed her to the back of his mind, and went out to take his place in front of the band.

Elizabeth was sitting in a small box overlooking the orchestra. She had arrived at the last minute so that she wouldn't be spotted by Radley. She dreaded meeting him more than anything. That morning she had sent him a letter saying that she wished to end their relationship. She had made no decision as yet about the child, but somehow it had made her feel a little better to take this step. Henry would have to find out about her pregnancy at some time – she could see no way of hiding it, even if she decided to end it. There was always the chance that her father had become so firmly established in his job that Radley couldn't let him go. But she could no longer live with the hypocrisy that she had known for nearly a year now.

The show whirled before her eyes in a kaleidoscope of colour, from which she couldn't distinguish the individual acts. The events of the tour and the problems that faced her occupied her consciousness to the exclusion of everything else.

It was not until the interlude before the last act that she noticed Henry signalling to her to attract her attention. Once he had caught her eye, he brought the band in with a jaunty introduction. Soon the little orchestra was filling the theatre with the strains of 'Melody for Lizzie'. Elizabeth's hands gripped the edge of the box as the spotlight swung round to illuminate her, while the audience responded with a burst of applause. She nodded and smiled in acknowledgement, but the lump in her throat felt as if it would choke her.

Dear Father, if only he knew what a shock his darling Lizzie was preparing for him, she thought. What would he say when he discovered that his "pure" little girl was in fact a scheming loose woman? Suddenly she could bear it no longer. As soon as the music switched to the introduction to the last act, and the spotlight swung back to the stage, leaving her half-blinded in the contrasting gloom, she stumbled out into the brighter corridor. For a moment she stood trying to calm her gasping breath, then hurried off towards the exit. With her wrap slung over one arm, Elizabeth had no idea where she was going ultimately . . . all she knew was that she had to get away from that theatre.

Her feet tripped down the huge sweep of marble staircase into the vestibule of the theatre. As she stepped off the last tread, her flight was arrested by the grip of a hand on her arm.

"Elizabeth! I didn't know you were in the theatre until your father staged that little show! What do you mean by that letter?" Radley hissed the words angrily at her, not wishing to raise his voice in the vestibule where he might be overheard.

Annoyed and startled by the sight of his face so near to hers, the young woman shook free of his grasp with a brisk shrug. "Exactly what I said. It's over! I'm finished with this degrading role."

Radley's face flushed at the vehemence of her reply. "And what about your father?"

"You can threaten all you like! It won't make any difference." At that instant, they both became aware that they had attracted the attention of a young man, in a neat but sober suit, who had been looking at the posters inside the theatre door. Their eyes met across the expanse of the marble floor. The contact with Radley was broken, so Elizabeth swept away from him, and hurried out of the doors which were standing wide, ready for the audience to leave at any moment. The sound of applause from the last act drifted from the auditorium, while Radley and the young man stared defiantly at each other. Then, with a quick movement, the manager straightened his evening coat and turned on his heel to re-enter his office.

Blinded by tears, Elizabeth hesitated on the pavement outside the theatre. Already another music hall further down the road was spilling its hordes into the street. Horses drawing carriages trotted up the street, and a motor car chugged past. There was a taxi on the opposite side of the road. The urge to flee was her only feeling. Somehow she would persuade the cabbie to take her, even if he already had a fare booked. Looking into her purse, she stepped into the road. There was a shout behind her, another from in front, before something hit her hard on the shoulder, tossing her backwards on to the paving-stones, where her head hit the kerb with a force that brought pain and bright lights, then darkness.

The young man in the dark suit watched Radley's retreat into the office with resentment. He had recognised Elizabeth Belmont immediately from the photographs of her he had seen. He had been startled by the exchange he had witnessed. Obviously there was animosity between the two, though he hadn't heard their words from where he stood. His immediate reaction had been to intervene, to protect Miss Belmont, for hadn't he come all the way from Kent to meet her and her father that evening?

Then the young artiste had broken away, and run from the theatre. Hesitant, the young man had stared into Radley's eyes, and watched his retreat. Then he turned to follow Elizabeth, and had just been in time to witness the accident. In an instant several people had gathered round the injured young woman, while another tried to calm the terrified horse.

"It wasn't my fault! Gawd! She stepped right out in front of the horse! How could I see her?" came the shaken voice of the driver.

"Going far too fast!" came a mutter from another quarter.

The young man fought through the gathering crowd. "Is she badly hurt? Has anyone sent for a doctor?" he gasped.

"She's out cold. Better not move her," someone said.

Behind them, the first of the audience was leaving Radley's Palace. More and more people huddled round the scene of the accident.

"Keep back! Back off!" shouted one of the bystanders.

"But she's bleeding!" exclaimed the young man. He fumbled for his handkerchief, which he pressed to the jagged gash on Elizabeth's forehead.

One of the theatre staff had stopped Henry on his way from the pit. His breathless words had been garbled, and only gradually did Henry grasp that something had happened to Elizabeth. He hurried up the passage to the exit, fighting through the crowds who were trying to leave the theatre. He was oblivious of the exclamations and complaints that were directed at him as he pushed through, only aware that he had to get to his daughter.

"Let me through!" he cried as he reached the front of the theatre. Slowly the crowds parted, and silence fell as they moved back to form a passage for him. The last man moved aside, and Henry was presented with a vision of his daughter lying unconscious on the pavement, with a young man pressing a bloodied handkerchief to her forehead.

"Lizzie!" Henry murmured in anguish, and, pushing aside the young man, gathered her into his arms. He wept openly as he cradled her head, while the blood from the gash stained the front of his white shirt.

The young man moved back and disappeared into the crowd. He had no place here, now. He pushed his stained handkerchief into the pocket where lay a letter, addressed in Henry's hand to "James Adamson".

Henry paced up and down while the doctor attended to Elizabeth. There had been some sort of crisis, about three hours ago, when a nurse had been summoned. Since then he hadn't been allowed near the room. It was now nearly 5 o'clock on Wednesday morning, and it seemed an eternity since they had arrived home with Elizabeth half-conscious and moaning. For hours Henry had been unable to sit still, terrified for the welfare of his daughter.

At last he heard the sound of footsteps on the stairs. Flinging open the door, he anxiously searched the doctor's face for a sign of reassurance.

"Is she going to be all right, doctor?"

Dr Richardson's face was drawn with weariness, but calm. "Yes, Mr Belmont. Your daughter will recover. But she is very weak and has lost a lot of blood. Er . . . may I talk with you privately for a moment?"

"Yes, of course." Henry showed the doctor into the drawing room.

Dr Richardson walked over towards the fireplace and paused for a moment, as if uncertain how to continue. His features were grave when he turned to face Henry.

"Mr Belmont . . . I don't know if you were aware that your daughter was pregnant."

"What? What?" Henry was incredulous. "Lizzie? Surely . . . couldn't there be some mistake?"

"No mistake, I assure you. She miscarried a child about two hours ago."

Henry's legs would support him no longer. "I don't understand it . . . my Lizzie," he muttered as he sank into the nearest chair. Then he cleared his throat. "I can see you're thinking that it's the life we lead – the immorality of the stage. But she's not like that, my Lizzie. I brought her up to be a good girl." But then the irony of his words struck Henry. What example have I given her lately? he thought.

Dr Richardson stepped forward and gripped Henry's shoulder. "I'm not here to pass judgement on my patients, Mr Belmont, only to care for them. And I suggest that you go to bed now and try to get some sleep. Miss Belmont is sleeping now, and you'll be no good to her if you overtire yourself."

"Yes, of course," Henry muttered, dazedly. He fetched the doctor's coat, and saw him to the door. The sky was beginning to lighten as Henry stumbled upstairs to bed. Before he retired he scribbled a note to Ella, explaining that Elizabeth had been involved in an accident and wouldn't be coming to stay. He propped the letter on the hall-stand with a note for their daily servant to post it as soon as she arrived, and hoped that Ella would read between the lines. How could he ask her to come now, after the shabby way he had treated her? Sorrow and hopelessness closed in on him as he made his way up to his room.

Ella arrived a few hours after a telegram announcing her intention of coming at once, to find Henry in the throes of deep despair.

"She won't even say anything to me, Ella – she just turns her head away, weeping all the time. She won't eat, either."

Their first encounter had been agonising. Tentatively, Henry had crept into the bedroom and sat beside his daughter's bed. Their eyes, so alike, had met and held for an age of mutual misery. How frail she looked, propped up on the pillows, her hair in one long plait over her shoulder, with a voluminous bandage covering her forehead and part of her left eye.

Then at last Henry spoke. "Why didn't you tell me, Lizzie?" he asked brokenly.

Tears filled her eyes and spilled onto her cheeks. She just shook her head.

"Didn't you believe I would understand? I know there must have been a reason. I could have helped you, Lizzie."

Her only response was more tears, more sobbing.

"Won't you even tell me who the father was?"

She rolled her head from side to side in anguished denial. Sadly, Henry held out his handkerchief to her, which she accepted, but she shrank away from his attempted caress. Cut to the heart, he left her still weeping, and he descended the stairs slowly.

"Ella, what can I do?" he asked, once he had told her all the details.

"We'll just have to give her all the care and love we can, Henry. She's weak and ill, and has just gone through a traumatic experience, not to mention the trouble she was having before the tour. Maybe she'll tell us in time, but, even if she doesn't, she needs help to rebuild her life."

Henry gazed at her with tears in his eyes. "Ella, why is it that whenever we Belmonts are in trouble you're always there to help us through?"

Ella paused for a moment before answering. "Do you really need to ask that, Henry?"

"No, I don't suppose I do," he responded. With calm tenderness and a feeling of homecoming, they drew each other into an embrace, close in the warmth of their finally acknowledged love.

Gradually Elizabeth's fits of weeping became less frequent, as Ella sent away the nurse, filled the room with flowers from the garden, and let in the ever-increasing sunshine. But still Elizabeth lay there, weak and hollow-eyed, speaking little.

Two weeks after her ordeal, Henry was sitting with her in the dusk, quietly reading his newspaper to keep her company, when suddenly she turned and asked, "Father, why aren't you at the theatre?"

Henry sighed and folded his paper. He had known that this would come eventually. "I'm not going back there, pet. I've handed in my notice."

Panic crossed her face. "But why? What about your job?" What had Radley said?

"Hush, hush, my love. Don't worry yourself. I just decided I was tired of it all. I'm going to take you away from London. We're going to live in Kent – there's enough money to live on, and we'll rent a nice little cottage."

For a moment she was silent. "Are . . . are you going to marry Ella, Father?"

He smiled gently and nodded. "Yes, I am. We were going to tell you when you were stronger." Seeing the tears once more running down her cheeks, his tone of voice changed to dismay. "Why, whatever's the matter? Don't you want me to marry Ella?"

"Of course I do, Father!" she wept. "It's just that you've both made me so happy."

"Lizzie," he murmured, folding his arms round her, rocking her like a child, kissing her hair. For the first time in weeks, he felt hope stirring within him.

Chapter 19

"Morning, Mr Bell. Sad news about His Majesty, isn't it?"

Henry straightened up with a jolt from his weeding, realising that the postman was addressing him. It would be a while before he became used to his new name. He'd shortened it to "Bell" to preserve the family's anonymity.

"Oh, yes, Mr Potts. I read it in the newspaper yesterday. Seems the bronchitis weakened his heart."

The grey-haired postman shook his head. "My missus and I, we couldn't believe he'd actually gone. 'Poor Teddy,' she said. 'Hardly on the throne any time at all, because the old Queen lived so long.' You come from London, don't you, Mr Bell? Think you'll go back for the funeral?"

"No, I don't think so. We like the quiet of Oakridge. We're still settling in. I've a lot of planting to do in the garden before the end of May."

"I'm pleased to hear that. The last folk neglected the garden sadly. It'll be cheery to see a few flowers on my rounds. Sorry, no letters for you today. Must be on my way."

As Henry bent down to grasp another dandelion, he felt that at last they were beginning to make some contacts with the other residents. The local people regarded them all as "foreigners" – even Ella, born and bred not so far away in Sevenoaks.

Their new home was just outside the town of Oakridge, about fifty yards down the road from the nearest group of houses. It was a quiet town, not much larger than a village, but, if they required, they could always go by train to the market town of Bromley, which was not far away. The cottage suited Ella because she could walk over the hill to the village of Somerham, where her sister lived, and there was a pleasant little country church which she could attend, a luxury for which she had not had the time in her working days.

Still, they were happy to keep themselves private after the traumas of the last few months. Henry didn't want it generally known that they had been on the halls. He just told people he was a retired musician, and left it at that.

But his remaining worry was Elizabeth. She was still weak and tired after the shock of the accident and her illness. Thin and hollow-cheeked, she kept to the house, quietly going about the daily housework. Sometimes she would sit quietly reading a book, or sewing, but she showed little interest in music. They had moved her piano with them, for it was a better instrument than Ella's, yet she had never set a finger on it since they had arrived in Oakridge, two weeks earlier. Ella was happy to play it, but hesitated at first for fear of upsetting her stepdaughter. But the young woman showed no reaction when Ella played the old songs, while Henry hummed along, tapping his foot.

"We're walking into Oakridge, Lizzie. Why don't you come?" Henry asked, soon after their move.

Panic flickered through her eyes. "Oh, no, Father, please don't ask me. I couldn't."

"But whyever not, my pet? Nobody knows you here."

She shook her head. "But still they stare at me. I've seen their eyes lingering on me, and I can't bear it." Her fingers touched the livid scar that divided her eyebrow and ran into her hairline. "I don't mind being ugly, if only they wouldn't look at me and wonder what happened to me."

Henry circled her in his arms. "But the scars will fade, and no one will notice, then."

"Maybe, but I can't go out yet. I feel . . . safe here. Please, Father."

He kissed her like a small child. "Very well, I won't push. All in your own time."

In the summer days that followed she would sit in their small back garden, her face shaded by a huge hat, her fingers occupied by sewing or her eyes by reading. But it took her weeks to hem one handkerchief or to read a few chapters. Often she just stared at the grass or the flowers, her eyes looking only inward.

As the weather changed and winter approached, she retreated into the cottage. There wasn't much housework to do, for their home was small, and with two women to oversee the household time soon weighed heavily on Elizabeth's hands.

One afternoon, Henry was strolling back from the village with Ella when he stopped. "Hush, Ella. What's that? Can you hear music?"

Ella turned to him, her eyes radiant. "It's the piano. What's she playing?"

They paused at the gate, listening. "It's Chopin – Jessie's book. I haven't heard her play that for years."

They pressed their hands together silently, hardly daring to hope. Could it be, after seven months, that Elizabeth was at last emerging from the dreadful lethargy which had beset her since her accident?

From that day, they frequently heard her at the piano during the long winter evenings. Elizabeth began to learn some new pieces from the books she had used while at school. It was as if she could pour out her troubles through the music in a way she could not to her family.

Ella trudged up the path and into the welcome warmth of the cottage. Henry came to greet her, kissing her affectionately in the dim light of the hallway.

"You're just in time, love. Lizzie's made the tea, and it's all ready for you. Come and get warm."

Ella gratefully approached the fire, spreading her hands out in front of the radiant heat. While she warmed herself, Elizabeth entered, carrying the teapot, which she placed on the table.

"You look cold, Ella. Some tea will warm you up. Shall I pour it now?"

"Yes, thanks, that would be lovely. The wind is bitter over the hill today."

"And how was Vera?"

Ella had made the journey specially to see her sister, who was recovering from an attack of influenza. "She's definitely on the mend. Her neighbours have been very good. Mrs Hastings, who's also a widow, is staying with her while she needs help, and wouldn't hear of me stopping over. Thank you, love," she added as Elizabeth placed a cup of steaming tea in her hands, and offered her a slice of freshly buttered toast.

Henry joined them, slipping into his favourite chair which had been one of the items brought from London. Most of the furniture had been sold with the house, as it had been too big for the cottage. He bit into a slice of toast, while listening to Ella's news.

His wife sighed. "It's such a shame that Vera will miss the Christmas service at church tomorrow. She does so love the carols. I don't really fancy walking over there on my own, either."

"I would come with you, but I've arranged to collect our Christmas goose from the farmer at half past 10."

Ella laughed. "And how many years is it since you were in church, Henry? – apart from our wedding, that is. That would have been quite an event, to see you at a service!"

Henry smiled at her. "Well, it seems a shame for you to miss the service, after attending since April."

"There's no need for Ella to miss it . . . I'll . . . I'll go with her."

They looked up in astonishment, hardly daring to believe what she had said. Elizabeth stood by the table, fingers nervously stroking the teacloth, aware of their startled expressions.

"That would be delightful, Elizabeth. I'm sure you'll enjoy it, too. I just hope that the weather stays dry for our walk." Ella's face creased into the smile that was never far from her features.

"Well . . . yes . . . I . . ." Elizabeth's voice trailed away.

"Then that's all settled! Good!" Henry said quickly to hide the moment of tension, lest his daughter should take fright at what she had promised. "How about some of that fruit cake – it looks absolutely delicious! Cut me a piece, will you please, Lizzie?"

The cake was handed round, and the talk turned to other matters. But, the moment Elizabeth turned her back, Henry and Ella exchanged glances of hope silently across the fireplace.

The weather on their walk to Somerham that Sunday was windy, but at least it was dry. They arrived early and took their places in a free pew towards the back of the church. Elizabeth crouched in the corner, keeping her head bent so that no one could see her face properly. She was thankful that large hats were still in fashion. Her heart was pounding, and her hands cold and damp with fear.

Why did I choose to come here? she thought in anguish. It was only natural that a stranger should cause speculation amongst the other churchgoers. She was slim and young beside Ella, quite obviously not Vera.

The organ music began discreetly, filling the church with a warmth of sound. The church was nearly full now. Ella pointed out one or two people she recognised, and also the landowner's family in their special pew near the front.

The church was small, built of grey stone, and decorated with fine wood carvings. It was mostly plain, save for the beautiful altar cloth in white and gold, and a warmly coloured tapestry behind showing a representation of the creation of the world. When her eyes had taken all this in, Elizabeth finally brought herself to look round. To her relief, everyone seemed engrossed in their own neighbours, and not in this stranger who had appeared in the congregation.

The service was cheerful and bright, with the Christmas hymns and readings, and a word of seasonal charity from the vicar. A small choir sang a Christmas anthem, impressing Elizabeth with their performance.

"We have a fine organist and choirmaster here," Ella whispered to her.

Finally the service was over, and the congregation left the church to the joyful strains of the organ.

"May we sit and listen to the music for a while, Ella?" Elizabeth asked, unwilling to mingle with the people.

Ella sat down again. "Why, of course. He's very good."

Gradually the congregation filed out, one or two nodding to Ella and glancing curiously at the silent figure beside her. The music finished. They were alone now in the church, save for the organist putting away his books.

"Are you ready to go now, love?" Ella asked. It was enough that Elizabeth had come so far today, without pressing her to meet people too.

"Yes. Oh, just a minute, Ella, I've dropped my glove. Can you see it?"

They hunted for a moment or two under the pew before the missing article came to light, tucked under the hassock in front. Puffing and laughing at her exertion, Ella led Elizabeth to the aisle.

"Why, Mrs Bell, how nice to see you. Did you enjoy the service?"

He was a tall man of around thirty, dressed in a smart dark suit that had seen better days. His face was pleasant, his eyes genuinely welcoming as he greeted Ella.

"Very much, Mr Jameson, and so did my young companion. May I introduce my stepdaughter? Elizabeth, this is Mr Jameson, our organist."

"I'm delighted to met you, Miss Bell," he said, leaning forward to grasp her hand. As Elizabeth raised her head to look at him, he gasped, and the book he was carrying slipped from his fingers to the floor. "Oh dear, how stupid of me!" he exclaimed, fumbling to retrieve it.

Elizabeth blinked back tears, and swallowed. I didn't think I was that disfigured, she thought in misery.

Embarrassed, the organist hurriedly grasped her hand, seeing that he had upset her. "I do hope you will come again, Miss Bell," he added quickly. "Your stepmother has told me how musical you are. Maybe I could persuade you to sing in our choir?"

Shocked, Elizabeth drew back her hand. "Oh, no, I couldn't!"

"It's early days yet," Ella interposed, calming her. "Thank you so much for your music, Mr Jameson. We must be leaving now, as we have to call on my sister, and ours is a long walk home. The compliments of the season to you." So saying, she linked her arm with Elizabeth's and led her into the cold winter air again.

Throughout the Christmas season, Elizabeth brooded over her meeting with Mr Jameson. She would stare at her face in the looking-glass, once more repeating the movement she had made when she lifted her eyes to his. What had he seen to make him gasp so? She had known that the scar had disfigured her, but surely it wasn't as bad as that?

Ella noticed that Elizabeth often lapsed into long silences. She would look up to find her stepdaughter staring into space, her book lying forgotten in her lap. Ella had also been upset at the organist's reaction, an uncharacteristic rudeness on his part. She had never known him to be anything other than kind and polite. Surely he could have seen that it would upset Elizabeth?

Snow set in after Christmas, and Ella was unable to walk over to Somerham again for several weeks. Already the first snowdrops were peering through the ground when the weather finally cleared, and she arrayed herself for church. She walked into the parlour to say goodbye to Henry and Elizabeth, to find her stepdaughter dressed in her out-door clothes.

"I'm coming too, Ella."

Ella smiled. "That's lovely, dear." She said no more, but kissed Henry, and took Elizabeth's arm. It was the start of many visits to the church. But they never stayed as late as they had done that first day, so there was no further chance of meeting the organist.

Apart from this, Elizabeth still kept close to home. But Henry felt much less anxious about her, for she was at least meeting some people, and talking a little to them. Of course, she wasn't like his darling Lizzie used to be, but occasionally there was a flash of her old warmth beneath the new nervousness. What made him happiest was to note the loss of her haggard appearance, the soft rounding of her cheeks and shoulders, and the return of physical health. The scar would always be there, but it was fading gradually, and didn't detract from her looks.

While Elizabeth was arranging a bunch of bluebells in a jar on the hall-stand, two letters tumbled onto the mat by the front door. Swiftly she picked them up. One was a circular for Henry, and the other . . . she drew in her breath sharply. It was for her! Since they had moved to Kent, there had been just two letters for her, both from Belinda. But this one was postmarked Marylebone.

Could it be from Frances? Her pulse quickened as she hurried into the front parlour. Ella and Henry were in the garden, so there was no one to disturb her as she tore open the envelope.

A horrified stillness overcame her as she read the words, "*IF YOU WANT TO KEEP YOUR PAST LIFE A SECRET FROM YOUR FINE NEW FRIENDS, THEN SEND FIVE POUNDS IN NOTES TO MR DAVIDSON AT MARYLEBONE POST OFFICE BY FRIDAY.*"

It was printed in block capitals, with no signature. Elizabeth's breath came in short gasps. Bright lights danced in front of her eyes, and for a moment she thought she would faint. Dear God! Who could it be from? Who knew her secrets? A wild litany of names whirled round her mind. Radley? No, he was rich enough. Five pounds would be paltry to him. Nora, the artiste she had confessed all to in Sunderland? But what would she be doing in London? No, she had been genuine and kind. Florence Royle? That was more likely. But had she known, had she guessed?

Shaking, she ran upstairs and pulled open her bedside drawer, and withdrew her bank book. Yes, she could do it. She would send the money to the mysterious "Mr Davidson", and that would be the end of it. She dreaded Henry ever discovering that the father of her child had been Frederick Radley. What was more, if it became common knowledge her shame could disgrace them all, and they would have to move again.

Henry came across her pinning on her hat in the hallway. He kissed her cheek. "And where are you off to, my pet?"

"Into the town – I've written off for some new music." She kept her voice light, marvelling that she could act in such an unconcerned manner when inside she was trembling with anger and fright.

"Oh, will you get me some more tobacco while you're there?"

He pressed a florin into her hand. "Are you sure you don't want me to come with you?"

She turned round with a slight smile. "I have to go on my own at some point, Father. Now is as good a time as any."

He nodded. "Well, take care. There aren't many carriages around, but there are some sharp bends in the road, and they can take you unawares."

Elizabeth knew that he was referring to her fear of traffic, especially horses, since the accident. She kissed him gently. "I promise I'll be careful."

Elizabeth bought the tobacco first, then hurried on to the small bank. It was a simple matter to withdraw the money, then to seal it in the envelope she had already addressed to Marylebone Post Office. It hadn't been a lie when she had told Henry about sending off for some music, as she'd written the order quickly before leaving the house. The two letters were duly stamped and sent, and Elizabeth let her breath out with a great sigh.

Some of the tension began to leave her as she emerged from the post office. There was a horse and trap standing on the opposite side of the road, but she had passed it on the way in, with only a small quiver of nervousness. It would do her good to pass it again. Checking that nothing was coming, she crossed the road to begin the walk home.

Suddenly there was a shout, and a commotion behind her. She turned her head to see what was happening. Two boys were chasing a dog up the road, the animal barking excitedly at their pursuit. It ran round Elizabeth, then in front of the horse, which pawed the air nervously. With a cry, she ducked away, dropping her basket into the dusty road, her hands shielding her head.

The boys and dog made themselves scarce at the sound of an angry shout. Then strong hands guided her to safety.

"Wait there. I'll get your shopping." With a quick word of comfort to the horse, the man retrieved the basket and the spilt contents. Elizabeth put one hand to the wall, trying to steady herself. Her heart still pounded furiously.

"Here you are. I believe it's all intact. Why . . . Miss Bell!"

Raising her head, Elizabeth found herself gazing into the concerned face of Mr Jameson, the organist.

"You look pale . . . and you're trembling." He took her hands solicitously. "I'm so sorry my horse frightened you. Those wretched boys!"

"I shouldn't be so afraid – it's stupid of me! But I can't help it . . . not since the accident." Elizabeth knew that the upsetting letter had brought back many old fears that she had begun to conquer. But she could never tell anyone.

"Why of course," he consoled her. "Here, you must let me take you home. It's the least I can do. Where do you live?"

Elizabeth explained while he put her basket into the trap, and then he helped her up after it. She glanced nervously at the horse, but it seemed docile again. Then he strode briskly round to the other side, and with an agile leap joined her in the trap.

After a moment or two, Elizabeth looked at her rescuer as he drove along in silence. He wasn't handsome, she surmised, but his face was genial and kind. If only she wasn't weighed down by her past, this man was one she could have made a good friend.

"This is surely out of your way, Mr Jameson."

"Why, no, it's on my way home to Somerham."

"No, I mean that it's a long way for you to travel, into Oakridge."

"Oh, yes, but we don't have a post office in Somerham, and I brought over some letters from the school. I also took my shoes to be soled at the cobbler's."

"The school? But I thought that there was no school in Somerham."

"The village children have to come to school in Oakridge, but I'm talking about the boys' boarding school over the other side of the hill. Didn't you know that I teach history there?"

Suddenly, Elizabeth felt foolish. How ignorant she must seem. "No, I didn't. But you live in Somerham, don't you, and not at the school?"

"Yes, I lived in Somerham when my mother was ill, and they didn't mind when I stayed there after she died. I didn't want the house to be empty. Anyway, I like the people, and I've been organist at the church for eighteen months."

They drove on in silence, until the Belmonts' cottage came into view. Then he turned to her again. "Miss Bell, I hope you don't mind me asking this."

Her heart sank. What could he want to know?

"Your stepmother told me that you play the piano well. I wonder . . . the vicar of Oakridge has asked me to teach the piano to his two young daughters, as the organist here is a crotchety old fellow, whereas he knows I'm used to children. But it occurred to me that, if you might consider it, you would be a far more suitable teacher. It seems to me that two little girls would be much happier learning from a young lady, and you're so near, too."

"Oh, I don't know! I've never had any experience. How old are they?"

"They're seven and nine years old."

Elizabeth paused as the trap drew up to the gate. "I . . . really couldn't say yet, Mr Jameson. Would you give me some time to consider it?"

"Of course. Tell me next Sunday at church. There's no hurry." He jumped down and went round to help her to the ground. He handed her purchases to her, then leaped back into the trap. "Goodbye, Miss Bell. I hope you've recovered from your shock."

"Oh . . . yes, thank you. Goodbye."

As he took her hand in farewell, Elizabeth suddenly felt a stirring within her, almost as if she were drowning and losing her breath. Then the bond was broken, and she was left standing by the gate, watching the trap as it rounded the corner.

All at once a new horizon was opening for her. Could I . . . could I really teach those girls? she wondered.

Elizabeth began to teach the vicar's daughters two weeks later. Margaret and Mary were quiet girls, used to strict discipline at home, and, though not exceptionally gifted, were interested enough to learn well. Elizabeth found their curiosity a joy, and was surprised how she herself responded to teaching. She had discovered a fascinating new interest.

"Good morning, Miss Bell, and how are your pupils?" Mr Jameson enquired a month later at church.

She turned a radiant face to him. "They're doing very well. Margaret, being a little older, is quicker, but she's inclined to be careless, while Mary is slower and more accurate. But they're nice girls and I enjoy teaching them."

"Good, I'm glad to hear it." His face creased into that warm smile which was so attractive. "I was looking through my books and found one which gives hints on piano teaching that you might find useful. I'll drop it in at your cottage next time I'm passing."

"Oh, there's no hurry, I can collect it next time I'm at church . . ."

"No, it's no trouble. I'll be driving into Oakridge during the week, and will be passing your way."

"That's very kind . . ."

True to his word, Mr Jameson brought the book, and stayed to chat to Elizabeth for a few minutes. A week later, it was followed by some piano music that he thought she might enjoy playing. Gradually a friendship grew, as the books and music passed between them, especially once the school term ended and Mr Jameson was free during the week.

Elizabeth looked at the flyleaf of one of his books to discover his name. "Adam Jameson" was written in a gently sloping copperplate script inside the cover. It was a nice name, she decided, flowing well off the tongue.

Elizabeth handed the book back to him on his next call, when he brought some Beethoven and an arrangement of a Strauss waltz.

"I've found it very interesting, Mr Jameson. Thank you."

"But you must keep it as long as you want. I'm not using it now." Then he added, "And couldn't you bring yourself to call me Adam?"

Her fingers curled round the brocade curtain in a tight fist. Already they were growing too intimate, and it was what she had wanted to avoid at all costs – it was not for her now. The shame of her past was too great. Yet she couldn't resist his kind manner. Panic fluttered within her. "I . . . really don't know."

"Oh, please. I confess I've thought of you as 'Elizabeth' for many months now. Surely we are friends."

"Yes . . . I suppose so. Very well, I'll try to remember to call you . . . Adam."

The smile that rewarded her reply seemed to flood the room with brightness. How could anyone have such a beaming smile? she wondered as she took back the book, and shook his hand in the doorway.

Ella looked curiously at the letter addressed to Elizabeth. Marylebone. She shook her head, and took the letter into the kitchen where her stepdaughter was kneading some bread dough. She looked up, brushing a strand of hair away from her flushed face with the back of her hand.

"For me, Ella?" She wiped her floury hands on her apron, reaching out for the letter. She blanched visibly as she recognised the writing on the envelope.

Ella had never seen anyone change colour so dramatically. "What is it, love?" she cried in concern.

Elizabeth swallowed, covering her shock. "Nothing, it's nothing, Ella. Just a letter from a former fan. My agent must have given them the address." She thrust it into the pocket of her apron, returning to her kneading with renewed vigour.

Ella was not convinced, but said nothing, as Elizabeth's expression was closed and forbidding.

This time the demand was for twenty pounds. Elizabeth was horrified. There wasn't enough money in her account to cover that. She would have to ask Henry for some money from their bank account. That would be impossible! He must not know about the blackmail.

She tore the letter into tiny shreds, and threw it in with their rubbish. Maybe Mr Davidson would leave her alone if she didn't reply. She needed time to think about how to get hold of the money without anyone knowing.

Perhaps she could tell Henry that she wanted to buy a lot more music. Another five pounds would cover the demand. Maybe Adam Jameson could give her a list of musical pieces, and she could show it to Henry and ask him to authorise her withdrawal of some money from the bank in Bromley. The thought of seeing Adam once more gave her spirits a much-needed lift, though she didn't pause to examine the reason why.

The road was dusty and rutted after the warm dry weather. Luckily, there were few vehicles or horses on the road to raise the dust, and no other walkers to disturb the shimmering heat of the day. Birds called in the hedgerow, while in the distance cows were being driven lazily back to the meadow. The occasional hum of an insect swelled then diminished on the still air.

Adam Jameson's house was one of the few in Somerham which could boast a second storey. It also had a small front garden, displaying roses of several hues. Closing the gate with a sharp "click", Elizabeth hurried to the porchway, and raised her hand to knock on the heavy oak door. For a moment she hesitated – what was that piano music she could hear? It was something familiar, but its name eluded her. She must ask him. Quickly she grasped the knocker and tapped it twice.

The music stopped. In that instant it came to her what the tune was – it was one of Vesta Tilley's famous numbers, which Elizabeth had heard her sing so many times. Suddenly, she went cold. How come Adam Jameson was playing a music-hall song?

There was no more time to speculate. The door swung open, and she found herself looking at the organist. His features immediately broke into a welcoming smile.

"Miss Bell . . . Elizabeth! What a charming surprise. Do come in!"

The hallway was dark, panelled in a sombre wood, with a red patterned carpet running up the centre of the stairs. With a smile, she removed her light coat and handed it to him.

He showed her into the drawing room. Immediately her eyes were drawn to the grand piano which dominated the room. It stood in the broad bay window, quite dwarfing the brocade settee and two chairs which huddled round the fireplace, where an unlit fire was laid. Her hand stretched out as if drawn by magnetism to touch the glossy surface of the piano. "Oh, Mr Jameson . . . I mean, Adam. What a beautiful piano."

"I'm afraid it's too large for this room – in fact, for the whole house. But I couldn't bring myself to part with it when I moved here after my wife died."

Shocked and surprised, she snapped her head round. "Your wife – but I didn't know you were married!"

His mouth twisted ruefully. "Not many people here know that. It's three years now since she died. We were married very young, but unfortunately her health deteriorated quite soon. The last year of her life we spent completely abroad."

"Oh, I'm so sorry," Elizabeth murmured, aware of an unusual clenching in her chest.

He shook his head. "You mustn't be, for my sake. I only wish I could have made her life with me happier. In the four years that we had, it was all too obvious that we had made a dreadful mistake. Sarah hated being a schoolmaster's wife, being used to a much more opulent way of life. It was a great trial to her to be buried in the depths of the country – I had a post in Sussex. I fear we were both to blame, too young to see that our ways of life would not mix." He stopped and looked at his visitor, as if he half-feared what her reaction would be.

But her eyes were distant, looking upon a time long past in her own life, thinking of William. Would theirs have been a terrible mistake, too? They also had been so young – he just twenty-one, herself eighteen.

"I'm sorry, I've been talking about myself too much and neglecting my guest. Won't you sit down?"

Quickly she gathered her wandering thoughts. "Thank you, but I can only stay for a short time. I called to return your Beethoven which you kindly lent me."

"Oh, but there was no need – I'm not using it at present. But of course, I'm glad to have your company. I feel that the house is really too big for just me."

"But it is a beautiful house."

"Yes, it was a good idea to move here when my mother was ill, and there is room for my belongings, much more than I would have had if I had lived at the school."

Elizabeth sat down on the settee. "You have lost so many people close to you," she ventured.

"Yes, it's true. But it's distracting to have the boys at the school, demanding attention, and to feel that I have some use in guiding them. Tell me, how do you enjoy teaching?"

"It's so little, but it's wonderful. I never believed I could give knowledge to others."

He smiled. "Then I must find you some more pupils. How shall I put it? 'Beautiful young lady desires to impart musical knowledge to genteel girls.' "

They laughed.

"But I'm not beautiful!" she exclaimed.

He turned to her in amazement. "But of course you are! How can you say otherwise?"

Her fingers wandered over her forehead. "But this – you know it's there, you've seen it. I've grown used to being ugly, there's no need to flatter me."

"Elizabeth." Seriously, he sat down beside her, and touched her hand. "Look at me." She obeyed, silently. "Never, never tell me you're ugly. Seldom have I seen a more lovely young woman. A blemish . . . can only emphasise the perfection of your looks. You must accept this and face the world with pride in what you've been given."

Her eyes faltered, unable to hold the earnestness of his gaze.

"Now, enough of the lecture. You must be thirsty. Would you like some lemonade?"

A smile touched her mouth. "That would be lovely."

"Then I must desert you, if you'll forgive me. My housekeeper isn't here today. I won't be long."

Elizabeth sat immobile, going over his words in her mind. He had said that she must face the world with pride. If only she could! It had been possible to do that before she became involved with Radley. But since the accident it had seemed to her that her disfigured face was the outward manifestation of her inner ugliness. Maybe she could grow to forget it as the years went by, though the writer of those dreadful letters was keeping the shame fresh in her mind. Perhaps she should never have left the halls – after all, other women managed to have liaisons which were recognised, if not condoned. Yet she believed that what she had done was doubly wrong. She had sold herself to a man she hated.

Thinking of the music hall reminded her of the song she had heard Adam playing while she was coming up the path. She had to know now if she was right. Jumping to her feet, she went to the piano and turned the music over so that she could see the title.

Her breath caught sharply. 'The Piccadilly Johnny with the Little Glass Eye', announced the title-page. It was one of Vesta Tilley's most famous numbers. How did a man like Adam Jameson come to have such music? It was a new copy, too.

"Ah, I see you've caught me out."

Elizabeth started as Adam's voice rang out from the doorway. "I . . . didn't know you liked this kind of music."

He walked across to her and laid the tray with the jug and two glasses on a small table beside the piano. "Elizabeth . . . I have deceived you long enough. There is something you ought to know. I . . . wrote 'Melody for Lizzie' and 'Skylark Waltz'."

With a gasp, she sat down on the piano stool.

"Yes, I know that you're Elizabeth Belmont. I recognised you that first time we met in church. It's no wonder . . . look." He reached to a bureau drawer, and brought out several postcards showing her in various poses, which had been printed during her most popular period on the stage. There was even one which she had signed, and sent with the letter thanking him – as James Adamson – for 'Skylark Waltz'."

Her voice broke the silence, a hoarse undertone. "Then why didn't you say anything before now?"

He shrugged. "You were introduced to me as 'Miss Bell', so I gathered that you wished to remain unknown."

"James Adamson – Adam Jameson," she murmured.

"Yes, I wondered if you might guess."

"I had no reason to expect to find the composer of my two greatest successes working as a schoolmaster and church organist in a tiny country village," she said accusingly. "You keep a lot secret, don't you? First your wife . . . and now this."

"My wife," he replied quietly. "I didn't tell people about her because it was a painful episode in my life, and I felt I didn't want, or deserve, their pity. But the music-hall songs are a different matter. It was something I enjoyed, some extra money earned lightheartedly. Surely you realise that it wouldn't have been deemed . . . seemly . . . for the church organist, or for that matter a master in charge of the moral upbringing of young boys, to be seen to be composing for the music hall."

"Oh, yes, I know that," Elizabeth responded bitterly. "All along . . ." But she could go no further.

"It meant such a lot to me, to be a part of your success. I must confess, I was half in love with you while you were a successful artiste, though I knew I could have no chance with you. But now I've met you, spent time with you . . . I see what a charming, unaffected young woman you are. Elizabeth . . ."

"No! Don't say any more! You don't know what I'm like, at all! I want to forget all that, the music hall, and just live quietly with my father and Ella out of sight of the world."

"But why?" He reached for her hand. "You're so talented – how could you leave such a successful career?"

Snatching away her hand she pushed him aside. "Please – don't you understand? I'm not a beautiful image on a stage. I'm flesh and blood, with real feelings, and real faults. If you knew all about me, you would hate me. But . . . I don't want you to hate me. So I think it's better if we don't meet again, and you can keep your dreams. I'll send you back the rest of your music."

In a moment she was gone, the slam of the door and the receding footsteps on the path echoing in his ears. Adam sank on to the piano stool on which she had so recently been sitting, and gazed unseeing at the tray of lemonade. Then, softly, he picked out the notes of 'Melody for Lizzie' on the piano, gently at first, then gathering speed and volume as he poured out his frustration at being so powerless.

Chapter 20

Elizabeth parcelled up the remaining books and music that Adam had lent her, leaving them on his doorstep when she knew he would be at church practising. She found the landscape blurring before her eyes on the way home. The future stretched out bleakly in front of her, friendless and lonely. Perhaps she ought to take up Belinda's much-repeated invitation to visit her in Australia. She loved Ella and Henry so much it would be a wrench to leave them. But the shameful secrets she kept to herself were devouring her.

There was her father, coming from the village. Elizabeth waved to him as they both neared their cottage. He held up an envelope. "Look, there was a letter for you at the post office. It's been re-directed from your agent. I suspect it was delayed by the strikes, too." There had been unrest at the docks, and the railways had been on strike for a few days.

Not another blackmail letter! Fear stabbed her momentarily. Then, as she took it, she realised that the writing was different, and the post-mark was Belgravia. She frowned as she entered the cottage, closely followed by Henry.

"I'm thirsty. I think I'll get a drink," he muttered, and left her to open the envelope in private.

Henry returned a moment later, carrying a glass of water, to find his daughter finishing the letter, obviously dismayed by the contents. "Father, it's from Gerald, Frances' brother. He says that she's been in prison . . ."

"In prison!" Henry exclaimed.

"Yes, apparently the suffragettes see it as a noble sacrifice for their cause. There was a demonstration, and she was arrested with several others. Then they went on hunger strike – and, do you know, they had tubes forced down them and food poured into their stomachs. Isn't that horrible, Father!"

Henry shook his head in disbelief. "What a thing to do to young ladies. Whyever did she become involved in such affairs?"

"Frances was always so fervent for a righteous cause. But listen to what Gerald says. '*Frances has been quite ill due to this treatment, and will be released on August 29th. She expressed a wish to see you, and is sorry for the quarrel which interrupted your friendship. My sister does not know that I have written to you, but we are all concerned for her well-being, and know that it would be a great comfort to her to know that you forgive her for her hasty words.*'"

Elizabeth's eyes glistened with tears. "When's the 29th, Father?"

"It was yesterday."

"Oh, then she's been released! I must go to see her at once!"

"But to Sheffield, Lizzie?"

"No, she's in London, at her aunt's house. You will let me go, won't you?"

"Why, of course, my pet. But be sensible. Pack a bag today, and send word – a telegram – saying that you'll be coming tomorrow. Then they can send back to say if it's inconvenient. Stay overnight, or even for two nights, and I'll collect you from the station on Monday."

"Thank you, Father. I'll go to Oakridge now to send the telegram."

Henry gazed out of the window in wonder as she hurried down the lane towards the town. Was this the same young woman who had refused to leave the cottage last summer? Now she was proposing a journey to the Smoke, and on her own, too! Silently he thanked the crisis which had caused her to undertake such a trip. Maybe she would stop moping and look ahead instead.

While Henry was feeling happier at seeing Elizabeth's confidence returning, Ella was brooding over the arrival of another letter postmarked Marylebone. She had put it into her pocket yesterday morning, and hadn't had the courage to give it to her stepdaughter, remembering the reaction Elizabeth had had to the previous one.

She'd had tea with her sister in Somerham, talking of trivialities, it seemed to Ella. Now it was nearly 7 o'clock, and time she was making her way back to Oakridge. As she turned towards the road to begin the walk home, a voice cut across her preoccupied thoughts. "Mrs Bell!"

"Mr Jameson! You look anxious. What's wrong?"

"Did you bring this parcel?" He had ripped back the brown paper to reveal some music and books.

Ella frowned. "Why, no. What makes you think I did?"

Adam sighed in exasperation. "Then Elizabeth must have been here while I was at the church. She's returned all that I lent her, with just this note."

Ella read the paper he showed her. "*With thanks. These have been most useful – E.B.*" She frowned. "Have you quarrelled?"

He sighed heavily, pushing his hair back from his brow. "I don't know exactly. I just know that she seems to have severed our friendship. I can't understand it. I thought there was something special between us, but maybe I was mistaken."

Seeing his concern, Ella decided that she could confide in Adam. "Mr Jameson, is there somewhere we could talk? I need your advice – it's to do with Elizabeth."

"Of course. Come inside."

He settled her into an armchair beside the grand piano. Ella looked round with approval, seeing the room of a true music lover. Then she explained. "This letter came yesterday for Elizabeth. I know it was wrong of me, but I kept it back from her. There was an identical letter last week, and I've never seen anyone go so white as she did when I gave it to her."

Adam held out his hand for the envelope. "Hmmm . . . Marylebone. Is there anyone she knows there?"

"That's just the point. No one at all. She said it was from a fan, but I don't see why it should upset her so much. She's been more nervy recently, and I wondered if the letters were anything to do with it. That one couldn't have been the first."

Adam held it up to the light. "I can see some writing through the paper. Let's try steaming it open."

Ella looked shocked. "But it's a private letter. Should we?"

"Well, if you think it's wrong, then you'd better give the letter to Elizabeth."

A frown creased her forehead. "It does feel wrong, but if we can help her . . ."

He nodded, leaving her to go to the kitchen. Ella kneaded her hands anxiously during the next few minutes, until he reappeared.

"It's coming apart now." He slid the note from the envelope. Together they examined it, both drawing in their breath as they read the contents.

"*You didn't send the money last week. If you don't send twenty-five pounds by Thursday then your secrets will be revealed. Mr Davidson of Marylebone.*"

"Blackmail!" Adam raged. "Who's this Davidson fellow?"

Ella mopped her brow with her handkerchief. "I've no idea. Oh, Mr Jameson, what are we going to do? Poor Lizzie."

Adam sat down opposite Ella, deep in thought. "I must speak with Elizabeth. If we can persuade her to arrange to meet this fellow, then we'll discover his identity, and put him in jail."

"It's strange you should say that. She's going up to London tomorrow to spend two nights with her friend Frances, who's been ill."

"That's ideal. I think I know how we can do it. Listen . . ."

The Whittinghams had cabled that they would welcome Elizabeth, and would be delighted to have her for two nights. Henry took Elizabeth to the station to catch an early train.

"Now remember, don't stint on the cabs – promise me!"

"Yes, Father. And you'll be here to meet me from the train on Monday?" She kissed his cheek.

Henry nodded, returning her embrace. "Take care, now!"

The train left the station with a loud grinding of wheels and hissing of steam.

Neither of them saw a last-minute passenger slip into the end carriage. Elizabeth had just settled down onto her seat when the door to her compartment was slid open, and she started to her feet in surprise.

"Adam! What are you doing here?"

"I've been wanting to talk to you. This is very important, and you must listen to what I have to say."

She laughed mirthlessly. "So you thought you would trap me here where I couldn't run away."

"Something like that." Adam swung round to the door as he heard voices approaching, and pulled down the blinds briskly, to the outrage of the couple who had been about to join them in the compartment. They went further down the carriage.

With a sigh, Adam threw himself down onto the seat, drawing Elizabeth down with a sharp tug on her hand. "Elizabeth, we need time to talk. Please hear me out."

She gazed sadly at her gloved hands, then nodded silently.

"I know there are parts of your life that you wish to keep secret, and I have no wish at all to cause you any pain. But if you could just cast your mind back to the night of your accident. Do you recall that your father had arranged for us to meet after the show?"

"Yes, I do remember now. I'd forgotten."

"Well, I was waiting at the front of the theatre towards the end of the second house, looking at the posters to while away the time . . . when you came hurrying from the auditorium. I could see you were upset, and then the manager stopped you before you could leave."

With a cry, Elizabeth buried her face in her hands. "I remember now! I saw you too, but I didn't recognise you when I met you in the church."

"This secret – it was to do with him. Isn't that true?" When there was no reply, he went on. "Elizabeth, I realise that there was something between you, but what I saw was . . . the fear in your face. He had some terrible hold over you."

Uncovering her face, she implored, "Adam . . . have you told anyone else what you saw? Tell me, please! I must know."

"Why, no . . . of course not. I wouldn't reveal such a thing."

"Then you must never tell anyone. Especially my father, or Ella." Fear contorted her features.

"But I assumed your father knew everything."

"My father knows some, but not all. It would kill him if he knew that I had been . . . associated . . . with Radley."

"Then you were having an affair with him?"

She closed her eyes. "Don't put it that way."

"Did you ever love him?"

"I hated him! If it hadn't been for . . ." She broke off, with a sob.

Adam put his arm around her shoulder, letting her cry for a few minutes. "What was the hold he had over you?"

"My father's job. Adam, you will despise me for what I'm going to tell you, but you might as well know, now." She pushed him away, wiping her eyes. "When my father was so ill, and was told he couldn't perform again, it broke him. I couldn't bear to see him like that, the man I had adored and leaned on all my life. He . . . he was a shadow, a wraith. There was only one way to put back the life in his eyes, and that was to make him believe in himself. I knew Radley admired me; he had already offered twice to become my . . . my protector, you might say. I went to him, and asked him to give my father the job of musical director at his music hall. When he hesitated, I did the only thing I could think of – I offered myself as payment."

"Oh, Elizabeth." The soft words were barely audible above the rattle of the speeding train. Then his hand touched her hair. "You poor child. No man should have accepted that of you."

"I broke it off – but it was already too late." The tears still ran down her cheeks.

"Too late?"

She remained silent for a few moments. Then she whispered, "I can't tell you, Adam. I just can't. I don't want to see the disgust in your eyes when you know what I have been."

Adam reached out and took her small gloved hand in his. "Dear girl, I won't press you now. But there is another reason why I'm here today. I need to ask your forgiveness." With his free hand he withdrew an envelope from his pocket. "Your stepmother brought this letter to me yesterday. She was terribly worried about you." He paused as he saw Elizabeth's face grow rigid. "It was a gross breach of manners on my part, but when she told me that you had been distressed by the last letter like this I took the liberty of opening it."

Elizabeth snatched her hand away from his clasp. "Adam, how could you! That was private!"

"Yes, it was private, and I apologise. But I think you need someone to help you in this matter. Read it."

She reached for the envelope, taking it as if it would singe her fingers. Slowly she withdrew the letter, but, once she'd read the contents, her hand flew to her mouth. "Twenty-five pounds! Oh, Adam, what am I going to do? He'll never let me be free!"

"Do you know who he is?"

She shook her head, unable to speak.

Adam couldn't bear to see her cry. He drew her into his arms. "Dear

Elizabeth, don't worry. I know how we can trap this wicked man. Trust me."

"But Adam, you don't know how bad it is. If people knew!"

The train hurtled into a tunnel. Holding her more tightly, Adam spoke. "Those who love you will not condemn you. Can you bring yourself to tell me? Then we will be in a stronger position."

"Oh, Adam . . ." she waited until the train emerged from the tunnel. "When I said it was too late . . . I was . . . I was going to have a child. When I had the accident . . . I lost the baby. My whole body felt defiled. Living in Oakridge . . . I felt I was beginning to cleanse myself. But this has brought it all back."

Adam held her close. "And this is what you are worried they will tell people?"

She nodded.

"Obviously your father knows."

"Of course."

"Well, to the rest of the village we can deny it as malicious gossip. There is no proof. Did . . . Radley . . . know?" He spoke as if the name would poison his tongue.

"No. I wouldn't have told him, and he couldn't have guessed, as I was on tour when I discovered." She turned slowly to face him. "Adam . . . doesn't this make any difference to you?"

He smiled slowly. "It doesn't change the way I feel about you, Elizabeth. I'm just sorry that you have suffered so much."

The train drew into a station. They sat in silent suspense, wondering if their solitude would be disturbed. Eventually the slamming of doors stopped and the shrill whistle of the guard cut through the air. Movement in the corridor ceased as the train lurched forward, and soon they were rattling towards the capital again.

"I want you to send this fellow a letter."

Elizabeth sat up. "The . . . blackmailer?"

Adam nodded. "Tell him you will have the money for him on Monday afternoon, as you need time to obtain it. We're going to surprise him, and put him behind bars."

Elizabeth shivered. "Adam, I don't want it in the newspapers. Must we involve anyone else?"

He was touched by her anxious plea. "Well, we might be able to do it ourselves. If we wait at Marylebone Post Office, you ought to be able to identify him, and we can confront him."

"But he may send a servant, or a friend."

"We'll get the clerk to signal to us when he arrives, and we can follow him."

"Do you think it will work?" she asked forlornly.

He squeezed her hand. "We won't let him get away with it. And I'm sure we can do it with no further pain to you. Now I must leave you." The train was drawing into Victoria station. "Would you like me to get you a cab before I go?"

Hastily, she dabbed the last of her tears from her eyes. "No, I think I shall manage."

"Dearest Elizabeth, try to forget this until Monday. Enjoy your stay with your friends. I'll meet you at the bookstall on Monday, at about 1 o'clock. Just send the letter. I'll do the rest."

She was prepared to leave now. They stood up. Gently, Adam leaned forward and touched his lips to hers briefly. "Go carefully, now." A brief smile flickered over her mouth. Then she picked up her overnight bag, and passed through the door that he held open for her.

Elizabeth turned once, to give him another tentative smile through the window before she disappeared into the crowd. Adam watched her as long as he could, until she turned the corner and was lost from sight.

Outside the station, the noise of the traffic was so much louder than Elizabeth remembered. Taxi horns blared, motor engines roared, trams rattled, and horses' hooves rang against the road. The air was clogged with fumes and dirt. For a moment Elizabeth stood, too dazed to collect her thoughts. Then she spotted a motor taxi cab point, and hurried to engage one before she lost her nerve.

Her encounter with Adam had left her trembling, though she could not quite identify all the emotions that whirled within her. The thought of Monday's confrontation with the mysterious Mr Davidson filled her with dread, but she would try to do as Adam had urged her, and attempt to put it from her mind.

He had not spurned her in disgust! Now he knew everything, and he still seemed to care for her. Dear Adam! Once her composer, the root of her success, and now her dear friend. Surely, if anyone could help her in her dilemma with this vile blackmailer, Adam could.

It was only a short ride to her destination in Belgravia. The cabbie took her bag up to the door, for which service she tipped him generously, before ringing the bell.

A young maid in a black dress and white starched apron opened the door, and ushered Elizabeth inside. "May I take your coat, Madam? What name shall I say?"

"That's all right, Mabel. I'll see to Miss Belmont," a male voice announced, and Gerald hurried across the hall to greet her. "How lovely to see you. Frances will be so pleased that you've come."

Elizabeth thought he looked agitated, and was surprised that the confident Gerald should show such anxiety. But, a moment later, she realised why.

"Would you like to come into the drawing room for a moment . . . there are some . . . other visitors here. I thought you might prefer not . . ."

"Why, it's Elizabeth Belmont."

Her heart twisted inside her at the sound of that half-forgotten voice. She turned her head quickly to find herself face to face with William Hareton. He looked no different from the day when he had cast her off and broken her heart all those years ago.

Trembling, she held out her hand. "How nice to see you, Mr Hareton. I trust you are well?"

"Why . . . your eye . . . what happened?"

Elizabeth stared him full in the face, surprised to find that she could face him with confidence. Suddenly the scar didn't matter – Adam had said she was beautiful. "It was an unfortunate accident with a horse cab. But I'm quite recovered now." She smiled graciously.

"Oh . . . er . . . yes. Well, I'm glad to hear that." He looked rather flustered, and glanced almost furtively back to the parlour, from which there came the sound of female voices.

"Miss Belmont, would you like to step this way?" Gerald intervened.

"Of course. Goodbye, Mr Hareton."

"Er . . . goodbye."

As Elizabeth swept into the drawing room, she caught sight of a young lady emerging from the parlour. Gerald apologised briefly, saying he would be back in a moment. Elizabeth waited until they left the house and walked down the front steps. Then, from a well-hidden point behind the curtains, she scrutinised William's companion as she linked arms with him and waved back to the house vivaciously. There was a proud tilt to her head, and her lips were a beautifully moulded bow shape, such as Elizabeth had longed for as a child. The hair which was swept up beneath the wide-brimmed hat was a fashionable rich brown. Elizabeth smiled to herself. Well, William had always liked pretty women, and now he seemed to have excelled himself. No doubt this time he had found one with a pedigree to match her looks.

She returned to the sofa and sat down, so that Gerald should not discover her gazing through the curtains like a shop-girl gawping at a duchess.

"I'm so sorry to have kept you waiting, Elizabeth. I hope you don't mind my addressing you in so familiar a manner."

"Of course not. We've known each other since we were children . . . and perhaps we were rather too familiar." She smiled roguishly. Kent and Adam and the sick remembrance of her problems began to fade.

Gerald responded with a laugh. Then he was serious again. "And I must apologise for hiding you – or at least, attempting to. I thought you mightn't wish to meet William. It was an unexpected visit, otherwise I would have put them off."

"Not at all. But I fear that there was more embarrassment on his part than on mine. Who was the young lady?"

"That was Miss Catherine Fowldes-Watson, the daughter of one of his clients."

Elizabeth grinned wickedly. "A much more suitable match than a music-hall artiste," she commented.

"That may be, but imagine marrying such a paragon! I fear that William may have some expensive tastes to meet if he throws in his lot there!"

They laughed. But then the levity dispersed as Elizabeth recalled the reason for her visit. "Frances – how is she?"

Gerald took Elizabeth's arm and began to guide her towards the parlour. "Much better, but I'm afraid you'll be shocked by her appearance," he warned in a low voice as they approached the door.

Even this warning did not prepare her for the first sight of her friend. Reclining on a couch before the fireplace, Frances was combing her hair, which hung loose. Its former shining splendour was dulled and lifeless, and the thick locks only emphasised the fleshless face. Her cheekbones protruded from her hollow skin, and her eyes were deeply shadowed.

"Frances," Elizabeth uttered softly, horrified by the spectacle of the young suffragette.

The emaciated features broke into a welcoming smile, and it was the old Frances. "Oh, Elizabeth! I'm so happy to see you!" she cried, and held out her arms. The girls embraced, tears on their cheeks. "Oh, look at me, crying like an infant!" Frances exclaimed, and blew her nose in a handkerchief which she had fished out from under the blanket that covered her legs. "I just seem to howl at the least provocation, these days."

"You're weak, that's all. It'll be better once you're stronger."

Gerald had faded into the background, leaving the two young women alone.

"Oh, Frances – was it worth it?"

Frances played idly with the coverlet. "You know, Elizabeth, I've always been so involved in the movement. Yet you should have seen the others, how uplifted they were by all the privation, and the harsh treatment by the authorities only served to strengthen their resolve not to give in."

"But not you?"

"I had to keep it up – I couldn't let them down. But I've never been so thankful for anything than when I had word that I would be released. I was so ashamed."

Elizabeth pulled her chair closer to the couch, and took Frances' hand. "You didn't let them down, Frances. It was very brave of you to stick it out when your feelings weren't with them."

The sick woman looked up. "I suppose you're right. You remember how it was Aunt Victoria who introduced me to the movement for the vote? She hasn't reproached me at all. I think she finds imprisonment a little too extreme a measure. I still support the cause, after all." Then a small smile touched her mouth. "Do you know, it wouldn't have seemed nearly so bad if I hadn't missed a boating party on the Thames with Philip – Mr Leighton."

"Who's Mr Leighton?"

"Oh, I'd forgotten how long it was since I saw you. It really feels as if we saw each other only last month. How long is it since that silly quarrel?"

Elizabeth considered. "Nearly two years."

"What? It can't be! Oh, Elizabeth, what a fool I was. How can you ever forgive me for being so pig-headed?"

"There's nothing to forgive. Let's forget any differences we had."

"But listen, I want you to know that, whatever you do in your life, that's up to you. I shouldn't judge others."

"Please, Frances. I don't wish to remember that time. It was a very unhappy phase of my life." She felt a wild lurch within her as she remembered her talk with Adam, and what she would have to face on Monday. "Of course I'll forget it, anything you wish . . . as long as we remain friends."

That evening, after dinner, Gerald went out, while Frances' aunt entertained three friends to bridge in the drawing room. The young women were happy to have time to catch up on their two lost years, though Elizabeth kept some things to herself. She mentioned the church and her two young piano pupils, but nothing about her friendship with Adam. Frances, understanding now that her friend did not wish to talk of some parts of her life, was happy to hear what she would tell.

"What are you going to do now, Frances?"

Frances sighed. "I'm not sure. Mother wrote to me yesterday to say that she had seen a post advertised for teaching English in Sheffield. I think it may be just as well for me to go home and settle down for a while."

"No more suffragette rallies?"

"Only if they take me to Cambridge."

Elizabeth smiled. "So what – or who – is in Cambridge? Is it Mr Leighton?"

With a laugh, Frances retorted, "It didn't take you long to discover that. Am I so transparent?"

"No. It's just that I've never heard you talk of a young man before. So he must be important."

Frances brushed back her hair from her face. "I'd like to think that, but I'm not sure if he still feels as interested in me as he was before I was in prison. But, if he still cares for me after all that, then his feelings must be deep, don't you agree?"

"Yes." Elizabeth's eyes were far away, seeing another face, remembering the comforting feel of Adam's arms as he held her close on the train. Could she dare to hope for happiness in the future?

They took Frances for a carriage ride on the Sunday, down by the river, and across to Battersea Park. She had said she would prefer the gentler movement of the horse to the motor car. It would give them more leisure to enjoy the sights of the city. Elizabeth was delighted to see Battersea again, and to remember the happy times she had spent as a child here.

"So you haven't been back to London since you moved to Kent?" Frances asked.

Elizabeth shook her head. "No, I was nervous of traffic for so long after my accident that I certainly couldn't face the city. But I have grown to love the countryside. It's so beautiful, and the air smells so fresh."

"Well, as you are returning there tomorrow, would you like to have a look at the West End now?" Gerald offered.

Knowing that Elizabeth wanted to forget much of the past, Frances turned to her with an anxious expression.

Her friend was silent for a few moments. Then she said, "Yes, I think I would. Thank you."

Frances leaned over and grasped Elizabeth's hand. She understood that it would not be an easy trip. They smiled at each other, then settled back for the drive back across the river.

Gerald took them back through Belgravia, up to Green Park, then to all the old familiar places – Piccadilly Circus, Leicester Square, the Strand. The famous theatres and music halls, vivid with posters advertising the current attractions, flashed past. Then finally he drove them past Radley's Palace.

"Just stop here for a moment," she requested. Her eyes took in the front, the posters, the lights, and the now-darkened foyer. It looked almost derelict in the afternoon sunshine.

Frances was still gripping her hand. "It was here you had the accident?"

"Yes," Elizabeth replied softly. "A taxi cab ran me down. I lay there, on the pavement, bleeding." Her free hand touched the disfiguring scar gently. To think that Adam had held her in his arms then, while she lay unconscious.

Somehow the thought of him softened the bitter memories. It all seemed like a dream now. The music hall was like a great empty husk. She turned to Frances with a half-smile. "I've seen enough now. Thank you for bringing me."

Gerald nodded, turning the carriage back to Belgravia.

Elizabeth sat quietly for the rest of the ride home, Frances silent beside her, leaving her to her thoughts. But she was not reliving her old successes. Her mind had turned to the frightening task that lay before her. She shrank from discovering the identity of her blackmailer, though she longed to be free. Again she went through those who knew some, if not all, of her secrets. Florence Royle still came out as the most likely. She suppressed a shudder, and forced herself to banish her troubles from her thoughts as they drew up once more outside the Belgravia house.

The two young women parted fondly the next morning, promising to stay in touch. Gerald took Elizabeth to Victoria Station in the motor car, and would have seen her to her train, but she insisted that she would manage perfectly well on her own. With a good-natured shrug, Gerald declared that she was becoming as emancipated as Frances, and left her with a firm handshake.

It was only 11.30. Elizabeth found her way to the station buffet, and ordered a cup of tea. She also forced herself to eat a slice of fruit cake, though it could have been sawdust and flies for all the enjoyment she gained from it.

When she felt she could justifiably occupy the seat no longer, she emerged into the station, and spent fifteen minutes browsing at the bookstall. Eventually the hands of the station clock crept round to 12.50. She jumped as she felt a hand on her arm.

"Adam!" Her nerves jangled at the sight of him, though she felt relief at his comforting presence.

"The train was early. Are you all right?" His face registered concern.

"Adam . . . I'm scared."

He took her arm, leading her through the bustle of the station. "Don't worry. I'm sure we can do this. Did you send the letter?" She nodded. "Good. Well, let's get a tram."

When they reached Marylebone Post Office, Adam withdrew a bulky envelope from his pocket.

Elizabeth gasped. "Adam, you didn't get the money!"

"No, this is just paper. It should be enough to deceive our quarry for a while." He gave her a pen, so that she could address the envelope in her own writing.

He spoke for a while with the clerk at the poste restante counter, and Elizabeth saw him slip something into the man's hand. When he returned to her, he gave her a grave nod, then moved her to a dark corner of the office, where they could observe the counter without being seen.

They stood without speaking, watching the customers coming and going about their business. The hands of the clock moved slowly round. Elizabeth began to fidget. Her feet were beginning to pinch in her boots with standing for so long.

"It's nearly a quarter to 3, Adam. Are you sure the clerk hasn't forgotten to signal to you?"

"Perhaps I could find you a seat. We could be here for hours yet."

"No, it would make us conspicuous. Maybe if I went for a breath of air?"

He nodded. "Keep your head down. We don't want you to be recognised before we execute the plan."

Elizabeth walked for a few moments by Regent's Park, gazing longingly at a bench she could see by the grass. But after about five minutes she forced herself to return to the Post Office. Adam was still waiting.

Time dragged on. "Half past 3," Elizabeth stated grimly. She was beginning to wonder if Adam's plan was going to work after all. Suddenly, he gripped her arm tightly.

With her heart pounding, Elizabeth looked quickly towards the counter. The clerk was nodding in their direction, pointing to a man who was leaving the post office, stuffing their envelope into his jacket pocket.

Adam grabbed her hand, edging from the post office slowly. Their quarry headed towards Regent's Park, moving at a brisk pace. He was a young man, with mousy brown hair growing over the back of his collar. His long, skinny legs kept up a steady lope.

"Do you recognise him?" Adam asked as they hurried along at a reasonable distance. The young man seemed to have no suspicion that he was being followed. The thought had probably never occurred to him.

"No," Elizabeth gasped a little breathlessly. Her feet still ached from the long wait. She hoped that his destination was not too far, otherwise she might not be able to keep up. "He must be a messenger."

"Look, he's getting on that tram."

"Oh, Adam! We're going to lose him!"

"No, we won't. We're in luck." He raised his arm, calling out to an empty cab passing opposite. The cabbie wheeled his horse round, drawing up beside them smartly.

"Where to, Guv?"

Adam helped Elizabeth into the cab, calling as he leaped in behind her, "Just follow that tram, but not too closely."

They trotted at a good distance behind the vehicle. About two miles further on, Elizabeth cried out, "Look, there he is."

Adam quickly paid off the mystified cabbie, and the two set off in pursuit on foot once more. The city centre was now far behind them, and they were in a poorer residential area, which soon became more run-down as they left the main road.

Adam drew Elizabeth to a stop as they saw the man turn down an overgrown path, closing a rickety gate behind him.

She turned to him with frightened eyes. "What now, Adam?"

He didn't hesitate. "We're going in after him."

"Oh, no, what if he gets violent?"

He took her hands firmly. "I'm going in – but I need you, dearest, to identify the blackmailer. If you like, we can call the police."

"No, no, I don't want it to become known. All right, Adam, I'll come with you."

He squeezed her fingers. "Good girl. We'll get to the bottom of this."

The paint was peeling off the side door, and a few more flakes floated to the ground as Adam hit the knocker loudly. Within moments the door was opened to reveal the young man.

"Yes? What do you want?" he demanded curtly.

From behind Adam's back, Elizabeth frowned. Surely she had seen this fellow before somewhere?

Suddenly the young man's eyes widened as he recognised Elizabeth. He made to shut the door, but, before he could act, Adam had placed his foot over the threshold. Being taller and broader than his adversary, Adam pushed the young man back into the corridor, and pursued him inside. Elizabeth followed hard on Adam's heels, drawing the door shut behind them.

"Perce? What's happening?" A woman's voice floated out of the main room.

Breathless with shock, the young man stood rigidly in the doorway to the front room. "It's 'er! She's found us!" he stuttered.

Adam pushed the man roughly into the room, at which the owner of the voice stood up in surprise. Elizabeth saw a small parlour, the carpet and suite showing threadbare in the pale light that filtered through the grimy lace curtains. It would have been quite a pretty room when the articles were new, but now it just looked shabby.

The woman stumbled forward with the awkward gait of late pregnancy, one hand to her swollen abdomen. Her face was puffy, her hair lank and unkempt. With a shock, Elizabeth realised at last the identity of her blackmailers.

"Gertie! Gertie Harris! It was you!"

Her aunt's former maid stared at the newcomers in horror. "How did you find us?"

"It was an easy matter to follow your friend," Adam stated grimly. "But we want some answers from you, unless you want to find yourselves in the hands of the law."

At this, Gertie gave a loud wail, and sat down once more, her head in her hands. "Oh, please, don't do that. We didn't mean no harm. We were desperate, we've got nothing, not now I'm having the baby."

Elizabeth looked at Adam in anguish. What problems Gertie had caused her! "You may not have wished me any harm, Gertie, but you certainly caused it – and I only ever gave you help."

"I know, it was wrong. But Perce said it would be no trouble to get a little bit of money from you. Then he got greedy, and wanted more."

Sheepishly, Percy came and stood beside Gertie, one arm clumsily round her shoulders. "Please, you won't get the law, will you. I only did it for 'er."

"Why did you do it? And what secrets were you going to tell?"

Gertie wiped the tears from her eyes. "You'd better sit down." When they had done so, she explained. "You know that Perce and I worked for the old magician?"

Elizabeth nodded, remembering that last meeting in Sunderland.

"Well, last year the old man died. Perce and I tried to keep up the act, but we weren't very good. He'd promised to tell Perce the secrets of the act, but he'd only learned a few by the time he went. We had to sell all the stuff, and Perce thought it would be a good idea if we came to London.

"We got married, and took these rooms with the money we had. We both looked for work. It weren't too bad at first. I went to your old agent – Carter Willson. He didn't have anything on his books for us, but he said he needed a pretty woman for the office, to look after his clients with cups of tea, and such. Perce didn't have such good luck. He's been looking for work all this time. But at least we managed on my wages."

Looking at Percy Parker, Elizabeth thought he was a very unprepossessing sort of fellow, colourless and gangly – though he did have a burning defiance in his eyes. Maybe that was just because of their discovery.

"Then I got pregnant, and Mr Willson didn't want me at the office any more. We were really desperate. I were going to write to you – I got the address from the files – to ask for money to tide us over, but Perce had the idea that, if we . . . if we said we'd tell on you, then you'd send as much money as we wanted." She fidgeted anxiously with the strands of her lank hair. "I didn't want to, as you'd been a friend to me, but he said you'd not remember me, and it would be the only way." Her eyes filled with tears again. "I'm sorry, really I am."

"But how did you know – what did you know?" Elizabeth demanded.

Gertie looked from Elizabeth to Adam, who watched the scene grimly. "I know a lot – d'you really want me to say in front of him?"

"I know all about Miss Belmont's past. Nothing you say can diminish my respect for her."

With a small nod, Gertie wiped her eyes once more, then continued. "It were at the Sunderland Empire – you know, when you were took badly. I saw Nora Davies take you up to the dressing room, and I followed. I didn't mean to spy on you, but, when I arrived, you were tellin' her all about it – the baby, the manager, and how he was making you do it because of your father's job."

Elizabeth gasped, her hands on her cheeks, burning with shame. She had never dreamed that all her guilty secrets were known by so many. Adam's arm enfolded her tightly.

"So you thought to make it common knowledge, Miss Belmont's private life?"

"No, no, we thought you'd pay, we wouldn't have, really."

"Really?" Adam frowned menacingly.

Percy squirmed. "She wouldn't have let me. Gert was firm about that, threatened to leave me if I told anyone. It was just for her, and the baby – we were down to our last shilling. It seemed unfair that someone else should have so much, and that we might starve. Fair shares for all!" He finished pugnaciously.

"Oh, Gertie, I would have sent you some money, even tried to help you with a job," Elizabeth declared.

"But not now!" Adam stated firmly. "You can't let them play on your warm heart."

"Adam, I can't let them starve. I've got five pounds in my purse. Have you any money?"

He sighed. "Very well. I have another five pounds I can spare, but that's to be the very last." He took the money from Elizabeth, adding his own. "Here, and make good use of this. I suggest you go back north, to your family, Gertie. Surely they could find something for your husband."

"Oh, thank you, Mr . . . Mr . . . ?"

"You don't need to know my name. The less you know, the better, it seems to me."

Gertie had the good grace to look ashamed. "I'd like to go back to Sheffield. I've wanted to for a while. But the baby's due soon."

"That money should tide you over for some time. But we don't want to hear from you again. Miss Belmont has had quite enough upset from you to last a lifetime. If you try it again, it'll be the police, for sure."

"We promise we won't, isn't that so, Perce?" Gertie nudged her husband, who seemed to have fallen into a trance.

"Yes, thanks, mister. We're not criminals – we did try to get work."

Feeling suddenly disgusted by the whole business, Elizabeth stood up. "We're leaving now. Good luck, Gertie – but this time, do it on your own merits. You might not be so lucky next time."

Leaving the dejected pair sitting in the dim room, they saw themselves out. As they walked back to the tram stop, Adam became aware that Elizabeth was trembling. He put his arm round her shoulders, heedless of passers-by.

"Take me home, Adam," she whispered, the only words she spoke on their journey to the station. Understanding that she was near breaking-point, he sat quietly holding her hand, saying nothing. They could only have spoken of trivialities in public, so it was better to remain silent. He hoped that he was conveying his support through the pressure of his fingers.

Thankfully the train was quiet, just before the first rush of office workers reached the station. Adam did as he had on their journey together on Saturday, choosing an empty carriage, and pulling down the blinds. They still sat in silence until the train drew away from the platform.

"I'm sorry you had to go through that, dear," Adam said gently once they were on the move. "But I still believe it was the right thing to do."

"Do you think it's really over?" Elizabeth murmured.

"I think so. I believed Gertie. Who is she, anyway?"

Elizabeth explained about her aunt's maid, obsessed with the music hall, though having no talent except her looks. "Losing her figure was the worst thing that could have happened to her. I don't think Percy Parker has much to offer either."

"But he has ambition, and some ingenuity . . . though he could have employed it better than to devise a blackmail plan."

She shuddered. "Oh, don't remind me, please. I hope I can forget this now."

"It's time to look to the future," Adam said softly.

"The future? I just want to lose myself in the country, and be normal."

Adam took her hand again. "I was hoping you might see your future with me."

Her heart was pounding. She turned her head slowly. "After all you know about me, how can you want me to share my life with you?

What if anyone were to find out about my past? I'm hardly a suitable wife for a schoolmaster."

He stroked a strand of hair away from her face. "These troubles will recede into the past. I know you did everything out of love. I don't condemn you – I've made mistakes myself. Anyway," he added with a smile in reply to her last statement, "I'm not an ordinary schoolmaster."

The train was drawing into a station. The platform was lined with rows of men in their city garb, poised to invade their seclusion. Giving Elizabeth a fleeting kiss, Adam smiled ruefully, then raised the blinds.

"I have a small favour to ask of you," he spoke quickly as the train lurched to a halt.

Her mind still reeling at the thought of a future with Adam, she stammered, "What?"

"May I call you Lizzie?"

Her eyes widened in surprise, and a chuckle burst from her. "Of course you may. No one has the right more than the composer of my own tune."

"And your answer to my other question?"

Their eyes locked. "Yes, Adam . . . yes to everything."

Adam leaned back with a self-satisfied smile, and began to hum. The carriage was filling with frock coats and top hats. Before the slamming of doors drowned Adam's voice, Elizabeth recognised the tune he was humming, and returned his smile.

It was 'Melody for Lizzie'.